My Hope Secured

Theresa Hupp

Copyright

ISBN for paperback edition: ISBN: 978-0-9853244-5-2

ISBN-10 for paperback edition: 0-9853244-5-7

Rickover Publishing

My Hope Secured

Dedication

My Hope Secured is a romance, but sibling relationships play a critical role in the lives of both main characters.

This book is dedicated to my siblings, Rosemary and Michael. The large age gap between us kept me from feeling close to them as we grew up. But as adults, they have been there when I needed them, and I am blessed to call them sister and brother.

Family Relationships, as of October 1850

The Pershings and Purcells:
Franklin Pershing, former Army sergeant from St. Charles, Missouri
Amanda Purcell Pershing, Franklin's second wife
Franklin's children:
   Zeke Pershing, age 23
   Joel Pershing, age 20
   Esther Pershing Abercrombie, age 18
      Daniel Abercrombie, Esther's husband (see Abercrombies)
      Their children: Cordelia, age 2, and Samuel, age 1
   Rachel Pershing, age 16
      Robert O'Neill, Rachel's husband
      Their son: Bobby O'Neill, age 1 month
   Jonathan and David Pershing, twins, age 13
   Ruth Pershing, age 11
   Noah Pershing, age 7
   Jonah Pershing, age 3, raised from birth by Esther and Daniel
   Franklin Pershing, Jr. (Frankie), age 18 months
Amanda's children from her first marriage:
   Sarah Purcell, age 14
   John Purcell, age 11
   Henry Purcell, age 7

The Bramwells:
Hannah Bramwell, from Cincinnati, age 24
Jacob Bramwell, Hannah's brother, storekeeper from Cincinnati
    Alice Bramwell, Jacob's second wife
    Jacob's children from his first marriage:
        Faith Bramwell, age 13
        His younger children: Oliver, Adam, and Charity
Jane Bramwell Goring, Hannah's sister, resides in Cincinnati
    Charles Goring, Jane's husband in Cincinnati

The McDougalls:
Caleb (Mac) McDougall, attorney from Boston
    Jenny Calhoun McDougall, Mac's wife
    Their children: William, age 3, and Maria, age 7 months

The Abercrombies:
Samuel Abercrombie, farmer from Tennessee
    Harriet Abercrombie, Samuel's second wife
Samuel's children:
    Douglass Abercrombie
        Louisa, Douglass's wife
        Their children: Annabelle, age 13, and Rose, age 9
    Daniel Abercrombie
        Esther Pershing Abercrombie, Daniel's wife (see Pershings)

Oregon City in the 1850s

Chapter 1: In the Churchyard

Zeke Pershing sat in the back pew of the little Methodist church in Oregon City, his fists clenched. October sunlight streamed through high narrow windows, adding golden highlights to Jenny's brown hair. Jenny sat in the front row, smiling at the man sitting beside her. Zeke recognized him—Mac McDougall, who deserted Jenny in early 1848, almost three years ago, to prospect in California. Now, it seemed, Mac had returned.

A baby's face peered over Jenny's shoulder—where had the baby come from? Jenny didn't have a baby. Zeke should know—just weeks ago, he'd asked her to marry him, but she turned him down.

Had she known Mac was coming back? Surely she would have told Zeke if she'd known. And she hadn't said no when Zeke asked her if someday she might reconsider his proposal.

One question after another flashed through Zeke's mind. Why was Mac here? Whose baby was it? Would Jenny stay with Mac? Would Mac leave again?

Zeke heard nothing the preacher said. He was startled when the service concluded and the congregation stood for the last hymn. Then the fifty-some worshipers gathered in the bright church courtyard chatting in small groups. Zeke seethed while Mac shook hands with acquaintances welcoming him back.

Rage built in Zeke's gut when Mac guided Jenny toward her wagon. Zeke should be the one escorting her home, as he'd done since Mac left.

Jenny's three-year-old son William trundled after the couple, and Jenny still carried the unfamiliar infant. Mac had abandoned Jenny for so long— why the hell was he back? Mac had never committed to her—what right did he have to touch her now?

Zeke strode across the churchyard and pulled Mac away from Jenny.

"You bastard!" he said through gritted teeth as he punched Mac in the jaw. The blow hurt his hand and felt so good, relieving the pain in his heart, if only for a moment.

"Zeke!" Jenny screamed. "Don't!"

Mac staggered against the wagon. He shook his head as if to clear it and pulled himself upright. He held his fists in front of his face defensively, but made no move to strike Zeke. "I guess I deserved that," Mac said.

"No," Jenny said, touching Mac's arm. "You didn't." She moved between the men, clutching the baby to her shoulder, and faced Zeke. "We were married," she whispered. "This morning."

With that, the sunshine left the sky.

Zeke turned away. He didn't have answers to his earlier questions, but he had the answer that mattered most—Jenny would never be his.

As he headed for his horse, everyone stared at him, including a tall thin woman he'd never seen before. Her mouth stretched wide in horror. As he passed her, she pulled her full skirt away as if otherwise his fury would taint her.

Hannah Bramwell recoiled when a stranger in homespun clothes strode across her path just after punching a well-dressed man. She recognized the fashionable victim of the blow—he'd been on the steamboat with her the day before.

Oregon City was rougher than she anticipated. Everything about the West was different than she'd expected, from the dank weather to the bare wooden church pews to her brother Jacob's remarriage. She'd traveled to Oregon believing Jacob would need her help after his first wife died of smallpox. But upon her arrival, she'd discovered he had already claimed another bride—a woman who made it clear she didn't relish a sister-in-law as a rival housekeeper.

Hannah watched the attacker rush across the churchyard and vault onto a horse. He was about her age, attractive in a rugged way—not like the men she'd known in bustling, commercial Cincinnati. She came from a family of storekeepers, and this man looked like he made his living from the land. Muscular build, shaggy hair under a wide-brimmed hat, worn farm clothes, and an angry frown twisting his clean-shaven face.

Hannah turned from the man when a young woman greeted her. "Miss

Bramwell," the woman said, "I'm Jenny McDougall." The petite woman's cheeks were pink, and she held an infant in her arms. "My husband says he recognized you from the steamboat from Portland."

"Jenny," Jacob Bramwell said from behind Hannah. "Allow me to introduce my sister Hannah, visiting from Ohio." Hannah didn't like his slight emphasis on the word "visiting," but even after just twenty-four hours in his household, she'd deduced she couldn't remain with her brother's family.

"Visiting?" Jenny McDougall's eyebrows rose. "So far? We don't get many visitors in Oregon. This is my husband, Caleb McDougall, whom everyone calls 'Mac.'" The woman took the arm of the handsome man beside her. "My son William." She patted a boy of about three on the head. "And daughter Maria." Now she gestured at the infant nestled against her shoulder. The infant's skin was as dark as a Mexican's—or even an Indian's.

"I hope your stay in Oregon will be as pleasant as my homecoming." Mr. McDougall spoke in educated tones as he bowed to Hannah. "I am newly reunited with my wife and son after a lengthy absence."

Hannah remembered Mac McDougall and the dark-eyed infant from the steamship. But his wife and son had not been with them, which seemed odd. And his words ignored the fight she'd just witnessed.

Maybe she looked skeptical, because Mr. McDougall continued, "I'm sorry you witnessed the argument. Zeke Pershing is an old friend with a score to settle." He rubbed his red jaw gingerly. It was swelling already. "But we'll work it out."

After a few minutes of small talk with the McDougalls, Jacob introduced Hannah to other churchgoers, telling her many had traveled with him on the wagon trip to Oregon in 1847. She couldn't remember most of the names, but there seemed to be many Pershing and Abercrombie family members in attendance.

When he finished the introductions, her brother herded his wife, four children, and Hannah back to his wagon. They began the short drive to their home above the general store Jacob operated in Oregon City. Her first twenty-four hours in Oregon had not gone as planned, and she wondered what other surprises she would encounter in the days ahead.

Chapter 2: Adapting to Oregon

Sunday evening after supper, Hannah sat beside the fire in her brother's parlor doing needlework. Jacob dozed in a chair on the other side of the fire, and his new wife Alice sat in a rocker beside him. Hannah could barely see her embroidery, but she was reluctant to ask for a lamp. She didn't know what luxuries were available in the emigrant town of Oregon City, and she hadn't yet inspected the inventory in her brother's general store downstairs.

Hannah smiled at Alice. "How did you and Jacob meet?" she asked.

"I came as a missionary in forty-nine," Alice said. "Just afore the smallpox epidemic that fall. I helped nurse the suffering, including Jacob's wife. We met then."

"And when did you marry?" This time Hannah turned to Jacob, whose eyes had opened when the women spoke.

"Last December," he said, shifting in his chair.

"When Beulah had been dead only two months," Hannah murmured, as much to herself as to her brother.

The silence grew uncomfortable. They needed to talk about her future, but Hannah decided to let Jacob raise the issue. "Why did you come here, Hannah?" he finally asked.

"Your letter arrived in February of this year," she said. "Telling us Beulah succumbed to smallpox, as had dear little Hope and baby Richard. We didn't even know of the baby's birth until the letter came saying he'd died with his mother and sister. Jane and I mourned all three." Their sister Jane had in fact taken to her bed at the news, leaving Hannah to handle the household as best she could.

"I didn't know you were coming. I would have told you—"

She sighed and raised her eyes to meet his. "I thought you would need a woman's help. You had four children remaining, and no wife. And with one arm—" She gestured at his empty left sleeve. "Jane and I knew you would have difficulty raising the children and managing the store by yourself. We agreed I should come."

"You should have written."

"I did. But it seems I arrived before my letter." Hannah clutched the linen cloth more tightly and stabbed her needle into it. "It makes no difference. I wasn't needed in Cincinnati."

"You've lived with Jane and her husband since Father and Mother died. Weren't you comfortable there?"

"It wasn't my home." She'd had no home since her parents died, and no, she had not been comfortable in their sister's home—not with her brother-in-law's lustful glances and hugs.

"You aren't suited for the West, Hannah."

Jacob's bald statement surprised and irritated her. "Why not? You keep a store now, as you did in Cincinnati. I worked with you there. I continued with Jane and her husband after you left. I can work in the store here also."

"Your leg."

She arched her brow as she glared. "When has my leg ever prevented me from doing anything? Except marrying." She couldn't quite keep the bitterness from her voice. "If you can manage the store with one arm, then a limp shouldn't keep me from working the counter."

"This is a rough land, Hannah. Surely you see that."

She nodded, lips thin. "I'll adapt." She fought the weakness in her leg every day. She didn't expect the future to be easy. But she was educated and willing to work. Those traits had earned her the respect of her friends in Ohio.

Beside Jacob, Alice shifted in her seat restlessly. "Jacob," she said. "We agreed—"

"We're delighted to see you, Hannah," Jacob said. "But we don't have room. Perhaps we should arrange your passage back to Ohio. I'll check the ship schedules for you later in the week."

Hannah crept into the bed she shared with her two nieces, thirteen-year-old Faith and six-year-old Charity. It was true her brother's quarters above the store were cramped—only a parlor and two small bedrooms. Jacob and

Alice slept in one room, Faith and Charity in the other. The kitchen was downstairs off the storeroom for the shop, and eleven-year-old Oliver and ten-year-old Adam slept on cots in the kitchen.

She'd had no idea of the conditions in Oregon when she left Ohio. At age twenty-four, she wanted to find something useful to do with her life—serving as a clerk in her brother-in-law's store and aiding her sister with household tasks had not given her any significant purpose. She'd hoped helping her one-armed brother and his children in the West would give her a meaningful occupation. And get her away from her licentious brother-in-law.

Surely on the frontier an intelligent, educated woman could find a place. Even one maimed and unlikely to attract a man.

"You could marry, you know," her niece Faith whispered as Hannah slipped under the quilts. "There's ten times the men here as women. You don't have to go back to Ohio, if you don't want to."

Hannah chuckled softly. "You've seen me limp, child. What man would want me? I haven't had any offers."

"I'm not a child," Faith said. "I'm likely to marry myself in another year or two. And you're able enough. Lots of men out here would have you."

"Are you unhappy, Faith? So unhappy you'd turn to marriage when you're barely out of braids?"

Hannah felt the girl's nod. "Since Ma died. Since *she* came here." The dark didn't hide the resentment in Faith's voice.

"How did your father come to marry her?"

"I heard her tell you—she nursed Ma and the babies. And comforted Pa." The girl's emphasis on the word "comforted" gave Hannah some idea of what must have happened. "She moved in almost as soon as Ma was buried. Pa wrote you and Aunt Jane about Ma's death, but she was here by the time the ink on his letter dried. Now we're supposed to call her 'Mama Alice.' I can't." Faith's shoulders shook with sobs, and Hannah put her arm around her niece.

"Please find somewhere to live in Oregon," Faith whispered. "And let me come live with you until I marry."

True to his word, Monday morning Jacob went to the maritime office in Oregon City. When he returned, he told Hannah, "There are regular steamboats from here to Portland, but ships from Portland or Astoria to the East don't keep to a schedule. Not many of them traveling, now winter's almost here. You should have booked your passage home when you landed in Portland."

"I hoped to be of service to you, Jacob. I thought you would need me. I had no plans to return."

He sighed. "You'll have to stay till I can take you to Portland to see what's available. Maybe next week."

"I don't mind bedding with the girls through the winter. You have fine children, brother." She'd always enjoyed his family when they lived in Ohio, Faith especially. The girl treated her new stepmother sullenly, but otherwise seemed much the same as when she was younger.

"You'll have to work in the shop some. Take Alice's hours, since she'll have more work around the house with you here."

Hannah nodded. "I'm happy to do that, Jacob. I can help both you and Alice. I came to be useful."

They agreed Hannah would work in the store from after breakfast through the midday hour, then eat her meal after the rest of the family had finished while Jacob spelled her. Then she would return to the store until it closed. In the evenings she assisted Alice with household tasks.

Men and women alike patronized the shop, but many more men than women. Most of the men were courteous, though Hannah saw them eyeing her as they selected goods. It seemed any woman was worthy of attention in Oregon—she knew her features were more often called "handsome" than "pretty," and she was sensitive about her limp.

The women inspected her also, but Hannah thought they cared primarily about the fashions she wore from back East. They were friendly, and one invited her to a Women's Temperance Meeting the Wednesday after she arrived. Hannah accepted—she wasn't a teetotaler, but she wanted to make the acquaintance of other women in town.

On Wednesday Hannah and Alice arrived at the Methodist church for the Women's Temperance Meeting. Jenny McDougall came over to greet Hannah and introduced her to another young woman, Esther Abercrombie.

"We all traveled to Oregon together in forty-seven," Jenny told Hannah. "Esther's father, Franklin Pershing, led the wagon company. Her mother died along the way. And Esther married her husband Daniel at Independence Rock, about halfway through our journey."

"I can't imagine the hardships," Hannah said, shaking her head. "By comparison, I think the sea voyage I took must be easy." She'd been seasick at times, but otherwise her journey had simply been tedious. She'd traveled by steamship down the Ohio and Mississippi to New Orleans, by ship through the Gulf of Mexico south to Panama, by land across the Isthmus, then another ship north to Oregon.

"I'm told many people die in Panama," Jenny said. "My husband met many ocean travelers when he worked in California."

"So that's why you and your husband were separated?" Hannah asked. "I knew he returned to Oregon on the same steamship that brought me from Astoria, but I didn't know where he'd been."

"Yes. He prospected in the gold fields, then ran a store in Sacramento awhile."

"And you stayed here to manage the land claim?" Hannah thought it unusual for a woman so young as Jenny—who looked several years younger than Hannah—to run a farm. And where had the infant come from? Mr. McDougall had carried the baby on the steamship.

Alice snorted softly. Hannah wondered what Alice knew about the McDougalls.

"Zeke Pershing, Esther's brother, helped me with the farm. And I'm teaching the children near my cabin," Jenny said, then sighed. "Mac wonders whether I should continue the school, now that he has returned. I made a commitment to those families, and I hate to abandon them. But he wants to build a house in town."

"Send Mr. McDougall to talk to Jacob," Alice said. "He's been keeping an eye on land parcels in town. We might build a bigger store soon."

That was the first Hannah had heard of Jacob's expanding the store. Perhaps there would be room for her to stay with her brother's family after all. More to discuss with her brother.

"You must come to visit us," Esther Abercrombie said. "See what a pioneer farm looks like. The town is growing, but so are the acres of cleared land. Soon we'll rival farms back in the States in prosperity."

Jenny seconded the invitation, and the women agreed Hannah and Alice would come for the midday meal the following Monday at Esther's home.

As they walked home after the meeting, Hannah asked Alice, "Is there a story behind Mr. McDougall's travels to California? He had the baby girl with him on the steamboat from Astoria. If he'd been gone almost three years, the baby can't be his wife's."

"No one knows," Alice said, puffing up as if indignant. "Jenny McDougall is well-liked, but there's something fishy about their relationship. I wasn't here when it happened, but I hear tell Mr. McDougall left Oregon suddenly. Now he's returned just as unexpectedly. And Zeke Pershing—Esther's brother—was paying attention to Jenny the whole time her husband was away."

"Was Mr. Pershing the one who hit Mr. McDougall in the churchyard?"

Alice nodded. "Jacob tells me Zeke hung around Jenny even on the wagon trek, even when Mr. McDougall was with her. Then soon as Mr. McDougall left, Zeke spent all his time on that farm." She lowered her voice to a whisper. "It's a wonder Jenny didn't have a surprise baby after her husband left, if you know what I mean."

Having heard what Faith said about Alice and Jacob, Hannah thought Alice was hypocritical to malign Jenny. But she didn't know any of them well enough to judge. "I wonder what the truth is," she murmured to herself.

Chapter 3: The Pershing Household

Zeke tried not to think about Mac and Jenny in the week after he saw them at church. As he gleaned his harvested fields for stray grain and fodder for the coming winter, he told himself to forget Jenny. But knowing she was on the homestead in the next valley only two miles away made it impossible.

On Friday afternoon he was about to saddle his horse, ready to ride to Jenny's cabin to see if she needed anything—just as he'd done several times a week for the past three years.

"Never mind, Red," he told the sorrel gelding. "Let Mac worry about her woodpile. I'm done with her." The horse snorted in response.

But Zeke itched to find out what had happened between her and Mac and whose child she held at church on Sunday.

As he ate a lonely bowl of stew in his small cabin at noon on Saturday, his dog Blackie barked. Zeke heard a horse trot into his barnyard and went outside.

"Zeke!" his sister Esther called. "Come help me down." She huddled on her husband's mare with her infant son Samuel in front of her on the saddle. Zeke lifted them off the horse. After they entered the cabin, she set Sammy on the floor to play, poured herself a cup of coffee, and dug a letter from her pocket that she waved at Zeke. "From Joel," she said. "He's coming back to Oregon."

"Why's he leaving California?" Zeke asked. Their brother Joel had prospected with McDougall in California and seemed to have embraced the life of a gold miner.

"Says there's gold in Oregon now. Down south. But he says he'll come for a visit afore he settles there."

Zeke grunted. "I'll believe it when he gets here. He's done everything

16

he could to stay away from us since we arrived in Oregon."

"Well, he ain't saying he'll settle here. But at least we'll get to see him. He's never met my children, nor Pa's little Frankie. Maybe you can talk him into farming with you."

"Not likely." Joel, two and a half years younger than Zeke, was the sibling between Zeke and Esther. He'd left home the spring after they reached Oregon, saying he didn't want to farm. Zeke wasn't sure he wanted his adventuresome brother working with him anyway—Joel was apt to quit and leave when the notion struck him. If Joel wanted to farm, he could file his own land claim.

Esther finished her coffee. "I'm off to tell Jenny. And Mac. It's so odd to have Mac here."

Esther, a gossip who spoke her mind freely, would know more than he did, so Zeke asked, "Who was the baby with them at church?"

"She's Mac's adopted daughter, or so he says. Jenny seems to accept it—she told me on the way to our Temperance meeting on Wednesday. Says the mother was a friend of Mac's in Sacramento, but I wonder . . . ."

"You think the girl is his?" Zeke asked, anger on Jenny's behalf surging through him.

"I suppose we'll never know." Esther squinted at Zeke. "Are you all right, Zeke? Everyone saw you punch Mac on Sunday. They did marry, you know. Doc and Mrs. Tuller said they witnessed the vows."

"Mac should never have left her." If Mac had stayed, Zeke wouldn't have courted Jenny. If Mac had stayed, Zeke wouldn't be feeling the pain of her rejection now.

"I know you were sweet on her. And I'm sorry she turned you down."

"Well, that's in the past," Zeke said, wanting the conversation to be over. "You go on and do your visiting."

Not only did Jenny haunt Zeke's thoughts, he also worried about his father and younger siblings. He was the oldest of Franklin Pershing's many children. The next three—Joel, Esther, and Rachel—were grown, but thirteen-year-old twins Jonathan and David had become headstrong, and his father seemed incapable of handling them. Ruth and Noah, the two youngest siblings living with his father, were all but invisible—lost amidst their older twin brothers, the three children of the widow his father had married, and toddler Frankie born to her and his father.

On Sunday, the day after Esther visited, Zeke decided to check on his father. He didn't feel like going to church, fearing Jenny and Mac would be there again. Best to let the gossip over his punching Mac die down.

He trotted Red toward his father's farm, still seething over Mac's return. Esther had confirmed Mac and Jenny were wed. Why had Jenny rushed to marry Mac after being abandoned for so long? And was the infant girl Mac's child? What business did Mac have foisting his bastard on Jenny? Wasn't her son William enough?

Only a few others besides Zeke knew Jenny's history before their Oregon Trail trek, when she and Mac traveled together. Mac and Zeke were friends on the trail, and they scouted together often. But Zeke never thought Mac was good enough for Jenny.

Zeke hitched his gelding to a post outside his father's home, then knocked on the door. Shouts sounded from inside, but no one answered his knock, so he pushed the door open.

"What in Sam Hill did you mean by letting the milk cow out of the barn?" his father bellowed as Zeke entered.

Zeke stepped back, befuddled, until he realized his father's shouting was directed at the twins.

"Sorry, sir," Jonathan said. David looked contrite.

"Well, go find the beast," his father muttered, then slumped into a chair.

The twins brushed past Zeke as they rushed outside. Their absence didn't make the scene any quieter. The toddler Frankie wailed in the corner. High-pitched shrieks came from the loft above—they could be from Ruth or Noah, or from one of his three stepsiblings. Those five squabbled constantly.

His father looked up. "Zeke—what brings you here?"

"Just stopping by."

"We'll need more biscuits," his stepmother Amanda said, with a loud sigh. She turned toward the loft. "Ruth, Sarah, y'all come down and help me. One of you start on the biscuits, the other see to Frankie."

He could have skipped the meal, Zeke thought. Mother Amanda—the name stuck in his craw—never made him feel welcome. She made it sound like feeding him was a huge imposition.

Zeke sat in a chair beside his father. "Have you heard? McDougall's back."

Pa's eyes lit up. "Mac McDougall? Back from California?"

Zeke nodded. "Saw him last Sunday. I thought sure Esther would have told you." He'd omit the part about hitting Mac first. Pa would hear about that soon enough.

"I wondered if he'd ever come back for young Jenny," his father mused. "Did you talk to him?"

Zeke shook his head. "No. I left after the service."

The twins returned, reporting that the cow was safely back in the barn. The younger children bickered, the baby cried. Somehow Zeke got through the meal, and departed as soon as he'd eaten.

Chapter 4: An Opportunity for Hannah

Hannah and Alice set out for Esther's farm shortly after breakfast on Monday, October 28. The Bramwell children had gone to school, and Jacob minded the store. "I suppose the laundry can wait till tomorrow," Alice said with a sigh.

"I'll help you with it," Hannah said, thinking Alice had probably hoped to provoke an offer of assistance with her remark and sigh. "If Jacob can mind the store while I do."

Alice drove the wagon, and the two women sat mostly in silence. Hannah gazed at the wild land on both sides of the road. This was her first opportunity to travel beyond Oregon City since she arrived. Some fields along their path were cleared and tilled, but tree stumps dotted even those open areas at varying heights. Tall forests of virgin pine flanked other points along the rough road, their dark needled boughs looming above. Colorful maple and oak limbs twined with the evergreens so the sky was almost invisible, except for directly overhead.

"How do you tolerate the dreariness?" she asked Alice. It wasn't merely the absence of sky that struck Hannah, but also the damp gloom—she'd seen gray and mist at least part of every day since she arrived. Sometimes it rained steadily, but even when the clouds held back their moisture they threatened and blocked the sun.

Alice shrugged. "I don't usually leave town. Don't even go outside much. No reason to, with our store and living quarters in the same building. Just for church and marketing."

"But you planned to be a missionary." Hannah wondered what Alice had expected, leaving the States and moving to Oregon. "That would have required you to move about in all weather."

"I'd hoped to teach in the mission school," Alice said. "But nursing was the greater necessity when I arrived. And thankfully, I met your brother, and he hired me to care for his family. Then we married."

Hannah thought again of what Faith had told her and wondered whether the child had slandered her stepmother. Alice's missionary intent seemed laudable, though her sister-in-law had not behaved charitably toward Hannah since her arrival.

The women arrived at Esther's farmstead, a few miles from Oregon City. They climbed down from the wagon, and Alice tethered the horse to a hitching post outside the small cabin.

Esther came out of the cabin, a little boy and girl clutching her skirts and another baby in her arms. Hannah had been introduced to the children at church the first week, but she couldn't remember their names. She bent over and held out her hand to the oldest, a boy. "I'm Hannah Bramwell," she said. "And who are you?"

"Jonah," he said. "I'm three."

"And who is this?" Hannah turned to the little girl next to Jonah.

"That's Cordelia. She's only two." Jonah spoke for the girl.

Esther laughed. "And this is Sammy, my baby." She nuzzled the infant she held. "My baby for now," she amended. "I'll have another in late March."

For the first time, Hannah noticed a slight swell under Esther's apron. The poor young woman, she thought. Four children under four years old.

Hannah's surprise must have shown in her face, because Esther continued, "Jonah is my brother, but Cordelia and Sammy are my children. I'm raising Jonah—our ma died when he was born." She ruffled the boy's hair. "So he's mine also."

Jonah took Hannah's hand and pulled her toward the cabin door. "We got cake," he said. His enthusiasm made her smile.

While Esther served coffee and cake, Hannah looked around the cabin. All she could see was one large room, though another door stood on the far wall opposite the door they'd entered. One side of the room contained a hearth with a banked fire, a worktable, a washbowl on a stand, and the table and chairs where they sat. On the other side, a bed stood half-hidden behind a curtain, a rocking chair beside it. The far door must open to another room, probably smaller, Hannah surmised. And a loft covered half the downstairs, with a ladder to it in one corner.

"We're all on top of each other here," Esther said. "Like most folks in

Oregon. We started with just this room." She swept her hand around the space they occupied. "Daniel built on the room out back for the children. Come next summer, we might move 'em there, but for now, Jonah and Cordelia still sleep in the loft where it's warmer."

After they ate, Esther showed Hannah and Alice the barn, which was twice as big as the house. "We have Daniel's mare and her colt and a pair of oxen for the plow. Some folks use mules, but Daniel likes oxen. And a milk cow." Chickens clucked in the barnyard, and a dog sleeping under the eave of the barn lifted a lazy head as they passed and flapped its tail half-heartedly in the dirt.

"Your house might be smaller than most homes in Ohio," Hannah said. "But otherwise it looks like a fine farm." She smiled. "Though I'm a city girl—I've never lived in the country."

"Nothing but country here," Esther said. "Will you be staying in Oregon City then?"

Alice stiffened beside Hannah and opened her mouth as if to speak. Hannah hastened to say, "I don't know yet. I came West to be helpful. Depends where I can be of most use."

For the next few days, Hannah divided her time between the store and helping Alice with household tasks. Alice took advantage of Hannah's labor, but spoke frequently of "when Hannah would return to Cincinnati."

At the end of each day, Hannah rubbed her aching leg. She could do anything she put her mind to, but the scars from the burns she'd suffered as a child still pained her when they were stretched. Although the limp was the more noticeable outcome of that terrible experience, it bothered her less than the damage to her muscles and ligaments.

Still, she refused to let physical deformities define her. Her older sister Jane, whom family and friends called the beauty in the family, was more limited by her emotional frailties than Hannah was by the weakness in her leg. Jane took to her bed at the slightest indication of difficulty, but Hannah did not follow her sister's example.

She should write Jane a letter. But what could she report beyond her safe arrival in Oregon? That Jacob had not expected her and that he and Alice did not relish Hannah's presence? That he had remarried with unseemly speed after Beulah's death? That Faith was unhappy? It would be a bleak letter.

And what of Hannah's future? Should she tell Jane she would return in the spring? Or should she commit to staying in Oregon and finding another place to live and a situation to occupy her time? If so, where and what?

Given her druthers, Hannah would stay in Oregon. If she returned to Ohio, Jane would expect her to live with them, and Hannah did not want to spend her days and nights dodging her brother-in-law Charles. But without Jacob's approval, she had nowhere to live and no means of supporting herself.

After they went to bed, Faith continued to confide to Hannah about her unhappiness. "Mama Alice"—she said the name spitefully—"uses me as a servant girl. I do her washing up and mind Charity whenever she asks."

Hannah tried to be neutral. "Didn't you help your own mother with the household chores?"

"But Ma would joke and laugh about it. She didn't order me about like Mama Alice does."

"You're at school most of the day."

Faith heaved a deep sigh. "The girls at school don't like me. I don't have any friends."

Hannah suspected Faith was exaggerating, but she kept quiet. She knew how miserable thirteen-year-old girls could be when they felt alone and friendless. She had spent much of her teenage years with her nose in a book, hiding from the girls in her class who ignored her once they became interested in flirting with boys and dancing—activities her limp kept her from pursuing.

Late on Thursday morning, three days after her visit to Esther's farm, Jenny McDougall entered the store while Hannah minded the counter. "Hello, Mrs. McDougall," Hannah greeted her. "May I help you find something?"

Jenny seemed hesitant. "It's a personal matter," she said. "Is there somewhere we could speak privately?"

"I have to stay at the counter," Hannah said. "My brother Jacob will relieve me at one o'clock. Will you still be in town then? You could join me upstairs and eat with me." She assumed there would be enough of the noon meal remaining for them both, though Alice's meals were usually not lavish. Hannah could add a jar of canned goods from the store.

Jenny agreed to return at one, and when she did, Hannah escorted her up the stairs to the small apartment. Hannah told Alice she would clean the dishes after she and Jenny ate, but Alice said, "No, no. Don't trouble yourself. I'd be delighted to chat with you and Jenny, then you can return to work."

Hannah had no choice but to acquiesce to her sister-in-law's suggestion. As she and Jenny ate, Jenny said, "My husband is making plans for us to move into town as soon as he finds suitable quarters. Then he plans to build another home for us here."

"You and he will be a welcome addition to society here, I'm sure," Alice said.

Jenny smiled, then turned to Hannah and said, "I have a proposal for you, but I don't want you to feel any obligation to accept."

Hannah waited.

"I have been teaching a school for the children on claims near my cabin," Jenny said. "But Mac wants me and our family with him in town. I do not feel right leaving our claim without finding another teacher. Could you teach the school in my stead?"

Hannah raised her eyebrows. She'd never been a teacher. Could she handle it?

"You would need to live on the claim, I think," Jenny continued. "It's too far from town to be an easy ride before the children arrive each morning. But we would not charge you rent, because you would be doing me a favor. The parents pay mostly in produce and services like chopping firewood. I think you could live on what they give you or trade their goods for what you need."

"My, what a fine opportunity for you," Alice said to Hannah.

Could she teach? She'd been a good student as a child in Cincinnati, but had no training as an educator. And could she live in a primitive cabin like Esther Abercrombie's by herself? "Might I have a few days to think about it?" Hannah asked. "And visit your home before I decide?" Preferably without Alice, she thought.

They agreed that Hannah would visit Jenny the following Tuesday afternoon. "I'll dismiss the students early," Jenny said. "So I can show you around."

Chapter 5: The Pershings' Problems

The following Sunday, the first week in November, Zeke made himself return to church. He couldn't skip it every week, or people would begin to talk.

After the service, Esther accosted him before he could get to his horse. "Did you hear what the twins did this week?"

Zeke shook his head. He hadn't seen the boys since the day they'd let the milk cow out. With the weather turning cold and damp, he didn't need their help on his claim. Pa sent the twins to Jenny's school mostly to reduce the trouble they caused at home.

"They burned off the stubble in the cornfield by the house. Pa told 'em to do so. But they left it burning and went fishing. By the time Mother Amanda saw it, the fire had spread to the side of the barn. If it hadn't been for the horse trough, she couldn't have put it out. She and her older two young'uns. Ruthie helped, too."

"Those boys know better." The twins weren't bad lads, but they seemed to get in a lot of mischief at home.

"Yes, they do." Esther nodded emphatically. "You've got to do something with them."

"Me? They're Pa's sons. He would have licked me or Joel if we'd done such a thing. Or if he weren't around, Ma would have whupped us." Zeke felt a pang of grief remembering his mother, who died on the journey to Oregon.

"Well, he ain't doing nothing to the twins. And Mother Amanda says they can't stay at the farm no more."

"It ain't hers to say. What's Pa say?" Pa ought to be disciplining those boys. Zeke wanted no part of the task.

"He don't say nothing. You know he lets her rule the roost. He may not be drinking anymore, but he ain't acting like a parent to any of the young'uns." Esther grabbed Zeke's arm. "It's up to you, Zeke."

"Maybe you should take 'em." But as soon as he spoke the words, he knew what she would say.

"We don't have room. And I have Jonah." She'd raised their youngest sibling Jonah since Ma died. Jonah was now three and a half, and was as much Esther's child as the two she had borne. "Daniel thinks the twins should live with you."

Zeke sighed. He could use the boys' help—if they would help and not burn down any more buildings—but he didn't want the responsibility of raising them. "I'll talk to Pa," he said.

After church, Zeke rode again to his father's claim. The household was as topsy-turvy as it had been the week before. Seven-year-olds Henry Purcell and Noah Pershing were teasing Ruth, though at almost twelve she should have been able to defend herself. Sarah Purcell rocked Frankie, whose squalling dwindled to whimpers. Mother Amanda bustled about the stove, shouting to the children.

"Where's Pa?" Zeke asked as he doffed his hat inside the door.

"In the barn," Mother Amanda said. "You tell him to come get these rascals." She nodded at Henry and Noah.

Zeke put his hat back on and walked outside. He scrutinized the side of the barn, scorched from the ground to about waist-high. They were lucky it hadn't burned entirely.

The barn's normally pleasant scents of horses and hay were lost in the odor of charred wood. Pa sat on a stool puffing on his pipe. "Ain't you afraid you'll set the place on fire again?" Zeke asked.

His father grinned. "Can't find anywhere peaceful for a smoke in the house. Guess I need to add on a room or two."

"Esther says Jonathan and David been in trouble again."

Pa shrugged. "No more'n usual."

"Setting the barn afire seems a tad more trouble than usual." Zeke pulled another stool beside his father and sat. "Esther says Mother Amanda don't want 'em here."

"More like Esther don't want the boys here. You know she's never cottoned to Amanda nor her young'uns."

"Do you want me to take the twins to my place for a while?" Zeke asked. He was reluctant, but he thought he should make the offer.

"Thanks, Zeke. I know I can count on you. But Amanda will calm down. Hate to split my young'uns up any more'n they already are. Let's wait and see."

"If you need me to take 'em, you send 'em over. I got room in the loft." After living in a room in his barn for two years, Zeke had built a cabin on his claim, thinking he'd have Jenny there with him soon—he'd even bought a fancy stove for her. The loft above the main cabin room would hold beds for the twins.

His father nodded and puffed his pipe.

"Will you tell Esther we talked?" Zeke asked. He wanted her to hear Pa say he'd keep the twins. Otherwise, she would light into Zeke again.

"All right, son. Now, let's go eat our meal."

"I'll pass, Pa. Got to get home."

Chapter 6: Hannah's Next Steps

For days, Hannah stewed over whether to accept Jenny's proposal to she teach school. Hannah yearned to be away from her brother's house, but wondered whether she could cope with the primitive farm life she'd seen at Esther Abercrombie's cabin. At the McDougall cabin, she would have to manage all alone.

One night as Hannah tossed in bed, Faith whispered to her, "If you decide to teach, may I come live with you?"

"What do you know about living on a farm? Or teaching?" Hannah asked.

"I helped cook and wash and did other chores on the wagon train," Faith said. "And I was only ten then. Ma showed me everything." The girl's voice cracked—she must miss Beulah terribly, Hannah thought. "The log cabin will be sumptuous compared to a wagon."

She smoothed a hand over her niece's hair. "If I take the position, I would relish your company. We'll talk to your father."

"Oh, do teach the school, Aunt Hannah, please!" Faith's face beamed as she hugged her aunt.

Sunday afternoon after church, Hannah sat in her brother's small parlor with pen and paper. She needed to write Jane, though her plans were still uncertain.

> *November 3, 1850*
> *Oregon City*
> *Dear Jane,*
> *Since I last wrote you from California, I have made it to Oregon. In case my earlier*

letters have not arrived due to the uncertain mail service from the West, I will start by telling you my travel by ship from New Orleans to Panama was uneventful. I suffered some from seasickness, but recovered soon enough. The heat and mosquitoes during the crossing of the isthmus made me more uncomfortable than I have ever been in my life, apart from the weeks just after my accident. But my traveling party reached the Pacific without serious illness or injury, unlike many voyagers, and the scenery along the coast of California was beautiful.

From San Francisco I found a berth on another ship heading to Oregon. Most travelers stay in California because of the gold. While the land was stunning, the City of San Francisco teemed with the worst types of adventurers. I feared for what kind of life our brother might have in Oregon, particularly after losing Beulah.

Imagine my surprise when I arrived in Oregon City and found Jacob remarried. His new wife Alice nursed Beulah in her last days, and they married just two months after Beulah's death—shortly after he wrote us. He wrote again to inform us of his nuptials, but the letter did not arrive before I left. Perhaps you have received it by now.

What would I have done had I known of his marriage? They do not need me here, and though Jacob professes to be glad to see me, he and Alice make it clear my stay with them can only be a visit. When a ship becomes available, he says I should return to Ohio.

However, I have been offered a teaching

position—yes, I a teacher!—and I believe I will accept it.

As she wrote, Hannah discovered she relished the possibility of finding independence as a teacher. Escaping the cramped quarters where her brother and his family lived was another inducement to accept Jenny's offer.

> *Our eldest niece Faith may live with me. She is unhappy at home and at school, and I have always been partial to her. She reminds me of myself as I was before the accident.*
>
> *I shall write further when I am settled in my new abode. The teaching position comes with a small log cabin, much ruder than anything in Cincinnati. Faith assures me it is better than the covered wagon in which she and her family traveled for six months. I hope I can endure the privations of the West.*
>
> *Your loving sister,*
> *Hannah*

On Tuesday morning, November 5, Hannah convinced Jacob to send Faith with her instead of Alice to evaluate Jenny's premises. "Faith would be better able than Alice to judge the features of the cabin," she told him. "If I'm to move to the country, I want someone who has roughed it. Alice came by ship and has always lived in town. At least Faith has your wagon company experience."

"If living in the wilderness concerns you, Hannah, you shouldn't take this position."

"Alice isn't happy with my being here. It would be better for me to move. But would you consider letting Faith go with me? I imagine she could learn as much helping the younger students as at the girls' academy in Oregon City."

"Are you decided on teaching then? Do you think you can?"

"I'm leaning that way."

Jacob sighed, then nodded. "Take Faith. I know she's unhappy at home now."

After the noon meal, Hannah and her niece set out. Hannah drove the wagon—Jacob's old mare moved slowly, but responded to the same commands and reins as the horses she'd driven in Cincinnati. Faith chattered excitedly the entire way, stories about the people in the wagon company, including Mac and Jenny McDougall.

"Captain McDougall was the handsomest man in our company. He took over as captain after Captain Pershing got drunk at Fort Hall. Samuel Abercrombie wanted to be captain, but the men voted for Captain McDougall instead."

"Is Mr. McDougall really a captain?" Jacob had told Hannah about Mac McDougall taking command of the wagons, but he'd said McDougall was a lawyer, not a military man.

"Oh, that's what we call anyone who led a company. And they stay captains forever, it seems." Faith prattled on, "And Mr. Abercrombie got to be a captain, too, later on, when he joined the Oregon militia. He wants everyone to call him 'captain.'"

Hannah couldn't keep all these people straight yet. "And what relationship is Samuel Abercrombie to Esther?"

"Her father-in-law. Her husband Daniel's father. Old Mr. Abercrombie—Captain Abercrombie—caused grief to everyone. He's not an easy man, though Daniel is ever so nice. So is Douglass Abercrombie, Daniel's older brother. But I'm not fond of Douglass's two daughters."

When they arrived at the McDougall cabin, Hannah was dismayed to discover it was smaller than Esther's. And an even tinier shack stood across the clearing. "Who lives there?" she asked, nodding at the shack.

Faith shrugged. "I'm not sure, but I think that's where the Tanners lived. They were the Negro family in our company. They've gone to California now. They stayed with Miz Jenny after Mr. McDougall left. They and Zeke Pershing helped her out."

Hannah remembered that name—he was the man who'd hit Mr. McDougall in the churchyard. "Zeke—another Pershing?"

Faith nodded. "He's Esther's oldest brother. There's some scandal around him and Jenny McDougall, though Pa won't tell me what it is."

Hannah hitched the mare's reins to a post, like she'd seen Alice do at

Esther's cabin. As she finished, Jenny came out of the cabin. "Welcome," she said. "Please come in."

The cabin was neat and clean, but only a single room with a loft above, similar to Esther's home, though without the addition of a back room. The place was furnished much like Esther's, except that benches were stacked on one wall.

Jenny waved toward the benches. "We put those out when the students are here. But we couldn't move around if we left them out."

"How many students are there?" Hannah asked. She wondered how big a task she would be assuming by taking the teaching position.

"You'll have twelve. The four youngest Pershings, their three Purcell stepsiblings, two Abercrombie granddaughters, and three Binghams. William was also a primer student, but of course he'll be moving to town with us, so you'll have one less little one."

"Thirteen students, with Faith," Hannah murmured. "How old are the children?" she asked.

"From fourteen down to seven. I usually divide them into older and younger students. I work with one group while the other group studies on its own."

"Were you a teacher back East?" Hannah thought Jenny too young to have taught before moving to Oregon in 1847.

Jenny laughed. "Oh, no. I studied with my papa at home. Otherwise, I only attended school briefly in New Orleans as a child."

From New Orleans to Missouri to a wagon train to Oregon—Jenny McDougall had quite an interesting history. Perhaps someday Hannah could learn more about her new friend's past. And maybe find out the scandal Faith had alluded to.

The school would last until March, Hannah learned. Then most of the children were needed for farm work. So teaching would not be a permanent solution to her problem. But it would delay her decision whether to return to Ohio and provide her with a livelihood in the meantime.

She and Jenny talked about books and paper and slates. They climbed to the loft. "William sleeps here now," Jenny said. "But you could sleep upstairs, if you don't want to haul the benches out every day."

"I'm thinking of bringing Faith to live with me," Hannah said.

"That would be wonderful!" Jenny smiled. "Esther's sister Rachel assisted me the first year I taught, until she married. She was a godsend.

And her older brother Zeke was also—Mac will talk to him today about helping you with the wood-chopping and other heavy chores. I couldn't have managed the farm without Zeke."

The relationship between Zeke Pershing and the McDougalls must be friendlier than the melee in the churchyard had indicated. Hannah remembered Alice's slander again. Would she ever learn the truth in the relationship between Jenny McDougall and Zeke Pershing? "When will I meet Mr. Pershing?" Hannah asked.

"Zeke is very nice, Aunt Hannah," Faith said. "You'll like him. Everyone does."

Chapter 7: Zeke Talks to Mac and Jenny

At the sound of a horse cantering toward him, Zeke Pershing glanced up from mending his barnyard fence. Mac McDougall rode into the yard on the fancy stallion he'd brought from Boston. The stallion was the best horseflesh Zeke had ever seen. Several mares from their wagon company produced colts as black as the stallion, and all the offspring finer animals than their dams.

Zeke waited for Mac to dismount and approach. What the devil did the man want? He already had what Zeke cared most about—Jenny.

Mac let his stallion into the paddock where Zeke's gelding grazed, then stuck out his hand.

It would be churlish to refuse to shake, and Zeke had shown his feelings more than he should have in the churchyard a few weeks back. He took Mac's hand, squeezing a little harder than necessary. Mac's palm was calloused. Zeke hadn't expected that. The man had worked during his years away from Oregon, even if he'd made more money than Croesus in the California gold fields.

"It's good to see you, Zeke," Mac said. "I always enjoyed working with you. Scouting on the trail. Clearing our fields and building our barns."

The last day before Mac left for California in February 1848, Zeke and Mac helped build Samuel Abercrombie's barn. They'd drunk too much, Zeke remembered. "Yeah," was all he said now.

"Thank you for helping Jenny while I was away," Mac said. "She's told me how you kept her woodpile high, and how you tilled the fields. We both appreciate your assistance."

"She paid me in crop shares." Zeke didn't want Mac or Jenny beholden to him.

"I know." Mac nodded. "But you didn't have to do it." He leaned on the top fence rail Zeke had just replaced and gazed into the paddock toward the horses. "And I know you asked Jenny to marry you. That's what made me come home."

"Huh?" How would Mac have learned of Zeke's desire to marry Jenny in California?

"Esther wrote Joel you'd proposed to Jenny. When Joel showed me the letter, I headed back here as fast as I could. I couldn't let you have her. I love her."

Zeke couldn't help snorting. A man should be constant in his love, not be a dog in the manger. "After leaving her alone with a baby for over two years you finally realized you loved her?" he said in disgust.

Mac shrugged. "I can be stupid sometimes."

They stood staring into the paddock awhile. Zeke's gelding and the stallion made their reacquaintance without any seeming tension. But Zeke wasn't ready to let go of his resentment toward his former friend.

Mac blew out a breath. "I need a favor."

Zeke turned to him, eyebrows raised.

"I want to move into town with Jenny. We need a bigger house, and I have to find something to do with my time. But she's teaching the school and doesn't want to leave it."

"I ain't a schoolteacher."

Mac grinned. "Didn't think you were. But there's a woman in town, Jacob Bramwell's sister Hannah. She's at loose ends, too, and might teach. If she does, she'll be alone on my claim like Jenny was and will need the same help Jenny did."

"You want me to stock her woodpile, muck the stable?" Did Mac really expect him to continue the work he'd done mostly for love of Jenny?

"If you would."

"How much you paying?" Zeke asked. He might as well get something for helping the new schoolmarm.

Mac cocked an eyebrow. "You worked the land for shares before." He sighed. "I'm taking our horses to town, but I'll pay you a dollar a day to care for the mules and cow and to keep the woodpile full. Your brothers can help you."

Zeke shrugged. "Fine. When's she coming here?"

"I'm not sure she'll take the position," Mac said. "Jenny is talking to her on our claim now. Why don't we go meet her?"

It would be the first time Zeke had seen Jenny since the day in the churchyard. It had to happen sometime, but not yet. He shook his head. "Let me know if Miz Bramwell decides to teach, and I'll go meet her. We'll work it out then."

Two days after Mac's visit, Zeke's twin brothers, Jonathan and David, came to help him clear a field so he could plant more winter wheat. It was late in the season to be planting, but it wouldn't hurt to try. The thirteen-year-old twins had urged Zeke to let them work with him. "Anything but school, Zeke," David said. "We don't need more book learning."

"I hope you ain't causing Miz Jenny no trouble," Zeke said.

"She ditched you," Jonathan said. "So what do you care?"

"I care," Zeke said. "She done us a favor, teaching all you young'uns."

"We ain't young'uns," David protested. "We're full grown." In fact, the boys were as tall as Zeke, who was above average height, but he outweighed them each by thirty pounds. At thirteen, their shoulders were just beginning to broaden, and he didn't think either of them had ever shaved. Still, they could work hard when they put their minds to it, and he welcomed their help in clearing stumps.

"I hear you'll likely get a new teacher," Zeke said. "According to McDougall, he and Miz Jenny are moving to town."

The boys nodded. "Miz Jenny told us the new teacher's starting Monday," Jonathan said. "Do we have to go?"

"What's Pa say?" Zeke asked. The twins seemed to listen to him as much as to their father, but he didn't want to assume a parental role.

"He says we have to go. Unless he—or you—have something for us to do. Can't we clear another field?" Jonathan continued to whine, though David didn't voice any more objections about school.

"Let's get this one planted first. You go to school Monday. I'll go with you and meet your new teacher."

Zeke couldn't let it rest until Monday. He wanted to talk to Jenny before she moved to town. Friday afternoon, about the time she usually let school out, he showed up on her claim. Sure enough, he caught her at home alone with William and the baby girl Mac had brought from California.

"Got a minute?" he asked, when she opened the door to his knock.

She nodded. "Mac's out checking on the fields. He said he'd try to shoot some quail or grouse to leave for Miss Bramwell."

"You're really moving to town?"

Jenny nodded. "That's what Mac wants."

"What do *you* want, Jenny?"

She smiled and gestured at the children playing at her feet. "My family is everything I want."

Her comment seared Zeke's heart. He'd once hoped *he* would be what she wanted. He realized now it could never have been. She'd always been Mac's, since before Zeke had met her.

He heaved a sigh. "What do you need me to do for Miz Bramwell?"

She explained Hannah Bramwell had never lived on a farm, and likely didn't know anything about caring for the plow team or chickens or cow on the claim. Nor could she chop wood.

"That means being here twice a day," Zeke complained. "Doing both morning and evening chores. Can't she do anything for herself?"

"She has a limp, Zeke," Jenny told him. "I don't know the cause, but I doubt she is able to do much physical labor."

Jenny was small, but she'd always done for herself as they traveled the continent. Except on river crossings—she'd been afraid of the water. Zeke smiled at the memory. This Hannah Bramwell didn't seem like much of a woman compared to Jenny. "You think she'll last long out here?" he asked.

Jenny shrugged. "I hope so. All I really need is for her to stay until school is out in March. Next year, families can make other plans. But I don't want the children left without instruction this winter—not after I made the commitment to teach."

Zeke grinned. "Jonathan and David wouldn't mind."

She frowned. "Those boys need discipline, Zeke Pershing. If your father won't provide it, then you need to. Why don't you have them come live with you? They'd be closer to school, and they could do the chores for Miss Bramwell. It would be good for them to be useful."

With a sigh, Zeke said, "I'll bring the boys early Monday. We'll talk to Miz Bramwell then." He tipped his hat to Jenny and rode home.

Monday morning Zeke and the twins arrived at the McDougall claim an hour before school started. A wagon pulled into the yard right behind them, driven by a tall, slender woman with young Faith Bramwell sitting beside her.

"That must be the new teacher," David said. "Why'd she bring Faith along?"

Chapter 8: First Days of Teaching

Hannah and Faith left Oregon City just after dawn on Monday, all Hannah's possessions packed in the carpet bag and large trunk she'd brought from Ohio. Her stomach roiled in anticipation of the new task ahead. She had accepted the teaching position, and she and her niece would be living in the wilderness in a cabin barely larger than Jacob's parlor. Faith chattered on the wagon bench beside her, seeming excited about the adventure. Of course, as Faith had said, the cabin was a luxurious abode compared to a covered wagon.

Jacob was unable to drive them to the McDougall claim. A ship from the Sandwich Islands had arrived in Portland, and he'd taken the steamboat to the port town to buy supplies and arrange shipment to Oregon City. He loaned Hannah his wagon and mare and said he would retrieve them later in the week. Alice complained about losing the family's wagon for several days, but when Hannah stated she had no other way to move to the McDougalls' farm, Alice quieted.

As Hannah steered the horse and wagon into the McDougalls' yard, a man standing in front of the cabin door turned to face her. She gasped. It was Mr. McDougall's churchyard assailant.

"There's Zeke Pershing," Faith said, waving to him. "And his brothers." Faith turned to greet two boys about her age who raced around the barnyard, pushing and shoving each other.

Hannah knew the McDougalls and Pershings had been friends since their travels to Oregon. Yet it seemed odd Mr. McDougall was still on good terms with the man who'd pursued Jenny while he was away, the man who'd been so upset at his return that he'd hit Mr. McDougall.

Now she and Faith would be beholden to Mr. Pershing. Well, she would have to keep an eye on him at all times. She didn't need a brutish philanderer nosing around her—and especially not around Faith.

"Hello, Faith," he said, helping Hannah's niece out of the wagon. Then he turned toward Hannah. "Miz Bramwell? I'm Zeke Pershing."

She held out a hand. "Mr. Pershing." Before she could say more, he'd put his hands around her waist and lifted her down. She staggered on her bad leg, and he caught her.

"Sorry, ma'am. I didn't realize you weren't steady."

"I'm perfectly steady, when I've had a moment to prepare," she said, letting starchiness show in her voice.

Jenny came out of the cabin, as her husband stood in the doorway behind her. "Glad you're all here. We can talk with Zeke before the other students arrive. After I introduce you to your pupils, our family will get out of your way." Hannah, Zeke, Mac, and Jenny entered the barn, leaving Faith in the cabin with the two McDougall children. The two Pershing boys still ran about the yard.

Hannah's head spun with everything the McDougalls told Zeke about daily chores, but he seemed to take it in stride. "Can you heft an axe, ma'am?" he asked her.

She shook her head.

"Then I'll make sure you have wood enough to burn each evening. I know Jacob don't like Faith chopping wood, after he lost his arm in forty-seven. Though in a pinch, I suspect she could manage. She's a fine girl, that niece of yours." A mark in Mr. Pershing's favor that he liked Faith, Hannah decided.

Jenny explained how to feed the chickens. "I always took care of them, so Zeke never did, though he would if you need him to. Can you and Faith scatter the grain for them and check the nests for eggs?"

"I'm sure we can," Hannah said timidly.

Zeke Pershing grinned, making Hannah wonder if he mocked her. "If you need anything and I ain't here," he said, "you get those twin brothers of mine to help you. Or they can come find me." He shouted at the boys, "Jonathan, David, come meet your new teacher."

The boys were almost identical, Hannah noticed when they approached. "Which of you is which?" she asked, shaking each boy's hand in turn.

"I'm Jonathan," one said. "I'm the elder."

"I'm David," said the other. "I'm the smart one," a remark which earned him an elbow in the ribs from his twin.

"We'll see about that," Hannah said, smiling. The boys were mirror images of each other, but Jonathan was marginally taller. She thought she'd be able to tell them apart with a little practice. "Will you boys help us set up the benches in the cabin? And tell me about the other students."

Perhaps being a teacher wouldn't be so difficult after all.

As the students arrived, Jenny introduced them to Hannah while Mac took care of the little McDougall children. In addition to the thirteen-year-old Pershing twins, there were two younger Pershings—eleven-year-old Ruth and seven-year-old Noah. With them came their stepsiblings, fourteen-year-old Sarah Purcell, eleven-year-old John Purcell, and seven-year-old Henry Purcell. Shortly after, two Abercrombie girls arrived—thirteen-year-old Annabelle and nine-year-old Rose. The three Bingham children were the last—two girls about the same ages as the Abercrombies and a boy of about seven. With Faith, that made thirteen students, ranging from fourteen to seven years old.

After introductions, the McDougalls left. Jenny drove a wagon pulled by a small mare with a young black horse tied to the rear, and Mac rode a prancing black stallion. The schoolchildren waved good-bye, then turned expectantly to Hannah.

"Well, children," she said, wondering how she would remember all the names. "Please be seated."

They swarmed to the benches, then looked at her again. She took a deep breath. "I'd like to get to know you better. So take some paper and write an essay about how you came to be in Oregon. Where did you live before? What does your father do now?"

Little Henry Purcell raised his hand. "Miz Hannah, I can't write that good."

"You will all call me 'Miss Bramwell,'" she said. "And, Henry, it's 'that well,' not 'that good.' You should use what's called an adverb."

"But we called Miz Jenny 'Miz Jenny,'" Noah Pershing said.

"You knew her better than you know me," Hannah responded. "As for writing"—she turned back to Henry—"Faith and I will help the younger students. Faith, you work with Noah, and I will assist Henry."

41

The first few days passed in a blur. Hannah was exhausted by the time she and Faith finally went to bed each evening. Cooking over the open fire in the hearth was a challenge—at least Jacob had an iron stove in his kitchen. No wonder the McDougalls wanted to move to town, though they'd left their household utensils and dishes for Hannah. Faith seemed adept at making biscuits, and Hannah managed to cook a stew or soup each day.

They slept together in the bed in the main room. Hannah offered Faith the option of sleeping in the loft, but Faith said she liked the coziness downstairs. She whispered her opinions of her new classmates to Hannah each night after they retired. Faith knew the children from their wagon travels, but she'd never gone to school with them before.

On Thursday of Hannah's first week of teaching, her brother Jacob arrived riding a borrowed horse. Faith ran out to hug her father, then chattered to him about her new classmates. The girl seemed genuinely happy staying with Hannah and helping with the country school, instead of living with her family and attending school in town.

"Well, Hannah, have you become a teacher now?" Jacob asked.

"It seems so, brother. Whether I'm any good at it remains to be seen. Most of the children are trying their best."

"Though not that stuck-up Annabelle Abercrombie," Faith said. "I didn't like her when we traveled in the wagon company, and I still don't."

"She's had a hard time of it, lass," her father said, pulling his daughter's braid gently. "Those smallpox scars ruined her face. She'd been a pretty girl, and that can't be an easy change."

Hannah had mixed feelings about Annabelle. The girl was thoroughly unpleasant, but Hannah sympathized with the girl's disfigurement. She hoped she could help the child, if Annabelle would let herself be helped.

"And the Pershing twins are as devilish as ever," Faith said. "They don't want to spend their time learning, and they make it hard for the rest of us to listen to what Aunt Hannah says."

"Those boys need a good thrashing," Jacob said. "Always did. And their father lets them get away with murder. Though so far they've only killed a few hens."

"Maybe I should put their skills to use," Hannah said, smiling. "There's an old hen that's not laying. I could stew her. How are Alice and your other children?"

Jacob told Hannah and Faith about the rest of the family and about goings-on in Oregon City. "McDougalls are staying in the hotel near our store," he said. "Best suite in the place. And McDougall bought a lot on top of the hill to build a new house. Construction begins next week. He must be paying a pretty penny to get laborers so fast. You doing all right out here?" His question seemed directed at both his sister and his daughter.

"It's wonderful, Pa!" Faith responded before Hannah could say a word. Soon, Jacob hitched his mare to the wagon, tied the extra horse to the back, and drove off. Now Hannah and Faith had only the plow team of mules and a small cart the McDougalls left behind.

Zeke Pershing stopped by every morning that first week. Hannah guessed his farm must be close, if he could visit the McDougall claim so frequently. He tended the barn animals and checked her woodpile. And each afternoon before the twins left, the boys replenished the woodpile and mucked out the barn. Faith and Hannah managed to milk the cow and feed the chickens, though Hannah sometimes had trouble with the cow and had to call Faith to do the milking.

Friday afternoon, however, the twins ran off without chopping wood, and the kindling stack dwindled. Hannah feared the fire might go out during the night and need restarting in the morning. So she decided she should chop more kindling.

Hannah stood a log on the chopping block, and held it with one arm while grasping the heavy axe in the other. She could barely lift the tool to her shoulder. "Do you have any notion how to do this?" she asked Faith.

"Keep your arm out of the way, Aunt Hannah," Faith said. "Or you'll end up one-handed like Pa. And use the hatchet. It's easier. Let me show you." The girl took the hatchet and chopped the log into kindling, though her pieces weren't split evenly.

"All right, let me try," Hannah said. The hatchet was lighter than the axe, but her weak leg kept her unbalanced. She couldn't get much power into her swing, and the hatchet stuck halfway into the log. It took all her strength to pull it back out.

She sighed and tried again, aiming for the same place in the log, but striking it differently. It took many tries to splinter the log into decent-sized kindling.

As she finished, Zeke Pershing rode into the yard. He sat on his horse watching her.

She glanced at him, then picked up the kindling and carried it to the front door.

"Need some help, ma'am?" he asked.

"I think we have enough wood for the evening," she said. "I didn't expect you."

"I was afraid those lazy brothers of mine hadn't chopped you enough wood. Seems I was right."

"We've managed," she said haughtily.

"You should have seen Aunt Hannah," Faith said. "This was her first time chopping kindling."

"Maybe I could show you how," Zeke said, dismounting and hitching his sorrel gelding to a post. He took the hatchet and with a few strokes split a log into eight even pieces. "Like that." He grinned.

"I don't seem to have the strength for it," Hannah admitted. "Is there an easier way?"

"Just make sure you get me or the boys to split it into halves or quarters. Then you should be able to manage. Let me see your stroke." He split a log into half and handed her the hatchet.

She swung, but the hatchet stuck again.

"You're not putting your back and legs into it," he said. He came up behind her and held her arms above her head, then swung her arms in his while pushing her forward with his chest and thighs. She'd never been this close to a man—it was closer than dancing—and she gasped and shied away.

"Did you feel that?" he asked. "How I used my legs?"

"I-I'm not sure I c-can," she stammered, feeling a blush rise to her cheeks. "M-my leg sometimes gives out."

He stepped back and looked at her. "Then make sure the twins or I leave you lots of kindling. Or get Faith to do it." He turned and headed for the barn.

Hannah sighed. She hated to let her leg become the subject of discussion. And she hated to show any weakness in front of a man like Zeke Pershing.

"We should ask him to stay for supper," Faith murmured to Hannah. "Shall I?"

Hannah nodded. They had a stew simmering, and it was only neighborly to feed a single man working for her, even if she felt uneasy around him.

Chapter 9: Ruth's Birthday

On Saturday, Zeke hunted in the morning, returning around midday with a deer and a few birds. Then he busied himself inside his house and barn in the afternoon. In a few spots, the mud cement designed to keep wind out of the house had crumbled, so he caulked the holes. He repaired leather harnesses that were only mildly worn.

All the while he fretted over his family. He didn't know whether his brother Joel would visit from California as promised. And what good would it do to have Joel here? He hadn't shown much interest in the family since his departure in early forty-eight. He'd sent a paltry few letters to Pa and to Esther and had never written Zeke.

The twins only went to school because they hated being home with their stepmother and her brood. The boys preferred spending time with Zeke, but this time of year he didn't have enough work to keep them busy. Though, come to think of it, the boys had expressed more interest in attending school since Faith Bramwell appeared with her aunt. Zeke hoped they wouldn't both get sweet on the same girl, which would cause trouble for certain.

Hannah Bramwell. Zeke didn't know what to make of her. She was a prickly one, much like Ma had been. A man could tell where he stood with her, and Zeke didn't think he stood very high in Miz Bramwell's regard. He wasn't sure why, until it dawned on him perhaps she'd been in the churchyard when he struck Mac. He vaguely recalled a tall woman pulling her skirts out of his way.

Hitting Mac hadn't been wise. He'd regretted it ever since. He and Mac had made amends, but Zeke would have to live with whatever others thought of him. Including Miz Bramwell.

He'd enjoyed supper with her and Faith last Friday. Hannah behaved primly, but politely, and the food had been good. Faith chattered away, like Esther had at that age. Faith was a natural at conversation, though he liked Hannah's plain-spoken common sense when she opened her mouth. Zeke wondered why she limped and what made her so reserved.

When he'd put his arms around her to show her how to use the hatchet, he'd been surprised at first—she was a tall woman, and there was substance to her. Not like Jenny, who was a tiny thing. But the proper Miz Bramwell all but froze in his arms, as if his touch sullied her. So he'd ended the kindling-chopping lesson quickly. Faith would have to cut their kindling, if the twins failed in their responsibility to their teacher.

After church on Sunday, Esther rushed over to talk to Zeke. "What is it?" he asked.

"I need to talk quick," she said. "I don't want Ruthie to hear." She hugged her wool shawl around her. "It's Mother Amanda. Ruthie was sobbing on my shoulder afore the service this morning."

"Why?" Their sister Ruth was typically a quiet one—it took a lot to get her going, though once she started it was equally hard to get her to calm down.

"Yesterday was her birthday. She turned twelve."

Zeke swore. "I forgot."

Esther sniffed. "Well, you're a man. Pa forgot, too. I took her a new pocketbook I'd sewn. It was the only present she got. I even whispered to Mother Amanda it was Ruthie's birthday, but she didn't do anything about it. No cake. Nothing special for supper. Nothing."

"Is that why Ruthie was upset this morning?"

Esther nodded. "When any of Amanda's children have birthdays, she goes whole hog. Treats 'em special all day. But our kin—she does nothing."

"Why don't Pa say something to her?"

Esther shook her head and bit her lip. "He ain't paying much attention to any of his young'uns. Nor to mine—his grandchildren. And *she*"— Esther's lip curled as she referred to their stepmother—"just says she'll do for hers and he should do for his. Can't you make Pa do something?"

"I don't see what I can do." Zeke sighed. "I'll go see Ruthie. Take her to town one day this week."

"Talk to Pa—he might listen to you. You know he thinks the world of his sons."

"He does you, too, Esther."

"But you're his oldest. His lead scout on the trail. That means more to him."

Zeke scratched his chin. "I'll talk to him."

As the congregation left the churchyard, Zeke found his father. "Hear tell we forgot Ruthie's birthday yesterday," he said by way of opening.

Pa shook his head. "Esther won't let me forget it ever again. She read me the riot act this morning."

"Thought I'd take Ruth to town this week, if the weather's decent. Stores ain't open today, or I'd do my brotherly duty now."

"That's right nice of you, son."

"You might give her two bits to buy herself something," Zeke suggested. "Unless you got another notion for a present."

"I don't know what to give her. But I'll do just as you say. Fine idea." His father hacked and spat. "Wish I could get rid of this cough of mine."

"You feeling poorly?" Zeke asked. He wondered if Pa was drinking again—he'd been drunk more often than not in the months after Ma died, but Amanda seemed to keep Pa away from alcohol most of the time.

"Ain't felt good since the damp weather hit. Only thing that helps is a belt of whiskey, and Amanda don't let me have but one a day." Pa looked around furtively. "You wouldn't buy your old pa a bottle when you go to town, would you?"

"Pa, I ain't sure—"

"Don't be a mother hen, Zeke. A man needs to quench his thirst when he's ailing."

"Just don't forget to give Ruth her two bits, and I'll do the same." Zeke resolved he would see Doc Tuller before he took Ruth to town—find out if the doctor knew what was wrong with Pa.

Tuesday afternoon a cold wind blew under a cloudy sky. After working through the morning and eating a warmed-over noon meal, Zeke hitched his mules to his wagon and drove to Doc Tuller's claim. After he saw the doctor, he would stop by the McDougall cabin to surprise Ruth at school and take her to town. Maybe his other siblings would want to go also, but he would make sure Ruthie knew she was the reason for the trip. And he'd have to see if he could take just his kin, and not Mother Amanda's brood also.

When he reached the Tuller farm, he knocked on the door. "Why, Zeke Pershing!" Mrs. Tuller said. "Doc's out in the barn, but should be back in a moment." The older woman bustled about to get him a cup of coffee.

By the time the coffee cooled to drinkable and a plate of flapjacks sat in front of Zeke, Doc entered the cabin. "What brings you here, boy?" Doc asked.

"Saw Pa yesterday," Zeke said after swallowing a syrupy bite. "He was coughing. Said he weren't feeling well. Has he been to see you?"

Doc shook his head. "Nope. I got called over there a couple weeks ago to see to young Frankie's croup, but didn't hear of anyone else in the house ailing."

"Could you stop by to see Pa? But don't let on I asked you to."

Doc grinned. "Afraid he'll think you're an old woman?"

Mrs. Tuller clucked from beside the hearth. "Ain't nothing wrong with old women."

"Unless you're a healthy young man," Doc said. "Sure, Zeke. I'll check on your pa. But don't be surprised if he guesses you sent me."

"See if you think he's drinking too much also." Zeke didn't want to raise the possibility, but Doc knew Pa's history.

Doc frowned. "You think he is?"

"Hope not. But I don't see him often enough to know."

"Might be you should spend more time with your kin," Doc said. "Your pa's got too much to deal with—the farm, all his and Amanda's young'uns. Esther does her best to step in, but they need you, too."

Zeke nodded. "I'll try to see 'em at least once a week." Through the winter, he could do it. Before the farm needed him from dawn to dusk.

"You know," Doc said, "Congress passed a new land law. I ain't seen the specifics yet, but I hear tell it grants married men more land than a single fellow. Might be you should think about getting married."

Zeke snorted. "They'll make good on claims already filed, won't they? And you know I wanted to marry Jenny, but that won't happen, so just who do you suggest? Ain't many eligible women in these parts."

"Keep your eyes open, boy." Doc winked. "Got to be someone out there for you."

Zeke arrived at the school about an hour before classes let out, and told Miz Bramwell he had a family errand with Ruth.

Ruthie beamed at his words and jumped up from her bench to gather her belongings. Noah pouted when Zeke said the errand was just with Ruth. Miz Bramwell pursed her lips, but merely nodded.

Zeke drove Ruth to Abernethy's store and told her to find something she liked. "Pa said he gave you two bits, and I'll match it," he said. "Happy birthday, even if it's a tad late."

She grinned and started fingering laces and ribbons. She decided on a length of blue ribbon and then added some peppermints. "I'll save a few for the others," she said.

"It's your birthday," Zeke said. "If you've a mind to hide the candy, I won't tell."

"Not much chance of hiding anything from the other young'uns," Ruth said. "There's too many of 'em. Sarah and I share a drawer for our clothes, and Noah and Henry are into everyone's belongings."

While he waited for Ruth to make her choices and bought a few things for himself, Zeke heard talk of grizzly bear sightings. "They's coming out early this spring," a farmer said. "Only mid-February, and they're leaving their dens."

"Where?" Zeke asked.

"Not too far from your claim," the man replied. "Over by McDougall's land. Man named Devlin Feeney told me."

Zeke plunked his purchases on the store counter. "Did Feeney actually see a bear?"

The farmer nodded. "Says he saw old scat, too. So the bear's been nearby for a while. Not just passing through."

Zeke thought immediately of Hannah and Faith Bramwell alone on the McDougall claim. And of his siblings and all the other students passing through the woods on their way to and from school.

They should be warned.

The day after the trip to town with Ruth, Zeke drove to Douglass Abercrombie's claim to help with repairs to Douglass's barn. Douglass's younger brother Daniel was there as well.

As they worked, Zeke commented, "In town yesterday, a man told me there've been grizzly bear sightings. Either of you seen anything?"

"I been staying close to home most days," Daniel said. "Esther's mighty uncomfortable now."

"She ain't due till early April, is she?" Zeke asked.

"About then," Daniel said. "But she gets mighty tired by day's end, what with three young'uns to mind."

"I seen bear scat," Douglass said. "Down by the creek." He waved toward the back of the barn. A waterway ran about a quarter mile behind Douglass's cabin. It was a slow-moving stream and meandered through his claim, causing many acres of marshy ground. "Only a few piles, but enough for me to keep my rifle with me these days." He gestured at the gun on the barn floor.

"How come the word ain't got out?" Zeke asked. "Seems folks oughta know about a grizzly."

"There's always a chance of bears," Daniel said. "Most folks are careful. I told Esther to mind the young'uns outside."

"Do you know if Hannah Bramwell can shoot?" Zeke asked. "She and her niece Faith are living alone."

"The teacher?" Douglass said. "The McDougall claim's only a few miles from where I seen the scat. Bear could range that far, easy."

"I doubt she's ever fired a gun," Daniel said. "She don't have much experience outside of town life. Don't you and the twins have to chop her wood?"

"Most of it," Zeke acknowledged.

"Well," Daniel said, "you best teach her'n Faith to shoot, too, if they don't know how already. Can't be too careful."

Zeke stopped at the schoolhouse on his way home. By now it was late afternoon, but the Bramwell women were in the yard hanging out laundry in the deepening shadows.

He told them a grizzly had been seen in the area. "Be on the lookout whenever you're outside." He squinted at Hannah. "Can you shoot?"

She shook her head.

"I can, Zeke," Faith volunteered. "Pa taught me on the trail. Though I haven't had any practice since we arrived in Oregon."

"Do you have a rifle here?" Zeke asked.

Hannah nodded. "Mr. McDougall left one. But I would prefer not to use it."

"Best thing to do is to make a lot of noise," Zeke said. "Bear'll stay away from you most likely. But if it's riled, it might well charge. You'll only have one shot. You should keep a gun with you and know how to use it."

Hannah turned to her laundry tub, picked up a sheet and snapped it to unfurl it, then handed a corner to Faith. They hung it on the line while Zeke watched.

"How 'bout we have some target practice?" he asked. "It's too late today, but soon. Maybe tomorrow afternoon?"

Hannah sighed. "If you insist, but only after I release the children from class."

Zeke nodded. "I'll be here."

Chapter 10: Trouble in the Classroom

By the last week in November, her third week of teaching, Hannah thought she'd found a rhythm to her classroom activities. She started by following Jenny's suggestion of dividing the children into two groups—older and younger. She set the older students to an independent task—writing, or a series of algebra equations—while she worked with the younger on their reading. Then she instructed the younger children to work on arithmetic problems while she discussed history with the older ones.

But quickly she discovered the students fell most naturally into three groups. There was a cluster of middle students who were past their primers but not yet able to work without instruction. So she divided the children into three classes. The beginners consisted of Noah Pershing, Henry Purcell, and the youngest Bingham. In the middle group were Ruth Pershing, the younger Bingham girl, John Purcell, and Rose Abercrombie. And the oldest group included her niece Faith, Jonathan and David Pershing, Sarah Purcell, Annabelle Abercrombie, and the older Bingham girl.

This division did not satisfy Hannah entirely. The little Bingham boy was older than Jonah and Henry, but he'd had less formal education. Sarah Purcell and the oldest Bingham lagged the other older students in ability, though not in age. Annabelle Abercrombie had the ability, but whined about every assignment. And the Pershing twins clearly did not think they needed any education at all.

Still, by the start of this third week, Hannah felt she'd adapted to the school well enough, and the children adapted to her. She sometimes struggled to stay ahead of the older ones, but that was part of the satisfaction she obtained from her role as teacher.

On November 28, the last Thursday of the month, a blustery and rainy day, Hannah faced a classroom of fidgety children. Jonathan and David Pershing were late that morning, with no good excuse. Their younger siblings and stepsiblings had been on time, and when Hannah asked the twins where they'd been, they shook their heads.

"Sorry, ma'am," Jonathan muttered.

David added, "Lost track of the time."

As soon as the twins settled on the back bench, Hannah told the older children to write an essay on the importance of punctuality and turned to help Henry Purcell and Noah Pershing read their primer. The little boys stumbled through the words.

"Eew," Annabelle Abercrombie said. "Something stinks in here." As the girl spoke, Hannah noticed a terrible stench coming from the coals on the hearth.

Hannah went to investigate. A smoldering black lump smoked in the back of the fireplace. She pulled it forward with iron tongs. "Is that a skunk?" she shrieked, as the full odor of the lump hit her. From the look of the varmint, it was not only several days dead but had been sodden when placed in the fireplace.

Snickering sounded behind her. She turned. Jonathan pasted an innocent expression on his lips, but his eyes gave him away. "What is it?" she asked.

"Don't know, ma'am," he said.

She turned to David, the less incorrigible of the twins, and glared.

"Found it along the path this morning. 'Twere already dead, ma'am. We didn't hurt it." David didn't look quite so innocent as his brother.

"Find a towel, and take whatever it is outside," she ordered. "Quickly."

The boys did as requested, but the rest of the students now either giggled or retched. Annabelle rushed outside after the twins, and Hannah followed to find the girl heaving into a bush in the yard. The twins guffawed as they watched.

"Boys," Hannah said. "Go to the barn and wait for me."

She returned to the classroom, told Faith to work with the younger children on their reading, and donned her coat to go back outside, leaving the door open to air out the room. Once away from the children, she took a deep breath. She would have to punish the twins, but didn't relish the chore. A part of her wanted to laugh at their antics, but she couldn't allow her authority in the classroom to be diminished.

She cut a switch from a tree by the house and went to the barn. After entering, she told Jonathan, "Lean your hands against the wall. Your back toward me."

"Ma'am—"

"Now." She pointed the switch at the boy. Hannah was tall for a woman, but Jonathan was taller than she was, though skinny. Her only power was in her voice, and she would have to make good use of it.

Thankfully, Jonathan complied.

She struck him three times across the back of his thighs. On the third strike he whimpered.

Then she turned to David. "You next."

David moved in silence to the wall and took his three whacks without a squawk.

"I will be talking to your father about this incident. For now, leave the premises. When you return tomorrow, I expect a written apology from each of you."

The boys nodded. "Yes'm," one of them mumbled.

Hannah watched the twins amble out of the yard, then she returned to the cabin. Annabelle now sobbed in the corner, while the rest of the children stared at her.

"Did you whup 'em?" Noah Pershing asked in awe. The twins were his big brothers, and Hannah wondered where the little boy's sympathies were.

"Let's keep the door open until the odor dissipates," Hannah said, not answering Noah's question.

"I can't stay, Miss Bramwell," Annabelle said. "My dress is soiled." Vomit stained the front of her skirt. "Rose and I have to go home."

"Come with me, Annabelle," Hannah said, and took her behind the curtain where the washbowl stood. She sponged off the girl's dress, but Annabelle insisted on leaving with her sister.

"And we might not come back!" Annabelle declared as she and Rose flounced away from the school. "My folks won't make me if those Pershing boys are here."

It occurred to Hannah teaching would be easier without the twins or Annabelle. And if she had to choose, she wasn't sure whether she'd pick the Pershing boys or the Abercrombie girls.

Not much learning happened for the rest of the day, though Hannah tried her best.

Chapter 11: Shooting Lesson

Thursday afternoon Zeke rode Red into the McDougall yard again and hitched the horse to a fence post, ready to give the women a shooting lesson.

Ruth and Noah had told him about the incident at school that morning, and he'd yelled at the twins until he was hoarse. But no matter his brothers' shenanigans, Hannah Bramwell and her niece still needed to be ready to deal with a bear.

When he knocked, Hannah opened the door. "Yes?" she said. "Did you want to talk about the twins?"

"Miz Bramwell, I came to teach you to shoot, like I said I would."

"I'm sorry, Mr. Pershing. I forgot. I have more pressing matters—"

"Ain't nothing more pressing'n dealing with a grizzly, if it comes at you."

"Mr. Pershing," Hannah said. "Did you hear your brothers made Annabelle ill today? They caused the entire room discomfort with the noxious odor—"

"I heard, Miz Bramwell. Ruth and Noah made sure I knew about it." His lips twitched, though he tried not to grin.

"It was extremely disruptive," she said primly. "Annabelle Abercrombie was sickened."

Zeke shook his head, thinking of what Ruth had said about the girl's dramatics. "That girl sickens whenever it's convenient for her."

"I doubt it was convenient for her to get smallpox."

"Smallpox was a true misfortune for Annabelle," Zeke acknowledged. "But she makes use of her disfigurement when it suits her. Unlike you."

Hannah stood straighter, a shocked expression on her face. "What do you know about me, Mr. Pershing?"

He shrugged. He hadn't meant to make her mad. "If you was like Annabelle, you wouldn't've come to Oregon. You wouldn't be learning to milk cows and chop wood. You wouldn't be teaching in a place you know nothing about."

"I know enough—"

"I'm trying to pay you a compliment, Miz Bramwell. You're a brave woman for following your brother west and for teaching when you ain't done it afore. But if you can't—"

"I'm sorry, Mr. Pershing. It's been a trying week."

"And I'm sorry for my brothers' part in it, ma'am. Now, can we get on with the shooting lesson?"

Faith looked up from the table where she sat writing. "I found the ammunition Mac left. We're ready."

Zeke smiled at Faith. "You got a target set up?"

Faith shook her head. "No, but we can shoot at the trees across the yard. Nothing beyond them but the creek and a cornfield. Nothing in the cornfield this time of year."

"Get a board," Zeke said. "I'll hang it up for us to shoot at while you ladies get your cloaks and gloves."

Hannah didn't move. "Mr. Pershing, I must deal with your brothers. They have disrupted my classroom and caused injury to another student."

He looked at her. "Miz Bramwell, Jonathan and David will bring their apologies to you tomorrow. You can't do anything afore then."

"I must talk to your father and to Annabelle's parents as soon as I can."

"Pa can wait. So can Annabelle Abercrombie and her parents. I come to teach you to shoot. Now, get your wrap."

She turned on her heel and took her cloak off a peg by the door.

Zeke nailed the board Faith found onto a tree about a hundred feet away from the cabin on the far side of the barnyard, then he checked to be sure no one wandered in the creek bed or the field beyond the tree.

Mac had left his single-barrel rifle in the cabin. He'd taken his newer gun to town, Zeke supposed.

Faith went first with target practice. She hit the board five shots out of ten, and managed to reload the weapon in between shots, though she was too slow. "You better hope any bears you see give you a second chance," Zeke said, chuckling at her.

Faith grinned. "I'll work at it. Next time I'll hit eight out of ten."

"Still not good enough," Zeke said. "Now, Miz Bramwell." He handed her the rifle and warned her, "It's got a kick. Brace yourself."

She frowned at him, aimed, and pulled the trigger. The recoil sent her to the ground on her rear.

Zeke smothered his grin when he realized she was in pain. "That's what I meant by a kick." He reached out a hand to help her stand. "Are you all right?"

She nodded grimly, but limped as she took a step or two. "I don't know if my leg can handle this."

"You'll be ready this time," he said, as he reloaded the rifle. "Now you know what to expect."

He helped her correct her stance to better absorb the shock. She was as rigid as she'd been with the hatchet a few weeks back.

She aimed again, taking her time. Her finger stayed still on the trigger as if she was afraid to pull it.

"Shoot," Zeke ordered.

Hannah hesitated, glanced at him, looked back at the target, and fired again. She staggered this time but stayed on her feet. Her shot went nowhere near the target.

"You reload this time," he said, and showed her how. That part, she learned quickly.

"Well," he said, "I guess you can load and Faith can shoot. If the bear'll stand still while you do."

"Let me try again," Hannah said, her jaw clenched.

Zeke was impressed with her grit, if not with her aim, and handed her the gun.

They practiced for an hour until dusk made it too dark to see. By the end, Hannah could hit the target about as well as Faith. She'd been knocked down twice more, but got up gamely each time. The woman had pluck, Zeke decided. She might not know anything about living on the frontier, but she didn't back down from a challenge.

Still, he hoped the bears would stay far away from the McDougall cabin. The women would be better off shouting at the beasts than trying to shoot them.

As he left, he tipped his hat at Hannah Bramwell. "I'll speak to Jonathan and David again," he said. "Make sure they know not to cause any more ructions in your classroom."

Chapter 12: Hannah Visits the Parents

Friday morning, all her muscles sore from the shooting lesson, Hannah girded herself to deal with whichever pupils returned to the classroom. She was surprised when the Pershings and Purcells were the first to arrive—the twins leading their younger siblings and stepsiblings.

"We're sorry, ma'am," Jonathan said, handing her a note. David mumbled the same and handed her a paper as well. She opened the notes to find neatly written letters of apologies.

"Did you tell your father about yesterday?" she asked.

They shook their heads. "Just Zeke," David said. "He said we had to apologize, like you said. He gave us the paper and ink."

"So your father doesn't know?"

The boys shook their heads again.

"This afternoon when school is out, I will visit him."

The Binghams arrived, as did Rose Abercrombie, but Annabelle did not come to class. At the noon break, Hannah stayed in the cabin with the girls, but the boys went outside despite the wind and rain.

As some of the girls played in the corner, Rose and Ruth Pershing approached Hannah. "May we speak with you, Miz Bramwell?" Ruth asked. "In private?"

"Put on your coats, and we'll walk outside," Hannah said.

The three went out in the yard. The boys climbed the paddock fence and raced around. "What is it?" she asked the two girls.

"It's Annabelle," Rose said, her voice barely above a whisper. "She's sensitive about her face. You know, her pockmarks."

"Annabelle was so pretty afore she had smallpox," Ruth said. "She hates for people to stare at her now."

"Then when she got sick yesterday, she thought everyone was laughing at her," Rose said. "Those Pershing twins are so awful."

Ruth nodded. "They're my brothers, but I don't like 'em much sometimes. Zeke's the only one what can make 'em mind."

"Not your father?" Hannah asked.

Ruth shook her head. "Not since Ma died. She could. And Esther used to, but the boys don't listen to Esther no more."

"Anymore," Hannah said, absentmindedly. "Your mother died along the trail west, didn't she?"

Ruth nodded. "And we don't like our stepmother."

It seemed to be a common complaint, Hannah thought—Faith didn't like her stepmother either. Women died young so often, leaving their children behind to be raised by others. "I'll go see Annabelle after school," she said.

After the break, Hannah told the Pershing twins, "I'll take your letters to Annabelle this afternoon. Do I have your assurances you will treat her kindly if she returns?"

The boys nodded, Jonathan in particular looking abashed. "We didn't mean her no harm, ma'am. Just having some fun."

After dismissing the children early, Hannah asked Faith, "What can you tell me about Annabelle's parents?"

Faith shrugged. "Her folks are all right. Douglass and Louisa Abercrombie. It's Douglass's pa who's the problem. Old Samuel Abercrombie—Captain Abercrombie—was a beast to everyone in our wagon train. He and Franklin Pershing argued the whole way, until Mr. McDougall took over as company captain. The Abercrombies and their platoon left us for a while when Captain McDougall detoured to Whitman Mission. Life was much more peaceable then. But then we met up again and the Abercrombies came back."

"What's the relationship between the Abercrombies and Pershings now?" Hannah asked.

"It hasn't ever been good, Aunt Hannah. I feel for Esther Abercrombie, stuck in the middle. But between you and me, I'd rather have the Pershings in our school than the Abercrombies."

Hannah hitched the plow mules to the cart. A cold rain fell, but she couldn't delay this trip. She decided to travel alone to see the parents, fearing Faith's presence would be a distraction. First she headed for Annabelle Abercrombie's home.

When she arrived, she found Annabelle and Rose at home with their mother Louisa. She showed Louisa the apologies from the Pershing twins and apologized herself. "The boys have been punished, Mrs. Abercrombie, and I hope Annabelle and Rose will return to school on Monday."

"Please, Ma," Rose said. "I like school."

"And you, Annabelle? What do you want?" Louisa asked her older daughter.

"Will those Pershings be back?" Annabelle asked petulantly.

"I hope so," Hannah said. "I'm going to talk to their father after this, to impress on him how important good behavior is in the classroom. Won't you give it a try?"

Douglass Abercrombie entered the cabin, his face and hands red from the cold. At Louisa's request, Hannah went through the situation again for him.

Douglass turned to his older daughter. "You should return to class, Annabelle. Your grandmother Harriet values education. She made me go to school as long as Pa permitted."

"Pa—" Annabelle whined, but her father insisted. After much pouting by Annabelle and many reassurances from Hannah, the girl agreed to return on Monday.

Buoyed by Douglass Abercrombie's support, Hannah set out for Franklin Pershing's claim, hoping for the same success. Despite the frigid drizzle, several of the Pershing and Purcell children chased dogs and chickens around the muddy yard. Inside the cabin, a toddler squalled, and Amanda Pershing shouted at Hannah's two youngest students, Noah Pershing and Henry Purcell, as she stirred a pot on the stove.

"Is Mr. Pershing here?" Hannah asked.

Amanda Pershing sniffed. "Think he's in the barn. Where he is most days. Smoking his pipe, most likely."

"I'll take you to see Pa, Miz Bramwell," Noah said.

"Then you get back here, young Noah," Amanda said. "You and Henry ain't done cleaning up what I asked you to."

Noah pulled on Hannah's hand to lead her out to the barn. "Are you gonna talk to Pa about the skunk?" he asked. "Can I stay?"

"You should return inside," Hannah said. "Mind your stepmother." As they crossed the yard to the barn, she noticed one wall of the building was partially singed.

Noah's lower lip poked out, but he didn't argue. "Pa," he shouted after opening the barn door. "Teacher's here to see you." He ambled toward the house, leaving Hannah in the doorway.

"Mr. Pershing?" she asked, peering inside. Dim light entered the barn through the door and one window in the hayloft above. She caught a whiff of pipe tobacco and saw a man's vague silhouette in the shadows.

"Over here," the man said as he stood. She'd been introduced to the Pershing patriarch at church one Sunday, but he seemed smaller now. He stretched out his hand. "Hear tell my twins been causing you a ruction."

"Did they tell you?"

He grinned. "*They* didn't, but the rest of the young'uns were happy to fill me in. Said the skunk were more noxious dead than alive."

"Your sons caused Annabelle Abercrombie to become ill."

Mr. Pershing coughed. "That girl is just like her grandfather. Takes offense at anything."

"Mr. Pershing, I can't have—"

"I ain't excusing my sons, Miz Bramwell. But they're only boys. And without a ma to teach 'em how to behave."

"Aren't you their parent also, Mr. Pershing?" Hannah couldn't imagine her father letting any of his children—son or daughter—get away with a prank like the Pershing twins had committed. "And they have a stepmother also."

"Amanda and me, we agreed we'd each see to our own brood," he said. "But boys will be boys. I talked to 'em. Told 'em not to cause you no bother. I'm sure it won't happen again."

"Annabelle has agreed to return to school, and I've assured her the twins will not cause her any more difficulty." Hannah drew herself to full height, almost as tall as Mr. Pershing, and said, "If the boys misbehave again, I will expel them."

Hannah was sorely disappointed in Mr. Pershing's response to the twins' misdeeds. She grew more irate as she drove home. Over supper, she described her afternoon visits to Faith.

"Don't mind Captain Pershing, Aunt Hannah," Faith said. "He hasn't been the same since his wife died."

"You mean the twins' mother?"

Faith nodded. "He was a good captain when we started out. After Jonah was born and Mrs. Pershing died, he started drinking. That's when Captain McDougall took command. And Esther took the baby."

Hannah had heard the story before, but listened to it more carefully now. "It sounds like no one has given those boys any real guidance since their mother died," she mused.

"That's right." Faith sighed. "At least my pa tries. Theirs doesn't."

"All the more reason their brother Zeke ought to step up," Hannah said.

Faith sniffed. "Zeke is single, Aunt Hannah. He can't make much of a home for David and Jonathan."

Hannah frowned. "But you would have preferred your father hadn't remarried—that he raised you on his own."

"Yes, but Pa had me to help. After Esther and Rachel left home, the Pershings didn't have any girls except Ruth. And she was too young."

"Maybe if their father had married someone else . . . " Hannah murmured.

"It surely makes a difference who a man marries." Faith nodded vigorously. "You should hope Zeke picks a good woman who can help with the boys. Otherwise, they'll continue to torment us all."

"What about Annabelle?" Hannah asked. "How do I get her compliance in school?"

Faith shrugged. "She's a harder nut to crack. She's never been happy, long as I've known her. But she's been worse since the smallpox. She was vain before, and now she has nothing to be vain about."

Hannah stared into the fire. "Maybe there is a way . . . "

On Saturday, about an hour before Hannah was scheduled to dismiss her pupils, a knock sounded on the cabin door. She opened it to find Jenny McDougall smiling at her. "I was visiting Esther, and thought I would pay you and the students a call. I left my children with Esther while my husband walks his timberland with Esther's husband and some other men. Mac wants to find the best wood on our property for our new home."

"Come in," Hannah said, though she felt awkward ushering Jenny into her own cabin.

The children voiced a chorus of greetings, "Good afternoon, Miz Jenny," and Hannah knew the rest of her lesson plans for the day would have to wait. Jenny spent the next hour talking with her former pupils. After the students left, Hannah offered Jenny a cup of tea.

"I'd welcome that, Hannah," Jenny said. She sighed, "I've missed the students. And teaching."

Hannah put the kettle over the fire. "They miss you as well. I'm afraid I don't have your knack for teaching. The younger pupils are eager to learn, but the older ones are a challenge."

Jenny laughed. "Are the Pershing twins causing trouble?"

"Yes," Hannah said ruefully. "And I don't know how to manage them."

"They're fine boys, really," Jenny said. "But Captain Pershing lost interest in his children after their mother died, and their stepmother . . . well, she favors her own offspring."

Hannah turned to the hearth for the kettle. "You'd think men would give more consideration before foisting a stepmother on their sons and daughters," she murmured, thinking of Faith's difficulty living with her stepmother Alice.

"How true," Jenny said. "Though mothers can impose unfortunate stepfathers on their children also." A faraway look in her eyes made Hannah believe Jenny spoke from experience. Then Jenny brought her gaze back to Hannah, and asked, "How are the Abercrombie girls?"

Hannah smiled. "Rose is a delight. Or tries to be. But Annabelle is another challenging student, and Rose often follows her older sister's lead."

"Annabelle is too much like her grandfather," Jenny said. "He was difficult to live with on the trail, and he has not improved since we settled. He's something of a tyrant."

"And Annabelle's parents?" Hannah asked. "Her father argued for her return to school, though I think her mother would have let the girl do whatever she wanted."

Jenny shook her head. "Harriet Abercrombie is one stepmother who did well in rearing her stepsons. Both Douglass and Daniel are fine men." She sighed. "Douglass tries to raise his daughters as he was raised, but Louisa often defers to Annabelle's whims. Unfortunately, Annabelle has been peevish since she had smallpox—though any girl would hate having pockmarks on her face."

"Yes," Hannah said. She'd been grateful often enough her own scars were hidden, though they still caused her pain and stiffness in her legs.

Chapter 13: Joel Arrives

The first few days of December continued cold and blustery, with rain falling off and on. Tuesday afternoon, December 3, the rain turned to sleet—the first solid precipitation of the winter. When Zeke saw the leaden sky, he spent the afternoon hunting to make sure his meat cellar was adequately stocked for a lengthy storm.

He returned to his claim around supper time with a few rabbits and two geese—enough to keep him and his dog Blackie from going hungry. He curried Red dry and gave the gelding an extra scoop of oats. The horse snorted his appreciation. Zeke slapped the horse on the rear and went to clean the meat.

After throwing the entrails into the yard for the dog to eat, Zeke hung most of his kill in the meat cellar. He took one rabbit inside and put it on a spit in the hearth. He poured himself two fingers of whiskey and sat to sip it while the meat cooked.

Blackie set up a ruction, barking outside. Zeke sighed, heaved himself to his feet, and went to investigate.

"Zeke!" a man's voice shouted. "Open up afore your dog kills me!"

Joel! Zeke knew his brother's voice. His younger brother had returned.

Zeke opened the door and Joel caught him in a hug. Blackie continued to bark until Zeke told him to be quiet, then the mutt began to whine.

"When did you get in?" he asked his brother. "Come in, come in. Have you eaten?"

Joel laughed as they entered. "I'm hungrier than that mongrel you got outside. And I could do with a shot of something warm," he said, pointing at Zeke's glass on the table.

Zeke poured his brother a glass of whiskey and refilled his own. "I've put a rabbit on to roast. It'll be ready soon."

Joel gulped the whiskey and groaned his approval. "Is there a spare stall in the barn? My horse could use a rub-down."

"You planning to stay here tonight? Have you seen Pa?"

Joel shook his head. "You're as much family as I can tolerate at the moment. I'll ride to Pa's tomorrow. That all right with you?"

"Guess it'll have to be." Zeke was glad to see his brother, but wondered what complications Joel would bring to the rest of the Pershings.

Wednesday morning Zeke ate and did his chores. Up in the loft, Joel slept late, so Zeke took care of Joel's mare along with Red. When he returned from the barn, his brother was stirring. Yawning over the railing, Joel asked. "What's for breakfast?"

Zeke shrugged. "Got another rabbit, if you want to cook it. Or mush."

"Mush like Ma made?" Joel's voice perked up. "I ain't eaten mush in a long time. Had plenty of meat as I rode, but no porridge."

"There's the pot," Zeke said, pointing to an empty Dutch oven and then at the stove he'd bought for Jenny. "Suit yourself."

Joel came down the ladder and stumbled outside. When he returned, he began to cook unenthusiastically. "Thought you might cook it for me."

"I ate already. When you want to head for Pa's?"

Joel sighed. "No need to rush. According to Esther's letters, he ain't doing well and Amanda Purcell has made his life miserable."

"That's just Esther," Zeke said. "Pa got what he wanted—a woman to help him raise the young'uns. Though Amanda don't pay ours much mind, only hers."

"Should I go see Esther first?"

"Your choice," Zeke said. "She'll give you an earful, and you might want to see Pa's situation for yourself."

"I'd rather be prepared," Joel said. "Let's ride over to Esther's. You coming with me?"

"Might as well."

After Joel ate and dressed, the brothers saddled their horses and went to Esther's. She rushed out of her cabin when they rode into the yard. "Joel! Joel!" she shouted, and launched herself into his arms as soon as he dismounted. "You're here! Have you seen Pa? What do you think of how the young'uns have grown? Come see Jonah. And meet Cordelia and

Sammy." She dragged Joel into the cabin while Zeke tethered the horses.

Esther poured her brothers coffee and set the children to playing on the floor after introducing them to Joel. "How does Pa seem to you?" she said when she sat at the table with them.

"Ain't seen him yet," Joel said. "Going there next. Tell me what you think I'll find."

"You'll notice how run down the claim is, at least compared to mine or Zeke's. And whichever young'uns are there will be dirty." Esther continued to malign her stepmother's housekeeping and childrearing, until Zeke finally put an end to it.

"We'd best be on our way, if we're going to get there afore noon," he said. "You want to come?" he asked Esther.

"Give me time to wash the children's faces, and they can go, too." It took another half-hour for Esther to clean up the children and wrap a venison pie to take, while Zeke and Joel hitched a mule to her wagon. Then they all set out.

As they approached his father's claim, Zeke said, "Let me go ahead to warn Pa we're all coming."

"No," his brother said. "I want to catch him unawares." When they pulled into the yard, Joel let out a shout and leapt out of the wagon.

Pa came out of the barn. His face lit up. "Joel! Son, you came!" He pounded Joel on the back as they embraced.

Mother Amanda stood in the doorway of the cabin, lips pursed. "How many of you are there?" she asked wearily. "I just washed up after breakfast. But there's bread and butter."

"I brought a pie," Esther said. "We'll make do. I wanted Pa to see Joel as soon as possible. He got in last night."

"Why didn't you come here first, son?" Pa asked.

"Thought I'd bother Zeke instead," Joel said. "He's all alone on his claim."

The school-aged children were gone, but little Frankie squalled in the cabin, putting Esther's baby Sammy into a similar mood. Cordelia and Jonah whimpered, and Esther led her stepmother toward the hearth. "The children need to eat. Let's slice the bread."

Pa tried to question Joel about his travels, but the toddlers interrupted. After the meal, Zeke suggested the men adjourn to the barn to talk. Esther frowned at this, but didn't argue. "Mother Amanda and I'll clean up. Then

I need to take the children home," she said.

In the barn, Joel recounted his adventures traveling on horseback from the gold fields outside Sacramento to Oregon City. "Took six weeks," he said. "I left it a little late, and got caught in early snows in the Klamath Mountains. Had to hole up at a fur trader's camp on the Rogue River. They've found gold near there—that's where I'm going next."

"You won't be staying here?" Pa said, disappointment evident in his voice.

Joel shook his head. "I ain't a farmer." He turned to Zeke. "I thought you might want to come with me, now Jenny married Mac. Ain't no reason for you to stay here no more."

Zeke shook his head. "I *am* a farmer," he said. "I prefer plowing to prospecting."

But did he want to stay in Oregon, where every day he was reminded of what he might have had with Jenny?

Joel badgered Zeke all week about leaving the Willamette Valley to mine with him near the Rogue River. Zeke told his brother no, but Joel pressed harder.

"How can you stand the weather? All it does is rain," Joel complained on Saturday evening as they sat by the fire after supper sipping whiskey. "What's left for you here, now Jenny's married? You can make more money mining than farming. And Pa said the *Spectator* reported the new land law won't let single men claim as much land as you staked out in forty-seven."

"I don't see you living the life of a rich man," Zeke responded. Privately, he wondered what impact the Donation Land Act would have on his claim, but he'd just have to wait and see.

"I made a lot in California, then I lost it," Joel said. "I wasn't as smart as McDougall. Mac didn't spend his nuggets on gambling and whores. After mining, he bought a store, and later he transported gold from the mines to the towns. All his ventures seemed to make money."

"I thought he sold you the transportation business."

"Yeah, but that was too tame for me." Joel sipped his whiskey. "This goes down mighty smooth," he said, tipping his glass at Zeke. "You ain't letting Pa have any, are you?"

Zeke grimaced and shook his head. "Mother Amanda ain't good for much else, but she does keep him from getting drunk." He frowned at his brother, debating whether to ask the question on his mind. Finally, he did. "Do you know who the baby's parents are—the little girl Mac brought back with him?"

Joel shrugged. "Maria? Her mother was a whore in Sacramento. No one knows who the father was."

"Could she be Mac's daughter?" It ate at Zeke that Mac might have brought his bastard home for Jenny to raise.

"Mac says no. He was friendly with Consuela, even hired her to work in his store and cook for him. But he didn't partake of her favors at the saloon." Joel took another sip of his drink. "Now, I, on the other hand . . . " He winked.

"You mean the girl could be your daughter? My niece?" That notion upset Zeke more than he expected. If the child was a Pershing, she should live with his family, not with Mac and Jenny.

Joel shook his head. "Not likely. I'd moved on to other girls by the time Consuela got knocked up. Nope, Maria's pa is likely to remain a mystery."

"Why did Mac adopt the girl? If that's what he did."

"Like I said, he and Consuela were friendly. She died after a customer stabbed her. Hear tell she asked Mac to take the baby on her deathbed."

So Jenny was raising a whore's child. Even if the girl's existence wasn't Mac's fault, the notion of Jenny mothering the baby bothered Zeke. But he had no say in the matter—Jenny had refused to give him that right.

Sunday morning Zeke and Joel rode into Oregon City for church, despite the continued rain. After the service, members of their wagon company clustered around Joel to greet him and learn first-hand about the gold fields of California.

Zeke grew bored with the conversation, still not interested in accompanying Joel to the new lodes along the Rogue River. He went to find Doc Tuller. "Have you looked in on Pa yet?" he asked the doctor.

Tuller nodded. "Stopped by yesterday. He's looking a little jaundiced. He ain't drinking again, is he?"

"Mother Amanda says only a glass here and there."

"He ought to lay off altogether," Doc said. "Though now might be too late. His liver is probably already pickled. And I don't like the sound of his cough."

"Then he's sick?" Zeke asked in alarm.

"He's old enough, anything could happen any time." Doc gave a wry smile. "Though he ain't as old as I am, and I ain't dying yet." Doc struck a match on the sole of his shoe and lit a pipe. "By the way, did you see last Thursday's *Spectator*? New land law limits single men to three hundred twenty acres. Married men still get six hundred forty. Maybe you need a wife."

"I saw it," Zeke said.

Mac McDougall joined them in time to hear Doc's question. "No one can say yet what the legislature will do for existing claims. Safest thing would be for single men to marry."

Zeke crossed his arms and scowled at Mac—the last person in the world he wanted advising him about marriage. "Three hundred twenty is still more land than I could have owned in Missouri. I ain't cleared even near half of my claim yet." He smiled wryly. "And if I don't like the laws here, I could abandon my claim."

"Where would you go?" Mac asked.

"Joel wants me to go with him to the Rogue River."

Mac frowned. "Have you talked to your brother about how he lived in California?"

"What do you mean?" Zeke asked.

"He sowed some pretty wild oats," Mac said, cocking his head in Joel's direction. "My recollection is you didn't behave that way. You might not be comfortable partnering with him."

Part of Zeke agreed with Mac, but he had to defend his family. "He's my brother. I think I know him better'n you."

Mac shrugged, then he and Doc began debating the meaning of the land laws. Zeke spied Hannah Bramwell across the churchyard with Faith and the rest of her family. He might as well pay his respects, and he wandered toward them.

"Morning, Miz Bramwell," he said, tipping his hat when he reached her.

"Good morning." She nodded.

"Hello, Zeke," Faith said. "Isn't it exciting to hear about your brother's adventures in California? I would love to see a gold nugget. Has he shown you one?"

"I think he spent all his nuggets afore he left," Zeke said. "He has a bag of gold dust, though there ain't many stores here in Oregon City that'll take it. Hard to know the value."

"Have you thought any more about our discussion regarding your twin brothers?" Hannah asked.

"I ain't had time, what with Joel's visit," Zeke said. "But I'll talk to my father about the boys."

"They need a firm hand," Hannah said with a frown. "Maybe more than your father can manage."

Zeke resented her meddling. "We Pershings take care of our own," he told her, and walked away.

Chapter 14: More Trouble in the Classroom

The second Monday in December began with yet more rain, but in late morning sunshine turned the sky a sparkling blue. Hannah let the children outside after they ate the food they'd brought for their noon meal. The boys played ball in the mud, while the girls sat on the barnyard fence and talked. Hannah was glad for the break from the classroom.

"Miz Bramwell!" Annabelle Abercrombie shouted. "Jonathan hit me with the muddy ball. Now my dress is filthy!"

Jonathan hung his head, looking sheepish. "Didn't mean to, Miz Bramwell. My throw went bad."

His twin David snickered. "Went bad 'cause you wanted to bother Annabelle."

Hannah raised an inquiring eyebrow at Faith.

"I don't know if it was an accident or not, Aunt Hannah." Faith grinned. "I couldn't tell where Jonathan aimed his throw."

Annabelle sobbed, and her sister Rose piped up. "We'd best go home, Miz Bramwell. Ma don't like us to stay in dirty clothes." At that, both girls jumped off the fence and ran into the cabin to gather their belongings.

Hannah followed. "I'm sure I can get the mud off your skirt, Annabelle. You can stay, if you'd like."

Annabelle shook her head. "Jonathan Pershing is a troublemaker. Always has been. Him and David both."

"He and David," Hannah corrected.

"I don't want to look a fright," Annabelle said. "And he knows it. I have an ugly face, and I don't want ugly clothes, too."

Hannah remembered the unkind looks and comments she'd received after her accident, the whispers the other children made. "What matters far less than your face is your character," she said, realizing she sounded priggish as she spoke. The same words from her teacher a decade earlier had not lightened her heart any.

Annabelle shrugged and left school, Rose trailing behind.

Hannah called Jonathan Pershing inside. "You know, you hurt Annabelle's pride, more than her clothes," she told him.

"How'd I do that, ma'am?" Jonathan asked. "How can her pride be hurt by a little mud?"

"She wants to look nice at school."

"I think she looks fine. Me and David just wanted to play ball with her."

"David and I," Hannah said.

"You wasn't there, it was me and David," the boy protested.

"I'm correcting your grammar, Mr. Pershing. She wouldn't play ball with David and you."

"That's right, ma'am. I asked, and she ignored me. So I threw the ball at her, thinking she'd catch it and throw it back. But she weren't looking—"

"Wasn't looking."

"Why won't she pay me no mind?" Jonathan's words went up an octave as he spoke. Hannah wondered whether he was about to cry like Annabelle, or if his voice was simply shifting between a boy's and a man's.

"She is very self-conscious about her appearance," Hannah said.

"I think she looks fine," Jonathan said again. "She looks as fine as any girl does."

His words stopped Hannah. Was Jonathan sweet on Annabelle Abercrombie? That might be the making of both young people, though Hannah wasn't sure how to get them to improve each other instead of causing trouble.

Maybe Faith would have some suggestions.

After supper that evening, as Hannah and Faith sat knitting beside the fireplace, Hannah raised the subject. "What was going on between Jonathan and Annabelle?" she asked her niece.

"What do you mean, Aunt Hannah? It was just a playground spat. Jonathan teased Annabelle, like he always does. And she got mad, like she always does."

"Then he pesters her frequently?"

Faith nodded. "He and David both, but Jonathan is worse about it."

"Do you think he likes her?"

Faith's eyes grew round. "Do you think so? But David is so much nicer than Jonathan."

"Really?" Hannah asked, surprised yet again by her students.

"Oh, yes. David talks to me about books and things. Jonathan is so wild. And Jonathan used to bother Annabelle back before she had smallpox. Then last year he ignored her, and this year he's teasing her again, like he used to."

"How do you know all this if you went to school in town and they lived out here on the farms?"

"Jonathan pestered her after church, too. And sometimes I saw them in town."

"Hmm." Hannah finished the round on the stocking she was knitting, then asked, "How do you tell the twins apart?"

"It's easy, Aunt Hannah. Their hair swirls differently," Faith said with a shrug. "And, like I said, David is nicer. You can tell them apart also, can't you?"

"Yes," Hannah said. "But a lot of people seem to have trouble."

"Once you know them," Faith said confidently, "they don't look anything alike."

"I'm not sure that's true," Hannah said. After knitting another round, she asked, "So you like David better?"

Faith blushed. "Well, he *is* nicer," she said for a third time. "And smarter." The girl gasped. "Now, look, you made me drop a stitch with all this talk."

Hannah worried the Abercrombie girls wouldn't return to school the next day, but they strolled in as she was about to begin the lessons.

"Let's try to get along today," she said to the class at large. Then she turned to the older students. "I'd like you to work on the algebra problems with partners. Faith and David, you're one team. Annabelle and Jonathan, you're another." And she paired the oldest Bingham girl with Sarah Purcell. "Now, which team can solve the problems the quickest?"

"That's not fair, Miss Bramwell," Annabelle protested. "David works harder than Jonathan. Why do I have to work with Jonathan?"

"I'm just as fast as he is," Jonathan said. "Let me show you, Annabelle."

"You won't tease me?" Annabelle's voice quavered.

"Not if you're my partner. I want to win, too."

The three teams set to work. Hannah assigned the middle group of students to write out their spelling words, then she began reading to the primer class. Except for the sound of her voice, all was quiet for about a quarter hour. Then she heard David snickering. She glanced over at the older children, but they looked at her innocently.

A guffaw sounded from David.

"Miss Bramwell!" Annabelle shrieked. "He cut my hair!"

"Did not!" Jonathan said. "Those are Sarah's scissors on the floor!" He pointed at his stepsister.

"I didn't do anything!" Sarah said. "What did you do, Jonathan?"

Jonathan shook his head.

David pointed at Annabelle and chortled. "Well, she surely has a chunk of hair missing."

Hannah walked behind Annabelle to look. A large lock of hair in the back had been cut about neck level. The shorn lock lay strewn on the floor next to a small pair of scissors. "Did you see what happened?" Hannah asked the other girls.

Faith and the Bingham girl shook their heads.

"No, ma'am," Sarah Purcell said. "But those are my sewing scissors. They been missing at home."

"I want both you boys out in the barn," Hannah said, pointing at the door. Fury at the twins threatened to make her say more than she should. She'd deal with them later.

Annabelle sobbed. "I'm going home. Come on, Rose."

Her sister stood and slowly picked up her belongings. Annabelle tucked her ragged locks into a knit cap, put on her coat, and stalked out without a word. Rose followed with a backward glance.

"Faith," Hannah said, "help the younger children with their reading. The rest of you, keep working."

She heaved a deep breath as she followed the twins to the barn. She had no idea how to handle these boys. It seemed no one did.

"Jonathan," she said when she had them alone, "it appears you did cut Annabelle's hair. Didn't you hear anything I said the other day? You mortify her when she is singled out for attention, particularly when you harm her appearance."

He hung his head. "I just want her to notice me. To like me. She was so danged—"

"Language, Mr. Pershing."

"—so blessed sure I couldn't do the algebra. Then she worked the problem, not paying me no mind."

"And you thought it would help to cut her hair?" Hannah shook her head in amazement—not even a thirteen-year-old boy could be so stupid.

Jonathan sniffed, seeming near tears.

"And you, David." Hannah turned to the other twin. "You should have stopped this."

"But he's my brother, ma'am."

"Blood is not thicker than water when you see someone about to make a foolish mistake." She sighed. "You should help each other be better young men, not bigger rapscallions."

"Yes'm," David mumbled.

"You have two older brothers," Hannah said. "They seem to be respectable men. Can't you follow their example?"

"Zeke's good enough, ma'am," Jonathan said. "But Joel ain't. I heard him talking about going to whorehouses—"

Hannah held her hand up. "I don't want to hear any more, young man. You keep your family's problems at home." Placing hands on hips, she continued, "As your punishment, you boys will muck out the stable. I want it completely clean by the noon hour."

"Yes'm," both boys grumbled, though David gave a sidelong glance at his twin.

"I'll dismiss school early today, and you both will accompany me to the Abercrombies' claim to apologize to Annabelle, and then to your home, where I will talk with your father again."

That afternoon, when Hannah and the twins arrived at the Abercrombie cabin, Louisa Abercrombie lit into Hannah. "Have you no control over your students? My poor daughter has been maimed! As if she didn't have enough problems without shorn hair."

Annabelle stood behind Louisa, peering around her mother's shoulder.

All of the girl's hair was trimmed now, and her curls hung softly to just below her ears. It actually looked pretty, Hannah thought. The blonde ringlets framed her face and softened her expression far more than when she'd worn her hair pulled back from her scars. Now it was possible to look beyond her pockmarks to see an attractive child.

Hannah bridled at Louisa's description of Annabelle as maimed, though she was in no position to argue with the irate woman. "Mrs. Abercrombie, I am sorry—"

"Sorry? That don't make up for my poor daughter's disfigurement."

The twins looked stricken at the woman's words. "Ma'am," Jonathan said, "I didn't mean her no harm."

Louisa turned to him. "You, young man—don't you ever come on my land no more. Stay away from Annabelle. And Rose, too. I'm of a mind not to send my girls back to school. They ain't learning much anyway."

Hannah fought the urge to correct Louisa's grammar.

"Ma'am," Jonathan said, his voice cracking. "Please give me another chance. I won't tease her no more."

Hannah escorted Jonathan and David to their home, but their father wasn't there. Their stepmother said she'd send her husband to see Hannah the next day. She didn't seem to want to hear what Hannah had to say about the boys' behavior.

Despite his wife's promise, Captain Pershing did not come with the boys to school the next day. Hannah waited for him throughout the day, but he did not appear. Nor did he come on Thursday morning. The twins came to school early both days and were on their best behavior. They chopped wood. They cleaned the stable. They gathered eggs with Faith.

The Abercrombie girls did not attend, and Hannah worried she'd lost those pupils for good. She would have to make another trip to their farm to plead with their parents to let them return. Perhaps their father would agree the girls needed more education, and after hearing Louisa Abercrombie describe Annabelle as maimed, Hannah wanted to help the girl.

Thursday afternoon Zeke arrived at her cabin after the students had gone home. "I just learned last night what happened on Tuesday," he said. "This was the first chance I had to stop by."

"Then the twins didn't tell their father about the most recent incidents?"

she asked.

"No, ma'am. We've been going hither and yon with Joel here. We ate supper at Esther's last night. She wheedled it out of them, why they'd been going to school early. Then Mother Amanda told us you'd been to Pa's house Tuesday afternoon. I'm mighty sorry about their behavior."

"In fairness, it's mostly Jonathan," Hannah said. "Though David eggs him on."

Zeke nodded. "Yes'm, it's always been that way."

"Throwing the muddy ball could have been an accident," she said. "But not cutting Annabelle's hair."

"No, ma'am. I agree. But Jonathan did apologize."

"He did." Something about Zeke Pershing made Hannah want to argue with him. "But they can't stay at school, if they cause any more trouble. They distract the other children. They prevent everyone from learning."

"I understand." His lips twitched, as if he found humor in the situation.

"Can't you take a hand in their upbringing, Mr. Pershing?" She wanted to force him to see the seriousness of the situation. "The boys look up to you."

"At the moment, Miz Bramwell, the family is celebrating Joel's return. I'm sure the boys'll settle down once he leaves."

"Then your brother isn't staying?"

"He's a miner, ma'am. Not a farmer."

"The boys need some stability. If your father can't provide it, perhaps they should live with you." Zeke could handle them, she was sure, if he would do so.

"Now, Miz Bramwell, that ain't yours to say."

"Perhaps not. But Jonathan and David are my students. And I can see what they need. They need a firm parental hand."

"I ain't their pa."

"You may be the only one who can save those boys, Mr. Pershing." She was overstating the risk—the twins would probably develop into law-abiding men as they matured. She was placing a bigger burden on Zeke than he deserved, but he seemed to be the only one other than their father who could assume the responsibility. She liked the twins and didn't want them to acquire a bad reputation that would stay with them into adulthood.

"I can't take 'em, ma'am. I'm thinking of leaving the Willamette Valley," Zeke said. "Might go mine with Joel."

Chapter 15: Zeke Changes His Mind

On Saturday, two days after Zeke talked to Hannah Bramwell about the twins, Joel announced he would leave for the Rogue River valley on Monday. "I got to get through the mountains afore it's too late," Joel said. "It ain't snowing here yet, but there's plenty higher up."

"Pa and Esther won't like you leaving afore Christmas," Zeke said, dishing up their supper. Joel stayed with him for his whole visit, arguing there wasn't room for another body at their father's house. Zeke had to agree with Joel on that.

Joel helped Zeke on the claim every day, morning till supper. The two brothers felled trees, shot game and smoked the meat, and repaired fences. But Zeke knew Joel wouldn't last on the farm. Joel had always had the wanderlust, just like Pa.

Joel shrugged. "I'm full grown. Pa can't stop me, and Esther never could." He squinted at Zeke. "You shouldn't let 'em tell you what to do either."

"I don't," Zeke protested. "But Pa's sick."

"Me staying won't get him better. And Esther'll drag you around by the nose if you let her."

"I'm the only one holding the twins in check," Zeke said. "Their teacher told me so."

Joel chortled. "Now you're letting a schoolmarm tell you what to do? She taking Miz Jenny's place in your heart?"

Zeke almost threw the stew pot in Joel's face. He'd given up on Jenny, he told himself daily. She was happy, and he would have to be happy for her. He didn't need Joel rubbing his face in his loss.

And Zeke had other worries, beyond his father and the twins.

He'd purchased a copy of the December 12 issue of the *Oregon*

Spectator newspaper. In it was more about the Donation Land Act. The men in town speculated about what the new law would mean for existing land claims. Would earlier settlers be able to retain their six-hundred-forty-acre plots, or would unmarried men be restricted to the new three-hundred-twenty-acre limit?

Mac McDougall would probably know. Zeke would have to seek him out, even if it meant seeing Mac and Jenny together again.

The next morning, Zeke and Joel went to church. They'd been invited to eat at Esther's house with the whole family for one last meal before Joel left. Neither brother looked forward to the gathering, but there was no polite way to refuse.

After the preacher read marriage banns for a couple soon to be wed and blessed the congregation, Zeke wandered over to see Mac. He couldn't help remembering how he'd punched Mac two months ago in October. This time, he stuck his hand out, and Mac shook it.

"Got a question for you, Mac," Zeke said, after he'd greeted Jenny and her three-year-old son. Seeing them with Mac and the infant Maria didn't hurt so much as he'd thought it might. "What do you know about the new land law?"

Mac shrugged. "Not much more than what's been in the paper. Text of the statute seems clear enough. Why?"

Zeke made his inquiry directly. "What'll they do about existing claims? Can I keep my six forty?"

Mac said, "Married men can still claim six forty. Three hundred and twenty acres in their own name, and three hundred and twenty in their wife's name."

"But I ain't married." Zeke sniffed at having to state the obvious.

"Law gives you a year to get married," Mac said. "Section Four of the Donation Land Act says specifically that if a current male settler marries within one year from December 1, 1850, he can claim six hundred and forty acres—one half titled to himself and the other half to his wife, if she resided in Oregon before December 1 of this year. So you have until December 1, 1851, to get married. If you do, there'll be no question—you can keep your claim."

Joel dug an elbow into Zeke's side. "Bet a lot of men'll be looking to get hitched this year. You better find a willing gal soon."

Zeke swallowed. He had no desire to marry, now Jenny was lost to him. But he also didn't want to see his hard work on the claim benefit someone else. He hadn't cleared anywhere near the six hundred forty acres he'd claimed, but he had plans for it. In his dreams he saw a fine spread—a large house, rolling fields of grain and fruit trees, groves of hardwoods and pine trees he could log for cash. His dream had become a lonely one since Jenny turned down his proposal, though surely someday he'd find another woman he could make a life with. Even if he'd never find anyone he loved like Jenny.

But he didn't want the timing of his marriage forced on him by the government. If he couldn't keep his land, maybe he should start over somewhere else.

After church, Zeke and Joel went with the rest of the Pershings to Esther's house. She didn't have enough chairs for everyone, so Zeke and Joel rolled large rounds of tree trunks from the woodpile into the cabin to use as stools. The children sat on the board floor while they ate.

Most of the food was plain—not like the Sunday dinners Ma used to serve back in Missouri. But the venison stew and home-baked bread were tasty, and Esther had baked fruit pies as well. They ate heartily, and the usual tensions between Amanda and the Pershing offspring were muted for the day.

"Where do you plan to settle?" Esther's husband Daniel asked Joel.

"Don't know yet," Joel said, sopping up stew gravy on his plate with a crust of bread, then stuffing it in his mouth. "Depends where the gold is."

"You're certain it's there?" Zeke asked.

Joel nodded. "Heard tell of some good finds already. Both on the Rogue River and the Umpqua. Might be as much as on the American River back in forty-eight."

"Let us know where you are," Esther said. "We need to be able to find you."

Joel ruffled her hair. "Don't you worry, little mother. I let you know my whereabouts in California, didn't I?"

She sniffed. "It worries me our kin being so spread out. Joel leaving. Rachel's claim so far away," she said, nodding at their younger sister and her husband Robert O'Neil. "I hardly ever get to see her and her baby."

"Why do you want everyone close?" Zeke asked. "We got more'n enough Pershings to fill up Oregon."

"It's only me holding this family together," Esther said. Tears welled in her eyes, though her voice remained quiet. "Ever since Ma died."

"Now, Esther," Pa said.

"It's true, Pa!" Her voice turned strident. "Joel won't stay. Rachel moved away. The twins are misbehaving. Ma would hate what's happening to us."

Pa glanced toward his second wife, who sat in a corner rocking Frankie. "We have Amanda's family with us now. And Frankie. The more the merrier."

"No, Pa, it ain't merrier." Esther sobbed openly now. "Our family is falling apart faster'n a waterlogged dam. And I, for one, hate it. At times, I wish we'd never left Missouri."

At that, her husband Daniel stood. "Esther, don't get so worked up. Your family'll do fine. We all take care of each other." He turned to Zeke. "Right, Zeke? You and I'll keep everyone together."

What could Zeke do but grunt his assent?

Later, as he and Joel mounted their horses to return to his claim, Esther clutched his arm. "You have to help, Zeke. You have to help with the young'uns—the twins, and Ruthie and Noah. And Frankie, he's ours, too."

Joel rode out the next morning right after breakfast, leaving Zeke alone on his claim. Although he disapproved of Joel's blustering, he missed his brother's company. The two of them had been close as youngsters—two boys standing together in a household headed by their mother while their father was away with the Army.

Zeke loved Oregon and he relished farming, but much of his satisfaction in the frontier life had left him since he lost Jenny. What was he working for, if not for the family they could have built together? Watching out for his younger siblings, as Esther wanted him to do, would be a poor substitute for having his own children.

Maybe he should join Joel, even though he didn't think prospecting would suit him for long. Still, maybe he could make some money, come back a rich man like Mac. Then maybe Jenny would regret rejecting him.

As he mucked out the stable, he heard a horse whinny outside, and his sorrel Red replied. He stuck his head out the barn door.

"Hey, Zeke," Mac McDougall said. "I need some help felling timber on my claim. Need more lumber for my house in town. You got time to help?"

"Maybe," Zeke said, scratching his head. With harvest over, he had time. But did he want to spend the next few weeks working with Mac?

"I'm paying top dollar."

Zeke swallowed. He could use the money, though Mac's offer stuck in his craw. Time was, the two of them traded labor on each other's claims. Now Mac acted like a land baron. "How long you think it'll take?"

Mac shrugged. "Two or three weeks. If you need to work on your own land, you can come and go as you please."

"You spending your time on the timber work also?"

"Sure am," Mac said with a grin. "I need to get out of town sometimes, or I'll go mad."

Didn't Mac appreciate Jenny? "Thought you was a happily married man now."

"I am. But that doesn't mean I don't want out of the house now and then."

"What are you going to do now you're back in Oregon, Mac?"

Mac frowned and sighed. "I haven't decided yet. Thought about opening a law office. Thought about running for the legislature or asking for a judgeship. But I want more than desk work. There's a railroad syndicate being formed. Maybe I'll look into that. Though it seems to me we need good roads in Oregon more than trains."

"I guess I can put off my chores around here a bit. When do we start logging?"

Zeke worked with Mac, the Abercrombies, and a man named Devlin Feeney felling trees on Mac's land. Zeke had never met Feeney before, though his name had come up regarding the grizzly sightings. He was a bandy-legged little man with a ready smile, but he handled his fair share of the timbering.

"Where'd you find him?" he asked Mac.

"Robert O'Neil knew him in the Army. Another sergeant. Feeney's getting out now, like O'Neil did two years ago. Came looking for work.

Seems a good man. And he knows some other ex-soldiers in the area, if we need more labor."

"Why aren't they claiming their own land?" Zeke asked. "It's free."

Mac chuckled. "I think they're used to having someone tell them what to do. Farming requires more initiative than they exercised in the Army. O'Neil was raised a farmer, like you. I don't think Feeney was."

Zeke nodded. He'd been bred to be a farmer, even if Pa had been a soldier. Ma and her brothers taught him how to work the land from the time he was Noah's age. Him and Joel both. Joel walked away from farming easily enough, but Zeke liked wresting his livelihood from the land.

Zeke and the others felled trees and loaded them into wagons to haul to the mill in Oregon City. He enjoyed the company of the two younger Abercrombies—Douglass and Daniel—though their father Samuel was full of bluster. The ex-soldier Feeney had enough blarney in him to mollify the older Abercrombie, which made working with old Samuel easier than it could have been.

Even though the days were short, they toiled hard enough to tire the muscles, and Zeke went home every evening exhausted. After fixing himself a cold supper, he fell into bed and was up the next morning to attack the trees again. Soon they'd stacked a large pile of logs on Mac's land, ready to haul to the sawmill.

Early one morning on his way to Mac's timber stand, he stopped by Hannah Bramwell's cabin on the McDougall claim. He wanted to check whether the twins were maintaining her woodpile. It was a little low, so he set to chopping logs into pieces she and Faith could manage.

Hannah came out of the cabin, a shawl wrapped tightly around her. "Mr. Pershing," she called, "you're here early. Would you like some mush?"

He put down the axe. "I'd be obliged, ma'am. I've been eating cold food for days now."

"Why is that?" she said, preceding him into the cabin.

"Sawing timber from dawn till dusk. For the McDougall house."

She nodded as she dished him a bowl of steaming cornmeal mush and set it on the table.

Faith had already tucked into her breakfast and looked up to smile at him. "I can't wait to see the house when it's finished," the girl said. "Miz Jenny showed me the plans. It's going to be grand. And sitting up on the bluff—they'll be able to see for miles."

Hannah cooked bacon and handed him a plate.

He enjoyed talking with the two Bramwells as he ate, then stood to leave. "Thank you, Miz Bramwell. I appreciate the meal."

"Might I have a word with you, Mr. Pershing?" she said, as she followed him out of the cabin.

He turned to face her. "Are the twins misbehaving?"

She shook her head. "There haven't been any more incidents with Annabelle or any of the other students. But the boys are not interested in their studies. Could you speak to them?"

"Ma'am, the boys don't think they need any more book learning. They want to farm or do other work outside. They ain't meant to be scholars."

"Your father says he wants them in school."

"That's because he don't know what else to do with 'em."

"And that's why you should step in. Either tell them to pay attention to their lessons, or find them something productive to do with their time. As it is, they aren't doing me or their classmates any good, with their sighs and moans every time I tell them to write an essay or do a math problem." She pulled her shawl around her again.

"You'd best get inside, ma'am. It's cold out here."

That evening, his muscles aching after another day of logging, Zeke poured himself a whiskey and sipped it slowly as he sat gazing into the fire. How had his life come to this? From the promise of free land and the hope of a family, he now worked for the man who'd stolen the woman he loved. Esther was right—their family was disintegrating and had been since Ma died in forty-seven. The government might take half his land. He had nothing to look forward to in Oregon.

He might as well join Joel prospecting.

Chapter 16: Christmas Preparations

In the days leading up to Christmas, Hannah's frustration with her Pershing and Purcell students grew. The twins were restless and unfocused on their lessons. Ruth and Noah Pershing and their three stepsiblings sat listlessly through class, though they did not create any disciplinary problems.

She assumed Zeke or Esther or another Pershing had chastened the twins, because the boys stayed far away from the Abercrombie girls. In turn, Annabelle was sullen, but did her lessons as instructed.

Annabelle refused to go outside when Hannah sent the children to run out their energy at recess. "No, thank you, ma'am," the girl said politely.

"Fresh air and exercise would do you good, child," Hannah said.

The girl shrugged, and pulled out her embroidery.

On the last Wednesday before the Christmas holiday, Hannah asked Faith to remain inside with her and Annabelle while the others played. "Sarah," she told the oldest Purcell girl, "you make sure everyone stays in the yard."

After the cabin door shut behind the others, Hannah said to Annabelle, "You must improve your demeanor, dear, or no one will enjoy spending time with you."

"I ain't causing any trouble, Miz Bramwell."

"No, you aren't," Hannah said, with a slight emphasis on the "aren't." She didn't want to be too obvious in correcting Annabelle's grammar.

She and Annabelle stared at each other uneasily. Hannah decided she should carry out the plan she'd considered for several days. She glanced at Faith. "Mind the door, Faith. Don't let anyone in yet."

Then she turned to Annabelle. "You may think your disfigurement permits you to be ill-tempered, but it doesn't. If anything, it means you should be more gracious and attentive to those you encounter in life. The beauty of your character is all you have to impress those around you. If you use it, they won't notice your pockmarks as much."

"How can you say that!" the Abercrombie girl exclaimed. "My face is all people see of me."

Faith hissed in a breath at Annabelle's impertinence. Hannah nodded at her to be still.

Then Hannah raised her skirt and petticoat and rolled down her stocking to reveal her thin, misshapen leg. The ropy burn scars wrapped from ankle to thigh. Tightness in the waxy, white skin kept her muscles weak even after fifteen years, causing her to limp.

As Hannah unveiled her leg, Annabelle gulped. "Miz Bramwell! What happened to you?"

"When I was nine, my skirt caught fire. My leg was burned. I lay in agony for weeks. It took me months afterward to walk again."

"My goodness," the girl murmured.

Hannah saw tears in Faith's eyes. Her niece had seen the disfigurement before and knew the story, but Faith was a kind and sensitive young lady.

Annabelle's eyes narrowed. "But your leg isn't visible. My face is."

Hannah nodded. "So is my limp. It sometimes slows me down, but your appearance doesn't hinder you from doing anything. You are strong and capable and intelligent. You can make anything of your life you wish."

"How can I ever marry?" Annabelle wailed. "That's what a woman's life is for, and what man will want me?"

"You can have pockmarks and a shrewish disposition, or you can have pockmarks and a pleasant personality. Which do you think a man would prefer?" Hannah fastened her stocking and lowered her skirt, then frowned at the girl. "It's up to you."

Then she went to the door and called the other students inside.

Hannah dismissed the students for the Christmas holiday at noon on Friday, December 20. The last few days had been difficult for both her and her students—they were all eager for their two weeks away from classes. As soon as she permitted each afternoon, the children bounded away from her cabin like wild deer.

"What am I doing wrong?" she asked Faith one evening.

"Nothing, Aunt Hannah. Don't you remember waiting for school holidays?"

Hannah sighed. "Not really. I didn't enjoy being with the other girls, but I loved my books."

"Why didn't you become a teacher back in Ohio?"

"My parents didn't think I could manage the students. They thought they were protecting me."

"But they let you work in the store." Faith's face wrinkled in a puzzled expression.

"They only let me sit at the counter. And I kept the books. I wasn't allowed to stock the shelves, not until after Papa died. Then Jane and Charles needed my assistance, both in the store and at home."

"Well, I'm glad you're teaching here. You're as good as the teachers at the Oregon City academy. And I don't have to live with her." The sneer in Faith's voice left no doubt she meant her stepmother Alice.

"At least the Pershing twins have stopped causing trouble," Hannah said.

"Zeke probably laid down the law with them."

"Maybe." Though Hannah wondered. Zeke hadn't seemed willing to put out much effort toward his younger brothers. He acted like he wanted to wash his hands of his family—even saying he would follow Joel to mine gold on the Rogue River. Mac McDougall had made a fortune prospecting, but Zeke didn't seem like a man willing to take many risks. Would he really leave his farm? He seemed rooted to his land.

Hannah and Faith had agreed to spend Christmas week in Oregon City with Jacob, Alice, and the other Bramwell children. Neither of them was eager to leave the snug cabin, though Faith told Hannah, "I will be glad not to have to chop wood. Pa buys his wood already cut. And I'm glad he isn't using an axe anymore. He learned to chop wood one-handed, but Ma and I always worried when he did it."

They returned to the cramped quarters above the store. Hannah put in hours behind the counter selling Christmas food and gifts to Oregon City residents and the farmers who traveled into town.

"Appreciate your help, Hannah," her brother told her. "I don't like worrying about you out in the wilderness."

"Faith and I are doing fine," she replied.

"Lots of ships bound for Oregon City now. I see reports each week in the *Spectator*. You should book passage back to Cincinnati right after Christmas."

"I can't, Jacob. I've committed to teach through the winter."

He sighed, shaking his head with a sniff. "Those country children don't need more book learning. They'll all end up as farmers or loggers. Or head south to search for gold."

"It's important for every child to read, write, and do their sums." She knew she sounded pompous, but she believed what she said. She'd always found solace in books, and she didn't see why everyone shouldn't have the same advantage.

"Have you seen the house the McDougalls are building on the bluff?" her brother asked. "We should drive up there some day. As fine a mansion as you'd find back East."

Hannah sighed, relieved Jacob had dropped his suggestion about her returning to Ohio.

Alice brought up Ohio at dinner that evening. "Have you decided when you're going back to Cincinnati, Hannah?" she asked as she carried the dinner of ham and beans to the table.

Hannah looked up in surprise. "No."

She caught a furtive glance between Jacob and Alice. "But I thought—" Alice said.

"I told Hannah there were many ships from Oregon now," Jacob said. He turned to Hannah. "You really should leave soon."

"Not until after the school term ends. Then I'll determine my options." To Alice, Hannah said, "Wouldn't you like more help in the store? Or around the house?"

"I'm managing," Alice said, then pursed her lips.

Later, when they were in bed and Charity had fallen asleep, Faith whispered to Hannah, "I don't want you to go. I want to stay on Miz Jenny's farm with you."

Hannah sighed. "If I'm not teaching, there's no reason for the McDougalls to let me stay there. And I couldn't pay them rent, if I'm not working. My only skills are working in a store—and now teaching."

"But I don't want to live here," Faith said. "Not with Mama Alice." Hannah couldn't see her niece's tears, but she heard them in the girl's voice.

"I'll stay until the school term ends in March. But then I'll need to find another reason to stay in Oregon, since your father and Alice are not able to keep me here."

Christmas dinner in the Bramwell home was a somber affair. Charity and the two boys were cranky after eating too many sweets from their stockings, and even Faith's mood was subdued. Alice looked peevish as she carried the turkey and mashed potatoes to the table. Jacob's blessing went on so long the food was cold by the time they turned to their plates.

They ate mostly in silence, though Alice eyed Hannah and seemed to want to say something. Once, Alice opened her mouth as if to speak, but Jacob shook his head at her. She shut her mouth again.

Hannah felt the tension between her brother and his wife. Had they argued over her? If so, did Jacob want her to stay? Or was Jacob simply trying to preserve family peace for the holiday and he'd raise the topic of her departure tomorrow? She wished again she'd known of his marriage to Alice before she'd left Cincinnati—though how could she have stayed in Jane's house with Charles leering at her daily?

It seemed Jacob only cared to keep the argument from spoiling the holiday meal. In the afternoon, as they sat quietly in the parlor, he told her again, "Ships departing every week for California. Not on a regular schedule, but you could book passage and be ready to go when the boat docks in Portland."

"Are they coming as far as Portland now? I disembarked last fall in Astoria."

Jacob nodded. "Portland is overtaking Astoria as the primary port in Oregon. The Columbia River is treacherous, but navigable by ocean-going vessels. Most captains are eager to get their cargo as close to the customer as possible. Makes my life as a storekeeper easier."

Hannah hoped he would move on from the topic of her departure, but he continued, "I'll see which ships are likely to arrive here in January."

Furious, Hannah stood. "Why are you in such a hurry to see me leave? I won't go before the school term ends. Faith and I'll head back to the

McDougall claim in the morning."

"Your school is on holiday until after the New Year."

"I can work on lesson preparations."

"What if I want Faith to stay in Oregon City?"

"She's your daughter. You have that right. But I'm returning to the claim tomorrow. Alone if I have to." Hannah marched into the small room she shared with Faith and Charity, unwilling to tolerate her brother's displeasure any longer.

Jacob did permit Faith to return to the McDougall claim with Hannah. Once they were settled in the little cabin, Hannah wrote her sister:

December 26, 1850

Dear Jane,

I spent a thoroughly unpleasant Christmas with our brother and his family. If it weren't for Faith, I should leave Oregon and return to Ohio.

I suppose I am overly harsh. Jacob means well, I believe, but he is under the sway of Alice, who is too concerned about her own place in the world. I fear she must have suffered mightily in her past to be so disagreeable now.

And I do have friends here. Jenny McDougall and Esther Abercrombie are fine young women. Jenny is well educated for one so young, and Esther has a generous heart, though her grammar is little better than that of my students.

Oh, the children, Jane—how you would dote on them! I must deport myself as their teacher at all times, but I yearn to hug the little ones.

Hannah went on to describe the classroom and the antics of little Noah Pershing and Henry Purcell. They made her ache for a child of her own.

She omitted any mention of Annabelle's pockmarks and self-consciousness, as well as the trials of the hard physical labor required to live in the West. She didn't want Jane to worry, nor did she want her sister to insist Hannah return to Ohio.

Chapter 17: Unexpected Tragedy

Zeke rode to his father's house for Christmas dinner, arriving about noon. The smell of roast venison wafted from the cabin as he led his sorrel Red into an empty barn stall. His little brother Noah entered the barn behind Zeke. "Can I ride your horse?" the boy asked.

"I just unsaddled him," Zeke said. "He needs his Christmas dinner, like you and me."

"Can I feed him?"

Zeke took a carrot out of his saddlebag and handed it to Noah. The seven year old fed it to the gelding, crooning as he did so.

"Why are you outside?" Zeke asked.

"Mother Amanda sent me out. Said I was too noisy. But I ain't as loud as Henry"—referring to their stepbrother—"nor as fractious as Frankie."

"That young'un does cry a lot."

"He sure do. And I usually get blamed for it, when I ain't done nothing."

"Maybe you can sneak back in with me. She can hardly keep me outside—I'm a visitor." Zeke frowned at his brother. "Where's your coat? It's cold."

"She ain't given me no time to fetch it. Just shooed me out the door."

Esther and her family arrived as Zeke and Noah left the barn. Zeke lifted Jonah and Cordelia out of the wagon, while Daniel took baby Sammy and helped Esther climb down the wheel. She moved awkwardly, though her pregnancy still had months to go.

"Why are you outside?" Esther asked Noah, who went through his story again.

Esther's lips thinned. "That woman," she muttered, as they all entered the cabin.

94

The smells of food made Zeke's mouth water, but he winced at the din inside. Noah hadn't exaggerated—Frankie bawled, while Henry made faces at him. Mother Amanda shouted for someone to tend to the toddler, but the girls had their arms full of dishes they carried to the table.

Esther picked up Frankie and cuddled him. "He's the only thing I like that's come from that witch," she whispered to Zeke. He patted his sister's shoulder, then went to sit beside his father near the hearth.

"Merry Christmas, Pa."

"Merry Christmas, son." Franklin smiled—a boozy smile, Zeke thought.

"You started the Christmas cheer already?"

"Only way to tolerate the day, my boy. Want some?" Franklin pulled a flask out of his pocket.

Zeke took a surreptitious swig. "Thought you'd laid off the drink."

"Christmas is a special occasion." His father beckoned to Daniel and handed him the flask also. "Good to see you, boy. How's your pa?"

Zeke shook his head. His father must have been drinking awhile to ask after Daniel's father—Pa and Samuel Abercrombie had been at loggerheads ever since they met.

"We're headed there for supper with Ma and Pa," Daniel said. "Ma's upset we're having the noon meal here. I suppose next year Esther and me should host everyone, so's not to cause trouble between our families."

"No trouble here, Daniel." Pa gave another sloppy grin.

The meal dragged on forever. His stepmother hadn't scrimped on food, and Esther brought bowls of beans and potatoes as well. When it came time for cakes and pies, Zeke could hardly manage a slice of cach.

The twins had no difficulty eating—they helped themselves to seconds of everything and dared each other to eat the most pie. Finally, Jonathan retched and bolted outside. Zeke got up to follow his brother, but Esther said, "Let him go. He done it to himself."

Zeke went after Jonathan anyway, and found the boy upchucking his meal. "Maybe a little more caution next time, huh?"

"I'm gonna die," the boy moaned. "It's David's fault."

Zeke grinned and returned to the house. Esther met him at the door. "Those boys are running wild," she said, hands on her hips. "They don't listen to anyone. Neither Pa nor Mother Amanda looks after 'em at all. They respect you—you should do something."

"Hah!" Zeke said. "They don't respect me any more'n they do anyone else. They'll learn about life the hard way, like Joel'n me did."

"You and me, Zeke, we're the only ones who care. Ever since Ma died, it's just been us." Esther sniffed. "I can't do no more. I'll have three of my own soon, plus Jonah. You need to handle the twins."

Zeke hadn't meant to say anything on Christmas, but Esther's bossiness stoked his ire. "Pa can handle 'em. I won't be here. I'm going to find Joel on the Rogue River!"

"You're leaving?" she shrieked so the whole house could hear.

"Where you going, son?" Pa asked.

He couldn't back down now. "I've decided to follow Joel. Try my luck prospecting."

"But your farm!" Pa stood unsteadily. "What'll happen to your land?"

"Government won't let me keep it all anyway. I'll start over in the south."

"Don't go, Zeke!" Noah threw his arms around Zeke's waist. "I don't want you to go."

Little Frankie started to wail. That clinched it. "I'm leaving as soon as I can pull my kit together," Zeke said.

Zeke wasn't surprised to see Esther walk into his barnyard the next morning while he repaired his paddock fence. "Morning," he said, as he fit the top bar into a slot in the fence post.

"You can't leave, Zeke."

"Where are your children?" he asked.

"With Daniel. He's taking 'em to his mother's for the day."

Zeke wedged the bar firmly into the slot, then pounded it farther down with a hammer. "Oughta stay now," he said.

"Zeke, you can't go."

He stopped and squinted at his sister. "Last I heard, I was a free man."

"We need you here." She waved her arms as if to encompass the whole Willamette Valley, then hugged herself tightly. "Pa's drinking again. You saw him yesterday. The twins are delinquents. Ruthie and Noah are ignored in that house."

Zeke sighed. "That's been true since Ma died. I can't fix it."

"No. But neither can I. And I certainly can't do anything more'n I already am." Esther came closer and grasped his sleeve. "I need you, Zeke.

Don't it mean anything to you our family is falling apart?"

Zeke glanced at his sister, then stared out into the woods beyond the barn, wondering how his life had gone so wrong in the last few months. "It bothers me. That's why I need to leave."

"You're giving up, then." Esther said. "Well, I won't. Someone has to keep us together." She turned on her heel, and trudged down the road toward her home.

Over the next week, Zeke stayed alone on his claim. He rummaged through his cabin and barn, gathering what he'd need on the journey—a canvas tent, tools, clothing, and blankets. And made a list of what he needed to buy—food, mostly. It would be cold in the mountains, but he thought he could manage the travel.

He'd take one of his mules as a pack animal and ride his gelding Red. He'd have to sell the other mule, or maybe leave it with Esther and Daniel. Or see if the twins wanted to take on caring for it—they could ride it to school. That'd prove Esther wrong—he was doing his part, trusting those boys with responsibility for a live animal.

He laundered clothes to take with him and hung them to dry. Often, he took his clothing to Esther for her to wash, but he didn't think she'd be willing to do it this time. And even if she were, he'd have to listen to her complain again about his leaving.

One morning he rode over to Doc Tuller's house and found the doctor boiling his medical instruments. "Got a minute, Doc?" he asked. "I'm leaving for the Rogue River soon. Hope you'll keep an eye on Pa for me."

"If you're so worried about him, why you leaving?"

Zeke shrugged. "Can't keep all the land I claimed. Decided I'd start fresh in the south of the territory. Maybe get rich."

Doc raised his bushy eyebrows. "You ain't never been a wanderer. Not like Joel."

"Don't mean I can't start."

"You running away because Jenny McDougall married Mac?" Doc's eyebrows frowned at him now.

"What? No!" Truly the thought hadn't occurred to Zeke. He wasn't one to run away. Was he?

"That's what people'll say." Doc busied himself with packing the instruments in his medical bag. Then he stared at Zeke. "What is it you want, boy?"

"Will you look after Pa?"

Doc nodded. "Been doing so since forty-seven. And I ain't going nowhere now."

Zeke rode home, deep in thought. Had Doc been right—was he running away?

By the first Monday of the new year, Zeke was ready to leave. He'd gone to church the day before and said good-bye to his friends. Esther refused to speak to him. Noah clung to his arm.

That afternoon he'd taken his extra mule over to his father's house to leave with the twins. He'd given them his mutt Blackie also.

Zeke spent some time sitting in the barn to say farewell to his father. As he rose to return home, he said, "I'm leaving tomorrow morning, Pa." He held out his hand. "Don't know when I'll see you again."

Pa shook his hand and clasped Zeke's shoulder. "You write when you get there, son. And take care of Joel."

"Yes, sir." After admonishing Blackie to stay behind, Zeke had ridden away, strangely reluctant to leave his father.

Monday he rose at dawn. He stashed the last of his belongings into his saddlebags and packs, then put water on the fire to douse the coals. He looked around his cabin—now and then the solitude had weighed on him, but often he'd relished being alone. He'd dreamed of Jenny living here with him, but that would never happen now. Sometimes a man needed to let go of old dreams, search out new ones.

He left the cabin, mounted his horse, and took up the lead for the pack mule.

"Zeke! Zeke!" Jonathan and David ran into his yard. "Stop, Zeke! Don't go—Pa's dead!"

Chapter 18: A Family's Grief

Hannah closed her school Wednesday for Franklin Pershing's funeral. The Pershing and Purcell children hadn't been in class since his death two days earlier, and she wasn't sure whether or when they would return. The Abercrombie and Bingham families would surely take their children to the funeral as well, so holding school would be pointless.

After breakfast she and Faith drove to the Pershing claim. A small crowd gathered on a hillside beyond the Pershing cabin. A grave had been dug under a maple tree near the top of the hill.

The minister from Oregon City spoke of Captain Pershing's role as a leader of the wagon train a few years back. Hannah had heard how his wife's death led Franklin Pershing to drink and to being usurped as wagon captain, but the preacher made no mention of the man's downfall in his eulogy, nor of the disheveled appearance of his farm. In death, every man was a hero.

After psalms and other prayers, the mourners sang "Amazing Grace." Jenny McDougall's sweet soprano led the congregants through all verses of the old hymn.

Hannah had never particularly cared for that hymn. No matter what her trials in life—and she'd had several—she didn't feel wretched, and she didn't like claiming to be a wretch before God. She sang perfunctorily in her mediocre alto, because not to sing would be disrespectful.

They came to the verse:

> *The Lord hath promised good to me,*
> *His word my hope secures;*
> *He will my shield and portion be*
> *As long as life endures.*

Promised good, Hannah sang the words, all the while doubting the Lord had promised much good to her. She was crippled, penniless, a spinster, and likely to remain so for the rest of her days. She possessed talents— talents she could use for the benefit of others. She could keep accounts, manage a store, and teach children. But because she was a woman, and a single woman at that, her talents were regularly ignored.

It was a shame women were so often seen merely as appendages of men. Once removed, Adam's rib became independent of his body, according to the Bible. But men seemed to need to keep women dependent nonetheless.

Hope secured? What hope did she have her situation would change? Jacob and Alice were hellbent on getting her to return to Ohio, where Jane's husband would be equally hellbent on bedding her. How she wished she could stay in the McDougalls' snug little cabin in the woods.

And when had that cabin changed from challenge into refuge? Surprisingly, she'd come to appreciate the hardships of pioneer life. She'd been happy the last several weeks living in the wilderness with Faith.

What did she hope for? She didn't bother hoping for a husband and children anymore—that hope had died in adolescence with the realization her leg would repel most men. All she wanted was a place of her own. A place where she was not beholden to anyone and could live independently. As a single woman, where could she find such a place? Her stay on the McDougall claim was only temporary.

After the service, mourners filed past the Pershing family, beginning with the widow. Amanda sagged against Zeke, who stood beside his stepmother looking uncomfortable.

"I'm sorry for your loss, Mrs. Pershing," Hannah murmured to the weeping widow, then she greeted Zeke. "My condolences, Mr. Pershing." His eyes stared at her bleakly, as if he would never see happiness again. Remembering her own parents' funerals, she pressed his arm. "It will get better," she whispered.

When Hannah reached Esther, her friend sobbed on her shoulder. After hugging Esther, Hannah moved on to Daniel and shook his hand.

Tables laden with food were set up in the yard outside the Pershings' cabin. Friends of the deceased ate and told stories of Captain Pershing, both on their journey to Oregon and since their arrival.

His children, even the twins, were more subdued than Hannah had ever seen them. She and Faith went to talk with Jonathan and David. "How are you boys holding up?" Hannah asked after expressing her sympathies.

"We're all right, ma'am," David said. "But the rest of our kin ain't. Ruthie ain't stopped crying since Pa died. And Noah don't say a word. Even the Purcells—Sarah, John, and Henry—they're sad, too."

"And Frankie don't know what to think," Jonathan added.

"It's a lot for your stepmother to take on, seven children still at home, and no husband," the doctor's wife said. She'd walked up behind Hannah.

"It surely is, Miz Tuller," Jonathan said. "Mother Amanda, she cries more'n Ruthie."

Hannah found Jenny McDougall and asked, "Will Mrs. Pershing be able to cope alone?" She realized the incongruity of her thoughts about herself during the service—she did not want to be reliant on a man—with how she spoke of Amanda Pershing now. But not all women were willing or able to manage on their own.

"I don't know." Jenny shook her head. "Her first husband drowned on our journey here. Amanda gave in to her grief then. But now—at least she has Zeke nearby." Jenny looked across the yard, and Hannah followed her gaze. Zeke stood alone at the edge of the yard, smoking.

"Zeke? I thought he was headed to the Rogue River." Hannah had heard the younger Pershings talk after the Christmas holiday about their older brother's imminent departure.

"He won't go now," Jenny said. "I know him better. He will stay to help, at least until his family is stable."

Hannah resumed classes on Thursday, the day after the funeral. The Pershing and Purcell children still did not attend, which did not surprise her. With only Faith and the Abercrombie and Bingham children there, she had little to keep her busy. The classroom was remarkably peaceful without the twins.

"You might need to stop the term early, Miz Bramwell," Annabelle said. "If you don't have enough students. Miz Jenny did after the smallpox epidemic."

"I hate to let you children down," Hannah said. The Bingham boy snickered, and she frowned at him. "Your parents had a contract with Mrs. McDougall, and I assumed her responsibilities to teach you. I feel obligated to continue."

But she resolved to visit Amanda Pershing on Friday to see when the Pershings and Purcells would return.

After classes on Friday, she packed a loaf of bread and a jar of preserves to take, and she and Faith set out for Captain Pershing's claim. They found young Sarah Purcell starting to make supper, with the help of still younger Ruth Pershing. The toddler whined in the corner, and none of the boys could be seen. Dirty dishes were piled near the washtub. "Where's your mother?" Hannah asked Sarah.

Sarah gestured toward the room in back.

"May I see her?" Hannah asked.

When Sarah nodded, Hannah told Faith, "You help Sarah and Ruth. I'll see to Mrs. Pershing." She went into the bedroom where Amanda lay huddled under blankets. The room was frigid—heat from the hearth in the front room could not penetrate the log wall. "Mrs. Pershing?" she offered.

"Who is it?" The woman's querulous voice responded, but the body under the blankets did not move.

"Hannah Bramwell. Can you sit up?"

The woman waved a hand as if to dismiss Hannah.

"Mrs. Pershing, your children need you."

"Sarah'll take care of 'em," Amanda mumbled.

"They need a mother," Hannah said firmly, and pulled the blankets back. "How long have you been sleeping?" A chamber pot stank in the corner. The woman probably hadn't left the room since the funeral.

"I don't know." But Amanda sat up at Hannah's prodding.

"Let's move you to the front room." Hannah took a shawl from a peg on the wall, wrapped it around Amanda's shoulders, and helped the woman stand. Then she pushed Amanda into the main room and sat her in a rocking chair near the fire. "Sarah, bring Frankie to your mother."

Amanda took Frankie when Sarah placed him on her lap, but sat woodenly. The toddler squirmed to get down, and Amanda let him go.

Hannah frowned at Sarah and Ruth. "How long has she been like this?"

"Since Pa died, ma'am," Ruth said. "We got her dressed for the funeral, and that's it. Otherwise, she's been in bed."

"Where are the boys?" Hannah asked.

"Noah and Henry are around, maybe in the barn playing. The twins and John only come home to eat. We ain't seen 'em since breakfast." Ruth did the talking, while Sarah stood silently with her lips pursed.

"Well, let's get this place spruced up," Hannah said. "I'll start on the dishes. Faith, you find a broom and sweep the floor. Sarah, the baby needs a new diaper. And dump the chamber pot." She and the girls worked for an hour, by which time a stew simmered on the cast iron stove and the dishes sparkled. Amanda Pershing sat staring at the fire the entire time.

"Goodbye, Mrs. Pershing," Hannah said, when she and Faith were ready to leave. "You need to get up and care for your children."

The woman made no response.

Hannah beckoned to Sarah and Ruth. "I want you children back in school on Monday. Maybe your mother will perk up, if she has to care for the baby."

Sarah looked stricken. "But what if she can't?"

Hannah shook her head. "I don't know, Sarah. If she doesn't, you get Doc Tuller over here."

As she and Faith left the Pershing claim, Hannah said, "Let's go find Zeke. Tell him what we saw."

They arrived at Zeke's claim at the start of dusk. He was in the barn caring for his horse and mule. "Your stepmother is melancholic, I'm afraid," Hannah told him. "She cannot manage the household or the children. Have you been to see them?"

"Not since the funeral."

"They need you, Mr. Pershing."

He sighed, and returned to mucking out his horse's stall.

"I trust your journey to the Rogue River will be postponed now."

He shook his head. "I'm still leaving. I'll put it off a week or two, but there's nothing for me here."

Hannah looked around. The barn was spotless, cleaner than Amanda Pershing's house had been. The yard she and Faith had walked through was free of debris. Something told her Zeke's cabin would be neat as a pin also. "Looks to me like you'd be leaving a well-tended farm."

He shrugged. "Government's taking half of it away from me."

"Why is that?"

"Land laws changed. Single man can only claim half a section now."

"That still leaves a lot of land, more than enough for you to prosper." She didn't know much about farming, but she knew three hundred and twenty acres was more than most men farmed back East.

"I've cleared the best fields. Still a lot I could do." She wasn't sure if his words were for her or for himself.

"Then why don't you set about doing it? Pick a parcel and get to work." She heard Faith muffle a laugh behind her.

Zeke raised his eyebrows and stared at Hannah. "Are you always this high-handed?"

"Only when I see the truth. And the truth is your family needs you."

Zeke turned suddenly toward his horse, grasping the gelding's mane. His knuckles turned white.

"Faith," Hannah said, "go inside and put on some coffee. Mr. Pershing and I will be there in a minute."

After Faith left, Hannah placed a hand on Zeke's arm. "I'm sorry about your father. I know what a terrible thing it is to lose your parents."

He nodded, then buried his face in the horse's neck. "We ain't been right since Ma died," he choked out.

"And now your father's gone also."

"I can't talk about him—I'm sorry." His words sounded thick, as if he swallowed a sob.

She hugged the arm she was holding. He turned, enfolding her in a tight embrace, and wept against the top of her head, his whole body shaking. She let him cry, remembering her bereavement after her parents died.

After a few minutes, he stood straighter and shrugged her away with a long sigh. "I'm sorry," he said again, seeming embarrassed. He pulled a handkerchief out of his pocket and blew his nose. "That's not like me."

"You have nothing to apologize for," she murmured gently. "Grief is not a weakness. It's a sign of affection for the one you mourn. But you can't let sorrow consume you as it has your stepmother. What you do next determines your strength, how you act in the midst of loss."

Hannah followed him into the cabin. She'd been right—Zeke's home was spotless. He owned a better stove than his stepmother's—bigger and shinier and cleaner. She wondered why a bachelor owned such a nice stove, when the McDougall claim merely had the hearth for cooking.

Faith poured them steaming mugs of coffee. Then the girl sat silently, while Hannah told Zeke what he could do to help the rest of the Pershing family.

He nodded at what she said, but she left with no commitment from him to stay on his claim for more than a few weeks.

Chapter 19: A Departure from Oregon

After Hannah and Faith departed, Zeke tidied up his cabin, washing the coffee mugs and drying them. Then he sliced some bacon and made himself supper. The cabin seemed close and confining, though he was alone. It should have felt more crowded with the two women there, but only after they left did he sense the walls pressing in on him.

He'd convinced himself he needed to get away, but he couldn't leave now. He hadn't agreed with Hannah when she talked to him about his family, but he admitted it to himself now. Amanda—did he still have to call her "Mother Amanda" now his father had died?—was not capable of raising her own children and his younger siblings as well.

He'd been embarrassed by his tears in front of Hannah. Her touch had given him the only comfort he'd felt since his father died. Still, a man didn't like to show weakness in the presence of any woman, let alone one who was little more than a stranger to him.

Truth be told, the father he'd loved and now missed had been less than adept at parenting. Had Pa always been so ineffectual, or had his father's incompetence increased after Ma's death? Looking back on his childhood, Zeke remembered the dashing sergeant who returned home after months away—he and Joel swarmed to their father's side, eager to be noticed by the strong man in uniform. Where had that man gone? Lost to grief and drink. Stifled by a second wife who needed more coddling than Pa could provide.

Zeke couldn't quite wish his family had remained in Missouri. He'd relished the journey west—at least until Pa disgraced himself by getting drunk at Fort Hall. Zeke grew into manhood as a scout on the trek. He made friends like Mac McDougall and Daniel Abercrombie, men he felt at ease with. He wished he still felt the same ease with Mac, though Zeke's feelings for Jenny might always stand between them.

Now, despite his love of the land, Oregon held no promise for him. He'd been ready to move on to the Rogue River, but he couldn't leave the young'uns. He couldn't put the burden of their care on Esther and Rachel—they had their own families to raise. As Hannah Bramwell said, he had a responsibility to his siblings and stepsiblings.

He would have to take up that responsibility. Esther had written Joel right after Pa died, but Zeke did not expect Joel to return to Oregon as a result. Joel might feel free to leave their family behind, but Zeke couldn't. He couldn't forget what Ma would expect of him. And he couldn't stop trying to be the man his father had failed to be.

His own dreams of adventure would have to wait.

After Hannah's visit, Zeke began stopping by his father's house daily to check on his younger siblings, usually after their school day ended. Zeke hadn't committed to Esther nor to Hannah Bramwell that he would care for the children, but he knew he must for his dead parents' sake.

The following Wednesday, Zeke rode his gelding to his father's claim. When he arrived, he found the four younger Pershings playing ball in the barnyard. The three Purcell children and Frankie were nowhere to be seen. When Amanda shooed the children outside, she usually sent them all. "Where are the others?" he asked.

"Packing," Ruth said.

"What do you mean?" Zeke asked as he dismounted and tied Red to the fencepost.

"She's leaving," Jonathan said. "Taking her young'uns with her."

Dumbfounded, Zeke stared at his siblings. He'd heard nothing about Amanda going anywhere. "Where's she headed?"

Jonathan shrugged. "She ain't said exactly. Back East, I reckon."

Zeke strode into the house, where he found clothes and bedding piled on the table and chairs, two trunks sitting on the floor. Frankie sniveled in the corner, while the older three Purcell children darted from piles to trunks, as Amanda barked orders.

"What's going on?" he asked.

"I'm taking the children back to Illinois. Got passage on the next ship to California. We need to be in Portland first Friday in February."

"What about the claim?"

She shrugged. "Sold my interest to Captain McDougall to get money for the passage."

"But it's Pa's land!"

"Captain McDougall says as his widow, I inherited his rights to the claim."

"What about the children?"

"I'm taking mine. You and Esther can care for yours."

"Amanda—"

She glared at him. "I've lost two husbands in this uncivilized country, and I can't take it anymore. I have family back home, and we're leaving."

Zeke thought they'd all made their homes in Oregon. "What do I do with my brothers and sister?"

"That's for you and your kin to decide."

After the brief conversation with his father's widow and reassuring his siblings he'd see them tomorrow, Zeke rode directly into Oregon City to find McDougall. He went to the hotel where Mac rented a suite of rooms while his new house was being built. Zeke strode up the stairs and pounded on the suite door.

Jenny opened the door, holding the baby girl in her arms. She looked as lovely as ever.

"Where's Mac?" Zeke demanded.

Mac appeared in the doorway of a back room and walked forward, his hand out as he smiled at Zeke. "You need to see me?"

"Why'd you buy my father's claim?"

Mac raised an eyebrow and dropped his hand. Jenny ushered the children toward the back room. "You two best talk," she murmured.

"Amanda was determined to sell. I gave her a good price—another man might not have."

"Why'd you buy it?" Zeke asked again.

"She said she's going back East."

"But Pa hadn't proved his claim yet. What's she got to sell?"

"Sit down, Zeke." Mac waved at a sofa and sat in a chair opposite. Zeke plopped on the sofa, then stood again, staring down at Mac. "This might take a while to explain," Mac said.

Zeke sighed and eased himself back down.

"It takes four years to prove up the claim, but your father built all the improvements necessary and has over three years into it. It's good land. I just have to keep it running until November in Amanda's name. Then I can sell it. She's given me her proxy."

"But Pa and I put all that work into it."

Mac shrugged. "You might not be able to keep all your own land, let alone take on your father's claim, too. It has to be in Amanda's name as his widow until it's proven up."

"Got anyone in mind to sell it to?" Zeke asked.

Mac shook his head. "Not yet. But I have until November to find someone. There'll be a whole new group of emigrants coming this fall. Someone will want land that's already partially improved. Or you and your kin can buy it off me—I wouldn't demand a profit from you."

Zeke didn't have any extra money to buy more land. "Who'll work the farm for you until then?"

"I'll find someone. Or let the fields lie fallow and cut the timber."

"She's not taking the young'uns."

Mac leaned forward, looking surprised. "What? She told me she and the children were all going back to Illinois, where she came from."

"She's taking her three, but not my kin."

Mac sat up straight at Zeke's words. "Zeke, I didn't know." He rubbed a hand over his face and sighed. "I thought I was helping your family— finding a way out for her and the children. I didn't mean to cause you trouble."

"Can you back out of the deal?"

Mac shook his head. "I paid her the money and took her proxy and quit claim deed. She was heading straight to the steamship office to buy the tickets."

From his meeting with Mac, Zeke rode to Esther's claim. His sister would be furious at Amanda, and Zeke hated to be the bearer of bad news to his sister in her delicate condition—a baby coming in just a few months.

When he entered Esther's cabin, her family was at supper, and she offered him a plate. He took it, but had trouble swallowing the food. "What's wrong, Zeke?" she asked, as he stirred the stew with a piece of bread. "You ain't eating."

"It's Amanda," he said, pushing his supper dish away. "She's leaving and taking her children."

"What!" Esther cried. "When?"

"Early February," Zeke said.

Esther's husband Daniel stood, picked up Sammy, and said to the older two children, "Let's go look at the horses." Then they left Zeke and Esther alone in the cabin.

"What's going on, Zeke?" Esther demanded.

He heaved a breath. "I stopped by Pa's claim this afternoon. Found the place topsy-turvy, trunks and boxes everywhere. She was packing. She's bought steamship tickets to California. Then returning East."

"What about the young'uns?"

"She's taking her kin, leaving ours. Told me you and me would have to care for 'em."

"And Frankie?"

Zeke sat stunned. "I didn't think to ask. Ain't it bad enough we have to manage the other four?"

"But Frankie's our kin." Esther stood and paced, clutching her swollen belly. "I kept Jonah because he's the last part of Ma. Well, Frankie is Pa's youngest. He's ours."

"He's Amanda's, too." Zeke couldn't deal with a toddler—he still couldn't fathom what they'd do with the twins, Ruth, and Noah.

"I'll go talk to her tomorrow," Esther said. "Get clear on what she's planning."

"What time you going?" Zeke asked. "I'll pick you up and go with you."

"Right after breakfast."

The next morning, Zeke drove his wagon to Esther's home. She greeted him tersely, and they rode to their father's claim in silence, broken only by bitter exclamations from Esther. "I never liked that woman," she said, and a bit later, "She's been a bad penny ever since we've known her."

When they arrived, Zeke helped Esther out of the wagon. She marched to the cabin door, knocked once, then entered. Zeke followed. The cabin was in a greater state of disarray than the day before. Amanda and her three children scuttled about, packing. The younger Pershing children, including Frankie, sat above in the loft. Apparently, none of the children had gone to school.

"What are you doing?" Esther said through her teeth. As always, his sister confronted conflict head-on.

Amanda straightened, hands on her hips, as spirited as Zeke had ever seen her. "Surely Zeke told you. We're leaving."

"You and your three," Esther said.

Amanda looked blank. "Four. My four."

Esther gasped. "You're taking Frankie? But he's our brother."

"He's my son. With his pa dead, I'm his only parent." Amanda turned back to her packing.

"You can't have him!" Esther cried. "Zeke, do something!" She grabbed his sleeve.

"Mother Amanda, let's sit down and talk about this," Zeke said. He didn't know how to handle his stepmother—he never had—and he didn't know whether she had the right to take her son with her if he and Esther objected. He didn't even know whether he cared if the little boy left, but Esther clearly did.

Amanda shook her head. "There's nothing to talk about. I bought his ticket already."

Zeke managed to get Esther out of their father's house and back to her own. She sobbed uncontrollably. "Esther, this ain't good for you. Not in your condition." She'd carried her first two children without any problems he knew about, but her despair couldn't be healthy for the child now in her womb. Daniel added his own soothing remarks, but Esther would have none of it.

Finally, Zeke said, "We'll go talk to McDougall. He can tell us the law, whether we can stop her or not."

"When?" Esther demanded, turning her tear-streaked face toward Zeke.

Zeke looked at Daniel. "Can you mind the children tomorrow morning? I'll take her then."

And so the next morning, Zeke picked Esther up in the wagon again, and they drove to town. This time Esther said nothing and merely sniffled occasionally.

At the hotel, Zeke escorted his sister to the McDougall suite. Jenny welcomed them in.

"It's Amanda," Esther said. "She's leaving and taking Frankie back to the States. We need to talk to Mac."

"Mac's not here," Jenny said. "He's at the mill arranging to have the logs from our claim cut into boards. The stone foundation is done, and we're ready to build the walls." She beamed.

"When will he be back?" Zeke asked.

Jenny shrugged. "Around noon? Would you stay to eat with us?"

Esther waved her arms. "I can't wait—Daniel's with the children. I need to know about Frankie."

Jenny put an arm around Esther's shoulders. "Let me get some tea."

And so they waited. Zeke felt uncomfortable sitting in Jenny's suite, but he couldn't leave Esther.

Shortly before noon, after they spent an hour or more in stilted small talk, Mac returned. He entered with a smile on his face as he looked at Jenny. Esther jumped up and ran toward him, clutching his coat sleeve before Jenny could reach him. "Mac, it's Amanda," Esther said. "She's taking Frankie!"

Mac looked over Esther's head at Zeke, a puzzled expression on his face.

"Turns out it ain't just her three going with her back East," Zeke said. "She's taking the baby also, and Esther don't like it."

"What can we do, Mac?" Esther said, pleading. "We have to stop her."

Mac sighed. "Let's sit down and talk."

Jenny took her children into the back room, saying, "You'll have an easier conversation without them." The others sat in the main room. Esther stood and began pacing almost immediately.

"Amanda is the boy's mother—" Mac began.

"But don't young'uns belong to their pa?" Esther interrupted.

"Yes, if he's alive. But your father died. Did he have a will?" Mac asked.

"Not that we know of," Zeke said. "We ain't found anything."

"Then it would be up to a court to determine who should be the guardian of all the minor children. The court could award the boy to his mother, while the other children go to you"—Mac nodded at Zeke—"or Daniel, since they are not her offspring."

"What about me?" Esther demanded.

Mac sighed. "You're a woman. A male relative would be named as guardian. Or another man, as trustee. But probably Zeke or Daniel."

"Can we go to a judge now?" Esther asked.

Mac shook his head. "We could. But it would delay her departure. Do you really want to do so? She'll be furious with you both."

"I reckon she already is," Zeke said.

Chapter 20: The School Term Continues

The Pershing and Purcell's attendance at school was spotty, even after Hannah's conversation with Amanda Pershing. On Monday, January 20, Hannah heard rumors from the Abercrombie girls the Purcells were leaving. "Miz Pershing is heading back East," Annabelle reported. "With her young'uns."

"All of them?" Hannah's school would disappear overnight, if the Purcell and Pershing children left. She would have to talk to Jenny McDougall about whether to continue teaching at all.

"No, ma'am," Annabelle said, puffed up with her status as purveyor of news. Hannah didn't stop the girl's gossip—she wanted to hear the whole story. "She's only taking her kin. Leaving the Pershings."

"What will happen to them?" Hannah couldn't help asking.

"Esther'll have to take 'em," Annabelle said.

"Or Zeke or Rachel," Rose chimed in. "How can Esther take 'em all? She don't have room."

The Pershings and Purcells did not attend classes that Monday or Tuesday. Wednesday after school, Hannah and Faith made the drive again to Amanda Pershing's home. She found the household in an uproar.

"Then it's true?" she asked Mrs. Pershing. "You're leaving?"

The woman burst into tears. "I've lost two husbands in this awful wilderness. I need the comfort of my family around me."

"Your family is here, Mrs. Pershing." Hannah gestured at the children filling the cabin. "You are responsible for them."

"For my offspring, but not for my husband's. They have Zeke and Esther to care for them."

Little Noah Pershing started sobbing. "I'll miss Henry. He's my best friend!"

113

Hannah put her arm around the little boy.

"Teacher, what'll happen to us?" he wailed. "I ain't got no parents now."

Exasperated, Hannah asked, "Mrs. Pershing, might we continue this discussion away from the children?"

Amanda shook her head. "They've heard it all. Ain't nothing I won't say in front of them. And I must say, Miz Bramwell, you ought not to be meddling in our family's business."

Hannah couldn't persuade Amanda Pershing to delay her plans. The best she could do was get the woman to send the children to school as long as they were in Oregon. But despite Amanda's agreement, only the twins, Ruth, and Noah returned to class on Thursday. The Purcell children remained absent.

"They ain't coming no more," Jonathan said. "Mother Amanda says she needs 'em to help her pack."

"When are they leaving?" Hannah asked.

"Next Friday."

Little more than a week left to figure out what would happen to the Pershing children and to the school. Hannah dismissed her students at noon and drove with Faith to Oregon City. Faith went to her father's store with instructions to replenish their flour and other supplies, while Hannah went to see Jenny McDougall.

"Can I continue the school with three fewer pupils?" she asked Jenny.

"I don't see why not," Jenny replied. "You have our cabin to live in. You'll still have the payments from the other families, and I'll make up any difference you're short."

"They almost all pay in kind. Faith and I can make do." Hannah wanted to be able to save money, but if she met her expenses, she'd be satisfied.

"Mac and I will make sure you come out whole, Hannah," Jenny said. "You've done us a favor this winter."

"What will happen to the Pershing children?" Hannah asked. She was gossiping herself now, but she justified it in her mind because they were her students.

Jenny shrugged. "Zeke and Esther are still sorting that out."

"Are you certain Mrs. Pershing will leave Oregon?" The journey was difficult, and Hannah hoped never to make the return trip to the States, though she might be forced to once the school term ended.

Jenny sighed and shook her head. "Her first husband—the father of her three children—drowned along the way. She collapsed after that tragedy and only survived with the help of the other families in our wagon company. She's a woman who can't stand alone. Captain Pershing married her soon after we reached Oregon City, and now she's lost him. I understand her fear."

"You lived alone for three years while your husband was in California."

"Yes. But I had no choice."

"Would you have taken your son and returned to the States?" Hannah asked.

Jenny shook her head somberly. "I had nothing back in Missouri."

"And I don't want the home my sister provided me," Hannah murmured. Her situation in Ohio had not been a happy one, and she wondered what problems Jenny had faced in Missouri. "A woman can have more independence in the West."

"We need more women like you," Jenny said, her face brightening. "And fewer like Amanda Pershing."

Hannah stewed all evening about the poor Pershing children. Amanda Pershing had correctly told her the family's problems were none of Hannah's business. But these were her students! Amanda could take her children out of the school, but she was apparently abandoning her dead husband's offspring—what would become of the rambunctious twins? Of sad little Ruth? Of sweet Noah?

Hannah decided she would have to talk to Esther and Zeke about their younger siblings—Esther first, as Esther seemed more likely to be concerned about the children. The next afternoon after school let out, Hannah hitched the mule to the wagon and explained the situation to her niece. "Faith, will you come with me? You can watch Esther's little ones while she and I talk." The January day was cool, but clear. The children could play outside.

"Esther and Daniel don't have room for four more, Aunt Hannah. What do you think they'll do?"

Hannah shook her head. "That's what I want to talk to Esther about."

When they arrived at the Abercrombie claim, Esther came out of her cabin, Sammy on her hip, and Cordelia and Jonah rushing past her to hug Faith.

"We'll play out here," Faith said, taking the two children by the hand. She'd picked up on Hannah's intention to speak with Esther alone. "Sammy can stay, too," she added when the toddler squirmed to be let down.

"Come inside," Esther said to Hannah. As they entered the cabin, Esther said, "So you've heard?"

"That Amanda Pershing is leaving Oregon without your siblings? Yes."

Hannah could feel anger seeping from Esther. "She's the most irresponsible, selfish biddy I know."

"What do you plan to do?"

Esther shrugged and waved a hand. "What can we do? They'll come live here. At least Ruth and Noah. I'm still trying to get Zeke to take the twins."

"Is he objecting?"

"He ain't agreed yet. But he will."

"How will you manage even two more children here?"

"I don't got a choice. They need a home. Though Daniel ain't happy about it—you should hear what he has to say about 'Mother Amanda.'" Sarcasm dripped from Esther's voice. No love lost between her and her stepmother, much like how Faith thought of Alice.

"What can I do?"

Esther's eyes welled. "Just be kind to them in class. I hate breaking up our family even more." She brushed a hand across her eyes. "The first step was when Ma died and I took Jonah. I wanted him, but 'tweren't easy starting married life with a baby. And then we had Cordelia, too, afore we'd been wed a year."

"You know I'll do anything I can to make life easier for them. And you." Hannah reached out to touch Esther's hand. Hannah didn't know anything about mothering, but she knew loss and grief. And homelessness, though she'd always had options—even if they were bad ones. The poor Pershing children were at the mercy of their elders.

Esther gave a wan smile. "Thank you." She sighed and hugged her belly. "Ruthie might be a help to me, especially when the next baby comes. And I love Noah to pieces—he's always been a cuddly child."

"Do you think it would help if I talked to your brother about taking the twins?" Hannah had no idea whether Zeke Pershing would listen to her—he hadn't the last time she tried.

"It couldn't hurt," Esther said with a shrug.

Hannah and Faith left Esther's home and rode through the sunny late afternoon to Zeke's claim. He was in his cabin mending a harness. He motioned for them to sit, then resumed his seat and took up the harness. "Those mules managed to chew through the leather again," he said.

"I thought you were letting the twins have one of the mules," Faith said.

Zeke grinned. "I took it back. The boys are too addlepated with the commotion in that house, and I ain't going to the Rogue River for a while."

"Esther says she's talked to you about staying and taking in the twins." Hannah saw no reason not to raise the issue directly.

"That's what she wants." Zeke continued to braid the leather strips.

"Is that your plan?"

Zeke looked up from the harness and frowned. "You're mighty forthright, ain't you, Miz Bramwell?"

The rustling of Faith's skirt let Hannah know her niece was amused. "I suppose I am, Mr. Pershing. Those boys need you."

He sighed. "You been telling me that ever since you started teaching."

"And it's still true."

He stood. "That's for me and my kin to decide. I'll be talking to Esther and Rachel, and our family will take care of our own. All you need worry about is whether they can do their sums."

The last week of January was cloudy and gray, and Hannah's spirits were low. Jonathan and David Pershing celebrated their fourteenth birthday on Wednesday, January 29, and Esther came to school with a cake for the boys. The other students all sang, and Hannah was pleased to see Annabelle smile at Jonathan as the girl joined in.

"It's bad enough they have to share their birthday," Esther said to Hannah while the children ate their treat. "I didn't want 'em to lack any celebration at all, just because we're all sixes and sevens."

"You're a good sister," Hannah said.

"Poor Ruth was ignored on her birthday, but there ain't no call for the boys to suffer on theirs. I won't let it happen again in our family. But it's better we celebrate at school than at home. That house is too discombobulated."

Hannah smiled. Her own birthday was in two days—on January 31. Jane wasn't there to recognize the occasion, and she doubted Jacob would remember.

As anticipated, Hannah received no gift or visit from her brother on Friday. Not even Faith wished her a happy day. Her niece probably didn't even know it was her birthday.

That night, after Faith went to bed, Hannah sat with her paper, quill and ink:

> January 31, 1851
> Dear Jane,
>
> I miss you this evening. I have spent my birthday like any other day—teaching and cooking and caring for the barnyard animals.
>
> Now I am twenty-five, I suppose I am officially an old maid, though I despise that term. Here in Oregon girls think nothing of marrying at fifteen. There are so many men and so few women.
>
> Though you are far away, I am fortunate to have two good friends in Esther Abercrombie and Jenny McDougall. Esther's family is in turmoil. Her father died, leaving a large brood of children, four of whom are my students. Their stepmother is returning to the States, and the only suitable guardian for the children is their oldest brother, a single man about my age. But he resists taking responsibility. I must admit I would hesitate to take on four youngsters without the support

of a spouse.

I hope you and Charles are well, and I hope to hear from you soon, Jane. Surely you have received my first letter from Oregon by now, written in early November. The dratted mail is so slow.

Your loving sister,
Hannah

Chapter 21: Zeke Comes Around

At church on February 2, the Sunday before Amanda Pershing and her blood children planned to leave Oregon, the conversation revolved around their departure. Zeke shrugged when people asked what he planned to do about his siblings. All he said was what Esther kept telling him, "We'll take care of our own."

The minister preached about a husband and wife cleaving unto each other, frowning in Amanda's direction as he spoke. The sermon seemed to imply the marital obligation lasted beyond death, though Zeke had thought "until death do us part" was all God expected.

Zeke heard little of the sermon's specifics. Once he realized the preacher meant to lecture the Pershing family, his thoughts turned inward. Maybe, if Esther took Ruthie and Noah, he could take the twins with him to the Rogue River. The boys would think it an adventure.

He daydreamed about the possibilities of finding gold—dreams that would have seemed alien to him before Joel's visit and the new land law caused him to rethink his ambitions. He knew farming. Life on the rich land in Oregon had been his dream, until Jenny rejected him and the fools in Congress decided to halve their original grant.

After the service, Zeke noticed all their clan—save the absent Joel—attended church that morning. Even Rachel and her husband Robert O'Neil had traveled to Oregon City from their farm several miles away. Esther must have sent Daniel to fetch them.

Esther grabbed Zeke's arm and told him. "Noon meal at my place. We'll all be there."

"I see you got Rachel here."

"She's one of the family," Esther said. "She needs to do her part." By her tone, Zeke concluded his sister didn't think he was doing what he should. "First thing is to see if we can get Amanda to change her mind about Frankie."

No chance of that, Zeke thought, but kept silent.

When all the Pershings and Purcells gathered at Esther's, she served a ham she'd cooked the day before, along with bread and beans and applesauce. Zeke heaped his plate full, though he knew the bounteous feast would come at the price of a miserable afternoon.

"We wanted to send you off in style," Esther told Amanda. "I don't agree with what you've done, but I wish you well. And I'd like you to consider leaving Frankie here."

"He's my son," Amanda said. "He's going with me."

"Then we'll have Captain McDougall file suit tomorrow morning," Esther said.

"Now, Esther—" Zeke began. They'd talked with Mac about a lawsuit, but Zeke didn't want to make an enemy of Amanda if he could help it.

Esther turned on him. "Don't you care about Pa's youngest? We'll lose him forever!"

"We been through this. And we shouldn't argue in front of the young'uns. " Zeke turned to the younger children, who stared wide-eyed at their elders. "You all go on and play. Stay in the yard or the barn. Jonathan and David and Sarah, you keep the little ones out of trouble."

He waited until the children had gone, leaving him alone with Amanda, Esther and Daniel, and Rachel and her husband Robert. Then he turned to Amanda. "McDougall says we could at least delay your journey. He thinks I might have a claim to guardianship of Frankie. But we don't want to make this hard on you."

Esther opened her mouth, but Daniel grasped her shoulder, and she didn't say anything.

"If you let me be named Frankie's guardian along with you," Zeke said, "we'll let you take him without a fight."

"Zeke!" Esther shouted.

Rachel shushed her older sister.

"A boy that young should stay with his ma," Zeke continued. "But like Esther says, we don't want to lose him. Will you agree?"

"And if I don't?" Amanda asked, her face grim.

"Then we will file suit. But if you agree, I'll have McDougall draw up the papers. All we want is for you to write us regular about Frankie's health and education. And a promise we can visit him if any of us go East, and he's free to come to Oregon when he's grown."

"Can't stop no grown man from leaving home," Amanda muttered. "That's what got me here in the first place."

"Zeke, how can we let him go?" Esther wailed.

"You heard McDougall," Zeke said. "We might win, but we might not. Let's not have a legal fight in the family."

"Family," Esther whispered bitterly.

"And I'll take the twins and Ruthie and Noah to live with me," Zeke said. He hadn't even known the words would come out of his mouth, but once they were out, it was done. He'd stay in Oregon and make the best of it.

Now, how was he going to manage four children?

Amanda consented to Zeke's terms for guardianship of Frankie, and the meal continued. Esther bustled about the cabin, but she seemed to accept his proposal as well.

Amanda and the children left as soon as they'd eaten. "I'll come get our young'uns' belongings mid-week," Zeke told his stepmother as he helped her into the wagon.

When they were gone, Rachel and Robert asked to speak to Zeke and Esther. "We want to move back here," Rachel said. "To help."

"I said I'd take 'em all," Zeke said. "We'll be all right."

Rachel shook her head. "It ain't just the young'uns," she said. "Though that's part of it. Robert and I miss being close to you. We want to buy Pa's claim from Mr. McDougall."

"What about your own claim?" Zeke asked. "You ain't proved it up yet. How can you buy another?"

Robert said, "You let me worry about that. I'll talk to McDougall. It may take time. I'll have to improve my claim enough for some man to want it. It's a good trade for me, if I can get someone to finish proving mine up. Your pa's land has more fields cleared. And a bigger house."

"It'd be right nice to have you closer," Esther said. "I worry about Zeke managing all the young'uns. You sure you don't want me to take Ruthie?"

she asked him.

Zeke shook his head. "Those children been tossed around enough. If I'm going to keep 'em, I'll keep 'em all. At least until you have your baby—if you need Ruthie's help then, she can stay with you awhile."

He turned the conversation with Daniel and Robert to planting crops. Esther and Rachel cleaned the dishes. By late afternoon, the children were back inside. Esther's and Rachel's little ones napped, and the other Pershings listened as they were told they'd live with Zeke.

Jonathan, David, and Noah all grinned, but Ruth sat silently, biting her lip.

"What's wrong, Ruthie? Won't you be glad to live with Zeke?" Esther asked her youngest sister.

"I'll be the only girl in a house full of boys," Ruth said. "Do I have to do all the cooking and cleaning?"

Esther and Rachel both shook their heads. "No," Rachel said. "We'll make sure the boys do their share."

As the sun set through hazy clouds, Zeke rode his gelding home from Esther's. He'd have to ride into town to see McDougall again in the morning. Had he done the right thing in allowing Amanda to have custody of Frankie without a battle? The boy was Pa's son, but Zeke didn't want to take the toddler from his mother, even if Amanda wasn't a strong parent.

Besides, he might have bitten off more than he could chew in taking the other four children. Somebody had to do it. Esther might talk about keeping the family together, but she had Jonah plus two—soon to be three—of her own. And Rachel would have enough to do moving her household back to the valley, if she and Robert followed through with their plan, which Robert said would take some time.

Caring for the four young'uns was up to Zeke.

He'd never really wanted to mine gold, anyway.

Where would the children sleep? For now, Ruth could have his bed, and Zeke could sleep in the loft with the younger boys. In the spring, he'd figure out something else.

Monday morning Zeke went to Oregon City to meet Mac McDougall again. "I need you to help me make it legal with the young'uns. So I can raise 'em," he told Mac. "And name me as co-guardian over Frankie, even if Amanda takes him."

"What agreement did you reach with her?" Mac asked, and Zeke outlined their discussion from the day before.

"If she has the boy back in Illinois, there won't be much you can do to enforce her agreement to stay in touch," Mac said. "Not unless you go to Illinois yourself."

Zeke nodded. "So I figured. But it saves us face. And it'll make Esther feel better. Amanda ain't a bad woman, she just can't cope on her own. I reckon she'll let Frankie know we care about him."

Mac leaned back in his chair. "Now, as for the twins, Ruth, and Noah, I can have you declared their sole guardian. Might take some time to have a judge approve it, but here in Oregon Territory no one will keep you from raising the children." He grinned. "No one outside your family will want the task anyway."

"Then you'll draw up the papers?" Zeke asked.

Mac nodded. "I'll have them ready tomorrow. I'll get Amanda's signature, then bring them to you to sign." He stood. "I'm sorry, Zeke. I'm sorry about your father, about Amanda's actions. It's a lot for you to take on."

Zeke shrugged. "What else can I do?" He sighed. "I suppose I'm head of the Pershing family now."

"Were you set on following Joel to the mines?"

Zeke shook his head. "Not really." He'd only thought about mining because of the uncertainty over his land claim.

And because of Jenny, but he wouldn't discuss her with Mac.

After they talked about the papers needed for Amanda, Mac asked Zeke, "Did you see the article in the February 6 *Oregon Spectator*?"

Zeke shook his head. "Ain't seen the paper this week."

"Here's a copy." Mac thrust the paper at Zeke. "Page three has a long description of the new land law."

Zeke looked at the text. As he skimmed it, he asked, "What's it say?"

"It confirms settlers who arrived through 1850 can each claim three hundred and twenty acres of land—men and women alike. A married couple together can claim six hundred forty. That doesn't change, merely because we haven't proved our claims yet, as long as we maintain residence in Oregon and cultivate the land for four years. Final title doesn't vest until the four years are up."

"If nothing's changed, why are you telling me this now?"

Mac pointed at the end of the article. "Says here what happens if a man dies. Like your father. The man's heirs take the land and can still prove it up. So Amanda's lease to me will be good, if we finish out your father's four years. I've asked Devlin Feeney to keep the crops alive this year, and Robert O'Neil says he wants the land by next year."

"Still don't understand how you got Robert to decide to give up his claim. Now he'll have to pay you for the land."

Mac shrugged. "He might be able to sell his interest in his existing land. It's good property, even if it isn't as close to Oregon City." Mac leaned back in his chair. "The article also confirms married women can file claims with their husbands. If you marry, you could keep your entire six hundred forty. But you only have a year after the law was passed to do so—that's December first of 1851."

"Ten months to find a wife," Zeke muttered.

"A little less than ten." Mac grinned.

"What are you doing to occupy your time, other than lawyering for me?" Zeke asked, ready to change the subject away from marriage.

"This same issue of the *Spectator* mentions the formation of a railroad company. I'm investigating whether to buy shares in it."

"A railroad?"

"You ever been on a train?" Mac asked.

Zeke shook his head.

"They're dirty and smelly," Mac said. "Far worse than steamships. But they're fast. We could get grain to Portland in a couple of hours. To Astoria within a day. Someday, trains will go all the way to California."

"I'm not holding my breath," Zeke said. "I just want the grain reaped from my land and sold to the mill. After that, I don't care how it leaves Oregon City."

Mac was as good as his word in handling the legalities with Amanda. On Friday, Zeke hitched his mules, drove to his father's claim to pick up his stepmother, Frankie, and her other children, and loaded them and their

125

trunks into his wagon. The twins, Ruth, and Noah drove behind him in the wagon from their father's claim, toting their belongings to take to Zeke's cabin after they saw their stepmother and her children off.

In Oregon City, Amanda and her children boarded the steamship to Portland. From there, they would go to California and on to Illinois. He didn't know their timetable, but the matter wasn't his to worry about. Amanda would have to get herself and the children back East.

Esther and Rachel and their families also came to bid farewell at the Oregon City dock. Tears streamed down Esther's cheeks as she hugged Frankie, though the toddler didn't seem concerned about the separation. Doubtful he understood anything of what was happening, Zeke thought.

Amanda said she'd write to let them know where she settled. Zeke reminded her of her agreement to keep him informed of the boy's whereabouts and well-being. "He's yours to raise, Amanda," he said. "But he's our kin, too. And I will seek to take over as his guardian if I think the boy's being mistreated."

After the steamboat left the dock, Esther told the others she'd brought a picnic. "We can eat on Abernethy Green," she said. "Remember when we pulled the wagons into town in forty-seven?" She waved her hand to encompass their group. "Now look at us—we're all that's left of the Pershings."

"It ain't that bad, Esther," Rachel said. "We lost Ma and Pa and Frankie. But we have our own babies now. And there'll be more." She touched her belly as she spoke those last words, and Zeke wondered if she was expecting again.

They sat on the lawn and ate, light clouds floating in the early February sky. The twins and the younger children played ball after the meal, Ruth minding the littlest ones. Meanwhile, the adults talked.

"You sure you want all four of them?" Robert O'Neil asked again. "Rachel and I'll take one, if you want. Ruth or Noah."

Zeke shook his head. "They should stay together. Your families are growing. I can manage." Though he wondered how he would. "But how are we going to handle four farms—Pa's, mine, Daniel's, and yours in the next valley? We'll have to give one up, with only three men left to claim them."

Robert answered, "As I told you, I'm giving mine up. Rachel'd rather be back with the rest of the family. I'll take on your pa's claim, if that's agreeable. But probably not till next year."

The men talked on—Daniel said his brother and father would help with the crops. Both Samuel and Douglass Abercrombie were diligent farmers, but Zeke remembered the animosity between his father and old Samuel Abercrombie. Would Daniel's pa be agreeable now or not?

"The twins are big enough to do men's work," Daniel said. "They're good workers when they have a mind to be."

The men's conversation continued. All the while, in the back of Zeke's mind, was the niggling worry about how he would manage four children and the land as well.

Chapter 22: The School Term Ends

Through the rest of February, after the three Purcell students left, Hannah's school continued with fewer pupils. Each of Hannah's classes had lost a student when the Purcells moved away. The remaining children seemed to feel the gaps—their group had been close-knit, despite the inevitable squabbles. Now her students were in turns subdued and antsy—unable or unwilling to answer her questions, unable or unwilling to sit still.

And the four Pershing children seemed particularly lost. Little Noah Pershing and his stepbrother Henry Purcell had played and studied together at school as well as at home. "How are you doing?" Hannah asked Noah one morning.

"I miss Henry," he said, his lower lip trembling.

"Don't you like living with your brother?"

The little boy, not quite eight years old, shrugged and wiped his eyes with his sleeve. "Zeke's all right. I like his mules. And his dog."

Hannah ruffled his hair. "At recess you can go to the barn here and see our mules. Would you like that?"

Noah nodded, but his eyes remained solemn.

Ruth Pershing also seemed overwhelmed by the changes in her life. One morning as soon as she arrived, she handed a comb to Hannah. "Could you please help me get a knot out of my hair?" she asked. "Sarah used to help me with the bad tangles."

Hannah took the comb. She thought Ruth, recently turned twelve, should be able to manage her hair on her own. But Hannah remembered the comfort of her older sister Jane brushing her hair for her as a child. Poor Ruth had no other women in the house with her now.

Only the twins were outwardly unchanged. They continued to cause minor disruptions among the other children, from hiding pencils in the classroom to chasing chickens in the barnyard during recess. Once, Jonathan threw a belligerent hen at Annabelle behind her back. Both Annabelle and the hen squawked at the impact.

As February drew to a close, the children's talk turned to sowing the fields. The weather remained gloomy, with rain or showers almost every day. Hannah slipped and slid in the thick mud covering the ground. Walking on the squishy grasses was no easier—hidden puddles soaked her boots. She was grateful she had nowhere she had to go, except church on Sundays, and if the Sabbath morning was too wet, she and Faith stayed in the cabin.

Finally, Sunday, March 2, was clear, with bright skies and a hint of spring warmth in the air. Hannah and Faith drove into Oregon City to the Methodist church. They met her brother Jacob and his family there. After services, Jacob took her aside and asked, "Your school ends next Saturday, doesn't it?"

"Yes," Hannah replied.

"Have you booked passage back to Ohio?"

"No. I plan to talk to the McDougalls about staying on."

"How will you support yourself?"

"You needn't worry about me, Jacob."

"You're my sister. I'm bound to worry. And we can't—"

Hannah knew what he was about to say and interrupted, "I won't move back in with you, Jacob. Tell Alice she can count on that."

On Monday morning, the last Monday of the school year, the students were particularly restless. All but Ruth Pershing, who sat glumly on her bench until the noon break. She said no more than two or three words when Hannah called on her.

When the other children raced outside into the pleasant early spring weather, Ruth stayed behind. Hannah watched the other students, then returned to the classroom to see Ruth. "What's wrong?" she asked.

"I'm dying," Ruth whispered.

"Don't you feel well?"

Ruth shook her head.

"Do you have a fever? Is your stomach upset?"

Ruth shook her head again, but she let out a small sob.

"Then what is it?"

The girl whispered, "I'm bleeding."

"Were you hurt? Where are you bleeding?" Hannah inspected the girl, but saw no blood on her skin or clothes.

"Down there." Another whisper, this time accompanied by a small gesture toward her private parts.

"Oh," was all Hannah could say. Hadn't anyone prepared the poor child for this? Why did it fall to her—the girl's teacher—to explain? Ruth had two older sisters and until three weeks ago had lived with a stepmother and older stepsister.

Hannah sighed and swallowed—she was the woman with Ruth now and would have to reassure the girl. "How long have you been bleeding?"

"It started Saturday."

"Has it happened before?"

Ruth nodded. "Once. But not as bad."

"And it lasted only a few days then?"

Ruth looked up at her. "How did you know?"

Hannah sat on the bench by Ruth and put her arm around the girl. "It's perfectly normal, Ruth. You're growing up. You're young to start, but sometimes that happens." And she explained.

Ruth's eyes grew rounder. "It's going to happen every month?"

Hannah nodded. "You'll be fine. Let's get you some clean rags, and we'll talk to Esther later."

After school, Hannah hitched the mules to her cart and drove the Pershing children to their sister Esther's house. She went into the cabin and told Esther to send her little ones outside with the schoolchildren, so the women could talk.

Once she and Esther were alone, Hannah told her about her earlier conversation with Ruth.

"Damn that woman!" Esther exclaimed.

"You mean your stepmother?" Hannah asked.

"Who else? She lived with Ruthie in that house for two years. She and Sarah must have had their monthlies. How could she not tell Ruthie? How could Ruthie not notice the laundry?"

"It's up to you and Rachel to reassure her now," Hannah said.

Esther sighed. "Of course, I will. Oh, poor Ruthie. I just assumed . . . "

"I think Ruth feels alone now, living only with her brothers. You and Rachel will have to help her adjust."

"And you, too. Thank you, Hannah." Esther pressed Hannah's hand. "We're lucky to have you here as a teacher."

Hannah shrugged. "Jenny would have done the same thing."

"You're stricter than Jenny was. Most of the young'uns need a little discipline. And I can't always manage." Esther cradled her belly—Hannah thought the woman was close to giving birth. Esther was younger than Hannah, but already in her third pregnancy. Hannah felt again the pain of not having her own family.

"When is your child due?" she asked.

"A few weeks." Esther sighed. "And Sammy's still in diapers." Then she smiled at Hannah. "Enough about the Pershing troubles. What will you do after school ends this week?"

"I don't know," Hannah said. "I have money enough to stay for a few months, if the McDougalls will let me remain in the cabin. But if I find a position in town, I'll have to move. Clerking in a store is what I know best. That and keeping accounts. I suppose I could keep house or tend children, though I've never done so before."

"I hope you'll stay on the claim. I'll ask Daniel if he knows anyone nearby who needs help. And you should talk to Zeke—he gets around to all the farms hereabouts."

By Saturday at noon when school let out, Hannah still had no idea what would come next for her. Faith wanted to stay on the claim with her, and they agreed they would ride to town that afternoon to talk to Jacob. Hannah needed to buy flour and other staples, but she would have to buy small quantities. She didn't know how long she would stay in Oregon, and she didn't fancy supplying Alice's larder free of charge.

She would try to talk to the McDougalls as well. Perhaps they would charge her a reasonable rent for the cabin.

Chapter 23: Zeke Struggles to Adapt

Zeke didn't know how he kept sane the first few weeks after Amanda and the Purcell children left. Adding four young'uns to his household had not been easy. With the weather still cold and rainy, he and his younger brothers all slept in the loft, and he gave his bed to Ruth. Fitting out the room in the barn could come later.

It was a scramble in the morning to get the four ready for school, complete with food for their noon meal. Supper was a thrown-together affair, sometimes cold sausage and cheese, sometimes eggs they hadn't had time to gather in the morning. After the children had been there a week, Ruth said they needed clean clothes, and he was forced to take a day off from preparing fields for sowing to do laundry—he saw the necessity, but hated to abandon the farm, even for a day.

His appreciation for his mother—who had managed twice as many children—grew daily. How did women handle all the work young'uns caused? And his four siblings were able to pitch in when he demanded it, unlike babies.

Zeke also recognized how little attention the four had received from their pa and Amanda. The twins obeyed Zeke's orders, but undertook no work on their own. Ruth did her best, but was overwhelmed. "Mother Amanda and Sarah did most of the housework," she told him. "I took care of Frankie, and watched over Noah and Henry."

At the mention of Henry, Noah started to cry. "I miss Henry," he said. Zeke remembered the two little boys frolicking on the prairie as their wagons moved west. They'd been chums since the day they met.

"I'm sorry, Noah," Zeke told his brother. "You want to come plow with me? You can ride the mule."

That kept Noah mollified for a few hours.

Perhaps it would be easier to develop a routine when the children's school term ended. The twins would help him in the fields, and Noah could either tag along or work with Ruth in the house. If Ruth wasn't helping Esther, who would soon have a fourth child at home.

On Tuesday, March 4, Zeke was at work in the barn when he heard Esther shout his name. The young'uns had just left for school. He went into the yard and found Esther in her wagon with a frown on her face.

"What is it?" Zeke asked. He tied her mule to the hitching post and helped her down. She landed awkwardly and grabbed her belly. "You ain't having your baby already, are you?"

"It's Ruth," she said with a shake of her head. "She's growing up."

Zeke nodded. "Almost as tall as you are now. Taller'n Rachel."

"Not that way." Esther seemed perturbed. "She's becoming a woman. That stepmother of ours didn't tell her nothing." She sighed. "And neither did I."

Zeke didn't understand for a moment, then it dawned on him what Esther meant. He felt a hot red blush rise through his face. "Oh."

"Can you send her to me this afternoon when she's home from school?" Esther asked. "I'll tell her I'm sorry, talk to her woman to woman. I ain't asking you to have that conversation with her. But you'll have to give her her privacy now. Like you would me or Rachel."

"Of course," Zeke said. "I gave her my bed already."

"It's more'n that," Esther said. "She'll need special laundering sometimes. Can you help her be discreet? Don't let the boys tease her."

"I've taken on their care, Esther. I can handle it." He reassured his sister, and kept his doubts about his ability to rear his siblings to himself.

Once school was out, the twins helped Zeke in the fields every day. Jonathan and David were eager to accompany him, if only to get out of the house. They'd worked with both their father and Zeke for the past three summers.

Because of their experience, Zeke expected them to be able to hitch the team to the plow and guide the mules in a straight line with little

133

supervision. Unfortunately, the boys rarely did as expected.

The first day he sent them to plow by themselves, he went to check on them at noontime. The furrows zigged and zagged. "What's this?" he asked, with a wave at the crooked lines. "Can't you plow straight?"

"Too many rocks," Jonathan said. "Mules couldn't plow over 'em."

"That's why there are two of you," Zeke said. "One to guide the mules, the other to haul the bigger stones away. You should know that."

"Pa never made us move the rocks," David muttered.

"I ain't Pa. And you've worked my land before. Last summer you both cleared the fields. We moved the big stuff then. This year should be easier." Zeke sighed. "Let's go eat. But make sure the rest of the field is tilled proper by suppertime."

Saturday, March 15, was Noah's eighth birthday, and Ruth attempted to make him a cake. She was in tears when Zeke and the twins returned to the cabin. "It burned," she sobbed. "I had the oven too hot."

Noah sniveled as they tried to celebrate. "I want Ma," he said. "Or Esther."

Zeke sighed. "Next time we're in town, I'll give you two bits, like I did Ruth."

"I can buy candy?" Noah asked.

"Yes," Zeke said, wishing his problems could be solved with a few sticks of licorice.

The mid-March weather remained cloudy and cool, with showers many days. Zeke often became chilled and wet as soon as he started in the morning, then grew heated from the heavy labor as the day progressed. He and the boys dragged with exhaustion each evening, and the twins grumbled if Ruth didn't have supper ready when they returned to the cabin.

"You told me I wouldn't have to tend all four of you," Ruth complained. "Noah ain't much help."

So on Monday, March 17, after a week in the fields, Zeke told the twins to stay home and help Ruth with the laundry, while he went to work with Daniel on his farm. "Stay here," he told Jonathan and David. "And don't get into any arguments."

When he returned at the end of the day, he found Ruth in tears and the three boys gone, along with one of the mules.

"Where are they?" he asked Ruth.

"Went hunting."

"Hunting? Why?"

"David said a venison stew would taste mighty fine for supper. I told him we didn't have any more venison. Jonathan said they'd go shoot a deer, and Noah cried to go with them."

"So the twins took Noah?"

Ruth nodded. "I told 'em not to go without asking you first. They didn't come see you?"

Zeke shook his head and swore under his breath.

Ruth gasped.

"Sorry, Ruth," Zeke said. "It ain't your fault." He muttered, "Am I going to have to whip them boys?"

"Don't whip 'em!" Ruth cried. "Ma wouldn't like it."

"Ma tanned Joel's and my hides often enough," Zeke said. "She didn't hold back none, either."

"But that's what Mother Amanda did. She made David cry once."

At his sister's words, Zeke's anger at his brothers evaporated. "Amanda beat the twins?"

Ruth nodded. "Harder'n she beat her boy, too."

Zeke closed his eyes. He hadn't been aware of his stepmother's cruelty to the children. "All right. I won't take a switch to 'em."

The three boys arrived home as the sun set, Noah riding one of the mules, with the twins trudging alongside. Behind Noah, a deer carcass perched precariously on the mule's back. Blackie barked and danced around the fresh meat.

"We shot our supper," Noah crowed.

The twins looked sheepishly at Zeke. "'Twas a clean kill," Jonathan said. "I shot it."

"I could've done it, if it'd been my turn with the rifle," David said.

Zeke looked at the boys, then at the carcass. "Did you field dress it?"

"Pretty well," Jonathan said. "Bled it some, then got most of the guts out."

"Take it down and shine a light on it," Zeke said. "Best do it right, or we'll all die from rotten meat. Ruth, you and Noah take the mule to the barn. And tie Blackie up somewhere out of the way."

When the younger two had gone off with the mule and hound, Zeke turned to the twins. "What in tarnation did you think—leaving home with Noah and a mule and a rifle without telling me?"

"We needed meat," Jonathan said defiantly. David hung his head.

"I told you boys to stay home today. Ruth needed your help."

"Laundry was done," Jonathan said.

Zeke helped the boys skin and butcher the deer and move it to the meat cellar. As they worked, he chastised them for disobeying him.

"You gonna whup us?" David asked.

Zeke sighed. "I should. I will if you run off again. This time, I'm making the two of you responsible for cooking our meals for the next week and washing up afterward."

"What about Noah?" Jonathan asked. "He went, too."

"He was your responsibility, so you two are to blame," Zeke said. "But I'll talk to him. He can dry the dishes."

True to his word, Zeke rousted the twins at first light the next morning and told them to start on the porridge. He had another day of work with Daniel planned. "When you're done with morning chores," he told his brothers, "muck out the stable, then do what you can to clear the south field. If we get it done in the next week or two, we should be able to plant more spring wheat."

The porridge was burned, but edible. Zeke gave Ruthie the best portion and took the next for himself, leaving the charred remains for his brothers. That'd improve their cooking skills faster than anyone's instruction.

Then Zeke saddled his gelding and headed to Daniel's farm.

"How do you handle your young'uns?" he asked Daniel as they burned stumps in a recently cleared field. "You got three, and they're all littler'n my family."

"Toddlers are simpler," Daniel said. "They can't get into as much trouble. Douglass and Louisa struggle with their girls at times, even though girls are easier'n boys, I think. I don't envy you taking on four young'uns—three of 'em boys."

"The twins took Noah hunting without permission yesterday."

Daniel chortled. "You don't say. My older brother took me fishing when I was younger'n Noah. I fell in the creek, and we both got walloped hard when we came home, me dripping wet and his boots ruined from pulling me out."

"Sounds like your ma was about like ours."

"'Tweren't our ma, 'twere Pa. And you know how big he is. He switched my backside something fierce. I never run off again, I'll tell you. And Douglass got it worse because he was older."

Zeke sighed. "A part of me wants to thank 'em for bringing home the venison. But a part of me says I can't let 'em get away with disobedience."

"Ain't that the truth." Daniel clapped Zeke on the back. "Now you know what being a pa is like. What you need, though, is someone to mother those children, so you're not in it alone. It's hard for a man alone to handle so many young'uns."

"They've had two mothers," Zeke said. "Not sure they need a third. But Ruthie can't do all the chores, and I need the twins' help on the farm. We can't go on like we have been."

Chapter 24: A New Life

On the Monday after the school term ended, Hannah drove into town to see the McDougalls. She and Faith had talked to Jacob on Saturday. He wouldn't commit to letting Faith stay with Hannah through the summer.

"Alice might need her help," Jacob said. "And Faith is old enough to work in the store."

Hannah couldn't object to Faith's father directing where his daughter lived. "Do you want my help in the store?" she asked, hastening to add, "I'd find a room in town. I won't burden Alice."

Jacob shook his head. "If I have Alice and Faith, I don't need another clerk. And the boys are big enough to help stock shelves."

"Then you won't mind if I ask at the other stores in Oregon City, to see if they need a clerk?"

Her brother frowned. "You're determined to stay in Oregon?"

"Yes." Hannah thought again of Charles's roving eyes and hands in Cincinnati. "I came west intending to make my life here. Even if you don't need my assistance, I should be able to find other work. And maybe I'll teach again in the autumn."

"Hannah—" Jacob began.

"I'm a grown woman," Hannah insisted. "You don't need to take care of me."

Since her brother seemed unwilling to help her, she went to seek the McDougalls' assistance. Mac McDougall had opened a law office in town, and she met him there.

"You can stay on the claim as long as you'd like," Mac told her. "I don't have need of the cabin. But it isn't safe for a woman alone without friends to assist her. You should arrange for Zeke or his brothers to continue to lend a hand with the chores. They'll be around often enough, because they're helping to farm my fields. There's a man named Devlin Feeney working with them also. He might help you."

"Thank you," Hannah said, relieved she would at least have a roof over her head until she found employment. "Do you know of anyone in town or near the claim who might hire me?"

Mac's eyes were kind, but she could tell he thought about her physical impediment. "Most work in the country is heavy farm work or chores," he said. "I don't have enough legal work to employ a secretary, and most folks would not accept a female law clerk if I did. I suggest you ask in the millinery and other women's stores in town."

So Hannah made the rounds of retail establishments in Oregon City, visiting stores catering to women as well as general merchants. None had any openings. Again, she suspected her limp made the proprietors hesitant to give her a chance.

By the end of the day, she grew weary from walking and stopped at the hotel for tea with Jenny McDougall before driving back to the claim.

"I suppose I could take in sewing," she told Jenny. "That's not a strength of mine, but I'm as capable as most women at basic stitchery."

"Mac isn't charging you rent, is he?" Jenny asked. "He shouldn't be. We need someone residing on the claim to help us prove it up."

Hannah shook her head. "He's been very hospitable. I could probably afford to feed myself through the summer on what I have in savings, though I would need to be assured of the school in the fall."

Jenny touched Hannah's arm. "Then talk to the families now about the school. And you can raise vegetables in our garden. Trade them for meat from farmers who don't have time to plant a garden."

Hannah sighed. She'd never gardened before. There was a first time for everything.

"I wish Pa would let me stay with you," Faith said when Hannah reported her conversation with Jacob to his daughter. "I dread going back home to live with Mama Alice."

"I can't go against your father's wishes," Hannah said. "The most I got him to agree to was letting you stay with me two more weeks to get the garden tilled and planted."

Faith chuckled. "It'll be the blind leading the blind. I've never planted vegetables before. We don't have much yard near the store."

"At least you're young and flexible," Hannah said. "I can manage the hoeing, but you'll have to do the bending to plant the seeds."

The next morning they tilled the garden area on the McDougalls' claim. Hannah cut rows in the damp soil, while Faith followed behind, squatting to plant the seeds Hannah had bought from Jacob. "Don't know why Pa wouldn't give you the seeds," Faith said. "They don't cost him much."

"I told him to charge me a fair price," Hannah replied. "I'm going to make my own way here."

They spent several days on the garden, and finally finished it on a showery Tuesday, March 25. Late that afternoon, Zeke Pershing rode into the yard between the cabin and the garden. He sat on his horse watching Hannah and Faith clean their tools while rain dripped off his hat.

Hannah followed his glance toward the garden. The furrows were ragged, but she felt a sense of accomplishment at finishing the task. She glared at Zeke, daring him to comment on the women's inexpert work.

All he said was, "The twins and I'll be working on McDougall's land tomorrow. Just wanted you to know. If you need any chores done, we'll handle those as well."

"Thank you," Hannah said. "Is there anything I can do to help you and your family?" With the garden planted, she would have time on her hands.

"We're fine," Zeke said curtly.

"I'm merely trying to be neighborly, Mr. Pershing," Hannah said. "I might visit Ruth tomorrow, if that's all right with you."

He nodded, touched his hat, and turned his horse to leave.

The next day after cleaning up their breakfast dishes, Hannah and Faith left to visit Ruth Pershing at Zeke's claim. Zeke and his twin brothers had arrived at Hannah's quarters while she and her niece were still eating. She'd heard them hitch their mules to Mr. McDougall's plow, then set out. "We'll start in the south field," she heard Zeke say.

The skies let loose a punishing sleet, but Hannah wanted to explore the area around the small cabin while she still had her niece for company. Hannah knew her way around the paths in the forest now, and there'd been no more sightings of bears, but she still preferred the security of having someone with her.

Ruth and Noah were by themselves in Zeke's cabin when Hannah and Faith arrived. "I'm mighty glad to see you, Miz Bramwell," Ruth said. "Noah and I get lonely when our brothers are gone."

"Do you get scared by yourselves?" Faith asked. "I would, I think, out here in the country, if I was alone."

Ruth shook her head. "I ain't scared. I just wish I had someone to talk to while I work."

"I'm here," Noah piped up.

"You're not much company for a girl," Ruth told him, ruffling his uncombed hair.

"Let's bake today," Faith said. "That'll help pass the time. If you have the fixings—flour and sugar and such—we can replace whatever we use from here next time we come."

"Cake?" Noah asked. "Will you make a cake? Ruth burned my birthday cake."

"We'll start with bread," Hannah said. "But there should be time for cake also."

The rest of the day went pleasantly, and several loaves of bread sat rising while the cake was in the oven. The women and Noah made a venison stew for supper, and Ruth insisted Hannah take part of it home. "I'll bring your bread loaves over tomorrow," Ruth said. "And you can replace your share of the flour and sugar then."

Hannah and Faith packed a pot of stew in their cart and arrived back at the McDougall claim just as Zeke and the twins came into the yard from the fields. The three farm laborers looked weary and cold, sodden from the snow and rain that fell most of the day. "Ruth has a stew waiting for you at your cabin," Hannah told them. "Venison. She told me the story of you boys shooting the deer." Hannah sent a stern glance toward the twins.

"Sounds mighty fine," Jonathan said. "That's why we went hunting."

"Looks like you have some of it here," Zeke said, lifting the Dutch oven from the wagon and handing it to Hannah.

"Ruth insisted," Hannah said, smiling. "It smelled so wonderful, I couldn't refuse. I'll return your pot tomorrow."

"Then you women had a good day?"

Hannah nodded. "We enjoyed spending time with Ruth. It's hard for her staying alone."

Zeke frowned. "She has Noah with her. And the two of them can visit

Esther—help her out. At some point, Rachel'll be nearby also. We're managing all right."

Next morning Hannah waited in the cabin for Ruth, but the girl did not come. She hadn't seen Zeke or the twins on the claim that day either. She wasn't too surprised the men weren't farming, because more sleet fell and the temperatures remained cold. After the noon meal, she and Faith hitched up the cart and went back to Zeke's cabin. No one was there.

She left the clean Dutch oven on the front stoop, and they turned to go. As they did, David came into the yard. "Howdy, Miz Bramwell," he said. "You looking for Ruth?"

"Yes, David."

"She's gone to Esther's. Esther is having her baby. Noah's in the field with us."

"You're outside in this weather again?" Hannah couldn't hide her surprise.

"Yes'm. I just come by the barn to get another piece of harness. A strap broke while we was plowing."

"Were plowing," Hannah corrected. "Does Esther have anyone else to help her?"

"I imagine Doc Tuller and his wife are there," David said. "But Esther's had lots of babies. She don't need much help."

"Shall we drive over, Aunt Hannah?" Faith asked. "I want to see the baby."

"All right." Hannah had never attended a birth and didn't think she'd be much help to the new mother or baby. But Faith seemed eager.

A wagon sat in Esther's yard and a horse grazed in the paddock outside the barn, nibbling for grass under the crust of snow. "I think that's Doc Tuller's horse and wagon," Faith said. "He or his wife must be inside."

Hannah knocked on the door, and Ruth opened it. From inside came a wail of pain. "The baby'll be here soon," Ruth said. "You're welcome to come in."

In addition to Esther's cries, three young children added their voices to the bedlam in the cabin. Hannah thought she remembered the children's names—Esther's brother Jonah and her two offspring Cordelia and Sammy. This new infant would join a crowded household.

Esther sat against the bed's headboard, knees drawn toward her chest and hands clutching the sheet draped over her. Beside her stood an older woman Hannah recognized from church—Mrs. Tuller, the doctor's wife.

"Good afternoon, ma'am," Hannah said, draping her cloak and Faith's over a chair near the fire.

"Oh, good," Mrs. Tuller said. "You two can help. I got water heating, but I ain't wiped down the cradle yet. Can you do that?" She pointed at a baby's bed on the table by the hearth. "This baby's come a little earlier'n expected."

Esther let out another cry, then called, "I need to push, Mrs. Tuller."

"Where's Dr. Tuller?" Hannah asked as she moved to do as instructed.

"Out on another call. Thank goodness he didn't take the wagon, or I couldn't have made it here in this weather." Mrs. Tuller turned to Ruth, "Are you minding those young'uns?"

"Yes'm," Ruth said.

"I'll help you," Faith said. "Let's take 'em out to the barn."

The two girls bundled up the three young children and led them outside. Hannah took a deep breath when the room became silent, except for Esther's groans and Mrs. Tuller's encouragement.

About twenty minutes later, Mrs. Tuller said, "Come here, Hannah. Baby's coming now. I need your help."

Esther gave a loud guttural moan that turned into a sigh. A baby cried, the newborn sound bringing a lump to Hannah's throat. Mrs. Tuller took the infant and handed it to Hannah. "It's a girl. Go wipe her down with a warm rag, while I deliver the afterbirth."

Hannah had never held a newborn before, though she'd seen her nieces and nephews within days of their births. She murmured with a sense of awe as she took the baby. Hannah treated the small wailing lump like fine china, as she carried the infant to the table. A soft blanket awaited, along with a pail of warm water and a towel. She carefully patted the baby, who stared back at her with solemn eyes and quieted when the warm towel touched her skin. When the infant was clean, Hannah folded the blanket around her and picked her up again.

"Bring her to me," Esther called from the bed, holding out her arms.

Hannah lifted the fragile newborn, her hands shaking now she'd managed the delicate task, and carried her to Esther. "What will you name her?" Hannah whispered to the new mother.

Esther touched her daughter's nose and fingers. "I don't know." She sighed. "We thought she'd be a boy. I was ready to name this baby Frankie, after the brother Amanda took from us."

Hannah and Faith remained at Esther's house until supper time, when Daniel returned. "We have a daughter," Esther told him, smiling. "Now, what'll we name her?"

"Cordelia is named after your ma," Daniel said, as he cradled his new baby in his arms. "What if we name this one after mine?"

"Abigail?" Esther nodded. "I like it." She turned to Hannah. "Daniel's ma died when he was born."

"I want to be sure my stepmother don't mind," Daniel said. "She raised me, and I don't mean to disrespect her. But I think she'll approve."

Hannah had seen how her sister-in-law Alice and Amanda Pershing treated their stepchildren, and she was glad to learn Daniel liked his stepmother. It must be terribly difficult to raise another woman's children, but perhaps Harriet Abercrombie had handled the role well.

"We should leave," Hannah whispered to Faith, as she watched the new parents with their infant. Ruth played with the other children on the floor near the hearth.

A knock sounded on the door, and Zeke Pershing stepped inside. He was still in his grubby work clothes and mud-caked boots. "Came soon as I could," he said, kicking off his boots. "Everything all right?"

"A daughter," Daniel said, beaming. "Think we'll call her Abigail."

Zeke stepped across the room and inspected his new niece. "Name fits," he said, grinning at Esther. "She looks more like an Abercrombie than a Pershing."

"She does not! She's one of us," Esther protested with a frown. "Just because we're giving her an Abercrombie name don't make her any less a Pershing."

"I'm teasing, Esther," Zeke said, dropping a kiss on his sister's head. "Are you well?"

"Well enough," Esther said, sniffing.

"I've come to take Ruth home."

"Can't you leave her here?" Esther asked. "For a day or two? She's a great help with the other three."

"What do you think, Ruth?" Zeke asked.

"Yes, please, I'll stay," Ruth said.

"All right then," Zeke said, putting his boots back on. "I'd best get home to the boys, or they'll burn my cabin down." He seemed to notice Hannah for the first time as she and Faith crept toward the door. "Might I escort you and Faith home on my way, Miz Bramwell?"

Glancing at the window, Hannah realized dark had fallen already, but it appeared the sleet and showers had stopped. "Oh, we'll be all right, Mr. Pershing."

But Zeke had already left the cabin and she found him hitching the McDougall mules to her cart. He boosted Faith up and lifted Hannah over the wheel as if she didn't weigh a thing. Then he tied his gelding behind and vaulted onto the bench beside her.

"Hie," he shouted at the mules, as he tapped their backs with the reins.

Chapter 25: Zeke Still Struggles

Zeke drove Hannah's wagon toward the McDougall claim in silence. He was chilled to the bone from laboring in the wet and cold all day. He and the twins had more than enough work in readying his own fields for planting and helping with those of his family and friends. By evening, all he wanted was a hot supper in his belly and to curl in his bed under a heavy blanket.

But he couldn't let Miz Bramwell and her niece drive themselves home in the dark.

He felt Hannah's warmth beside him on the wagon bench, while Faith chattered from behind them about the new baby. According to Esther and Mrs. Tuller, the starchy Miz Bramwell handled his newborn niece expertly, though she'd never attended a birthing before. As they rode, the woman relaxed beside him, leaning into him occasionally when the wagon lurched over a bump in the road.

"Isn't she precious, Zeke?" Faith asked.

"Huh?" Zeke said, with a sharp glance at Hannah.

Hannah's lips twitched at his look. "She's a lovely baby, Faith," she said, humor in her tone.

"I'm sure she is," Zeke hastened to add. "I ain't one to pay much mind to 'em that young. But I'm sure Esther is delighted."

"Probably mostly delighted to have the birthing over," Faith said, and she launched into another long prattle.

"I suppose you and the baby's father hoped for a boy to work with you in the fields," Hannah said.

Zeke shrugged. "Don't matter. It'll be years afore the child can be any help."

Only Faith broke the silence for the rest of the ride. As he drove, Zeke pondered what it would be like to be a father. He didn't feel like a parent to his younger siblings. Noah was sixteen years younger than Zeke, but Zeke remembered Ma chasing after Noah the same way she'd chased after him when he was young—their shared experience kept him feeling like Noah's sibling. And the same was true to an even greater degree with the twins and Ruth.

Esther often said she felt more like Jonah's mother than his sister. Of course, she'd raised their youngest brother since birth. And Daniel and Esther now had three young'uns of their own. What would it be like to know he'd caused a new life to come into the world? Would it make him feel more responsible than he felt now? How could that be, when he already seemed to have more weight on his shoulders than Atlas?

The next two days on Zeke's farm were chaotic. While Ruth remained at Esther's house, Zeke, the twins, and Noah had to prepare their own meals and tend to the household chores, in addition to their work in the fields all day. Noah resisted any instructions Zeke gave him. The twins teased the little boy and each other as well.

Finally, Zeke exploded. "Next lad who causes a ruction gets a beating." He immediately regretted his words, but once said, he had to follow through or lose his authority with his brothers.

The young'uns calmed down for an hour or so, but later in the barn, Zeke caught Jonathan squirting cow's milk at Noah. Zeke sighed, but pulled Jonathan off the milking stool by his shirt collar. He cuffed him once on the side of the head. "What did I say?"

"Are you really going to beat him?" Noah asked, eyes widening.

Jonathan stood defiantly.

"I got something worse," Zeke said. "Jonathan, you go chop wood. I want the pile chest-high and stacked neatly. The rest of us are going to the north field. You work off your orneriness afore you join us." He hoped the hard labor would slow the boy down.

The weather cooperated in the late days of March. Friday, March 28, was cloudy but dry, and on Saturday, showers held off until evening. But two days of baching it with the three younger boys taught Zeke how hard Ruth had been working.

Saturday evening, two days after the baby's birth, Zeke drove his brothers to Esther's house to fetch Ruth. The younger boys hadn't yet seen their new niece, and Zeke thought it would be good for all of them to get away from home. He took the last haunch of venison from the deer the twins had killed, certain Esther and her family could use the meat.

When they arrived, the boys gave a quick look at the baby, then were happy to take Esther's older children to the barn to play with kittens. Ruth went with the other children, leaving Zeke with Esther, Daniel, and the newborn Abigail.

"Ruth's been telling me about keeping house for you," Esther said as she rocked the baby. "She shouldn't be doing all that work alone."

"I leave Noah with her some days. And the twins help as well."

"She's only twelve, Zeke. She should be learning how to run a house, but she shouldn't have to cope on her own. Rachel and I didn't start so young. And even after Ma died, we had each other and the whole wagon company."

Zeke sniffed. "I recollect you complaining plenty on the trail after Ma died, when the Abercrombies wouldn't let you help our family. Rachel bore the brunt of caring for us all then."

Esther glanced quickly at her husband—Zeke wished he hadn't mentioned Daniel's parents being a thorn in Esther's side back in forty-seven. But it was true. Daniel's father had been the big problem, but Mrs. Abercrombie followed her husband's lead.

"You should hire a housekeeper," Esther said. "Someone to teach Ruth. Give Ruth more time to be a child."

Zeke leaned back in his chair. "And just who do you suggest I hire? Not many women in these parts. Not who ain't more slatterns than housekeepers."

"What about Hannah Bramwell?" Esther said, raising the baby to her shoulder. "She needs work, if she's to stay in Oregon."

"Miz Bramwell?" Zeke said. "The teacher?"

Esther nodded in time with her rocking.

"She knows books, but she's not much good at frontier life. Can't hardly chop wood. And can't shoot well at all."

"Hannah is a decent cook, keeps her cabin neat, and is good with the children," Esther said. "What more do you need?"

Zeke took the children to church on Sunday. He hoped the threatening clouds would hold off dumping their moisture until after they returned home. He'd thought about Esther's suggestion he hire a housekeeper all evening and into the night. It wasn't a bad idea, if he could find the right woman. He didn't cotton to Hannah Bramwell, but maybe a widow in town might be able to help. Though where he'd put another body in their house, he didn't know. He resolved to ask Doc and Mrs. Tuller who they might recommend.

After the service, he approached the doctor and his wife. They had no one in mind, but said they would think about it. Zeke then asked Mac and Jenny if they knew of someone he could hire as housekeeper.

"What about Hannah Bramwell?" Mac said. "She needs work, though she's looking for store or office clerking."

"Esther suggested her," Zeke said. "But I don't know."

"She's a fine woman," Jenny said, laying a hand on his arm. "She pitched in for me finishing out the school term, and the children became quite fond of her. Your younger siblings included."

"You don't think she's too delicate for farm life?" Zeke said. He didn't want to mention Hannah's limp, though he'd seen it limit her activities, both when he taught her to use the hatchet and also as she practiced with the rifle. Still, she did not let her infirmity stop her.

"She's planted a garden," Mac said. "I saw it when I inspected the fields this week."

"I think Faith did most of the work," Zeke said, though he wondered. Miz Bramwell's hems had been mighty muddy when he'd come across the women in the garden that afternoon a couple weeks ago.

"Faith is moving back to live with her father this week," Jenny said. "Hannah will be all alone on our claim. I'd feel better if she were expected somewhere every day—if someone watched out for her."

"I'll think about it," Zeke said.

As he hitched up the wagon to return home, he noticed Hannah Bramwell struggling with her mules nearby. He went over to help her, and she thanked him primly.

"Hear tell Faith is moving back to town," he said.

"Yes," Hannah said in a crisply clipped syllable. "Her father wants her with him."

"I'm sure you'll miss her."

"Yes," she said, equally crisply. But her shoulders slumped she spoke. "I will."

"Hear tell you're looking for work," he heard himself say.

She looked at him sharply. "I am."

"I need a housekeeper. Do you want the job?"

Chapter 26: Hannah's Quandary

Hannah was speechless at Zeke's question. A housekeeper? She hadn't really considered the possibility. She'd worked as a store clerk both in Cincinnati and in Oregon City. She'd taught. But she'd never been responsible for a large family's household.

Still, she'd assisted Jane when her sister's health didn't permit her to manage her home. Hannah had often directed the cook and maids, the coachman and gardeners. Of course, on the frontier, she wouldn't have servants. "You mean, you need a cook and maid and laundress?" she asked. She'd handled these things for herself and Faith while she taught in the McDougall cabin.

Zeke nodded. "That about sums it up. And milking the cow and tending the garden."

"I don't know . . . ." Hannah didn't mind menial chores for her own wellbeing, but did she want to take them on for Zeke Pershing and his siblings? And she struggled milking the cow on the McDougall claim.

Did she have any other options?

"Let me think about it," she said. She glanced up at the sky—clouds above them threatened rain. "I need to get back to the claim before it showers."

Zeke shrugged, lifted her into her wagon, then handed the mule's reins to her. "Take your time. I ain't got anyone else in mind for the job. Esther just suggested yesterday I find someone. Not even sure I cotton to the idea."

Hannah thought about Zeke's offer on her lonely drive back to the

McDougall claim. She continued to ponder it all evening and spent a restless night still considering it. Without Faith there, the little cabin was eerily silent, and she had no one to take her mind off her worries. She hadn't thought to ask whether Zeke expected her to live with his family or to continue on at the McDougalls' cabin. She couldn't see adding herself to the several Pershings in Zeke's cabin.

The next morning, as she cooked her toast over the fire, she thought longingly of the new cookstove in Zeke's home. Why did he—a bachelor—have better cooking facilities than Jenny McDougall? Jenny's husband seemed to have plenty of money for such luxuries, and Hannah didn't really think of a stove as a luxury, though its absence was certainly a deprivation.

She decided to talk to Esther—the notion of Zeke needing a housekeeper seemed to have originated with his sister. Besides, she would relish seeing the infant Abigail again. She would likely never have a child of her own, but she enjoyed mothering little ones when she could.

It had rained all afternoon and evening the day before, so Hannah did not need to water the garden. As soon as she washed and dried her few breakfast dishes and laundered a few dirty garments, she set out for Esther's.

Esther was up and looking physically stronger than when Hannah had seen her on Thursday right after Abigail's birth. But the young woman looked harried. "It's hard managing four little children alone," she said. "I should have asked Zeke to leave Ruth a few days longer."

"What can I do to help?" Hannah asked, taking off her cloak and bonnet.

"Would you find some bread and jam for the older ones? They only had bacon for breakfast."

Abigail mewled in the cradle in the corner. Cordelia, almost three, raced over to pat her newborn sister. Esther rushed after her. "Careful now," she said, lifting the infant out of Cordelia's reach. "Mustn't hurt the baby." Esther turned to Hannah. "She's so-o-o loving it frightens me. The boys ignore Abigail, which is fine with me."

Hannah sliced bread, covered the slices with jam, and handed them to Jonah, Cordelia, and Sammy, who had seated themselves at the table.

Esther collapsed with the baby in the rocking chair. "What brings you out this morning?"

Hannah smiled. "I thought you might need some help. I saw Mr. Pershing with your younger siblings at church yesterday. Ruth was with him, so I figured you were alone."

"Thank you." Esther sighed. "I forgot how much time a new baby takes. This one suckles constantly."

As if to prove her mother right, Abigail cried and rooted at Esther's chest. Esther pulled a shawl over her shoulder and put the baby to her breast underneath it.

As soon as contented grunts came from the infant, the older children clamored for milk. Hannah stood to tend to them.

"Thank you," Esther murmured, her eyes closed as she rocked gently.

"Mr. Pershing told me he is looking for a housekeeper," Hannah said after pouring three mugs of fresh milk.

Esther's eyes opened. "He asked you?"

"Yes." Hannah wiped Sammy's dribbles of milk off the table.

"I didn't think he would. He pooh-poohed the notion when I raised it."

"What do you think his household really needs?"

Esther laughed at Hannah's question. "Everything a woman does," she said. "Zeke is busy dawn till dusk with the farm. It'll only get worse now planting season's here. He needs the twins with him, or he can't manage it all. Particularly without Pa." Esther paused and her lip quivered. "Ruth can't take care of all of 'em. And I don't want her to. And I'll need her help also, so she'll be torn."

"Would I have to live there?" Hannah asked.

Esther shrugged. "That's between you and Zeke. But I shouldn't think so. Not unless you want those boys hollering at you day and night. Best agree with Zeke on your hours afore you start."

The next day—April 1, though the weather remained cool—Hannah was no closer to deciding how to respond to Zeke. She needed work, but she was not eager to take on the Pershing household. She rode into Oregon City to ask Jacob's advice—her brother wanted her gone, but if he could be convinced she had no intention of leaving the territory, maybe he would give her an honest opinion. They had once been close—before he left Ohio and lost his arm, before Beulah died and he married Alice.

"Oh, you should do it, Aunt Hannah!" Faith said, once Hannah told her of Zeke Pershing's proposal. "You can stay in Oregon, and I'm sure the McDougalls will let you live on their claim as long as you need."

"I don't know, Hannah," Jacob said. "Your leg—"

Hannah herself worried housework for an active family would tax her physical abilities, but having Jacob be so blunt about it incensed her. "I've always done everything I put my mind to, Jacob," she said. "I've learned to chop kindling and tend the mules since coming to Oregon. Faith and I planted a garden." She hoped her niece wouldn't let it be known she'd done most of the stooping, while Hannah handled the hoe.

"Now, Hannah, you know what I mean." Her brother sounded apologetic. "I'm only looking out for your interests. Will you earn enough to keep yourself?"

"I didn't ask what he'd pay. But I should be able to manage until school starts again in the fall," Hannah said.

"It's your reputation you need to mind," Alice said from the corner where she sat knitting. "That Zeke Pershing is a scandal."

Faith glanced surreptitiously toward her stepmother but kept her mouth shut. Hannah remembered Alice mentioning some impropriety involving Zeke and Jenny McDougall, but her sister-in-law had not provided any details. Perhaps both she and her niece would learn the story now. "What do I need to know about Mr. Pershing, Alice?" Hannah kept her voice pleasant.

"He and Jenny McDougall were closer than they should have been while Mr. McDougall was away," Alice said. "More than that, I won't say. Not in the presence of the young people." She arched her eyebrows at Faith.

"Faith," Jacob said. "Go down to the store and bring up a jar of pickles." When the girl left, he turned to Hannah. "Zeke spent a lot of time with Jenny McDougall while we traveled in the wagons. You know McDougall took over as captain after Franklin Pershing lost his wife and turned to drink. Zeke filled in, helping Jenny with the wagon. I didn't think much of it then, because McDougall was around and he didn't seem to mind. But then, after McDougall went to California for the gold—along with half the men in Oregon, I might add—Zeke farmed the McDougall claim. There were rumors he and Jenny were intimate."

"I see." Hannah refrained from mentioning Faith's comments about Jacob and Alice being as guilty of fornication as Zeke Pershing and Jenny

McDougall, though Jenny was a married woman at the time of their alleged indiscretion. She wondered whether her brother and Alice began their relationship before Beulah died, though she would never ask. "But you don't know whether they were?"

"Well, how could we?" Alice interjected.

"What do you suggest I do?" Hannah asked her brother, ignoring Alice.

"Do as you please," Jacob said. "You always do."

"Just remember the type of person you'll be dealing with," Alice added with a sniff.

Faith returned with the pickles. Hannah spent the night with her brother, and after she got in bed with Faith and Charity, Faith whispered, "Did they tell you the story?"

Hannah sighed. "It's nothing you need to know, Faith. I won't pass on gossip I don't know to be true."

"Well, if you stay on the McDougall claim this summer, will you ask Pa again if I can live with you?"

So Hannah asked her brother in the morning if Faith could return to the country with her.

Jacob refused. "I don't want Faith spending a lot of time with the Pershing twins, and I suspect she'd tag along with you to work most days. You heard what Alice and I told you—where there's smoke there's fire, and I won't have Faith caught up in rumors and innuendo. Besides, she shouldn't be working for another family when Alice says she needs her here at home."

Before returning to the McDougall claim on Wednesday morning, Hannah asked again in several Oregon City shops whether they needed a clerk. No one would hire her.

On her way out of town, she stopped at the hotel to see Jenny. She had no intention of repeating what Jacob and Alice had said, but she wanted Jenny's reaction to Zeke's proposal to hire her. Jenny sat with embroidery in her hotel suite, her two children playing on the floor.

"A housekeeper!" Jenny laughed when Hannah explained the situation. "Zeke is the neatest man I know. He must be truly overwhelmed by his younger siblings if he thinks he needs a housekeeper. But then, you and I know those children are a handful."

"I've spoken with Ruth," Hannah said. "Before Esther had her baby—"

"Esther's baby came?" Jenny interrupted. "I didn't know. I must go see her. Boy or girl? "

"A girl. Abigail." Hannah said, smiling. "I was there. Anyway, Ruth is too young to manage on her own."

Jenny nodded. "And with planting underway, Zeke doesn't have time either. Yes, I can see why he'd want a housekeeper."

"You say he's neat?" Hannah prodded, hoping Jenny would reveal more about the man.

"Yes," Jenny said. "Will you take my children and me to Esther's with you? I'll leave word for Mac to come retrieve us there."

As they rode to Esther's claim, Jenny recounted Zeke's assistance to her on the trail when Mac nearly died of cholera, how he'd saved her on a river crossing when her wagon mired in quicksand, and how he'd farmed her fields while Mac had been in California. It all sounded innocent, as Jenny told the story.

"He does seem to be a capable man," Hannah said.

"More so than anyone else I know in the territory," Jenny said. "I would rely on him completely."

Was that a statement of platonic friendship or of continuing affection for a former paramour? Hannah had no way of knowing.

But it seemed she had no alternative to the housekeeping role, if she wanted paid employment for the summer.

Chapter 27: Zeke Regrets His Offer

Thursday morning, Zeke fried potatoes and bacon and fed his younger siblings breakfast. As he and Ruth washed the dishes after the meal, a knock sounded on the door. "Noah, see who it is," he said.

When Noah opened the door, Hannah Bramwell stepped in. "Miz Bramwell," Zeke said in surprise. He wiped his hands on a towel and turned to her.

"May we speak, Mr. Pershing?" She took off her cloak and hung it over a chair as if prepared to stay awhile. "I've come to accept your position as housekeeper. Provided we come to terms."

He hadn't seen her since Sunday when he blurted out the offer, and now it was Thursday. "I didn't hear from you. I assumed—"

"I told you I needed time to think. Well, I have. And I'll take the position. If it's still open."

Ruth grinned. Noah pulled at Zeke's arm, whispering, "Say yes." The twins glanced from Zeke to Hannah, but continued to lace their boots to ready themselves for a day in the fields.

Zeke swallowed. He wasn't sure he wanted her as a housekeeper, but the young'uns seemed to be in favor. And Ruth would relish the help. He sighed. "All right, Miz Bramwell. Can you start tomorrow?"

"Terms first, Mr. Pershing," she said. She told him she'd work half days for the rest of this week, wanted Saturday afternoons and Sundays off, and would start a full day the following Monday. "Saturday afternoons are for my own business," she explained.

Zeke shrugged. "I don't mind if you handle your own affairs when you're in town getting our provisions. As long as you feed us and get the laundry and house cleaning done." The woman clearly had a plan in mind, and it might be best to let her have at it. He could fire her if she caused too much trouble.

"How much will you pay?" Hannah asked.

"A dollar a day, in cash or grain on account at the Abernethy store," he said.

She nodded. "Make that my brother's store, and I accept."

"Fine." He could open another account at Jacob Bramwell's store, though he thought Abernethy had better merchandise.

"And I want Ruth and Noah at my disposal."

He frowned. Miz Bramwell was not starting out on the right foot. "The purpose of hiring you is to take the work off Ruth."

"I'll let the children play, Mr. Pershing," she said. "You'll have to trust me on that. But I won't be your slave. They'll do their part, too."

"I'm willing, Zeke," Ruth said. She poked Noah, who nodded reluctantly.

"All right, then." Zeke stuck out his hand. If she was going to act as bossy as a man, she could shake like one.

She grasped his fingers with a surprisingly firm grip. "I'll be here tomorrow at seven."

Then she put on her cloak and left.

Friday morning, as she promised, Hannah showed up at Zeke's homestead promptly at seven. The Pershings had finished their breakfast by the time she arrived, and Ruth piled the dishes near the wash tub. As Zeke and the twins put on their boots to leave, Noah eyed them with a woeful expression.

Hannah looked at Noah, then at Zeke, then back to the boy. "Noah, would you like to join your brothers today? Ruth and I'll make up a weekly work plan, and I don't need you here for that."

The little boy grinned at her.

"But tomorrow, you'll stay in the cabin. We'll schedule your chores for tomorrow."

As Zeke looked at her with a puzzled frown, she added, "If it's all right with you for Noah to accompany you, Mr. Pershing? You'll have to tell me if he might get hurt in the fields. I know very little about farming or what's appropriate for children on a farm."

Zeke shook his head. "No, ma'am. He'll be fine." Yesterday she'd asked for Noah to be at her beck and call, today she foisted the boy on him. Noah wasn't much help with farming yet, but it made little difference where the boy spent the day, so long as someone watched out for him.

"Ruth and I will bring your noon meal out to the field," Hannah said. "Isn't that the usual practice?"

"Yes, ma'am," Zeke said. "Any time in the hour after noon would be fine."

"I'll be leaving after the noon meal, but your supper will be on the stove, so you and Ruth can dish it up when you're ready."

As the Pershing males left the cabin, Zeke heard her tell Ruth. "Now, then, let's take an inventory of your provisions and make up a plan to get the chores done regularly."

It remained cool and cloudy all morning, as the three Pershings plowed and sowed the spring wheat. The pale sun shone weakly through the haze high above them, when the wagon pulled up with Hannah and Ruth in it. Zeke's spirits rose and his mouth watered as he lifted a covered pot smelling of ham and beans out of the wagon. He carried the pot under a tree while Jonathan retrieved a spider pan full of corn pone from the wagon.

"Are those mint leaves floating in the water?" Noah asked after he clambered down from the wagon with the water jug.

Ruth nodded and smiled. "It was Miz Hannah's idea," the girl said. "She has lots of ideas."

They had just laid the meal out under a tree when rain began to fall.

"There's more of this for supper," Hannah told Zeke. "Ruth can keep it warm. I'm leaving now. I want to get home before it's too wet. I'll be back in the morning."

Zeke and his brothers fell into the food like they hadn't eaten in weeks. He hadn't had a meal this good since last he ate at Esther's house. His spirits lifted despite the rain.

Showers continued all Friday afternoon and evening. Zeke hoped it would clear by morning. But when he arose on Saturday, rain poured from the sky, even harder than the day before. It would be a miserable day. He'd hoped they could finish sowing the cleared fields, but it was probably too wet to plant the spring wheat. They might have to clear a new field instead—muddy work in this weather.

Hannah arrived promptly again. As on the morning before, the Pershings' breakfast dishes were still unwashed. Zeke saw her lips purse and her eyes narrow.

Hands on hips, Hannah said, "Jonathan and David, before you leave each morning, I want those plates scraped off. Ruth and I can wash them, but there's no reason to leave caked-on porridge on the bowls to make our job harder."

"Miz Bramwell—" Zeke started.

"I mean to impose order on this household. By autumn when school starts, the five of you should be able to tend to yourselves," Hannah said.

"Miz Bramwell—" Zeke tried again.

"I can't teach and tend house for you at the same time," she continued.

"I was going to tell you the twins make our breakfast," Zeke said. "It don't seem right they should have to clean it up also."

"Well, then, you and Noah can do the scrubbing," Hannah said.

Zeke bit his lip and beckoned to Noah. The two of them scraped the bowls and porridge pot, and Zeke went so far as to fill the pot with boiling water to sit until the high and mighty Miz Bramwell could get to it.

Zeke and the twins cleared brush and hauled rock in muddy fields all morning. He grew colder and wetter as the day wore on, and the twins provided little help. He should have left them in the house, though he suspected they would have been as little use there as they were moving stones.

The skies stayed gloomy through the morning, and only Zeke's stomach told him when noon was approaching. He'd about decided to return to the cabin for dinner, when Hannah appeared. She drove, with Ruth and Noah in the wagon bed behind her. She'd brought a canvas sheet. "I thought we should try to keep the food dry," she said.

Zeke grinned at her, as he and the twins tied the canvas corners to trees to provide some shelter. This time, Hannah stayed while he and the boys ate the hot, meaty stew and ginger beer she'd brought.

After filling his belly, he lay down for a nap. He tried to doze, but Miz Bramwell wouldn't let him rest until he approved her schedule of chores. "I need to leave now, Mr. Pershing," she said. "And I want to be ready for Monday morning. I have a full day planned." She handed him a piece of paper with tasks outlined in a neat script—Monday washing, Tuesday baking. He didn't read any further.

"Miz Bramwell," he said. "I hired you to keep house, not to bother me with the details."

"Mr. Pershing," she said, her voice colder than the damp air, "I need to know when I'll have the twins' and Noah's help, and when you'll need them."

"That depends, Miz Bramwell," he said, trying to match her icy tone. "If the weather improves, I'm likely to need all the help I can get. And some days, I'll promise my time and that of the twins to McDougall or to one of the Abercrombies. Farming is an uncertain business."

She stared at him. Then she walked to the wagon, calling over her shoulder, "I suppose I'll have to make do with Ruth and Noah. That's all the help you promised me."

That evening, when Zeke and the twins returned from the fields, filthy, sodden, and downcast, the only thing keeping Zeke from falling into bed immediately was the need to feed his younger siblings. For himself, he'd just as soon sleep as eat. They put the plow in the barn, took care of the mules, and traipsed to the cabin.

After stepping inside the door to remove his boots, Zeke smelled freshly baked bread and something savory—perhaps the remnants of the noon stew. "I thought you wasn't baking till Tuesday," he said to Ruth.

"Miz Hannah and I made the dough this morning," Ruth said. "Enough for the weekend."

"So it's 'Miz Hannah' now, is it?" he asked. "Are you happy she's here?"

"It's ever so nice to have someone to talk to," his sister replied, with a smiling sigh. "Someone besides a brother."

"She seems kind of bossy," Zeke said.

"She is!" Noah piped up. "She had me making beds and gathering eggs and all sorts of chores."

"She let you play marbles, too," Ruth said. "And after she left, you had the afternoon in the barn, while I baked the bread."

"Food's better'n we had it afore she came," David mumbled, pulling off his boots. "Can I have a slice of bread now?"

"Wash your hands," Ruth said, sounding as high-handed as Miz

Bramwell—make that, Miz Hannah.

But Zeke set the example for his younger brothers and moved to the washbasin.

They ate their supper mostly in silence. Ruth and Noah chatted, but Zeke and the twins were too tired to say much. As he ate, Zeke wondered whether Hannah Bramwell would be the making of the Pershing clan or cause him to follow his father's road to ruin in whiskey.

Chapter 28: Hannah Regrets Her Decision

As Hannah drove to the Pershing claim Monday morning, she worried she'd started off on the wrong foot with Zeke the week before, arguing with him about the chores and the help she would need. But she didn't think her role as housekeeper would continue into the fall after school started, and she was determined to leave the family in better shape when the summer ended than they were in now.

When she entered Zeke's cabin, she found the small residence in shambles. After a day and a half without her, dishes stood piled in the sink, dirty footprints tracked the floor, and clothes littered the floor at the foot of the bed. And Jenny had told her Zeke was a neat man, she fumed silently.

"I wanted it spruced up afore you got here," Ruth wailed when she saw Hannah. "But the washing ain't—"

"Isn't," Hannah said automatically, as she took off her cloak.

"—isn't sorted, and the breakfast dishes ain't—aren't—washed."

"I thought your brother Zeke washed the breakfast dishes," Hannah said, tying on the apron she'd brought with her.

"He had to help Daniel today, and he left first thing. Thinks it's going to stay dry for a change. Twins went with him."

"Where's Noah?"

The little boy's head popped over the edge of the loft. "Up here, Miz Hannah."

"Come on down. You can dry while I wash." Hannah shook her head with a sigh. Her schedule was out of kilter already. At least she could start heating the laundry water while she cleaned up after the Pershings' breakfast. But she'd need the washbasin from the dishes for the clothes. "Ruth, please sort the clothes, then mop the floor."

After finishing the extra chores, she and the two children started on

163

laundry. She was disappointed the twins weren't there—she'd hoped the older boys could haul the washtub for her. She and Ruth dragged it into the yard, though her leg was aching by the time they'd scrubbed the wash, rinsed out the lye soap, and hung everything on the line to dry.

While she and Ruth worked, she ordered Noah about the cabin and barnyard—tidying up inside, gathering eggs outside—"Carefully, now. We don't want any broken."

"Can we eat 'em at noon?" he asked.

Hannah looked at Ruth. "Are the eggs needed for anything in particular?"

Ruth shrugged. "We'll need more bread soon. But we have a few eggs left from yesterday."

After establishing from Ruth that Esther would supply the noon meal for Zeke and the twins today, Hannah decided, "We'll eat the old eggs at noon today. Save the new ones." So for dinner they had scrambled eggs and bacon.

In the afternoon, Hannah and Ruth made a ham soup for the Pershings' supper. "It'll keep until your brothers get home," Hannah said. Then the three of them brought in the laundry, which was still damp. As Zeke predicted, the weather remained fine, but the air was humid from the rain and clouds of the past few days.

"We'll iron tomorrow," Hannah said. "And bake again. Isn't that what's on the schedule?"

Exhausted by the day's duties, she left in late afternoon, as the sun lowered behind the high trees. Zeke and the twins still had not returned. She felt guilty leaving Ruth and Noah alone, but she'd set her hours with Zeke, and she didn't intend to deviate from them—not on her first full day. Zeke would have to learn to keep his part of their bargain, and he'd failed that morning by leaving the house in a mess.

The rest of the week remained cloudy, but the only rain came on Thursday evening. Hannah was able to stick to her schedule most days, though Zeke took Jonathan and David with him every day. "We need their help in the fields more'n you need 'em here," he told her. "If something around the house don't get done, it can wait. I don't care."

"I care, Mr. Pershing," she said. But she couldn't countermand Zeke's orders to his brothers.

At least the breakfast dishes were washed when she arrived each morning. Noah told her plainly he helped Zeke with them after the twins cooked. Ruth, apparently, had no responsibility for breakfast. "At least until harvest time," she explained to Hannah. "Then Zeke says I'll have to do more, while he and the twins bring in the crops."

By evening each day, Hannah's leg throbbed. She'd thought teaching was difficult, but now she was not only standing most of the day but also lifting and carrying from morning until dusk. The Pershings' cow was less docile than Jenny's. When Hannah attempted to milk her, the beast simply mooed and stepped away. That chore would have to be left to Ruth.

She tried to leave the Pershing cabin in time to get home and do her own work on the McDougall claim. But on her first Saturday afternoon off, she was appalled to see so many weeds sprouting in the garden she and Faith had planted. She pulled what she could before supper. She'd planned to do her own laundry, but now she would have to take her clothes to add to the Pershings' wash on Monday.

When Hannah arrived to begin her second week of work on Monday, April 14, Ruth and Noah greeted her with great excitement. "Cordelia's turning three on Friday, and Esther's having a party. Saturday at noon. You'll come, won't you? We're to bake a cake."

It took a moment for Hannah to remember Cordelia was Esther's oldest child. A cake and a party? That hadn't been in Hannah's schedule, though she was pleased the children wanted her to attend. She smiled. "We'll make the cake on Friday. But I can only go to the party if you two help me tend my own garden. Then we can cook some of my beans and peas here, once they're ripe."

"I don't like peas," Noah said.

"We'll help," Ruth said, nudging her younger brother. "We want you to come to the party. Everyone will be there."

"What about planting the crops?" Hannah asked.

"Esther'll make Zeke hold off for a day. She's even bossier'n you," Noah said.

Hannah raised an eyebrow at the boy's impertinence, but she recognized the truth of what he'd said. She was bossy. But it was the only way she knew to get all the chores done in the time she had available.

The next Monday, laundry went more smoothly than the week before. Though the skies remained cloudy, the temperature was warmer—they could work outside more comfortably. Hannah hoped spring had finally arrived.

When the sun shone on Tuesday, she announced, "Today we're going to my cabin. Time to weed while the skies are clear." As soon as the ironing was done—"Let's not bother doing the sheets today," Ruth whispered, and Hannah agreed—they set off for the McDougall claim in Hannah's wagon.

Hannah fed the children bread and cheese from her larder, then they worked in the garden until the sun began to lower.

"My," Hannah said as she stood and stretched. "I forgot about supper. What do you have at home, do you think?"

"You should know, Miz Hannah. You been doing most of our cooking," Noah said.

"We got some ham left," Ruth said. "We didn't eat it all last night. And I can make cornbread. Noah and I'll walk home by ourselves, then I'll do supper."

"Are you sure you'll be all right?" Hannah asked. "You'll head straight home?"

"We walked home all the time after school," Noah said. "We can do it." So the children set off.

"Why did you let Ruthie and Noah come home alone yesterday?" Zeke asked as soon as Hannah walked into the Pershing cabin Wednesday morning.

She stared at him, panicked. "They told me they'd be fine. Did something happen?"

Zeke shrugged. "Ruthie thought she heard a panther, but they didn't see anything."

Hannah sighed, shoulders sagging. "Then they're all right."

"The point is—"

"We almost got eaten by a painter," Noah said, hurtling down the ladder from the loft. "I heard it, too. And Ruthie was scared."

"I was not," his sister said, hiking her skirt as she followed him down. "We were never in any danger, Miz Hannah. Don't you worry."

"I don't want the young'uns in the woods by themselves after dark," Zeke said.

Hannah frowned at the two children. "You left my cabin in plenty of time to get home before dark. Did you go straight there?"

Ruth and Noah stood silently, eyes downcast.

Zeke glared at them. "Did you?"

Ruth shook her head.

"Why not?"

Ruth gave a sidelong glance at Noah, but said nothing.

"Noah?" Zeke's voice took on a threatening tone.

"I had a piece of string and a hook in my pocket. I wanted to see if I could catch a fish. For supper. But I didn't have no bait. We weren't out long, I swear it." The little boy's eyes grew big.

"Fishing?" Zeke shouted. "Don't you know enough to come straight home when dark is falling? And Ruth, you shouldn't have allowed it."

"I can't drag him, Zeke. He's getting too big." Ruth started to cry. "At least I stayed with him." She turned to Noah. "I didn't tattle. It's not my fault we're in trouble."

"I've got all I can manage with the farming," Zeke said, still shouting. "I can't handle disobedient young'uns, too. I've a mind to say you can't go to Esther's party on Saturday."

"Zeke—" Ruth said, crying harder.

"But what about the cake?" Noah said, tears forming in his eyes also.

"May I speak, Mr. Pershing?" Hannah said.

"You're partly to blame, Miz Bramwell. You oughtn't to have let them go off by themselves."

"I had no idea they wouldn't go straight home."

"You didn't tell us not to fish," Noah said, weeping.

"Might I suggest we talk about this tonight, Mr. Pershing?" Hannah said. "I'll stay here until you return for supper."

After Zeke left, Hannah sat Ruth and Noah down at the table. "Children must obey their elders," she said. "You both knew you were supposed to head straight home."

"Are you going to make us stay home from Cordelia's party?" Noah asked. Ruth sat beside him solemnly.

"It would be a shame to miss your niece's celebration," Hannah said. "But what do you suggest as a punishment?"

The children were quiet.

"I think you will go to the party, but not eat cake," Hannah said to break the silence. "Unless you can think of something else."

"We could scrub the floor," Noah said. "All by ourselves. I'll muck out the barn. And Ruth can iron the sheets."

"I'd rather skip the cake, Miz Hannah," Ruth muttered.

Hannah sighed. Disciplining the children at home was harder than in school. And she wasn't sure what their guardian Zeke had in mind. "You two put your minds to working today, and we'll talk to your brother tonight."

The children found the scrub brush and bucket. It took Ruth and Noah an hour to wash the main room's floor. "What about the loft?" Hannah asked.

"Noah should do it," Ruth complained. "The boys are the ones who sleep up there."

"But that ain't fair, Miz Hannah," Noah whined.

"Either both of you scrub the loft, or one of you do that, and the other muck the stable."

"We'll work together," Ruth said. "He likes doing the stable, so that ain't a chore for him."

Hannah waited until after dark for Zeke to return. She and the children had eaten supper and washed most of the dishes, leaving plates near the hearth for Zeke and the twins. When they arrived, she could see the three of them were fatigued, but she needed to talk to Zeke about Ruth's and Noah's punishment.

"Mr. Pershing—" she said.

"You're still here?" he asked in surprise.

"I told you we would talk this evening."

"Miz Bramwell, I'm plumb worn out. Can't it wait until tomorrow?"

She frowned at him. She didn't know much about how to deal with men, but she didn't think she would have a reasonable discussion with Zeke while he was hungry and tired. "All right," she said. "I'll see you in the morning." She turned to go hitch up her mule and drive home.

"Jonathan and David," Zeke called. "Get Miz Bramwell's cart ready for the drive. And saddle Red and hitch him to the back." He sighed. "Let me wash my hands, and I'll drive you home."

"I'm perfectly able—"

"There might could be a panther in the woods, Miz Bramwell. I won't have you riding by yourself, anymore'n I want Ruth and Noah out there alone."

He lifted her into the cart, climbed onto the bench, and took the reins.

As they rode, she told him the children had worked hard, and she was inclined to let them attend the party—and have cake—but she'd made no promises to them. "As their guardian, you should make the decision," she said.

"Do whatever you like, Miz Bramwell," he murmured.

"Mr. Pershing, you must take a firm stance with the children. They need discipline."

"I'd say they're getting it from you just fine, ma'am."

"But you're their—"

"I'm too tuckered out to think about it now. Let me chaw on it overnight." She couldn't get him to say anything more.

When they reached the McDougall claim, he got out of the little wagon slowly, and helped her down. "Go on inside," he said, untying his horse from the cart. "I'll put your wagon and mule in the barn for the night."

She waited inside the cabin until he came out of the barn, mounted his horse, and rode slowly away. As she watched him through the window, she wondered how long she'd be able to work for Zeke Pershing before they reached a serious disagreement.

Chapter 29: Crisis on the Farm

Zeke was glad for Esther's sake the weather improved Saturday afternoon. After an overcast morning, the skies turned bright, with only an occasional wispy white cloud. He and his younger siblings showed up at Esther's cabin at the noon hour. Already, several wagons lined her yard, with mules and horses in the paddock.

Noah bounced in the back as Zeke tried to find a place to park the wagon. Ever since Zeke told Ruth and Noah they could eat whatever sweets were served, the boy's excitement had known no bounds.

"Don't jostle that cake," Ruth told her younger brother. "Jonathan and David, don't you let Noah jump like that."

Zeke pulled forward to the far side of the barn, then instructed the twins to take the mules to the paddock. He lifted Noah out of the wagon, took the cake from Ruth and handed it to Noah, and helped his sister down. Then Ruth rescued the cake from Noah's exuberant grasp.

They entered the cabin and found most of Daniel's family already there, along with the McDougalls.

"Where's Hannah?" Esther asked. "Didn't she come with you?"

Zeke shook his head. "I gave her the morning off. She said she'd make her own way here."

Just then, the twins came in, and Hannah Bramwell with them. "We helped Miz Hannah with her wagon," the boys said proudly. "And unhitched her mule."

A shout came from outside. "Mule's loose!"

Zeke went out. Douglass Abercrombie, Daniel's older brother, rode at a canter down the road—presumably chasing the mule. Daniel, also on horseback, followed his brother.

"Is it mine?" Hannah asked.

Zeke shrugged at Hannah—he hadn't seen which mule escaped. "Didn't you shut the paddock gate?" he asked the twins.

"I thought we did," David said. "But Douglass's mule got out somehow."

Zeke and the twins entered the cabin, though Zeke had a hard time joining in the family gaiety. He frowned at the twins whenever he caught their eye. Old Samuel Abercrombie lectured them about the need to take care of their animals, and for once, Zeke thought Samuel was right.

A short while later, Daniel and Douglass returned. "Found it," Douglass said, grinning at the twins. "The old mule was more interested in grazing than running."

"All's well that ends well," Hannah said.

But Zeke glared at his younger brothers. He'd talk to them later—repeat old Abercrombie's admonishments. Inwardly, he sighed. If it wasn't one sibling in trouble, it was another. How had Ma and Pa dealt with eight children?

Privately, Zeke thought the party far too much hullabaloo for a three-year-old's birthday, but he didn't say anything. He took his plate and found a corner with a stool near Mac and Jenny. He sat and began to eat, chatting with them.

"Are all your crops planted, Zeke?" Mac asked.

Zeke nodded. "Got the last field done this week. Now it's hoeing and weeding as the seedlings come up."

While they conversed, Samuel Abercrombie came over. Zeke didn't much like the blowhard who'd made so much trouble on the trail four years earlier. But for Esther's sake he nodded politely.

"I mean to talk to you about your land, Pershing," old Abercrombie said. "You decided yet which acres you're giving up from your claim?"

"Ain't planning to give up any acres," Zeke said, sopping up gravy with a piece of bread. "I can't clear it all, but each year I farm a few more acres. And half of it's good timber."

Abercrombie took a swig from a flask he carried. "Well, you're going to have to give half back since you ain't married."

"That isn't certain, Abercrombie," Mac said. "We're trying to get clarity from Congress on the new land law."

Abercrombie snorted. "You ain't holding your breath, are you?" He turned back to Zeke. "Douglass's land ain't as good as yourn, so I'm aiming to make you a good deal, if you'll listen. We'll take the back sixty acres of woodland, farthest from your house. Won't be no loss to you. I'll buy it at the government price—dollar twenty-five an acre."

Douglass stood next to his father, but looked uncomfortable at his father's proposal.

"Zeke doesn't have title to the land yet," Mac said. "Why would you pay him for it?"

"Trying to keep the problem in the family," Abercrombie said. "Zeke being Daniel's brother-in-law. Douglass can take Zeke's woodland, cede some of his land that's swampy. But if you're going to spout law at me, McDougall, I might just take the matter to court."

"Doubt it would hold up, Abercrombie." Mac seemed relaxed on his stool, though Zeke felt himself tensing.

After the Abercrombies wandered off, Zeke asked McDougall, "Can he do that? Take me to court?"

Mac shrugged. "Anyone can sue. That doesn't mean he'll win. Honestly, I don't think Congress meant to impact any claims already filed, even if they weren't proven yet. But unfortunately, the statutory language isn't clear."

"Don't worry, Zeke," Jenny said. "You know Mr. Abercrombie talks more than he acts."

Zeke raised his eyebrows. "You told me he threatened to take your land, when Mac was gone. Same thing—he wanted it for Douglass."

"Yes," Jenny said. "But he never did anything."

Zeke worked his fields all week with the twins. His twenty-fourth birthday came and went on Friday, April 25. Either his younger siblings didn't know, or they forgot, because no one said anything all day. He'd half-expected a cake from the estimable Miz Bramwell, who seemed to know everything, but the occasion went unremarked.

The following Monday, Zeke took the day off from farming to go hunting—Hannah had told him the meat cellar needed filling. At dawn, despite the heavy rainfall, he put on his oldest boots and hiked through the wet forest to a clearing in the middle of his woodland acres. The ground was low and marshy, and ducks frequented the wetland.

He and his dog Blackie settled into the trees downwind of the pond. As he waited for birds to land, he thought again of Abercrombie's threat to dispute his claim for the six hundred and forty acres, all because the old man's son Douglass hadn't made a good choice back in forty-seven.

Zeke remembered when the men staked out their claims that November. In fact, Samuel had made the loudest noises about what land he wanted. He'd insisted his sons take claims abutting his, and Douglass and Daniel both did as their father instructed, though Douglass's land encompassed many acres in low-lying marshes.

After the Abercrombies selected their claims, the Pershing family's choices had seemed easy—Esther wanted her father and Zeke to claim land near her and Daniel. The McDougalls and Doc and Mrs. Tuller also selected land close to the Pershings, though none of them viewed proximity to Samuel Abercrombie as a plus.

Zeke staked out land with many acres of good soil, though it took backbreaking work to clear it. Each year, with the help of family and friends, he cleared more acres, and now had about forty acres in crops with more in hay and pasture. But most of his claim remained in its natural state. Some he would never clear—he would leave it for timber and hunting.

He gazed around at his land. Most days, he didn't see its beauty. The land was his livelihood, and wrestling it into productivity was his calling. It wasn't a romantic life, but it fed his siblings and himself. He liked working in the fields, grueling as it could be. He was a farmer—always had been, and, now he'd given up the notion of prospecting with Joel, he was likely to always be a farmer.

But today—today he relished the green of spring, the call of songbirds, the smell of pine trees all around him. He set himself up on the bank of a creek, shotgun in his lap. When a brace of ducks landed, he shot both birds. Then later, another brace. Blackie did his part retrieving.

He must have scared off the wildfowl, but after a bit, a deer came into the clearing on the far side of the creek. Zeke put down his shotgun, raised his rifle, aimed, and killed it. He'd bring home more than ducks for Miz Bramwell to cook tonight.

They'd eaten well Monday night. After he'd shot the deer, Zeke field-dressed the carcass and carried the best cuts home together with the ducks.

Then he'd taken Red back with him and loaded the rest of the venison onto the gelding.

Tuesday he worked in the fields again. The morning sun on this late-April day promised heat by midafternoon. As Zeke and the twins hoed the field of potatoes to manage the weeds, he was glad of his hat's wide brim to block the sun.

By noon, when Hannah and the younger children arrived with their midday meal, Zeke was almost as ready as the twins for a break. All six of them sat in the shade and ate the warm venison stew Hannah had brought in a Dutch oven. "I made the bread," Ruth proclaimed.

The food revived the twins, and they challenged Noah to see who could climb the highest tree. The twins were more daring, but Noah was lighter. As he watched them, Zeke remembered similar contests with Joel, which often resulted in one or the other getting hurt and Ma chastising them both.

But today, his brothers incurred no injuries other than one scraped elbow—Zeke thought it was David's. Each boy argued he'd won the climbing competition, until Zeke told them all to be quiet and get to work. He stood, picked up his hoe, and trudged back to the field.

Hannah, Ruth, and Noah packed up the food, and rode away in the wagon.

In midafternoon, when the sun beat down as hard as Zeke had feared in the morning, Ruth came running over to him, out of breath. "It's Noah," she gasped. "Come quick, Zeke. You need to come *now*."

"What's wrong?" he asked.

"Fell." She couldn't talk without wheezing. "Hayloft."

Dread seeped from Zeke's brain to his gut. He dropped his hoe. "Jonathan and David, take the tools back to the barn." He sprinted toward home, not waiting for Ruth or the twins.

He arrived at the barnyard, sweat trickling down his back, and burst into the cabin. Noah lay on the bed, his head wrapped in a bloody bandage, eyes closed, skin pale. Hannah sat beside him.

"What happened? Is he hurt bad?" Zeke said, kneeling beside his little brother.

"He fell out of the hayloft. I don't know what he was doing, maybe looking for eggs. Cut his forehead, and I think his arm is broken." Hannah's voice quavered as she spoke. "I washed his head, but I can't do anything for his arm."

"You moved him from the barn?"

"Ruth and I did. We heard him scream, but he's been unconscious since I cleaned the cut. I told Ruth to get you."

Zeke ran a hand lightly down each of Noah's limbs. When he touched the boy's left arm, Noah whimpered, but did not awaken. "Have you sent for Doc Tuller?"

Hannah looked at him blankly. "I sent Ruth for you. There was no one else to send."

Zeke sighed. "I'll go get Doc." He went out to the barn to saddle Red. He glanced up at the hayloft, but didn't see anything there to explain Noah's fall.

As he finished saddling the gelding, Jonathan and David arrived, with Ruth trailing behind. Her face was flushed, but she seemed to have recovered from her run. "Jonathan, ride Red to Doc's house," Zeke ordered. "I'll stay with Noah. Ask Doc to come quickly. Tell him Noah's got a broken arm and a cut on his head. Bring Mrs. Tuller, if Doc ain't there."

Eyes wide, Jonathan nodded, mounted Red, and trotted toward the road.

"Will Noah be all right?" David asked.

"I hope so," Zeke said. "Let's go see him."

An hour later, Doc arrived in his wagon, Jonathan on the bench beside him, and a lathered Red tied to the back of the wagon.

Doc examined Noah, who revived enough to moan. It had taken Zeke's strength to hold him steady until the doctor arrived—Hannah couldn't manage the boy's writhing.

"Arm's broken all right," Doc said. "I'll have to set it. You got any good, straight boards?"

Zeke nodded. "David, bring one in from the barn."

David retrieved a four-foot-long board, and Doc instructed Zeke what length and width to cut. "You find some rags and tear 'em into strips," Doc told Hannah, as Zeke left to get his saw. "We'll wrap the splint on to keep the bone in place."

After Zeke sawed the board, Doc pulled Noah's arm straight. The boy screamed and yelled. Zeke held his brother as Doc bound the splint to his forearm. The twins and Ruth watched with horror on their faces. Hannah sat at the table, staring toward the fire, her face drained of color.

"It's a clean break," Doc said when he was done. "Bone didn't break the skin. Boy's young—he should heal fine in a few weeks. I'll come again on Friday. Keep him quiet, give him willow bark tea for the pain, and send for me if you can't wake him up."

After Doc left, Zeke turned to Hannah. "Why wasn't he with you?"

"I'm sorry, Mr. Pershing," Hannah whispered. "I should have—"

"'Tweren't Miz Hannah's fault," Noah mumbled drowsily. "I was climbing the pole to the roof."

"What?" Zeke said. "Why would you climb the pole?"

"It's taller'n the trees Jonathan and David climbed. I wanted to show I was best. I guess I'm not . . . " Noah's voice trailed off into sleep.

"I'll stay the night here," Hannah said. "And sit with him. You'll need your rest so you can work tomorrow."

Zeke sighed and gently smoothed his snoring brother's hair. "We'll split the night. Like guard duty on the trail. I'll take the first shift after supper."

Supper was bread with more venison. Hannah made broth for Noah, but he barely woke to drink it and the willow bark tea she'd made. When it grew dark, Hannah and Ruth bedded down on a pallet near the hearth, since Noah slept in Ruth's bed.

Zeke sat beside his brother, wondering if he'd made a huge mistake assuming responsibility for his younger siblings. But what else could he have done? He worried Hannah Bramwell was not well-suited to maintain a household in the wilderness. Why hadn't she thought to send for the doctor? Though he had to admit he also would have been mad if she'd sent for the doctor instead of him.

Around midnight, Zeke tapped Hannah's shoulder.

She sat up groggily, hair disheveled, and looking not much older than Ruth, though she must be about Zeke's age. "How is he?" she asked.

"Sleeping."

"Did you try waking him? Doc said—" She patted her hair back into place.

Zeke shook his head. "The boy needs rest." He held out a hand to Hannah to help her stand.

She limped to the bed and sat by Noah. "I'm sorry," she said. "I feel terrible he was hurt."

Zeke shrugged. "His own recklessness caused it."

"But I was responsible for him."

"No," Zeke said. "I'm responsible for all of them." He headed for the ladder to the loft where the twins slept. "Wake me if he seems in too much pain."

Chapter 30: Hannah's Fears

While she kept watch over Noah that night, Hannah shed a few quiet tears. Despite Zeke's claim of responsibility, the boy had been under her care when he was hurt. She told herself his climbing in the hayloft was the kind of risky behavior little boys were known for—if Noah hadn't injured himself this way, he would have done something else foolish that might also have caused him harm.

But it did no good. She couldn't get the picture of the lad's limp body on the barn floor out of her mind.

And had she done the right thing in sending Ruth for Zeke instead of for the doctor? It hadn't even occurred to her to send for Doc Tuller. The country physician seemed capable, and she liked the crusty old man. But her first thought had been to get Zeke to see to his little brother. She trusted Zeke Pershing, though she wasn't sure why.

She still wondered what led Zeke to punch Mac McDougall in the churchyard last fall. It had something to do with Jenny, but why Zeke felt obligated to attack Jenny's husband was a mystery to her. Maybe she shouldn't trust the man, but nevertheless, at least with respect to his love for his siblings, she knew he was rock-solid and reliable.

Hannah dozed beside the sleeping boy until the rest of the Pershings rose at dawn. Then she made breakfast for the family while Zeke and the twins did chores in the barn. Zeke promised they'd care for the animals on the McDougall claim also.

Ruth sat beside her younger brother and stroked his hair above the bandage. "Will he be all right, Miz Hannah?" the girl asked.

Hannah looked at the sleeping child. His cheeks were still pale, but he breathed easily. "I expect so, Ruth. But only time will tell."

"I'm all right," Noah said, shaking off his sister's hand. "I'm hungry."

Hannah and Ruth stayed in the cabin with Noah all day, while Zeke and the twins worked in the fields. When the Pershing men returned—Hannah had started thinking of the strapping fourteen-year-olds as men—she left the family to return to the McDougalls' claim.

"I'll drive you," Zeke said.

She shook her head. "There's plenty of light, and you didn't get much sleep last night. I'm happy to walk."

"The mules are waiting," he said, paying her no mind.

They rode in silence. When they arrived, she said again, "I'm sorry about Noah."

"'Tweren't your fault," Zeke said. "You couldn't've known the boy would be so foolish. He'll mend."

"Good night, then." Hannah climbed down from the wagon before Zeke could help her.

After fixing herself a quick supper, she took out a sheet of paper, her quill, and ink, to write Jane.

April 30, 1851

Dear Sister,

I have been slow to write you. Since last you heard from me, the school term is over, and I am no longer teaching.

I have become a housekeeper for the Pershing family, who lost their father at the first of the year. There are five of them living in a small cabin. The oldest, Zeke, is a man of about my age. His twin brothers, Jonathan and David, are fourteen. The only sister still at home is Ruth, who is twelve, and the youngest boy Noah recently turned eight. Zeke, who is responsible for all his younger siblings, is a difficult man—taciturn and uneducated, though he loves the children dearly.

Yesterday Noah broke his arm in a fall in the barn. I feel responsible for his injury, though the boy's own foolhardiness caused it.

I am not sure I am suited for the frontier life. I can manage the cooking and laundry, but not the uncertainties I find all around me. A panther might live in the woods nearby. The only doctor is a curmudgeonly old man, who conveys his medical knowledge with words crustier than charred meat. No house is within a mile of me, chores are difficult with rudimentary tools, and the men track in mud from the fields every evening. It is a far cry from Cincinnati.

This incident with young Noah has brought back my memories of the time after my accident. His pain strikes close to home, and I recall my weeks of agony after the fire.

Our brother and his family seem well, though I only see them on Sundays at church. Faith has returned home to live. She seems unhappy still. Jacob's new wife Alice is not an improvement over Beulah, whom we all loved.

I do not know if I should remain in Oregon. There is nothing for me in Cincinnati except you, dear Jane, though I hate to admit defeat. But there is also nothing for me in Oregon, except hard work and loneliness.

Fondly,
Hannah

The next morning Hannah reread the letter she'd written to her sister. Perhaps she was too strong in voicing her fears about life in Oregon. She'd adapted well to some aspects of the wilderness, she thought. She had taught school successfully. And now she managed Zeke Pershing's household.

In the light of day, Noah's accident seemed one of those childhood experiences every family endured, and less significant than her own tragedy. She did not think Noah's injuries would be so long-lived as her own.

She hitched her wagon and drove to Zeke's cabin, where she found the Pershings all eating a peaceful breakfast.

"I waited for you," Zeke told her. "Didn't want to leave the young'uns alone, not with Noah feeling poorly."

"Is he feeling poorly?" she asked, rushing to feel the boy's forehead. "He doesn't have a fever."

"He's just fretful," Jonathan said. "Zeke told him he had to stay home, and the day will be a fine one."

"We'll find something to do outside," Hannah said, smiling at Noah and Ruth in turn. "Maybe even go fishing in the stream."

Noah's eyes widened. "Can you fish, Miz Hannah?"

"No, but I imagine you and Ruth can show me how." She thought Zeke smirked when she confessed her lack of experience.

After Zeke and the twins left for the fields, Hannah insisted they finish the household chores before they headed to the creek.

"How're you going to bait the hooks?" Ruth asked her brother. "I ain't digging up the worms, nor putting 'em on the hooks."

"Say 'I'm not,' Ruth, not 'I ain't,'" Hannah said. "And I don't think I relish those tasks either. Perhaps we should search for greens instead and fish another day."

Noah muttered his disgust at their female sensibilities, but his joy at escaping the cabin after spending yesterday inside brought his high spirits back soon enough. Hannah found him an anthill to watch while she and Ruth gathered a basketful of greens. Then they returned to the cabin and took cold ham, cheese, bread, and barley water to the fields.

The next day, a Friday, was again a warm day with bright sunshine, though it was only early May. Hannah managed to keep Noah from pulling off his splint.

Doc Tuller showed up after the noon meal on Friday, as promised.

"I can't keep him still," Hannah told the doctor. "But I assume if he wants to play in the sunshine, his head injury must not be severe."

"You figured right, Miz Bramwell," Doc told her. "Let the lad do as he feels able, within reason. And you, young man, if you can play, you can do your chores, so no whining when you're told to do something."

"Yes, sir." Noah sounded sincere, but Hannah wondered whether he would turn fractious on the next laundry day.

Doc Tuller examined the splint. "Keep the limb splinted at all times. Should heal in four to six weeks. Young bones mend fast. Let me know if there's much pain."

"Yes, doctor," Hannah said. "What do we owe you?"

Doc shook his craggy head. "Ain't yours to pay. Tell young Zeke I'll talk to him next time I see him."

Country ways were a far cry from those of Cincinnati, Hannah thought.

Saturday morning, while Ruth and Hannah baked bread and Noah played marbles in the corner of the cabin, Hannah heard a woman call from the yard.

Ruth went to the door. "It's Esther and her brood," the girl said, and she rushed out to help her older sister. Noah got up to follow.

Hannah had her hands in the dough and couldn't go outside, but soon Ruth and Esther came in, with Abigail in Esther's arms and Esther's three older children tagging behind.

"We came to see how Noah is," Esther said. She ruffled the boy's hair. "But I see he's fine."

"Dr. Tuller said to keep the arm splinted for the next several weeks," Hannah said. "But his head injury is not serious."

Esther sat. "That's a relief. All the other boys broke at least one bone at some point growing up, but usually just a finger or toe. I guess Jonathan broke an ankle. But this is our first arm."

Noah showed the younger children his splint and the bandage on his head. Little Jonah seemed awed, but after a glance the other little ones asked Ruth for a slice of bread.

"First loaves are out of the oven," Ruth said. "Shall I slice some?"

Hannah nodded, and Ruth fed the children while Hannah washed her hands and sat with Esther and Abigail. "How did you hear about Noah's accident?" Hannah asked.

"Zeke's working with Daniel today," Esther said. "And the rest of the Abercrombie men." She sighed. "Though Mr. Abercrombie is trying to make trouble for Zeke these days."

"What kind of trouble?"

"About the land. Old Samuel ain't satisfied unless he's got the best of everything. And he thinks Zeke's land is better'n Douglass's."

"But they each filed their claims already, didn't they?"

Esther nodded. "Yes, but the claims ain't proven up yet. Won't be till this November. And Congress cut back what a single man can claim. It ain't fair, but what can Zeke do?"

"It doesn't seem right," Hannah agreed. "Not when he's labored here for over three years."

"Still a lot of unimproved land on the claim. No man can work six hundred forty acres. So if Zeke has to give back part, he ain't out any labor." Esther shook her head as she lifted the baby to her shoulder. "But I surely hate to see Douglass Abercrombie get what Zeke claimed. No matter how nice Douglass is. Maybe too nice—he tends to do as his father commands."

Saturday provided their last fine weather in early May. For the next several days, it stayed cold and rainy. Forced to stay inside, Noah grew cranky. Hannah was at her wits' end trying to keep him occupied, while still getting the housework done. Once she took Noah and Ruth to see the Tullers to play with their barn cats. Another day she took the children to visit Esther, but Esther was too busy to spend time with them.

By Sunday, May 11, Hannah had had all she could take of the Pershings, and she spent her day off with her brother Jacob's family in town.

"How's your housekeeping job?" Jacob's wife Alice asked.

"The little boy's injury has us all out of sorts," Hannah admitted. "He's healing well, but he's unhappy he can't run and play."

Alice sniffed. "Our boys are working in the store. That child needs discipline, seems to me."

"Noah's younger than our boys," Faith piped up. "Younger than Charity, too. And she isn't working in the store yet."

"Would you and Charity like to come stay with me for a week?"

Hannah asked. "Charity could help me entertain Noah. She's only a year older than he is."

"I can't let Faith go," Alice said. "She's busy here—both in the house and in the store. And I don't have a mind to let Charity spend time with an ill-mannered boy like Noah Pershing."

Over dinner, Jacob said, "I hear you're tired of working for the Pershings, Hannah."

"Maybe I'm tired, but it's what I agreed to do," Hannah said. "Every job has its problems."

"You should consider going back to Ohio," Jacob said, cutting another slice of beef roast to add to his plate. "Weather's best for sailing now. You shouldn't wait until autumn."

"I'm hoping to teach again after harvest," Hannah said. She'd written their sister Jane about her fears, but she wouldn't confess them to Jacob. Particularly not with Alice around. But she wondered—would she still be in Oregon by harvest time?

Chapter 31: More Trouble

Zeke spent Monday morning with Douglass and Daniel Abercrombie clearing a field on Zeke's land. It was too late to plant crops on the field this year, but Zeke reckoned he might get a cutting of hay, if he could sow it within the next couple of weeks. The additional feed for the animals come winter would be a help.

Zeke and the Abercrombies wielded axes to chop down trees, while Jonathan and David sawed off branches and hauled away the brush. They'd have to bring the mules to drag off the logs another day. Despite cloudy skies and cool temperatures, the hard labor caused Zeke to work up a sweat.

"You know my pa's still itching to get part of your claim," Douglass commented as the men worked. "He blathered on about it over supper yesterday."

"What do you think?" Zeke asked. After all, Samuel Abercrombie couldn't claim the land for himself—he'd need Douglass's cooperation.

Douglass paused to lean on his axe. "I don't want to cause no trouble for you, Zeke. But Pa is determined."

"He is at that," Daniel said. "It's all he talks about."

Hannah, Ruth, and Noah brought lunch to the men at noon, but they didn't stay long.

After they left and Zeke and the others resumed chopping and sawing, Samuel Abercrombie rode into the field on his large gelding. "This one of the fields you clearing for me?" he said to Zeke. "I seen a lawyer last Friday. Says I can file suit to dispute your claim."

Zeke cast a glance at Douglass and Daniel, wondering why they hadn't mentioned a lawsuit. Maybe Samuel hadn't told his sons, but the man boasted about everything—he wasn't likely to have withheld the lawyer's comment from his family.

Zeke considered Daniel a closer friend than Douglass. Douglass would stay out of the argument as much as possible, though he stood to gain if his father was successful. Zeke and Daniel often scouted together on the trek to Oregon and became good friends. Zeke thought Daniel would have warned him about old Samuel's intentions. But now he asked himself, whose side would Daniel take in a dispute between his father and Zeke?

At Zeke's glance, Daniel shrugged in response. No telling what the shrug meant.

"I seen a lawyer, too," Zeke said. "Mac don't think any lawsuit's likely to boot me off the land."

"McDougall's a city lawyer," Abercrombie said, then spit a long stream of tobacco juice. "What's he know?" But he sounded less certain than his first remarks. They'd all learned to respect McDougall on the wagon train in forty-seven.

"Do what you think you have to," Zeke said. "And I'll do the same. Now, if it's all right with you, I'd like to clear more trees afore dusk. You want to help, seeing's how you think your kin'll own the land soon?"

"Got other work to do, boy." Abercrombie spun his horse around and left.

"Sorry," Daniel said. "He ain't told me about the lawyer."

"Me neither," Douglass said.

"No matter," Zeke said. "But I guess I need to see Mac again."

It took two more days of felling trees for Zeke and his helpers to finish clearing the field. As long as the weather cooperated, he wanted to work, so he put off the trip to town to see McDougall. But he grew more anxious every day, wondering if Abercrombie would follow through on his threat of a lawsuit.

Zeke didn't have money to pay a lawyer. Mac might not want to charge him, but Zeke didn't want to be beholden to anyone—he prided himself on paying his own way in life.

Clouds threatened Tuesday and Wednesday, but the rain didn't come. Thursday, however, it poured. Zeke peered out the window as he put on his oilskin to head to the barn for morning chores. He couldn't put off the trip to see Mac any longer.

Hannah arrived in her wagon—she and the mules sopping wet. He explained he needed to go to town.

"Might we all go?" she asked. "I've a mind to shop. Your household needs sugar and other provisions, and I need a few things also."

"In this rain?"

"The children are all outgrowing their clothes. Ruth and I should make new ones. I can handle the rain."

Zeke didn't relish the idea of people accompanying him to town. He wanted to mull over the dispute with Abercrombie, and he couldn't do so with Hannah and his siblings distracting him. But he couldn't politely refuse. He nodded curtly. "Get the young'uns ready."

They bundled into the wagon and left for town as the skies continued to pour. Zeke pulled his hat low on his face so he wouldn't have to talk to Hannah beside him. They rode in silence, huddled under wool cloaks and oilcloths, while he wondered what McDougall would tell him.

In town, he stopped in front of the Abernethy store, and they piled out of the wagon. "Do you mind if I also shop at my brother's store?" Hannah asked.

Zeke shrugged. "No matter. Buy as much as you can at Abernethy's— I've got an account there. But if your brother'll give me credit till harvest, I'll give him trade also." Then he walked up the street toward the law office McDougall had opened.

He entered the front room and shed his dripping hat and coat, hanging them on a nearby hook. Mac sat in the back room writing, and Zeke knocked on the door. "You taking customers?" he asked.

Mac looked up and grinned. "You look like a drowned dog." Standing, he shook Zeke's hand. "What brings you to town?"

"Abercrombie."

Mac gestured for Zeke to sit. "What's he done now?"

"Says he's going to sue me. Still wants my claim."

"We've been through this," Mac said, frowning. "I don't think he has grounds to sue. The government could boot you off the land, but not Abercrombie. Though there aren't any guarantees, once a judge gets hold of the issue."

"And I can't stop him from trying, can I?"

"No," Mac admitted. "Anyone can file a suit. Abercrombie can make himself a real nuisance, like he always has." He leaned back in his chair and put his feet on the desk. "Let me ask around, see what he's done so far. Maybe I can find out who he's hired as counsel—if anyone."

"What'll I owe you?"

Mac laughed. "For snooping around? How about you buy me a drink this afternoon?"

Zeke shook his head. "Can't today—got the young'uns and Hannah Bramwell with me. She wanted to shop, despite the rain."

"How's she working out as your housekeeper?"

"Fair enough," Zeke said. "She's kind of persnickety. But she gets along well with Ruth and Noah. Keeps the boy from hurting himself any more'n he already has."

"Think she'll stay on past harvest?"

"Don't know. She says she wants to teach again." Zeke realized he'd rather have Hannah working for him than teaching. "Say," he said, "anyone else we can get to teach? Is Jenny interested? Then Miz Bramwell could keep minding house for me."

Mac shook his head. "I don't want Jenny teaching. Our new home in town will be done soon. Then she'll be housekeeping herself. And I'm hoping William and Maria will have another brother or sister soon."

A pang of jealousy went through Zeke at the thought of Jenny having a child with another man. But the pang wasn't so strong as what he'd felt in the past. It'd been seven months now since Mac returned from California, and Zeke had given up forever his hope of marrying Jenny. He was over the worst of the pain, he realized.

Zeke spent a sleepless night stewing about Abercrombie and his conversation with Mac. There was no telling what Samuel would do—the man had had it in for the Pershings since they'd met in Independence four years ago. Abercrombie had made life hell for Pa, and now the bastard did the same to Zeke.

The rain ended by the next morning, and Zeke and the twins resumed clearing stumps from the new field. The mules did most of the pulling, but hacking through old roots and digging to loosen them was still backbreaking labor. Zeke wrestled the trees like they were Abercrombie himself.

By quitting time, all three Pershings were sweating, but they chilled in the cool temperatures on the walk back to the cabin. When they reached the barn to put the mules in their stalls, all Zeke wanted was a wash-up and a hot meal.

While they did chores in the barn, Hannah stormed in. "Might I have a word with you?" she said. She glanced toward the twins. "Alone."

Zeke sighed and nodded at his brothers. "Go on in and wash up." He turned to Hannah. "What is it?"

She waited until the boys left, then said, "Noah. He was disrespectful to me and teased Ruth all day. We were trying to sew, and I bought the wrong color thread yesterday, so we didn't get very far. He spent the day taunting us both."

"That's it?" He'd been fighting maple stumps all day, and she was frazzled over a little boy's teasing? "Can't you manage—"

She drew herself up to full height, which was middling tall for a woman. "Noah is your brother," she began, "If you can't be bothered—"

"Oh, I'm bothered, Miz Bramwell," he said. "I'm tired and I'm hungry. I'm paying you to take care of—"

"And I'm telling you your brother needs your discipline," she said, taking a step closer.

He stepped toward her also. "If you calm down and tell me what he done—"

"It's *did*, Mr. Pershing. What he *did* was—"

At her correction, Zeke saw red. Her dark eyes glared at him and her mouth curved in a pout. So he kissed her.

She was sweet. All the starch left her, and her hands came to his shoulders. She pulled back and gasped, and he lowered to her lips again. Her mouth opened, and she softened and leaned against him.

"Hannah," he murmured.

She removed her hands from his shoulders, twisted away, and slapped him.

Chapter 32: Aftermath

Hannah's hands shook as she hitched her mules to the cart. The gall of that man! Zeke had stormed out of the barn as soon as she slapped him, his mouth a narrow line, his blue eyes glittering—whether in fury or lust she didn't know.

Why did Zeke kiss her? He had been angry when she corrected his grammar. Well, the man should set a better example for his younger siblings—he must have been taught better somewhere in his childhood. He was a smart man, if bullheaded.

She'd never been kissed before, not even by Charles, who cornered her and pawed her but never bothered with a kiss. As she ordered the mules into a fast walk and rode out of the Pershing yard, she could still feel Zeke's arms around her. His lips were surprisingly soft, though the chest she'd leaned against was solid as an oak trunk. She'd wanted to sink into his softness and strength, but that would have revealed her weakness. When she'd slapped him, she'd meant to rally herself as much as to stop the kiss. Because she hadn't really wanted it to stop. Even now, riding home in the rain, she felt warmed by the memory of Zeke's embrace.

Hannah shook her head firmly. She would have to find another position. She couldn't continue to work for Zeke. Not when she would see him every day, would remember his kiss every day, would think of how comforting it would be to lean on a man like Zeke instead of making her own way in the world.

Making her own way—that was the problem. Without the housekeeping job, how could she remain in Oregon? She would have to talk to Jacob again, make the rounds of Oregon City to see what other positions might be available.

By the time she arrived at the little cabin on the McDougall claim, she'd made a plan. She would arrive at the Pershings' house late the next morning, after Zeke and the twins had already left. She would get their dinner on the stove, then leave—it was Saturday and she had the afternoon off anyway.

She relived the kiss over and over in bed that night. Each time it came to mind she told herself she couldn't keep working for Zeke. Her reputation would suffer, just as Alice intimated before Hannah began the job.

The Pershing house was quiet when Hannah pulled her mules and cart into the yard on Saturday morning, a carpet bag of her belongings stowed under the wagon bench. She planned to spend the weekend in town with her brother and his family.

Only Ruth and Noah were home. As soon as Hannah opened the door, Noah stood and said he was sorry about his behavior the day before. Hannah wondered whether Zeke had told him to apologize. She glanced inquiringly at Ruth, who shrugged and nodded.

"Thank you for your apology, young man," Hannah said. "It is important to say you're sorry, but even more important to resolve to change. I will expect better behavior in the future." Then, with a pang of regret, she remembered she wouldn't be working for the Pershings any longer.

Hannah set Noah to slicing potatoes, which he managed clumsily with one arm in a splint. She and Ruth put together the rest of the stew, while Hannah explained she had urgent business with her brother in Oregon City.

"I might not be available to work on Monday," she told Ruth. "Can you manage without me?"

"I'm sure I can, Miz Hannah," Ruth said. "But I'll miss you. I like having your company—it's better'n just me and Noah."

"I'm sorry to leave you," Hannah said—that much was true, because she cared about Ruth. She even liked Noah when he wasn't playing the rapscallion. "I will let you know when I can return."

As soon as the meal simmered on the stove, Hannah left. She drove to her brother's shop in town, arriving shortly before noon.

"What are you doing here?" Jacob asked in a surprised tone.

"I came to see if you are in any more need of a clerk than you were a month ago," Hannah said. It would be easiest to explain leaving the

Pershings if she worked for her brother—Zeke would surely understand her supporting her brother's enterprise.

Jacob shook his head. "The boys are handling the toting for me this summer. They're strong as oxen now. And Alice and Faith assist at the counter. The store can't support more than our family."

"Alice told me once you were expanding your store."

Jacob grimaced. "That's just her puffery. Someday, perhaps. But not now."

Hannah sighed. "I'll inquire at other shops then."

"What happened with the Pershings? I thought your situation there would last all summer."

"They don't really need me," Hannah said. It was a weak excuse, and she wondered if Jacob would accept it. "Ruth is perfectly capable of keeping house for them."

"Have they thrown you out?" Alice sidled over behind Jacob and interjected herself into the conversation.

"No, of course not," Hannah said. "But I hate to take their livelihood, if I can find a position where my services are more needed."

"Well, you're not needed at our store," Alice huffed. "You'd be taking *our* livelihood. You planning to stay here now? I'll need to water down the soup to stretch it, though we have plenty of bread, I think."

Hannah inclined her head. "Just for the weekend. I'll visit other shops this afternoon and go to church with you tomorrow."

Hannah found no work in town. Saturday afternoon she spoke with every storekeeper, inquired at the newspaper office whether they needed a clerk, and even asked Mac McDougall if he knew of anyone needing a secretary. He told her gently most professional men would feel more comfortable working with a male secretary. Hannah nodded—even in a large town like Cincinnati, female clerks and secretaries were unusual. A woman's education was good only for teaching, and then only until she married.

She hoped none of the Pershings would attend church in town. Although Esther and her family were there, she was relieved to discover Zeke and his household were not. She listened to the minister preach on the sinfulness of man and the value of humility in the face of God's great forgiveness. Had her sinfulness provoked Zeke's kiss? She couldn't see how—she tried to be a good woman and dressed modestly, though she knew she was prideful about her education and her deportment. Perhaps she should be modest about her intellect, but that was difficult, when she was so much better read than everyone around her.

What would it be like to be a woman like Esther or Jenny—a woman whom men found attractive and wanted to protect? The only other man who had acted lustfully toward her had been Charles, and she thought her brother-in-law merely desired to assert his dominance because she depended on him for a home.

When Hannah realized the self-pitying direction of her thoughts, she shrugged them off, and brought her attention back to the sermon. Sinfulness, she thought, came in many forms. Her pride was just one of them. Whining to herself about her troubles was another.

At dinner after the service, Jacob announced, "I've purchased you a steamship ticket to San Francisco, Hannah. I'm sorry, but it's for the best."

Faith gasped. "Pa, you can't send Aunt Hannah away!"

"This is not your decision to make, young miss," Alice said.

Jacob continued, "Alice and I agreed your prospects will be better if you leave Oregon, since you cannot support yourself here. I wish I could help more, but we cannot assume responsibility for you."

"What am I to do in San Francisco?" Hannah asked, the last bite of food she'd swallowed rising in her throat. "I know no one there."

"That's as far as I can afford to send you," Jacob said sheepishly. "I hope your savings will permit you to return to Ohio, but if not, perhaps you can find employment in California. I'm sure Mac McDougall could provide you with a letter of reference to his colleagues there."

"I still have employment at the Pershings," Hannah said. "I don't think I'm needed, but they will continue to pay me for the remainder of the summer."

Alice sniffed. "You've probably discovered Zeke Pershing's baser nature. I suspect that's why you're looking for another position. I'm surprised you don't accept Jacob's generosity and leave for California. Now, he'll have to turn in your ticket to get his money back."

Hannah had no alternative but to return to Zeke's house to work on

Monday. If she wanted to refuse Jacob's dictate to leave Oregon, she needed to support herself, and she'd found no other position. Kiss or no kiss, she would have to work for Zeke Pershing.

As she had Friday, she tarried at the McDougall cabin until Zeke should have left his home. She'd have to confront him sometime, but she didn't have the courage yet.

She and Ruth washed clothes and bedding until midafternoon, Noah helping as best he could with one arm. "I'm afraid I'll need to leave early this afternoon," she told the children once the laundry was dry and the bread for dinner rising. "Ruth, can you bake the loaves and fry the meat for supper?"

Ruth frowned, but nodded. "Is something wrong, Miz Hannah? You've seemed flustered all day."

Hannah shook her head, not trusting her voice. Ruth was too perceptive for comfort.

"Zeke's been surly all weekend," the girl said. "I think he's upset about Mr. Abercrombie, but he don't—doesn't say anything."

Hannah smiled at Ruth's self-correction. The twelve-year-old seemed to have taken Hannah's frequent admonishments to heart. Unlike the girl's oldest brother.

When she got home, Hannah took out paper, ink, and quill and wrote her sister:

> Monday, May 19, 1851
> Dearest Jane,
>   I am in the depth of despair, and my future seems grim. My position as housekeeper has become intolerable, though I hesitate to explain what has happened in a letter.
>   Jacob will not have me in his store, and there is no other position for me in Oregon City. Our brother seems determined to send me back to Cincinnati, so I may have no alternative but to return to you. I will write

should that become the course of action I take. But I hope . . .

Hannah's quill rose from the page. She could not continue the sentence. What did she hope?

The independent life she sought in Oregon seemed impossible to find.

Chapter 33: A Lawsuit

Kissing Hannah hadn't meant anything, Zeke told himself all weekend. She'd provoked him, and he'd wanted to make her stop talking. It worked, he thought smugly.

But the kiss lingered in his mind anyway. And not just in his mind. His hands remembered how she felt in his arms, while his tongue remembered her tart, sweet taste. His body . . . He tried not to think about how his body had reacted to the feel of her breasts against his chest, because he hardened again at each recollection of her softness.

Who would have thought the prim and proper schoolmarm could arouse him so?

The only other woman he'd ever kissed was Jenny. That had been a careful peck on her lips so as not to scare her away. With Hannah, he'd hoped she would leave him be.

And she had. He grinned at the memory of her palm slapping his cheek. He'd apparently aroused something in her as well, if only her ire.

When Ruth told him Monday night something was bothering Miz Hannah, he grinned again. "Did she say what?" he asked.

Ruth shook her head. "She says she's fine, but she almost put the bluing in with your pants instead of the whites."

Zeke never bothered with bluing when he did laundry, but Ruth seemed to think it a sign of Hannah's turmoil over some unknown botheration.

Tuesday morning Zeke and the twins went to help Daniel on his land. Douglass Abercrombie would be there also. Noah begged to go with them, and Zeke allowed it. "Just stay out of the way, since you can't be of any help," he said, tousling the lad's hair.

The men hoed Daniel's cornfield, hacking at weeds around the reed-thin stalks. Noah scrabbled behind the others, using his good arm to toss the refuse into piles to be fed to the pigs.

Esther brought them a basket lunch at midday, her children in the back of the wagon. She looked harried. "I'll leave you to eat in peace," she told the men. "Daniel, bring our dishes home tonight."

The sun shone brightly overhead, and Zeke relished the chance to rest from his labors while he ate. When he finished the meal, he lay on the ground, hat over his face, and dozed, while the twins and Noah chattered nearby. Daniel and Douglass Abercrombie rested beside him.

"Ezekiel Pershing," a voice said.

Zeke lifted his hat and squinted up at a man on horseback, silhouetted against the sun. "That's me."

"I'm here to serve papers on you, Mr. Pershing."

Zeke sat up. "Who are you?" Then he noticed the sheriff's badge. "Sheriff Thomas?"

"Yes, sir. I'm Sheriff Calvin Thomas. A lawsuit's been filed against you by a Mr. Samuel Abercrombie."

Daniel grunted as Zeke leapt to his feet. "What is this?" Zeke shouted.

The sheriff thrust a sheaf of papers at him. Zeke took them, noticed a fine copperplate script, but didn't bother to read the words. He shook the papers at Daniel. "Did you know about this? Is this why you asked me to work with you today?"

"I swear I didn't—" Daniel said, sitting up.

"I mentioned to Pa last night—" Douglass said, now sitting as well.

"You been served now, Mr. Pershing," the sheriff said. "Best read the document and take it to heart." With that, the man turned his horse and left.

Zeke stared at the Abercrombie brothers. "Fine repayment for my help." He gathered his tools and called to his brothers, "Come on, boys. We're leaving."

Though the sun was still high in the sky, Zeke stalked home, feet pounding the ground with every step. And with each step he grew angrier. At Samuel Abercrombie. At Douglass and Daniel, who apparently supported their father's thievery. At his sister Esther for marrying an Abercrombie. At his own pa for dying and leaving him head of the Pershing clan, when all Zeke wanted was to farm his land in peace.

Jonathan, David, and Noah trailed behind him, Noah whining about

Zeke moving too fast.

"I got business in town," Zeke said through his teeth when they reached their barn. "I'll saddle Red. You boys put the tools away and go on in the house. Tell Ruth I'll be late for supper."

He rode off at a fast canter to town, then hitched his gelding outside McDougall's office. He marched in and threw the papers on Mac's desk. "What's all this mean?"

Mac glanced at him, then picked up the papers and paged through them. "Abercrombie's done what he said he would. He's sued you, saying you don't have a right to six hundred and forty acres. He's asking the judge to partition your land, so you only keep three hundred and twenty. And for good measure, he's told the judge which three hundred and twenty to give you, freeing up the part of your claim he wants."

"What do I do now?"

Mac leaned back in his seat. "I'll file an answer and request the case be dismissed. But as I've told you before, I can't guarantee what the court will do. And it will take time to resolve, either way."

"Can I farm my claim or not?"

Mac nodded. "Keep working it like it's yours. Abercrombie wants some of the acres you've tilled, but most of what he's asking the judge to remove from your claim is still in trees. And in my answering papers I'll make it clear that equitable principles require you to receive the fruits of your labor."

Zeke sighed and sat in the chair across from Mac. "Can't you make this go away?"

Mac frowned. "The best way to do that is for you to marry. The law passed last year clearly lets married men keep six hundred and forty acres."

"Who would I marry?"

Mac shrugged. "Any woman who was in Oregon before December first of last year will do. Why not Hannah Bramwell?"

"Hannah Bramwell?"

"She's already almost a part of your family. Or aren't the two of you getting along?" Mac asked. "She was in town last Friday asking about a job."

"She's got a job," Zeke said in surprise. "She works for me."

Mac raised his eyebrows. "Maybe she'd be interested in something more permanent."

Zeke left Mac's office befuddled. He didn't want the lawsuit hanging over his head. It would worry him as long as it lasted. And much as he liked Mac, Zeke didn't want to pay the man to fix a problem caused by Abercrombie's belligerence.

But marry Hannah Bramwell? He'd liked kissing her well enough, but he didn't want to shackle himself to her for the rest of his life. She was too weak for life on the farm. She limped—he wondered what she hid under her skirt. And the notion of her correcting his grammar every day, of her arguing with him about his siblings' behavior, of her sleeping beside him every night . . . .

He found he couldn't complete that thought. The image of Hannah asleep the night Noah broke his arm came to mind. She'd looked much softer in sleep than when she was awake. Almost pretty. Her rigid posture melted into curves under the blanket. Her hair haloed around her face until she pushed it back into a bun.

Zeke had never thought of marrying anyone but Jenny. He knew he'd never have Jenny now, but he wasn't ready to consider another wife. Was he? If it meant keeping his land . . . .

Wednesday morning Esther appeared in the field where Zeke was cutting hay. He'd left the cabin before the others were awake, wanting time by himself to consider what to do next. Esther carried her infant daughter Abigail.

When he saw his sister, he asked, "What are you doing here?"

"It's not Daniel's fault," she said. "He didn't know."

Zeke snorted. "That's hard to believe. I was served the papers on his land."

"He and Douglass talked to their pa the day before, told him you'd be working with them yesterday. But Daniel didn't know his pa meant to have you served. You know how disagreeable Samuel can be."

Zeke shrugged and went back to swinging his scythe.

"What are you going to do about it?" Esther asked.

"I don't know." He sighed.

"Daniel says there's one way out for you."

Zeke straightened up. "What's that?"

"Marry."

"You, too!"

"What do you mean?" she asked.

"Mac told me the same thing."

"So are you going to?"

"Going to what?"

"Get married."

"And just who do you think I should marry?"

"Hannah Bramwell. She'd serve you well." Esther bit her lip after she spoke.

"That's who Mac suggested."

"Well?" Esther patted Abigail's back when the baby whimpered. "Why not?"

Zeke frowned at her. "You had this great romance on the trail, marrying Daniel as soon as you could, because you two couldn't keep your hands off each other—"

"Zeke!" His sister's cheeks flamed.

"Well, it's true, ain't it? Then I lost Jenny, and you think I should settle for whoever's handy."

"It's not like that. Hannah's a good woman. She'd make a good wife."

"How do you know what kind of wife she'd make? What a man wants in a wife?"

Her eyes flared. "I *am* a wife, you dunce. I think I know something about marriage."

"Aw, Esther," Zeke said, his voice softening. "I'm sorry. I'm finding it hard to move from asking Jenny to marry me because I loved her, to considering Hannah just because she's available. Can you blame me?"

"No," Esther whispered. "I can't."

Chapter 34: Out of the Frying Pan

The twins and Noah surprised Hannah when they ran into the cabin early Tuesday afternoon. "Zeke got sued!" Jonathan shouted.

"What happened?" she asked.

It took a while for the boys to explain, but Hannah gathered the sheriff had served court papers on Zeke having something to do with Samuel Abercrombie wanting Zeke's land. "How can that be?" she asked. "Didn't your brother file his claim properly?"

"I dunno, Miz Hannah," David said. "But Zeke rode to town to see Mac McDougall."

"Says he won't be home for supper," Noah added.

Hannah sighed in relief. Another day in which she wouldn't have to see Zeke—she still hadn't seen him since the kiss in the barn last Thursday. She told the twins to pick whatever early vegetables were ripe in the garden, then to muck out the stalls. Noah tagged along after his older brothers.

"What's a lawsuit?" Ruth asked her after the boys left.

"It's a way to get a judge to decide an argument," Hannah explained. "I didn't know your brother and Mr. Abercrombie had a dispute over land."

"Old Mr. Abercrombie hasn't liked us ever since we left Missouri," Ruth said. "He caused Pa all sorts of trouble on the wagon train. I was too little at the time to notice most of it, but Esther told me later. Then after Ma died—" The girl bit her lip and was silent a moment. "Then Captain McDougall took over. But Mr. Abercrombie wanted to be captain. He hasn't treated any of us kindly ever since."

"Then Zeke didn't do anything to the Abercrombies?" Hannah asked.

"I don't think so," Ruth said. "Zeke's as straight as they come. You know that." She scowled as if daring Hannah to dispute her characterization of her brother. Hannah might think the man uncouth and uneducated, but she knew he loved his family dearly. His kiss didn't change that fact.

"Well, I'm sure it will all get sorted out," she said. The problem wasn't her concern, no matter how curious she might be.

Hannah managed to avoid Zeke again on Wednesday. He and the twins left the house before she arrived. "Zeke says he needs to make up for the time he lost yesterday," Ruth told her. "They were away at dawn this morning. Jonathan and David didn't like it much, and Noah was glad to stay in bed."

But once he awoke for the day, Noah was ornery, unhappy to have been left behind with Hannah and Ruth. "I ain't doing no women's work," he grumbled when Hannah asked him to feed the chickens.

She chose not to correct the boy's grammar. "It's a warm day, even if cloudy," she told him. "You take the bucket of grain out and mind those birds."

"Will you stew a hen for supper?" he asked. "Old Brownie ain't laid—"

Her lips twitched. "Hasn't."

"—hasn't laid eggs in weeks."

Hannah sighed. She hadn't planned on plucking a chicken. "All right," she said.

"Can I wring its neck?"

"With only one good hand?" she asked.

He nodded, flexing the fingers of his still-splinted left arm.

"See what you can do, but call Ruth or me if you can't."

Noah rushed outside with the bucket of grain. Soon she heard squawking, then Noah squealed and Blackie barked. Hannah opened the door to find the boy in tears and the dog at his heels.

"She pecked me," Noah sobbed, clutching his cheek with his good hand. Blood trickled through his fingers. Hannah saw no sign of the brown hen, which she assumed had escaped its demise.

Hannah put her arm around the boy and led him inside, pushing Blackie out the door. As she washed his face, she said, "I think we'll have venison tonight. Brownie earned another day."

Despite her trepidation at encountering Zeke again, Hannah decided she should stay at the Pershing cabin until he and his brothers returned. She wanted to explain why Noah's face was bruised and cut. But Zeke and the twins did not return by dusk. "I need to leave to be home before dark," she told Ruth. "I'll try to get here tomorrow before Zeke leaves."

"It's all right, Miz Hannah," Ruth said. "Zeke'll understand. He won't blame you for Noah's getting hurt."

A cold hard rain beat down Thursday morning, making the air feel more like early March than late May. Shortly after dawn, Hannah scurried into the McDougall barn to hitch up the mule and cart. After avoiding him for a week, she now needed to see Zeke to explain about Noah, though she wondered whether the men would work in the fields in such miserable weather. Perhaps he would stay near the house all day—a thrill of anticipation went through her at the thought.

Her memory of the kiss had faded in the week since it happened. She no longer recalled the texture of his shirt beneath her fingers, though she remembered the comfort and strength of his arms around her. And a pang went through her belly as she touched her lips, trying to recollect the taste of him.

She shook her head at her own foolishness. Zeke had behaved inappropriately, but she had no reason to think the experience would ever be repeated. She didn't see him as a libertine like Charles, who she suspected seduced women into his bed whenever he could.

Hannah drove the cart into the rain, climbed down to shut the barn door behind her, returned to the bench, and slapped the reins on the mule's back to begin the drive.

Despite her wool cloak and the oilskin she'd wrapped around herself, she was drenched when she arrived at the Pershings. Her fingers were cold as she clambered shakily down the wagon wheel. Her damp boot slipped on a wet wooden spoke, and she grimaced as she caught herself.

A stinging hail began to fall. The mule brayed and shied. Hannah grabbed the reins to stop the beast from bolting. Ducking low against the icy pellets, she tugged the mule toward the barn and pulled the door open.

The door was wrenched from her grasp, and she shrieked as a man yanked her into the barn. Zeke.

"What do you mean by frightening me so?" she cried.

"I mean to get you out of the storm," he shouted. "Give me the reins." He took the traces from her and slapped the mule's rump to hurry it into the barn.

Hannah pushed the oilcloth back from her head. She shook it out and hung it on a hook on the wall. "I'm sorry about Noah's face," she said, turning to Zeke.

He stared at her. "What?"

"The cut. From the chicken." She gestured at her own face. "You must have noticed."

"Oh." Zeke cleared his throat, still staring. "Ruth told me. And Noah, too."

"The poor child keeps getting hurt when I'm in charge. You must think me a terrible housekeeper."

"Will you marry me?"

She couldn't have heard him right. "I'm sorry. What did you say?"

"I'm asking—will you marry me?"

Her mouth dropped open. She couldn't remember a single one of the pretty speeches she'd read in novels about how to turn down an unwanted proposal. "W-why?" she stammered, her heart pounding.

"McDougall said you were looking for a job. I thought you were happy here, but maybe you ain't."

"You want to marry me to keep me as your housekeeper?" She'd heard of stranger reasons for marriage, and she had never expected romance from a man. But she was puzzled. "You don't have to marry me. I'll stay on, if you really want me to. But after last week—"

"I need a wife to keep my land, and you need a job. Why shouldn't we marry?"

"You're serious." She was stunned. No man had ever proposed to her before. She may have yearned to marry and have children, but she'd never thought it likely, given her disfigurement. She swallowed. Zeke might not realize the full cause of her limp. "But my leg."

He shrugged. "You do most things all right around the house now, don't you?"

"But . . . in a wife . . ."

He stepped nearer. "It don't matter. Will you marry me or not?"

She held up her hand between them. "I need to think."

He sighed and stepped back. "Think all you want. But I need an answer soon. McDougall has to file my answer to Abercrombie's complaint within a couple weeks."

She frowned at him. He seemed sincere. "You really think we'll suit?"

He stepped toward her again, closer this time, and took her in his arms. He leaned over and kissed her. This is what she'd forgotten. The sweetness of his breath on her cheek, the searing touch of his mouth on hers, the press of his firm chest against her breasts.

"We'll suit fine," he murmured sometime later when she gasped for air.

Chapter 35: Zeke Has Second Thoughts

Hannah Bramwell brought out the worst in him, Zeke thought as he went about his chores Thursday evening. He hadn't meant to blurt out a marriage proposal. He hadn't even decided marrying her was a good idea. He'd wanted to ponder the problem a little longer.

Then he'd seen her struggling with the mule. After he took the reins from her, she'd stepped into the barn, hair dripping and face flushed. The proposal left his tongue before he knew what he'd said. He couldn't take the words back. He wasn't sure if he wanted to.

She'd clung to him when he kissed her as if she were drowning in the rain and he provided the only air available.

Truth be told, they'd both been left breathless. Same as after the first kiss. Which is why he didn't know whether he regretted his proposal.

Friday morning Zeke rode his gelding into town again. The weather had improved, but the road was muddy and the skies still gray. He entered McDougall's office to find the lawyer sitting at his desk and reading the newspaper. "Have you seen yesterday's *Spectator*?" Mac asked.

Zeke shook his head as he sat across from Mac. "Ain't been to town since I saw you Wednesday."

"This town is growing," Mac said, folding the paper. "One article says a steamship will be traveling daily between here and Portland. Some folks say we need a plank road from the docks to smaller towns nearby. Maybe even a railroad. An advertisement in this issue offers to insure risks of any sort. Some say we'll be bigger than San Francisco again soon."

Zeke raised his eyebrows. "That don't seem likely, based on what I've heard."

Mac grinned. "I agree. I think California has the best of us, now it's a state and we're still a territory. Unless significant gold deposits are found nearby, Oregon Territory will rise and fall based on farming and lumber."

Zeke shrugged. "Ain't nothing wrong with that."

"No. And there's money for men like me to make by supporting farmers and loggers. I'm planning some investments, though I don't want to get into the insurance business." Then Mac cocked his head. "What can I do for you today?"

"Just wanted to let you know I proposed to Miz Bramwell yesterday. So you can put that in your papers to Abercrombie."

Mac chortled. "You did? Has she accepted?"

"Not yet."

"Well, the judge won't care whether you've asked her. Not if she might reject you. Do you think she will?"

"Don't know." Zeke grimaced. "Don't even know why I did it."

Mac leaned back in his chair. "What have you told Miss Bramwell about Jenny?"

Zeke was sure his face showed surprise. "Jenny? Why would I tell Hannah anything about Jenny?"

"Lots of gossip in this town. We've kept it quiet Jenny and I didn't marry until I returned last November. But the fact you were courting her while I was gone has probably spread beyond our close acquaintances. Hannah Bramwell might be the answer to your land problem, but I would hate for you to marry her and her be hurt later on."

"There's nothing to tell, Mac. Jenny turned me down afore you got back here. You won her, fair and square."

"We have thirty days after you were served to respond to Abercrombie's pleadings," Mac said. "There's time for you to handle the situation with Miss Bramwell as a gentleman would."

Zeke left Mac's office and rode Red slowly back home as he thought about what Mac had said. Did he owe Hannah an explanation about Jenny? Since when did a man need to tell a woman about his past loves?

And what did he really know about Hannah Bramwell other than she relished kissing? It was a little late to be asking questions now he'd asked her to marry him, but he ought to find out what he could.

When he came to the cutoff to Esther's house, Zeke turned his horse toward his sister's. He found Daniel in the barn mending a leather harness.

"Morning, Daniel."

Daniel stood from his task. "Let me say it again, Zeke. I'm sorry about Pa. Ain't no call for him to file suit against you. He and Douglass chose the land my brother claimed. They should have known the low fields would be boggy and not grow much."

"Well, it's done now. And I need to find a way out of it." Zeke sighed. "Is Esther inside?"

Daniel nodded. "Noon meal'll be on the table in a bit. Stay and eat with us. You go on in, and I'll be there shortly."

Zeke put Red in a stall and went inside. Esther stirred something savory in a pot, while holding Abigail to her shoulder. He heard the older children playing in the loft. "Morning, Esther."

She turned and handed him his niece. "Hold the baby while I take this off the fire."

He fumbled with the infant uncertainly. As the oldest of eight children—nine, counting Jonah, and ten, counting Franklin, Jr.—he'd held a lot of babies, but the littlest ones still scared him. He was afraid he'd drop them or break something with his big hands. He nestled Abigail in the crook of his elbow. Then it dawned on him—if he and Hannah married, he might have a child of his own in a year. His grip on Abigail slipped.

"Have you come to apologize for talking to me like you did Wednesday?" Esther said as she lifted the pot, its handles wrapped in dishcloths to avoid burning her hands.

"I didn't mean to hurt you, Esther." He bounced the baby, tightening his hold. "And I done what you said."

"Hannah? You asked her?" He heard a laugh in Esther's voice. "What'd she say?"

"Nothing yet." He sighed. "Mac says I need to tell her about Jenny. Do you think so?"

Esther frowned at him. "How much of Jenny's story would you tell? Does Mac really want it all spread about town?"

"That's just it," Zeke said. "I don't know what to do."

"I'd say you should ask Jenny, not me."

Zeke asked his sister the other question bothering him. "What do you know about Hannah's limp? Or about how she and her family get along?"

Esther shrugged. "I'd say you need to talk to Hannah about those things. Or maybe Ruth knows something."

The proper thing to do would be to find Hannah, Zeke thought as he rode home after the noon meal. But he took Red to the barn and went to the fields to locate Jonathan and David. He finished the day with them. By the time they returned to the cabin, Hannah had left.

After supper, Zeke told his siblings he'd help Ruth with the dishes and sent his three brothers outside. As he dried the dishes, he asked, "How'd it go with Miz Hannah today?"

Ruth gave him a puzzled look. "Same as always. Though she's still bothered by something. Seems distracted, like she has a problem she's thinking on."

"Could it be her brother?" Zeke asked. "How do they get along?"

"Not so well, according to Faith. Back during the school term, Faith and I talked. Faith don't like her stepmother Alice, and Miz Hannah don't like her either. Faith wishes she could live with Miz Hannah, but her pa won't let her."

"Do you think Hannah will try to change Jacob's mind?" Zeke hadn't considered Hannah might want Faith to live with them after they married. Another thing to discuss with Hannah. Assuming she agreed to wed him.

Ruth shrugged.

"How'd she get the limp?" Zeke tried to sound like he didn't really care.

"That I know," Ruth said. "Faith told me. She was badly burned in a fire when she was a girl."

He felt a rush of pity—Hannah must have suffered terrible pain. And he muttered as much to Ruth.

"I think she did. Faith says she has horrible scars. Said it took her weeks to walk again."

Zeke swallowed. How would a scarred leg feel under his hands? But he found the thought didn't trouble him. Hannah had healed from the injury, for the most part. And bedding her would be enjoyable, if her kissing was any indication.

Chapter 36: Hannah Considers

Hannah worked at the Pershing homestead after Zeke's surprise proposal on Thursday, and returned on Friday and Saturday. She and Zeke did not speak of it again in those three days, but she thought of little else. "Are you all right, Miz Hannah?" Ruth asked Saturday morning after Hannah burned her hand taking a loaf of bread out of the oven.

"Yes," Hannah responded tersely. "I'm only woolgathering."

"So is Zeke," Ruth said. "He ain't—hasn't—put two words together all week."

He'd said a mouthful to Hannah in the barn on Thursday. And kissed her with that same mouth. But Hannah kept those thoughts to herself.

She worked in her garden on the McDougall claim Saturday afternoon, weeding rows of vegetables and picking early lettuce and carrots. She felt a sense of accomplishment harvesting food she'd grown from seeds. There was something to be said for farm life—a satisfaction in wresting food from the wilderness. As Hannah worked, she mulled Zeke's proposal again, but came to no conclusions about whether to accept.

It surprised her she was even considering marrying Zeke. He was rough and uneducated, and sometimes violent. Life on the farm was difficult. And, most importantly, she would lose what little independence she had as a single woman.

But marriage brought many advantages. She would have a home. She liked the Pershing children. She might have more children. At that thought, she felt a pang in her belly. She yearned for a baby of her own, but her body had disappointed her so often in the past, she wondered whether it was possible.

Sunday morning Hannah hitched the mule to the cart and drove to church. She'd decided to confide in her brother Jacob. He was her only family in the vicinity. No matter how unsympathetic he'd been since her arrival in Oregon, as her older brother he deserved an opportunity to voice an opinion. That was how they'd been raised, and though it stuck in her craw to ask his advice, she would.

After the service, Esther invited Hannah to eat with her family. Since spring arrived, the families at the Methodist church held a potluck meal whenever the weather was nice.

Jacob hadn't been at church, and Alice always made it seem as if they couldn't afford to feed Hannah when she visited. She would enjoy sitting with Esther's family more than seeking out her brother, but Hannah didn't want to cope with Zeke's presence under his sister's eye. "Will Zeke and your younger siblings be joining us?" she asked.

"Don't know." Esther nodded at a group across the churchyard. "Looks like he's talking with Mac and Jenny."

Hannah glanced in the direction Esther indicated. The three of them—Zeke, Mac, and Jenny—stood in earnest conversation, the two young McDougall children nearby. The little girl Mac had brought from California could now toddle a bit, and her brother William helped her up when she fell.

Hannah wondered if Zeke was talking to Mac about the lawsuit, but he seemed to be speaking to Jenny more than Mac. Jenny touched Zeke's arm as if to emphasize what she told him. Hannah remembered Alice's insinuations about Zeke and Jenny. There were depths to the relationships between members of the former wagon train she did not understand. Maybe Jacob could enlighten her, but talking to her brother could wait until later in the afternoon.

"I haven't brought any food to share," she said, turning to Esther.

"No matter," Esther said. "I have plenty."

So Hannah agreed to join Esther's family. They ate their fill, then Daniel left to speak with other men. Zeke stopped to say hello, but didn't stay, saying he needed to get home.

Esther's older children frolicked on the grass while Esther and Hannah chatted. The infant Abigail slept on Esther's lap. When the baby awoke, Esther retreated to the wagon to feed her, and the other children pestered Hannah with silly questions and prattling. Then Esther returned and handed the baby to Hannah. "You take her while I pick up the baskets," Esther said.

Hannah was cooing at Abigail when Esther spoke again. "I understand Zeke asked you to marry him."

Hannah looked up, startled. "Yes."

"What answer will you give him?"

Esther's directness caused Hannah to respond similarly. "I don't know."

"Please don't hurt my brother."

"I have no intention of doing so." Hannah's tone was as terse as Esther's, though she didn't want to be impolite.

"He's already had his heart broke once."

"By Jenny McDougall?" Hannah asked. "What happened there?"

"The story ain't mine to tell," Esther said. "You'll need to talk to Jenny. Or Zeke."

"Is it something I need to know?" Hannah was reluctant to raise the subject with either Jenny or Zeke, but after Alice's frequent hints, she didn't want to marry him unaware of his past.

"That's up to Jenny." Esther turned to her. "You'd be a fine match for Zeke, and he needs a wife. But I don't know if he's ready to marry."

If Zeke wasn't ready to marry, then why had he asked her? Hannah waffled until she decided there was no point in talking to her brother yet. Besides, she didn't trust Jacob to tell her the truth about Zeke and Jenny. Alice never offered more than insinuations, so perhaps Jacob didn't know the full story.

Hannah looked around the churchyard for the McDougalls after finishing the meal with Esther, but did not see them. So she headed directly home. She would have to talk to Jenny another time.

On Monday Hannah and Ruth washed and hung the laundry on the line, and in midafternoon Hannah left the Pershing house, saying she needed to shop in town. She stopped at her brother's store, but Jacob was not there. Faith sat at the counter, and Hannah made small talk with her niece while purchasing a few necessities.

"Won't you talk to Pa again about my living with you?" Faith pleaded. "I don't mind clerking in the shop, but I can't abide living at home. If it weren't for Charity, I'd run away."

"You mustn't," Hannah said. "I'll talk to him soon, I promise."

But her immediate concern was talking to Jenny McDougall. She drove the cart to the hotel, secured her mule to a post, then went inside to the McDougall suite. After greeting Jenny, Hannah asked, "Might we talk? In private?"

Jenny laughed. "With the children here? Not much is private. The weather is decent, isn't it? Let's take them to the park." The women and two children headed out, Maria in Jenny's arms. "She's walking some, but rarely makes it across the room before she falls. It'll be a few months yet before she can make it to the park on her own feet."

Once the children were occupied tossing a ball between them, Hannah said, "Zeke Pershing has asked me to marry him."

"Mac told me," Jenny said.

"I'll be blunt, if I may." Hannah paused, then continued, "I've heard rumors from my sister-in-law Alice about you and Zeke. I have no reason to countenance what she said, but before I make any promises to him, I want to know whether our marriage would create difficulties for him, for you, or anyone in your families. I do not want to step into any relationships unawares."

Jenny sighed and looked off into the distance. Then she turned to Hannah. "There is nothing between Zeke and me that should cause you any concern."

Hannah wanted to ask more questions, but Jenny's bald statement gave her no openings.

Then Jenny said, "You've probably been told Zeke proposed to me last summer. I thought for a while Mac might be dead. Zeke and I had been friends since our journey to Oregon four years ago. He helped me on the wagon train, particularly when Mac was busy as captain."

"Did you love Zeke?" Hannah asked.

Jenny shook her head. "He is a dear friend. But I did not love him in the way a wife should love her husband. I rejoiced when Mac returned. He and I are very happy." Jenny smiled and touched her stomach. "I am hoping to give him a child by year-end."

Hannah smiled as well. "You're expecting?"

Jenny nodded. "I believe so. But it's early." She looked into Hannah's eyes. "There is nothing to keep you from marrying Zeke if the two of you love each other."

But she didn't love Zeke, Hannah thought. And Zeke didn't love her either. If they married, they would be solving each other's problems—her need for a home and desire for a family, and Zeke's need for a clear claim to his land and someone to care for his siblings. Was that enough on which to build a marriage? This pragmatic match certainly wasn't what she'd hoped for when she and Jane had giggled about their future beaux. But many women settled for far less.

Hannah left Jenny and the children playing in the park and returned to her brother's store. Jacob was minding the counter by himself, which relieved Hannah. She didn't want to deal with Alice at the moment.

"Might we talk, brother?" she asked.

"Until a customer comes in," he replied. "Faith said you'd stopped by earlier. Is this about her living with you? I've said I don't want her keeping house for the Pershings with you."

"I have a different matter I wish to discuss. We'll talk about Faith another day."

He cocked an eyebrow and waited.

"I've been offered marriage by Zeke Pershing," Hannah said. "I am seeking your opinion."

"Marriage!" Jacob guffawed.

"Why are you so surprised?" Hannah had never shared her dreams with her brother the way she had with Jane, but certainly he should realize every woman wanted to wed, wanted a family.

"None of us ever expected you to marry. Not after the accident."

"Well, apparently Mr. Pershing thinks I have something to offer him."

"The right to his land, most likely." Jacob said gently, "Do you wish to marry under such circumstances, sister?"

"What other option do I have?" Hannah shrugged. "I'm working for him now, and I can't continue as his housekeeper if he finds another wife. And you won't have me live with you."

"It's not my choice, Hannah."

Hannah coughed to mask her laugh. "You let Alice make the decisions then?"

Jacob gestured helplessly. "What are you going to do?"

"I haven't decided yet."

That evening, alone in her cabin, Hannah started a letter to her sister.

May 26, 1851

Dearest Jane,

I have received a proposal of marriage from Ezekiel Pershing, the man for whom I am keeping house. Do you remember our long discussions about marriage—our hopes and dreams? In your case, your hopes were realized at an early age, though I know you regret no children have come from your union with Charles.

I, on the other hand, wondered if my dreams would ever be fulfilled. I had no real hope a man would want me as a wife, though I have always desired children. In Mr. Pershing's case, it is not love that motivated him to offer for me, but the need to secure his land under new laws in Oregon.

But then, I also would not be marrying for love, if I accept him. He is a good brother to his siblings, and I think would not treat me ill. But he is not a tender man, nor well-spoken, nor learned.

Under these circumstances, I question whether I should forgo my independence. Yet striving for autonomy has gained me little during my time in Oregon. The people here are no more receptive to a woman making her own way in the world than are people in Ohio.

To have a home to call my own is my biggest incentive to marry. And to have the possibility of children. But to marry without affection? Is that my best option?

I cannot tell you yet what I will do, but I shall write again as soon as I decide. Oh, I wish we were together so we could talk as we used to as girls!

Fondly, your sister,
Hannah

Chapter 37: The Decision

Zeke had seen Hannah in church on Sunday, but he merely greeted her briefly as she sat with Esther's family. He'd talked at length to Mac and Jenny, wanting to know what they thought he should reveal to Hannah. "Tell her you asked Jenny to marry you when you thought I was dead," Mac said.

"But we knew you weren't," Zeke said. "You'd written Jenny you weren't coming back to Oregon."

"You can't tell her Mac and I weren't married!" Jenny said, clutching Zeke's arm. "Then she'd wonder about William's father."

Zeke sighed. "All right. But I don't like starting my marriage with a lie."

"Then say as little as possible," Mac said.

"Alice Bramwell is a vile creature. She's been spreading gossip about Jenny and me for months." Zeke took a deep breath. "Why does a man need to take on another family, when his own is trouble enough? Pa and Jacob Bramwell made the same mistake." And now he worried he'd blundered as well.

But Zeke had had no opportunity to say anything to Hannah as of Wednesday morning. For almost a week after his proposal, she'd managed to stay out of his path.

Wednesday started with a heavy rain, and he told the twins to work in the barn instead of the fields. "Ruth," he said, "can you manage the house and Noah today? I have business with Miz Bramwell, and I'm riding to see her afore she gets here." He saddled Red and rode to the McDougall claim.

Zeke found Hannah in her doorway, just leaving her cabin, her head and clothes covered in a large oilskin cloak. "Oh," she said, "I was heading to your house now."

"We should talk," Zeke said.

She nodded. "All right. Come in." She entered the cabin and took off her cloak. "Would you like some coffee? I can make it quickly."

"Sounds fine." He sat at the table where he'd sat many evenings with Jenny and William. "Have you given any thought to my proposal?"

She laughed with a wry twist of her lips. "I've thought of little else."

"And?"

"As you said, we should talk." She put the coffeepot on the stove and got two mugs down from a shelf. "Sugar?"

He shook his head. "I wanted to—"

At the same time, she said, "I have a few—"

"You first," he said.

"I have a few questions," she said.

He waited, watching her.

"About Jenny McDougall. Alice has told me—"

"Don't believe everything Alice Bramwell says."

"I don't," she said earnestly. "I went to speak to Jenny myself on Monday."

"You talked to Jenny?" He was surprised not only that Hannah had gone to Jenny, but also that Jenny had apparently been willing to talk to Hannah. Jenny hadn't mentioned it on Sunday. "What did she say?"

"She told me you and she had been friends since forty-seven, and you'd asked her to marry you after you thought Mac died."

"Mm-mm."

"But did you love Jenny?" She hesitated. "I don't expect love from you, but I won't marry a man who is pining for another woman."

"Jenny has loved Mac since they first met, afore I knew either one of them. She is a fine woman, but I know I have nothing with her and never will." He'd repeated that speech to himself for weeks, if not months.

Hannah nodded, then sat silently.

"What other questions do you have?" Zeke asked. Might as well hear everything she could shoot at him.

"Your younger siblings will live with us, won't they?"

Zeke raised an eyebrow. "Where else would they go?"

"I expected as much. And I like them all."

Zeke grinned. "Even the twins?"

She smiled, too. "They're good boys. Just growing faster than they know how to." Her face turned serious. "But could we house one more relative, perhaps? If Faith came to live with us?"

"Does she need a home?" Zeke surmised there were problems in Jacob Bramwell's household, but he didn't know how severe.

"It isn't urgent, but she isn't happy with her stepmother. Surely you can understand."

"I do." Zeke thought of the troubles his stepmother Amanda had caused his younger siblings. "But the house is already bursting at the seams. We'll have to add on as soon as we can. Once I build another room, Faith and Ruth could share, if need be."

"Thank you." Hannah seemed to relax. "And what did you want to ask me?"

Zeke swallowed. Now that he was faced with asking, he didn't know how to raise the subject. "Your leg. Ruth told me you burned it as a child."

"Yes."

"Will it . . . will it keep you from a normal marriage?"

"What do you mean?" she asked, blushing.

"From bearing children, I suppose is what I mean." For the life of him, Zeke didn't know how to ask how damaged her leg was. Based on their kisses, he thought they'd manage the bedding just fine, assuming she was able, but he did want his own young'uns someday.

Hannah stood, her face still flaming. She raised her skirt, rolled down her stocking, and showed him her leg. "It's scarred and twisted," she said. "It pains me greatly at times. I worry it will give out on me. But no doctor has ever told me I could not have children."

He stood beside her, touched her calf, and tugged her stocking up to cover it. Then he pulled her against him gently. "I don't mind. So will you marry me?"

Zeke held his breath.

Hannah drew back from his chest and looked at him for a long minute. "All right," she said. "I'll marry you."

Zeke exhaled. "When?"

"Well, you mentioned adding another room—"

"Mac needs to respond to the lawsuit—"

She pulled away from him then and placed hands on her hips. "Mr. Pershing, I suggest when we are discussing our marriage, you leave the lawsuit out of it as much as possible. It tends to place our discussion on too practical a footing."

"I'm sorry, Hannah."

"We will not enter into this marriage precipitously. We will discuss the situation with our families—I assume you have not told your siblings yet?"

He shook his head.

"We will have the minister read the banns in church, and you will build onto your cabin. If we still believe we should wed a month from now, I will be honored to marry you."

"It isn't necessary to read the banns." Zeke wondered if she merely wanted to delay the wedding. "I'll need to purchase a license, but—"

"I would like the banns read. Our families and friends should know our intent. Besides," Hannah said, shrugging, "you will need the time to add to the house."

Zeke figured that was the best he could hope to negotiate.

After helping Hannah hitch her mule to the cart for her trip to his farm, Zeke rode into town and went to see Mac.

"She's agreed," he announced to Mac.

Mac grinned. "Miss Bramwell? She will marry you?"

Zeke nodded somberly.

"Come, man," Mac said. "That calls for celebration." He pulled a flask from his desk drawer and handed it to Zeke. "You drink first."

Zeke took a swallow and returned the flask. Mac sipped from it also.

"How soon?" Mac asked.

"She wants the banns read."

"It's not necessary—"

"That's what I told her. But she wants me to add a room onto the house."

Mac laughed loudly. "She's pulling you by a ring in your nose already."

"Now wait a minute—"

"It's a good thing, Zeke." Mac chuckled again. "When Jenny tells me what to do, I know she cares for me. It's what women do, they do their best to organize the men around them. Miss Bramwell must feel comfortable with you. Well done, man."

"When can you get the lawsuit dismissed?"

Mac shuffled some papers on his desk. "I'll file an answer Monday, but

I don't know if the judge will take up the matter until you are actually married. But if you are affianced to a woman who came to Oregon last November, it should be easy to obtain a stay on any motions filed by Abercrombie's attorney." Mac winked. "Just make sure she goes through with the wedding. Then I'll have more to tell the court."

Zeke gulped the whiskey when Mac handed the flask back to him, then said, "First I have to tell my brothers and Ruth. And Esther and Rachel also, I suppose."

"They won't be troubled by this, will they?"

Zeke shook his head. "Ruth talks only of Miz Hannah this and Miz Hannah that. And Esther told me to propose." He shrugged. "I doubt the boys care."

"Well, let me know if there are any snags. Meanwhile, I'll have the response ready by Monday."

When Zeke returned to his claim, he gathered the twins and worked in the fields until evening. Hannah had left by the time they returned to the cabin. Jonathan and David took Noah fishing after supper, but Zeke said he needed a word with Ruth. He'd decided to tackle his conversation with her first, as he suspected it would be the easiest.

While Ruth washed the supper dishes, Zeke dried. "I asked Hannah Bramwell to marry me, and she accepted," he said.

Ruth let the plate in her hands slip back into the suds. "Oh, Zeke!" Her broad smile shone at him.

"You don't mind if I marry?"

Ruth shook her head, continuing to beam. "No. I think it's wonderful. Miz Hannah is wonderful. How did you—? Well, I mean, how did you get her to agree?"

Zeke thumped his sister's head. "You don't think your oldest brother'll make a good husband?"

"Of course, I do. But you and she ain't—haven't got along all the time."

"She's a good woman. A strong woman. And she'll put up with the lot of us." Zeke paused, then said, "She says she might want Faith here, too. Does that bother you? Another girl?"

"Of course not," Ruth said. "Faith is my friend. I'd be delighted to have another girl here. And now there might be three—Hannah and me and maybe Faith." A puzzled expression went over her face. "Where will we all sleep?"

"I need to build a room afore Hannah will marry me. That's her one demand. So I'll start next week. I'm thinking two rooms—one down off this room, and another one upstairs connecting into the loft. What do you think? Hannah and me—" Zeke felt himself blush. "We'll take the new downstairs room. You and Faith could have the upstairs room, and the boys can continue in the loft. We'll take the bed out of this room." He gestured at the bed in the corner where Ruth slept now. "And we'll have more space for sitting of an evening. What do you think?"

Ruth threw her soapy hands around Zeke's neck and kissed his cheek. "I think that sounds perfect."

Chapter 38: Public Knowledge

After accepting Zeke's proposal, Hannah somehow got through the day with Ruth and Noah without letting them know she would soon be their sister-in-law. She and Zeke agreed he would talk to the children first.

She truly had not known how she would respond to his proposal until she said yes. But his tenderness when she showed him her leg won her. Pulling down her stocking in front of him was the hardest thing she'd ever done—not the most painful physically, but the most emotionally wrenching. Revealing the scars to Annabelle Abercrombie had been an act of instruction. Revealing them to Zeke bared her soul as well as her body. She knew she wasn't beautiful, but she didn't want her future husband to think her ugly, nor to worry she could not give him children.

Zeke said he didn't mind her scars. She had trouble believing a man could ignore such a frightful disfigurement, but he was kind to say so. It gave her hope. And so she said yes.

That evening she pulled out the letter she'd written to Jane and added at the bottom.

> *P.S. Sister, it is agreed. I will marry Zeke Pershing in a month's time. He is a good man, a loving brother and good provider for his orphaned siblings. As I told you in a previous letter, he took in three brothers and a sister after his father died, when his stepmother and her children returned to the States.*
>
> *He believes we will suit. I cannot be certain, but I have seen his family almost daily for the*

past month, and I think I know the challenges which lie ahead for me.

I regret you are not here to stand with me on my wedding day, as I did for you. I am glad to have Jacob, of course, but I always thought you would be at my side if ever I wed.

Pray for me, Jane,

Your loving sister, Hannah

(I shall write again after I am married.)

The next morning when Hannah arrived at the Pershing cabin, Ruth hugged Hannah. "You'll be my oldest sister," the girl proclaimed. "I'm so happy." The three younger Pershing boys shook her hand and mumbled their congratulations.

Zeke tipped his hat at her when he left with the twins for the fields. "See you later, Hannah." She noticed he'd dropped the "Miz Bramwell." She told Ruth and Noah to also call her "Hannah," since she would become their sister.

Other than what the children called her, there was no change in her activities next few days. She cooked, she cleaned, she gardened. Ruth told her Zeke planned to add onto the house—"Two rooms, he says. One for me'n Faith, if she comes to live with us. And another for you and him."

Soon Hannah would share a room—and a bed—with Zeke. She found the idea disconcerting, more because of the loss of her privacy than because of the physical intimacy. Ever since Jane's marriage, Hannah had had her own room. She'd roomed with Faith and Charity briefly after her arrival in Oregon, and with Faith during the school term, but those were her only experiences sharing a room since childhood. Now she would have a husband. And they would share a bed.

She didn't fear the marriage act—women had been tolerating it since Eve, though she wasn't sure how she would adapt. Zeke could be uncouth, but he could also be gentle, as she had discovered recently. He was good with his younger siblings, but how would he treat a wife? Particularly a wife whom he'd married for convenience?

Hannah had almost talked herself into backing out of her engagement by Saturday afternoon, three days later. To keep herself firm, she decided to go spend the night with Jacob's family and to tell her brother of her decision. The first banns would be announced on Sunday—Zeke told her he would arrange that—and then the engagement would be public knowledge. Jacob deserved to be told ahead of time.

She arrived at the store and found Jacob and his two sons stocking shelves. "Where's Faith?" she asked. "And Alice and Charity?"

"Fixing supper," Jacob said. When she asked to speak with him privately, he sent the boys upstairs. "Go tell Mama Alice we'll have Hannah with us tonight."

When they were alone, Hannah said, "I have agreed to marry Zeke Pershing."

"Are you sure?" her brother asked.

She nodded. "The first banns will be read in church tomorrow. It's the best option I have for a home here in Oregon. And I will have the possibility—" She swallowed, hoping she wouldn't blush in front of her brother. "The possibility of children, which I have always wanted."

"Will you take some time to think about it?"

"Do I need to?" Hannah asked. "Is there anything you know about him which might change my mind?"

Jacob shook his head. "Zeke's a good man, if rough. The talk about Jenny—well, I never put much credence in it. She was such a meek little thing on the prairie. I couldn't see her taking up with any man other than McDougall, and I never understood what Mac saw in her."

Hannah passed the night whispering with Faith, who'd grinned when she found out about the upcoming nuptials. "Once I'm married," Hannah told her niece, "I'll talk to your father again about your coming to live with us. Zeke has given his consent, and Ruth would welcome you, as would I."

During the church service, the minister intoned, "First banns read for Ezekiel Pershing, a farmer now of Oregon City, and originally from St. Charles, Missouri, and Hannah Bramwell, spinster, now of Oregon City, and lately of Cincinnati, Ohio." Hannah felt as well as heard the murmurs pass through the congregation.

Zeke sat somewhere behind her in the pews, but after a brief greeting in the churchyard after the service, they were separated as their acquaintances sought them out. Hannah received smiling congratulations and best wishes from Zeke's extended family—Esther and Daniel, Rachel and her husband Robert—and other friends.

Doc and Mrs. Tuller greeted her. "Zeke's a fine man, Miz Bramwell. He'll do right by you."

Jacob came over and cleared his throat. "I still have the ticket I bought you to travel to San Francisco. I've decided to cash it in and give you and Zeke credit in my store in that amount. As a wedding present. Tell him to come see me—I hear he's building onto his house. I can offer him a good price on lumber."

"Does Alice know?" The words left Hannah's mouth before she thought.

Jacob looked pained. "I don't tell her everything. But she wishes you well, just as I do. Have Zeke come talk to me. I want my sister to live comfortably."

"Would you consider letting Faith come stay with me until the wedding?" Hannah asked. "I could use her help with sewing and mending and other preparations."

"I'm still not eager to have her under the same roof as the Pershing twins," Jacob said. "Those lads are too boisterous."

"I'll not let anything happen to her," Hannah said. "I truly could use her help. And the boys behave themselves well enough with me."

Jacob agreed, and Faith hurried to pack a bundle of clothing so she could ride back to the little McDougall cabin with Hannah.

The McDougalls came to greet her as she and Faith were leaving. "My felicitations to you, Miss Bramwell," Mac said, tipping his hat.

Jenny smiled broadly. "I'm happy for you, Hannah."

"I suppose you'll need another tenant for your cabin," Hannah said. "I'm sorry if my marriage causes you any difficulty. Though I'd like to harvest the vegetables I planted."

"You are welcome to them," Mac said with a slight bow. "And I have a man in mind to live in the cabin. Name of Devlin Feeney, an ex-soldier like Robert O'Neil. He's been helping with the planting and timbering."

As Hannah and Faith climbed in their wagon to leave, Hannah saw the McDougalls talking with Zeke. They were all smiling broadly. The last thing Hannah saw as they left the churchyard was Jenny standing on her toes to kiss Zeke on the cheek.

Chapter 39: What Zeke Hears

Zeke hadn't had a chance to talk to Esther before church on Sunday. After the service, she rushed over. "So she said yes?" He barely nodded before his sister threw her arms around his neck, saying, "I'm so pleased."

Zeke grunted and patted her awkwardly on the back.

"I know Ruth must be happy. What about the boys?"

Zeke shrugged. "Twins ain't said much. Noah wonders if she'll still cook for us."

"How silly," Esther said. "Of course, she'll mind the house, just like now. But you treat her right, Zeke. She'll be your wife, not your housekeeper. A few flowers now and then wouldn't hurt you."

Flowers. Zeke hadn't thought about courting Hannah. He'd courted Jenny the year before, though she'd refused him in the end. Then he remembered Hannah's stiff back melting under his hands when he kissed her. A few flowers to make that happen once in a while wouldn't cost him anything. He'd have some for her tomorrow when she came to work.

Rachel joined them and offered congratulations also. "Well, brother," she said, flashing a smile, "you've done it now." She gestured at her infant son in his father's arms. "Perhaps little Bobby will soon have more cousins to play with. Along with a brother or sister." Her belly was now beginning to swell.

As Zeke stammered congratulations to Rachel, he felt a panicky surge from gut to throat. He wanted children, but how could he manage an ever-increasing household? He already had enough mouths to feed.

More friends joined them, and soon it seemed every member of the 1847 wagon train had greeted him and congratulated him. Hannah had a throng of well-wishers around her as well.

Doc and Mrs. Tuller led Hannah over to Zeke and the rest of the

227

Pershings, and Zeke found himself standing next to Hannah. She took his arm as if she'd been doing it for years, and they chatted with others in the congregation.

Then Hannah's brother Jacob pulled her aside, and Mac and Jenny McDougall joined Zeke.

"Mac told me your happy news after you met with him on Wednesday," Jenny said, smiling. "I am so pleased for you as well. Where is Hannah?"

Zeke gestured toward the Bramwell family.

"I'll make sure to tell her so myself," Jenny said. "When will you marry?"

Zeke explained his plan to add on to the cabin. "There are so many of us already. And Hannah would like Faith to join us."

Jenny nodded. "Mac and I also entered marriage with a ready-made family. It's not how most couples begin, but I'm sure the children you start with will bring you and Hannah as much joy as William and Maria have brought us." She touched Mac's arm and gazed up at him. Then she turned back to Zeke, her eyes shining. "I wish you happiness, Zeke." And she rose on her toes to kiss his cheek while Mac smiled at them benevolently.

What might have been, Zeke thought as Jenny kissed him. What might have been.

After his conversation with the McDougalls, Zeke turned to look for Hannah. The crowd in the churchyard had dissipated, and he couldn't see her. She must have left with her brother's family. Then he searched for his younger siblings, ready to drive back to the claim.

"Pershing!" came a call from nearby.

Samuel Abercrombie rode his tall gelding over to Zeke. The barrel-chested man loomed above Zeke. If Abercrombie intended to intimidate him, Zeke wasn't scared—he knew the gelding to be well-mannered, even if its owner was not. Zeke waited in silence for Abercrombie to say his piece.

The man couldn't be silent for long. "You must think you've beaten me, Pershing. I want your land, and this so-called marriage won't stop me."

"Are you threatening Miz Bramwell or me?" Zeke asked mildly.

"I'm just telling you what my lawyer told me."

Zeke shrugged. "Lawyers say a lot of things."

"I'm here to make you one decent offer, Pershing. Five hundred dollars for half your claim. If you won't sell, I'll see you in court."

"Thank you kindly, Abercrombie. But I'll keep the land."

Abercrombie wheeled his horse around, so close its tail brushed Zeke's face. "I gave you a chance. It's the only one you'll get."

As the cantankerous man rode off, Zeke shook his head. If his marriage to Hannah bothered Abercrombie so much, it must be a good thing. He smiled as he drove his younger siblings home.

Gray skies threatened overhead in the morning. Zeke needed to weed the crops, but he only had three weeks to build two rooms onto the house. He sent the twins out to the fields with instructions to do what they could with hoes, then hitched the mules to go to Oregon City. Hannah had arrived before he left. "Anything you need in town?" he asked as he helped her down. "I'm going to talk to Mac and buy the lumber from your brother."

She shook her head. "No, thank you. I got what I needed in Jacob's store yesterday."

Zeke set her on her feet, then leaned over and kissed her briefly. As his lips touched hers, she gripped his arms but didn't pull him closer. "Then I'll see you later." He felt husbandly talking about trips to town and shopping. And thinking about building her a room. But he'd forgotten the flowers, he remembered in dismay.

When Zeke got to Oregon City, he stopped at Mac's office. The lawyer confirmed he'd filed the answer to Abercrombie's lawsuit with the court. "Judge set a hearing for next Monday," Mac said. "It isn't the usual practice to hear a case so quickly. Perhaps he's thinking of dismissing the complaint."

"That's good, right?" Zeke asked.

"Yes. But we won't know what the judge plans to do until next week."

Zeke then drove to the Bramwell store. He didn't like this shop as well as Abernethy's down the street, but if Jacob Bramwell would give him credit on lumber, he'd take it thankfully. He removed his hat as he entered. "Morning," he said to Alice Bramwell, who stood behind the counter.

"Good morning, Mr. Pershing," she said with a sniff. "I suppose I should congratulate you. We will be related soon, I hear."

"Yes, ma'am. Thank you."

"What can I do for you?"

"Jacob offered me some lumber. I'm building onto my house. We're busting at the seams even without Hannah, and I want to do right by her."

"Lumber?" She seemed surprised. "Jacob is in the stock room. I'll get him." And she hurried to the back room behind the counter.

Zeke heard a whispered conversation in furious tones, but he couldn't make out the words.

Then Jacob appeared. "Let's go out back. I have some good boards there," Hannah's brother said. "I suppose you have logs for poles and walls. You'll only need the finished boards for flooring."

Zeke nodded. "That's my plan. The trees on my land are free, but your gift of the lumber is mighty kind. Thank you."

Jacob shrugged. "It's the least I can do for Hannah."

Chapter 40: What Hannah Hears

Monday afternoon, as Hannah, Ruth, and Faith wrung out laundry in Zeke's yard, Esther pulled her wagon in from the road, all four children with her. "I can't stay," she said. "But I want to invite the three of you to a party in Hannah's honor at my house Saturday afternoon."

"A party!" Ruth clapped her hands.

"To welcome Hannah into the Pershing clan," Esther continued. "Rachel will be there. And Jenny." She nodded to Hannah. "You should include Alice, if you'd like. I'll be inviting the Abercrombie women."

Hannah wasn't sure Alice would be a welcome addition to the festivities, but in the interest of family harmony, she nodded.

"But only women," Esther clarified. "We'll make sure you're outfitted to begin your new life. Everyone will contribute something—bedding, dishes. You might make a list of what Zeke's house needs."

Hannah shook her head, embarrassed. "I don't think we need a thing. I've been stocking up since I started working here."

Esther grinned. "If you won't let us bring housewares, then we'll just do for you—a pretty nightgown, perhaps."

The teenage girls tittered.

Hannah frowned at them, but feared a blush spoiled her attempt at sternness.

Faith and Hannah made another trip into Oregon City on Tuesday to convey Esther's invitation. While Faith gathered a few more of her belongings to stay in the country until the wedding, Hannah sat in the parlor with Alice.

Alice sniffed at the invitation. "I suppose I can come to the party. It's only neighborly. Though I don't know what good will come of your marrying Zeke Pershing." Alice shook her head. "I've done my best to warn you."

"He's been a gentleman with me," Hannah said. That might be an overstatement, given his poor grammar and lack of manners. But Hannah certainly did not have any cause to fear him. He'd behaved far better than her brother-in-law Charles, who'd tried to corner her every time he found her alone in a room. Zeke had made advances, but they hadn't been—Hannah realized with a twitch of her lips—unwelcome.

With Zeke, she knew their relationship did not include love. As long as he didn't love another woman, she could tolerate a practical marriage. Zeke had told her he wasn't in love with Jenny. Jenny gave her the same assurance—Hannah was sure Jenny's peck on Zeke's cheek in the churchyard on Sunday had meant nothing.

They had the raising of a family in common—Zeke's responsibility for his siblings and Hannah's need for a home and desire to help Faith. They had plenty on which to build a marriage.

Alice rambled on. "Jacob told me he'd given you the price of lumber for a wedding present. More generous than he need be, if you ask me," she said, crossing her arms across her lap. "I hope you are grateful. Zeke took him up on the offer quick enough—he was in the store yesterday."

"Mmm," Hannah said, not trusting herself to respond further.

"Mind you," Alice continued, "I'm not happy about Faith staying with you on the McDougall claim again. She'll have to return to town after you're wed. I won't have her living under the same roof as those Pershing twins. I've heard about their antics. Louisa Abercrombie told me . . . "

Hannah ignored her sister-in-law as much as she could, mumbling small sounds whenever Alice paused to breathe. When Faith returned to the parlor, Hannah stood. "Thank you, Alice. Faith and I must be going now." She ushered her niece down the stairs, and they left.

That evening over supper, Faith was full of questions. "Aunt Hannah, how do you know Zeke Pershing is the man you should marry?" Her niece's eyes were dreamy. "When did you know you loved him?"

Hannah sighed, not knowing whether to break the girl's illusions about her relationship with Zeke. "He and I have come to know each other while working together this year."

"But you've known a lot of men—"

Hannah laughed harshly. "Not so many, Faith. A woman with a deformed leg does not spend much time flirting and dancing."

"But you must care for him."

"I do." Hannah could say that honestly. "Zeke Pershing is a good guardian for his brothers and sister, and I respect his efforts to provide a home for them."

"But love—" Faith sighed.

"Love isn't everything, Faith. Zeke and I have an understanding, and I believe we will each do our part to keep our marriage bargain." No matter how much Faith prodded, Hannah wouldn't say more.

She hoped her niece would find love in marriage someday, but for herself, Hannah would be content to have a home with a man she respected. His kisses brought her pleasure. And she had the prospect of children. Many women settled for less.

And perhaps, someday, this practical marriage might even bring her happiness.

The weather had been cool for days, not even reaching sixty degrees although it was early June. But the day of Esther's party dawned bright and warm. Zeke agreed Hannah should not work that morning, because of the party. She and Faith heated kettles of water for baths.

"I'll be so glad when you move to Zeke's house. That stove of his is so much nicer than cooking over a fire," Faith remarked.

"How'd he come to buy the stove, a bachelor as he's been?" Hannah asked.

"I heard he bought it last summer when he was courting Jenny McDougall," Faith said, pouring a steaming kettle into the tub.

The pang of jealousy Hannah felt surprised her. No man would worry about cooking over a fire, but he might want to make life easier for a woman he loved. Well, she would have at least one benefit from Zeke's infatuation with Jenny.

Many women were already at Esther's by the time Hannah and Faith arrived. The only child present was Esther's daughter Abigail. "I made

Daniel and Robert take the other young'uns over to Douglass's house," Esther said. "The men can take care of 'em all. That way we're free to gossip as much as we want."

Hannah smiled politely. She didn't like to engage in gossip, though she supposed her marriage was now fodder for everyone in Oregon City.

Ruth took Faith to sit with Rachel O'Neil—the middle Pershing daughter—who sat hemming a garment. The Abercrombie women sat by themselves, but Hannah went to greet Annabelle and Rose. Annabelle blurted, "You're getting married, Miz Bramwell?"

Hannah nodded and smiled. She thought she understood Annabelle's surprise. "Someday it will be your turn, dear."

The girl's mother nodded. "I been telling her so, but she don't listen to me. Men here in Oregon will take any woman, long as she's breathing. Ain't enough of us to go around."

"Louisa!" Harriet Abercrombie, Samuel's wife, chastised her daughter-in-law. "Annabelle is a lovely young woman—any man would be glad to have her."

"Annabelle and I talked about the importance of character during the school session," Hannah said. "Character provides an inner beauty to all of us." Annabelle's mother, Louisa Abercrombie, riled her almost as much as Alice did.

Esther took Hannah's arm and led her to a chair by Jenny. "Have a seat here, Hannah," Esther whispered. "Where the company is more congenial."

Jenny laughed. "Are your in-laws causing you heartburn again, Esther?" she murmured.

"Same as always." Esther sighed, then turned to Hannah. "I'm glad Zeke picked you. You'll be my favorite sister-in-law, with very little effort. I thought Jenny would have that honor—" She gasped. "Beg your pardon, Hannah. I didn't mean to mention—"

Jenny put a hand on Esther's arm. "It's all right. Hannah knows Zeke courted me last year. I told her I worried Mac had died."

Esther looked slowly from Jenny to Hannah. "I'm glad you know," she said to Hannah. "I didn't want Zeke to hide it from you."

"Both Jenny and Zeke have told me there's no reason for their friendship to bother me," Hannah said, ignoring the jealousy she felt again. She smiled at Jenny. "Nothing will stand in the way of our continuing as friends in the future." Her smile encompassed Esther. "You both have been so kind to me."

A knock sounded on the door, and Esther went to greet Alice Bramwell. After her stepmother's arrival, Faith shrank deeper into the corner with Ruth and Rachel.

Esther later commented to Hannah, "Your family ain't done any better with stepmothers than ours did with Amanda."

"We all loved Jacob's first wife. Alice is an adjustment," Hannah said. "I hope I shall do better as a sister-in-law to your younger siblings. After all, I am the interloper in the household."

"No, you mustn't think that way," Esther said. "Zeke needs you. So do the children. You will be a blessing to our family, I'm sure of it."

Chapter 41: A Court Hearing

True to his word, Mac filed an answer to Samuel Abercrombie's lawsuit on June 2, the Monday after the first banns were read. Zeke spoke with Mac when he bought the lumber for his building project.

Wednesday morning, while Zeke and the twins hewed logs for walls on the house addition, Mac rode his black stallion Valiente toward them and hailed Zeke. "Good news," Mac called. "The judge has set a hearing for next Monday."

"Why is that good news?" Zeke leaned on his axe and mopped his forehead with a handkerchief. A fine mist had fallen all day, but he'd worked up a sweat chopping and sawing. The twins threw themselves on the ground at the respite from work.

"I didn't think he'd hear the case for weeks, if not months." Mac dismounted and tied Valiente to a tree. "Need some help?"

Zeke shrugged. "More hands are always better. But it's hard work."

Mac grinned. "I'm not too much of a city boy to get my hands dirty. What do you need?"

"Let's you and me fell the trees. The boys can then do the limbing and buck 'em into lengths we can pull."

The men worked until Hannah and the younger children arrived with food. "Oh," Hannah said when she saw Mac, "will you stay for the noon meal?"

Mac helped her unload the wagon and motioned to the twins to assist as well. "Thank you, Miss Bramwell."

"Feeding you is the least we can do, after you been working so hard," Zeke said. "You brung enough, ain't you, Hannah?" He saw her wince, but he didn't know why. "You all right?"

She nodded, then thanked Mac for lifting a big pot out of the wagon.

"And I have an invitation for you all from Jenny," Mac said. "We'd like to host a party to celebrate your upcoming nuptials in our new home next Friday."

The children responded with eager excitement, and Hannah agreed they would all attend. "Please thank Jenny," she said, smiling.

Zeke sighed to himself. He'd planned to have the roof raising on the day after the scheduled date for the McDougalls' party, but he nodded at Mac also.

They all sat on a blanket under a tree. Hannah dished food onto plates, while Ruth poured ginger beer. As they ate, Zeke and Mac talked about the upcoming court hearing. "You should be there," Mac told him. "I can handle it, and I can get a continuance if there's any need for testimony. But your presence will tell Judge Quinn you're serious about this matter."

"Will Mr. Abercrombie be there?" Hannah asked.

"I don't know," Mac said. "His lawyer is probably giving him the same advice I'm giving, so I wouldn't be surprised if he is."

"Should I attend?" Hannah asked.

Zeke looked at her in surprise. "Why would you go?"

"I would think my presence would be a sign of my commitment to proceed with our marriage."

Mac nodded. "You're right, Miss Bramwell. But most women find the courtroom a most unsavory place."

"I will be there." Hannah's tone was firm. Then she turned to Zeke, "Unless you don't want me to attend." He had the impression she didn't want to add those words, but thought she should let him decide.

"I don't mind," he said.

Zeke and his brothers worked on the house through the weekend. Ruth went to Esther's home for the women's party on Saturday and came home bubbling with stories. That was enough socializing for the Pershings, Zeke decided—he didn't want to stop working to make a trip to church, not when he needed to get the walls up. Besides, he'd be going to town for the court hearing on Monday.

Daniel and Douglass Abercrombie had helped him erect the walls for the lower room, and Zeke spent the weekend pounding floorboards into place. He found it awkward working with the Abercrombies after their father sued him. Nevertheless, Zeke considered Daniel a friend, and Douglass was a solid man also, though Douglass was closer to his difficult father than Daniel was.

By Sunday afternoon Zeke was ready to frame the second story walls. He would need men to help with those and with the roof. After the Monday hearing, he would see who he could drum up to assist him. He wanted to have the roof-raising the following weekend, party or not.

The morning of the hearing was cloudy and windy, but no rain fell. After instructing the twins on their chores and admonishing Ruth to take care of Noah, Zeke hitched up his wagon and drove to the McDougall claim to pick up Hannah. They hadn't had much time alone, so he looked forward to the drive to town.

"Do you mind if Faith comes?" Hannah asked as the two women exited the cabin. "She wants to see her brothers and sister."

Zeke swallowed his disappointment and smiled. "Not at all." And he helped them into the wagon.

Faith chattered all the way to town, while Hannah said little except to answer Faith's questions. Zeke said nothing. Most of Faith's comments related to the McDougalls' party.

"It's not just women, this time, Zeke," Faith said. "Men are invited, too. And all your family. You'll be there, won't you?"

"It's a lovely gesture on the McDougalls' part," Hannah said. "Of course, we'll all be there." She turned to Zeke. "I'm sure Mac and Jenny wouldn't have bothered, but for their friendship with you. I've become friends with them as well, I think, but they don't know me nearly so well as they know you."

When they arrived in town, Zeke left Faith at the Bramwell store, then drove with Hannah up the street to the courthouse. The building had been erected the prior year, and the lumber still smelled new when Zeke led Hannah inside. Mac waited in the vestibule and ushered them toward the judge's chambers. "Abercrombie and his attorney are with the judge now."

They followed Mac, and the men all stood when Hannah walked through the door. As each man was introduced, she nodded silently, then sat beside Zeke. He would have thought her demure, except for her flashing brown eyes.

"So, Mr. McDougall," Judge Quinn said. "Tell me your client's status."

Abercrombie's attorney interjected, "Shouldn't I begin by explaining why Mr. Abercrombie filed this case?"

"Your petition could well be moot, sir," the judge said. "If Mr. Pershing is in fact marrying."

Mac explained the wedding date was set for June 18, the Wednesday after the third banns would be read.

The judge turned to Zeke for confirmation. Zeke nodded.

Then the judge asked Hannah, "And is this marriage your plan also, Miss Bramwell?"

"Yes, Your Honor. Provided Mr. Pershing has added onto his house to my satisfaction before the wedding." Zeke noticed Mac try to hide a smirk at Hannah's words.

The judge laughed. "Then what is the status of your construction, Mr. Pershing?"

"Walls are up for the first level. Planning to build the second story this week. And put the roof on next weekend."

"Does that plan satisfy your standards, Miss Bramwell?" the judge asked.

"Yes, Your Honor."

"And to confirm what Mr. McDougall has written in his answer, you arrived in Oregon prior to last December first?"

"Yes, Your Honor." Hannah nodded. "In mid-October. The nineteenth, I believe."

Judge Quinn frowned at Samuel Abercrombie. "This lawsuit seems unnecessary, sir. She satisfies the requirements for the wife of a man claiming six hundred and forty acres. I won't dismiss your case yet, but will wait to see if Mr. Pershing does in fact marry Miss Bramwell."

"Then after their wedding, might I renew my motion to dismiss, Your Honor?" Mac asked.

"Most certainly," the judge said. "If Mr. Abercrombie does not see fit to withdraw his petition voluntarily." He stood and bowed to Hannah, "My felicitations, madam." The hearing was obviously over.

Outside the courthouse, Zeke asked Mac, "Why didn't he just dismiss the case now?"

Mac shrugged. "Abercrombie's rationale for filing is easier to overrule if you're actually married." Mac turned to Hannah. "So please don't back out, Miss Bramwell."

Zeke secured Mac's agreement to come for the roof-raising on Saturday. "Provided Jenny doesn't need my assistance after the party Friday night," Mac said. On the way back to his claim with Hannah and Faith, Zeke stopped to ask Daniel to help with the roof also. Douglass was working with Daniel, so Zeke requested the older Abercrombie brother's aid as well.

"What happened in court?" Daniel asked. After Zeke recounted the morning's events, Daniel said, "Don't know why Pa's being so obstinate. He ain't got a case."

"So you'll both be there on Saturday?" Zeke asked.

Douglass nodded. "But I doubt we can get Pa to help."

"I wouldn't expect it," Zeke said.

After a few more stops, he had several neighboring farmers committed to assist. Doc Tuller said he would be there, though Zeke didn't think the doctor was capable of much physical labor. Still, it would be a good thing to have a medical man around, in case anyone got hurt.

Through the week, Zeke, Jonathan, and David sawed logs and boards and split shingles. By Friday afternoon, Zeke had the logs and lumber and shingles stacked and ready, along with pegs and nails and panes for a window in each of the new rooms. He stood, hands on hips, trying to think if he'd forgotten anything.

"Zeke," Ruth called from the doorway. "Time to get ready for the party."

He sighed. The last thing his aching muscles needed was an evening in town. But Hannah and the McDougalls expected him.

Chapter 42: The McDougalls' Party

Hannah had mostly enjoyed the party at Esther's house the weekend before, but she didn't look forward to this one hosted by Mac and Jenny. The McDougalls had moved into their large new home on the bluff a few weeks earlier, and Jenny told Hannah they would roll back the carpets and hire musicians for dancing. Hannah smiled at Jenny's eagerness, but she wondered how she could politely avoid dancing at a party in her honor. She'd rarely danced in Ohio because of her leg—in part the quick movements were difficult for her, and in part it seemed no man wanted to stand up with her.

Friday afternoon, she and Faith bathed and dressed in their finest. Zeke and the rest of the Pershings planned to stop for them on the way to town. Hannah had thought about spending the night before the party with Jacob and his family, but Faith talked her out of it. "They'll be in a tizzy, and it'll be so much easier to take care of ourselves here on the claim," Faith said, and Hannah acquiesced. She didn't want to spend time with Alice any more than Faith did.

Zeke knocked on the door, and Hannah opened it. He'd shaved and wore trousers and a frock coat she'd never seen before. He handed her a bouquet of flowers.

"Thank you," she said, smiling, "You look very handsome, Mr. Pershing."

He bowed. "These were Pa's clothes. Ruth took 'em in so they fit." He seemed embarrassed.

Out of the corner of her eye, Hannah caught Faith motioning at Zeke. "You look mighty fine yourself, Hannah," Zeke said quickly.

She raised her eyebrows. "Thank you."

"The young'uns have it in their head you and I should take a separate wagon," Zeke said. "Jonathan and David are hitching your cart up now."

Faith grinned openly. "Shall the rest of us ride behind you as chaperons, Zeke?"

Hannah turned to her. "I'd say the other way around—Zeke and I should keep an eye on you children."

After Hannah and Faith gathered their shawls, Zeke handed Faith into the Pershing wagon, then Hannah into the cart. He climbed up beside her, sitting far too close for her comfort, and took the reins. She tried to make conversation with him, but Zeke's responses were short.

"Are you all right?" she finally asked.

"Just tired," he said. "Got the roof-raising tomorrow."

When they arrived at the McDougalls' house, Hannah marveled at the fine construction. It was not so ornate as the best homes in Cincinnati, but the rooms were spacious and the woodwork so polished it reflected light from the multitude of candles on wall sconces and tables.

"We just got the sofas and ottomans last week," Jenny whispered. "I feared we'd be sitting on benches."

"It's lovely, Jenny," Hannah said. "Every bit as nice as my sister's home in Ohio."

Soon the house filled with people, most of whom Hannah had met. Jacob and his family arrived, and Alice openly gaped at the new mansion. Hannah wondered at her sister-in-law's background—she'd never bothered to ask about Alice's upbringing. Although the woman had come to Oregon as a missionary, she certainly did not display much piety, nor did she seem comfortable in the fashionable McDougall home.

When supper was announced, Zeke brought Hannah a plate and sat beside her with his own. He was polite, but seemed distracted. He smiled whenever anyone congratulated them, but left the responses up to her.

Once, she saw him gazing across the room in Jenny's direction. She swallowed hard. She knew Zeke needed a wife, but did he still regret losing Jenny? Was he sorry he'd chosen Hannah? Or was he simply tired, as he'd said?

Music began, and Jenny and Mac stood to lead the first dance. Jenny urged Zeke and Hannah forward also. Hannah felt obligated to take the hand Zeke offered.

"Can you do this?" he murmured in her ear as they moved forward.

"Just don't let me fall," she said.

He smiled slowly. "I won't."

Zeke held her firmly throughout the dance. He wasn't a smooth dancer, but he was solid and took care to lead her so she could keep her weight mostly on her good leg. After the first dance with Zeke, Hannah danced once with Mac and once with her brother. Both men accommodated her leg as carefully as Zeke had.

Toward the end of the evening, she danced once more with Zeke. "Can we leave yet?" he muttered. "I got a long day ahead tomorrow."

"I think so," she said. "Let me thank the McDougalls."

"I'll go with you. Then we'll round up the young'uns. I saw Noah asleep in the corner."

They found Mac and Jenny saying farewell to other guests in the hallway. "Taking off now, Mac," Zeke said. "See you in the morning."

Mac grinned. "I'll be there. But maybe not too early."

Hannah thanked Mac as Zeke turned to Jenny. "It's been a nice evening," she heard him say.

"Can't stay away from her, can you, Mr. Pershing?" Alice's grating voice cut through the humming of other conversations. "Your bride is right beside you, and you're holding Jenny's hand. I've seen it all now!"

Jenny gasped. Mac put an arm around his wife. "Mrs. Bramwell, I think that's enough," he said in a quelling tone.

Zeke's mouth opened, but he didn't say anything.

Anger gave Hannah words she didn't know she had in her. "Zeke has known Mac and Jenny longer than he's known me, Alice. He treasures their friendship, as do I. I'll thank you to keep that in mind when you speak."

But inwardly, Hannah's heart sank as her inadequacies came to mind. She'd seen Zeke stare at Jenny earlier.

With an anguished glance at the McDougalls, Hannah let Zeke pull her away from Alice. He said nothing until after they ushered the younger Pershings into the wagons. Then he told Jonathan and David, "Take Ruth and Noah home and see to the mules and wagon. I'll expect you all in bed when I get back."

He was silent as he helped Faith and Hannah into Hannah's cart, got in, and slapped the mule on the rump to set out.

"Zeke—" Hannah said.

He shook his head, with a glance back toward Faith. So Hannah let Faith rhapsodize about the elegance of the evening they'd just experienced. "My first grown-up party," her niece said several times. "With ices and dancing."

When they arrived at the claim, Hannah sent Faith inside, telling her, "I'll help Zeke with the mule and wagon. I'll be in soon."

In the barn, Zeke led the mule to its stall. "I don't need your help."

"No," Hannah said, "but we need to talk. I'm sorry for what Alice said. I don't believe it."

The muscles in Zeke's jaw clenched, but he nodded. "I told you there's nothing between Jenny and me now."

"I said, I believe you. Jenny has told me so as well. It's clear she's happy with Mac. They're having a child."

Zeke's eyes widened. He nodded again. "So you'll still marry me?"

"Of course." What choice did either of them have? she thought. He wanted the land, and she had no alternative means of supporting herself in Oregon.

Zeke threw out his hands in a gesture of helplessness. "I want to do right by you, Hannah. But our families ain't making it easy. Between Esther's in-laws and yours—"

"I know," she whispered. She stepped closer and laid her cheek against his shoulder. "I know."

His arms came around her and he rested his chin on her hair.

Chapter 43: Raising the Roof and Tying the Knot

Zeke spent a sleepless night, worrying about the roof-raising, about Hannah and what she really thought of him, about what kind of husband he'd be. He respected her, and occasionally even liked her. Would that be enough to get them past the pettiness of people like Alice Bramwell? Enough to make a family out of the baggage each of them carried?

Saturday morning Zeke rousted his siblings out of bed before dawn. They ate a quick breakfast, then Ruth started cooking for the crowd that would soon arrive to help construct the roof. Hannah and Faith arrived not long after sun-up, bringing pies and a Dutch oven full of stew. Zeke and the twins made a table of planks on top of two stumps in the barnyard to hold the prepared dishes.

The farmers who'd agreed to help Zeke showed up not long after Hannah. Many of them brought their wives and children also. A short while later, Mac and Jenny and their children arrived from town.

Soon Zeke's yard teemed with people. Saws and hammers sounded, men shouted, children laughed. In midmorning the cacophony from the crowd stilled when Samuel Abercrombie rode into the yard on his large gelding. He swung off the horse and tied it to a fencepost.

"What are you doing here?" Zeke asked him.

"Come to help my neighbor," Abercrombie said, spitting tobacco juice. "Heard tell you're raising a new roof today."

"I don't want no trouble, Abercrombie."

"I don't aim to make any, Pershing." He pulled a hammer from his saddlebag. "Where should I start?"

"What about the lawsuit you filed?"

"I ain't claiming your house and barn. Just your timberland."

Zeke squinted at the beefy man, wondering whether he was sincere. He caught Mac's eye across the yard. Mac shrugged in a "why not?" gesture.

"Do you want my help or not?" Abercrombie spat again.

Zeke sent the man to help build the roof truss, and the sounds of men working started up again. Zeke wandered over to see Mac. "Do you think he's planning something?" he asked the lawyer.

"We'll see soon enough," Mac said. "He's not all bad. He saved my life on Laurel Hill, if you'll remember."

Zeke nodded. Mac's wagon had broken from its ropes as they'd lowered it down the hill. Only Samuel Abercrombie's brute strength kept Mac from being crushed under the wheels.

By noon, the walls to the upper story room were in place, and men began setting the rafters and crossbars for the roof. They worked in shifts, some on the roof, others moving boards below, still others eating and drinking. Every hour or so, they changed places, to allow another group to rest.

At one point, when Zeke took a break, he saw Hannah in conversation with Samuel Abercrombie. He didn't want the man harassing her, so he strode toward them. When he got within earshot, he heard Hannah say, "I don't know what you have in mind, Mr. Abercrombie, but I won't have you disturbing our household."

"You're taking a mighty uppity position, Miz Bramwell, seeing's how you ain't married Zeke Pershing yet." Abercrombie scratched his bushy beard as he spoke.

"Our wedding is in less than a week, Mr. Abercrombie. He is adding onto this house for me. I think I have a stake in what happens here."

"Well, ma'am," Abercrombie drawled, "I ain't got nothing in mind but being neighborly. I have my differences with the Pershings, but I ain't making a claim on this house of his. Just the acres he ain't using."

"It's my understanding the court is likely to dismiss your suit once we're married."

"We'll see. But in the meantime, Miz Bramwell, I'm happy to provide my labor to help with your roof. Zeke done the same for me when I built my house and barn."

"Then I thank you, Mr. Abercrombie."

Zeke moved closer to Hannah. "Is he bothering you?" he asked her.

She shook her head. "I think we understand each other."

Abercrombie grinned at Zeke. "This one reminds me of your ma. Another feisty woman. Hope Miz Bramwell keeps you on your toes, Pershing. And your bed warm at night."

Hannah's cheeks flamed, but she merely pursed her lips.

"I'm sorry about him, Hannah," Zeke said, after Abercrombie walked away.

"He's crude and he's a bully," she said. "But I can handle him. I'm only glad Jacob and Alice aren't here also. Alice's comments would likely have been worse."

"Come see the progress we've made." Zeke gestured at the house. Men were pounding nails into shingles now. They walked around the addition, and Hannah murmured surprise at the quick progress. "We worked even faster on the original cabin," he said. "But then, we had approaching winter to worry about." As they continued their inspection, he asked, "Did you expect your brother and his wife today?"

"No." Hannah sighed. "With only one arm, Jacob wouldn't have been much help. And Alice made her opinions known well enough last night. I'm sorry she insulted you and Jenny. And in Jenny's own home."

"None of it's true, you know."

"I know." She smiled up at him. "You've told me so often enough. And Jenny is one of the kindest women I've met. I hope she and I will be friends in the years ahead."

It was dusk before the last shingles were in place. Zeke would still have to caulk the seams, but he could do that in the weeks ahead. The hard work requiring many hands and backs had been accomplished that day, and his cabin was now half again as big as before, with two new good-sized bedrooms, each with a small window placed in the back wall.

The next morning, he took his siblings, Hannah, and Faith into town for church. During the service the third and last banns were read, and afterward Zeke and Hannah received congratulations from most of the congregation. The wedding was planned for Wednesday afternoon at Esther's house.

They spoke with Jacob. "Will you attend, brother?" Hannah asked him. "Bring your children, if you'd like. But not Alice."

Jacob coughed nervously. "I'll tell her to hold her tongue for the day," he said. "It would be awkward to leave her home."

"Will you close your store then?" Hannah asked. "Perhaps she should stay and mind it."

Jacob nodded. "I'll see if that will convince her to remain in town. I want to see you married, sister. And I'll take Faith back to my house. She shouldn't reside with you once you've wed."

"Faith is welcome to live with us," Zeke said. "Our first night, Hannah and I will stay on the McDougall claim. But we will return to my house the next day. Ruth is eager for Faith to join us."

"Let's wait and see. I might enroll Faith in the girls' academy in town this fall." Jacob nodded and left.

Mac and Jenny joined Zeke and Hannah. "I'm so pleased you'll start your married life in our cabin," Jenny said. "Mac and I were happy there."

"Have you made provisions for someone to live there once I move to Zeke's claim?" Hannah asked.

"Devlin Feeney has agreed to do more work on my crops," Mac said. "In exchange, I'm providing the cabin and a share of the grain."

"Why don't he file his own claim?" Zeke asked. "Plenty of land around here still."

"He's a soldier, like Robert O'Neil was. Says he's too old to hack a farm out of the wilderness, and he doesn't know a lot about farming. But he's happy to work the land we've already cleared. He'll keep my claim going and still hire out to help you, the Abercrombies, and anyone else who needs him."

"What about the school?" Hannah asked. "Who will teach this fall?"

Jenny sighed. "I don't know. And with Mr. Feeney in the cabin, there won't be a place to hold classes."

The twins wouldn't mind turning full-time to farming, Zeke thought. And maybe Hannah could teach Ruth and Noah in addition to managing the household. The other families would have to educate their own young'uns. He didn't want his wife teaching other folks' children.

Clouds rolled overhead Wednesday morning, the day of the wedding. Jacob Bramwell would drive from town to take Hannah and Faith from the McDougall claim to Esther's. Zeke's only responsibility was get himself and his siblings ready for the ceremony, though that felt like chore enough.

"Bath time," he announced as soon as they finished the noon meal. There would barely be time to clean them all up before they drove to Esther's. He hauled the tub into the new downstairs bedroom that would be his and Hannah's. Ruth heated water on the stove and filled the tub. She bathed, then Noah, then Jonathan, then David, and finally Zeke. They refilled the tub as needed to keep the water clean and warm.

By the time Zeke was dressed in Pa's old trousers and frock coat, the twins and Noah already looked disheveled. "Comb your hair again, boys," he said. "Time to go."

The twins hitched up the wagon, while Ruth packed the cake she'd made. Zeke fingered Ma's silver wedding ring and put it in his pocket. Esther had handed him the ring after church last Sunday. "You best give this to Hannah," she'd told him with a tremulous smile. "I didn't let Pa give it to Amanda. But Hannah is one who'll stick with us. Ma would've liked her."

"You think so?" Zeke said. "I hope we'll make a go of it."

Esther frowned at him. "There's no hoping, Zeke. Marriage is work, not hope. You treat Hannah right, and she'll do right by you." Those words returned to Zeke now, and he swallowed his nerves. Would he and Hannah do right by each other? He knew so little about her. But he needed a wife, and she was here. She had a backbone of steel, but a soft heart. She'd do her best, and so would he.

A crowd had already gathered in Esther's yard when Zeke and his siblings arrived. High clouds still floated overhead, but they were thinning. The afternoon promised to be pleasant—not warm, but not too cool either. The makeshift tables Zeke used for the roof-raising now lined Esther's yard, laden with food and pitchers of drinks.

"Come on, Zeke," Esther urged. "Hannah and Faith are ready. The minister's here." She looked around. "There's Jacob Bramwell. I'll take him inside, so he can escort Hannah out. Are we missing anyone?" She turned to her husband. "Daniel? Is everyone here?"

"Everyone that matters," Daniel said. "I think we're ready."

Zeke stood by the minister, with Daniel Abercrombie at his side. He'd thought about asking Mac to stand with him, but it felt awkward to have Jenny's husband be his witness. He watched Jacob Bramwell—his wife Alice nowhere in sight—escort Hannah from the house toward him. Faith walked ahead of them, carrying a posy of wildflowers and smiling broadly. Both Jacob and Hannah were somber.

When Hannah reached him, she handed her bouquet to her niece, took Zeke's arm and glanced up at him with dark, nervous eyes, a tremulous smile on her lips. He patted her hand. She presented a firm and competent face to the world, but perhaps she felt the weight of the day as much as he did.

"Dearly beloved," the minister began. And soon it was done.

Chapter 44: Making Do

The ceremony passed in a blur. Surely the most momentous event of her life thus far should take longer, Hannah thought. At the minister's prompting, Zeke said his vows, then she said hers. He leaned over to kiss her briefly, and they were married. The only proof it had happened was the silver ring on her finger. She hadn't expected a ring and wondered where it came from. It was a pretty thing, too pretty for daily wear on the farm.

Then she was accosted by well-wishers and swept into the wedding festivities Esther had planned—eating, singing, dancing. There'd been all too much celebration surrounding this marriage, with the women's party Esther hosted two weeks earlier, then the McDougalls' party, then the roof-raising, and now the wedding feast. Hannah had not anticipated her decision to accept Zeke's proposal would require so much socializing. She would rather slip slowly and privately into the role of wife—it would take some getting used to.

Soon enough, Zeke escorted her to his wagon and lifted her in. His hands on her waist were strong and steady. Her hands on his shoulders shook. She'd told herself before she didn't fear the marriage act, but now the time was here. Would they suit?

"Esther handled the wedding quite nicely, don't you think?" she said, once they were alone in the silence of the forested road.

"Mmm," was the only response Zeke gave her.

"Where did you obtain the ring?" she asked.

"It was Ma's. Esther kept it after Ma died."

"It's lovely. Thank you." She was touched he'd given her something from his mother.

"Esther thought you should have it."

His words dashed her earlier sentiment. What of you, Zeke? she wanted to ask. What did you think? They didn't speak again until they reached the McDougall claim.

"I'll put away the wagon and tend to the mules," Zeke said.

Hannah nodded. "Then I'll see to some supper." She went inside and found a basket on the table. It contained a ham, a loaf of bread, and a jar of wild strawberry jam, with a note—"Best wishes, Mac and Jenny." She smiled and laid out the food.

When Zeke came in, she told him of the gift. "Mighty nice of them," he said.

As they ate, Hannah tried to make small talk. But after getting only brief responses from Zeke, she stopped. She picked up their plates and carried them to the washtub to scrub.

"I'll do the evening chores," Zeke said, not meeting her eye. "Then shall we get on with this marriage business?"

"All right."

He hadn't returned from the barn when she finished cleaning up after supper. She donned her nightgown and sat on the side of the bed in the corner of the cabin, the bed she'd slept in for so many months, alone or with Faith.

Zeke came in. He walked over and pulled her to her feet, then slipped his arms around her. "I ain't never done this before," he said.

"You haven't?" she whispered, surprised and a little pleased.

He bent and kissed her, then slipped his hand up to cover her breast. She gasped softly. No man had ever touched her there before, though Charles had tried. It felt nice. Perhaps she and Zeke would get on all right after all.

It hurt, but not so badly as she'd been led to believe. Their first fumblings had been awkward, but pleasant. She relaxed as Zeke stroked her body. He didn't say anything about her leg, though she flinched when he first touched it. When he climbed on top of her, she felt ready for more, but it ended so quickly. A sharp pang, a few thrusts, his sigh. He kissed her, then fell asleep.

Once more during the night he'd turned to her. That time, she felt less pain, but it was over just as quickly. She barely awakened to the pleasure of his touches before he finished.

Was this all there was to it?

She wished she could talk to Jane. She had no friend in Oregon she felt comfortable speaking with about such an intimate act—she wasn't even sure she could tell Jane.

At dawn, Hannah rose. As she left the bed, Zeke stirred. "I'll do the chores," he said.

"Breakfast will be ready when you get back." She swallowed the lump in her throat and dressed.

He kissed the back of her neck as he left for the barn.

After breakfast, he said, "You best pack up your things. We'll leave for home soon as you do."

Everything she'd brought to the McDougall cabin fit in one carpetbag and her trunk. Zeke carried her belongings to the wagon. "Ready?" he asked.

She nodded.

Hannah and Zeke arrived home to find his siblings squabbling. "I tried to get them to pick up afore you got here," Ruth said. "But they won't do a thing I say."

"The loft is all ours now," Jonathan said. "You got your own room."

"But I have to walk through the loft to get to my room," Ruth said. "I don't want to see your dirty clothes on the floor. Least you can do is put 'em on your beds."

"I'm hungry," Noah said. "Will you fix pancakes, Miz Hannah?"

"I made you porridge," Ruth said. "You didn't eat it."

"I want pancakes, Miz Hannah."

Hannah sighed. "Call me 'Hannah.' I'm your sister now." She carried her carpetbag into the downstairs bedroom and took out an apron. She put it on and returned to the kitchen. "All right. Let's have pancakes."

Zeke shook his head. "Come on, Jonathan and David. We need to hoe the south field today." He turned to Noah. "You pick up the loft after you eat your breakfast. And don't give Hannah any trouble."

Zeke hauled Hannah's trunk inside, then he and the twins left Hannah alone with Ruth and Noah. Just like every other morning since she'd started as housekeeper. The only change married life brought was an ache between her thighs. She swallowed hard, wishing Zeke had kissed her before he went.

Chapter 45: Trouble on Zeke's Claim

Zeke thought he and Hannah got on pretty well in the first days after their wedding. She managed the house, as she'd been doing the past few months, and he and the twins worked the fields—either on his land or with Daniel or Douglass. Now that Hannah lived with them, she had supper waiting when they returned. Ruth seemed happy with the change—she had more leisure time, though she still helped Hannah clean up after the meal.

And he had Hannah in his bed at night. Her body pleased him, from head to toe. She'd shown him her leg before they married, but he found her scars didn't bother him at all. He relished everything about her. In fact, Zeke thought, smiling to himself, he might have wed sooner, had he known the satisfaction he could find in a woman's body. He fell asleep quickly each night after possessing her.

She seemed to like him well enough also. She didn't push him away, as he'd been told some women did their husbands. She kissed him back willingly enough, and seemed to enjoy his kisses more than Jenny had. She held him close while he made love to her.

On the Sunday morning after the wedding, Hannah had everyone ready for church on time. There was none of the rushing around that had often been necessary to get Jonathan and David to don clean clothes and Noah to slick down his hair.

After the service they all went to Esther's house for dinner. The meal also went smoothly, with Hannah helping with Esther's young'uns. Given how well the day had gone, Zeke was surprised to sense a tension in Hannah on the drive home. She sat stiffly on the wagon bench beside him, while the young'uns bantered behind them.

"Something wrong?" he asked her.

Hannah shook her head.

Ruth leaned over his shoulder. "Is Faith going to come stay with us?"

"She's welcome, you know that," Zeke said.

"It depends on her father," Hannah said. "I asked him again after church today. He's not willing yet."

"I'd dearly like to have another girl here," Ruth said, with a sigh. "And Faith is so mannerly and well-read."

"Yes," Hannah said, without anything further.

When they arrived home, the boys played outside, while Zeke took care of the animals. Hannah and Ruth went in the house. They'd started fixing a light supper when Zeke finished his chores and joined them. Ruth chattered about embroidery and fabric and other womanly things. He hadn't realized how starved his sister was for female companionship—one more good thing to come from his marriage to Hannah.

But Hannah remained quiet through the supper hour and into the evening. After the meal, the twins played checkers and Ruth read a book to Noah. Hannah sewed, darning one of Noah's socks.

Zeke sat watching his wife, imagining their night ahead. "Think I'll turn in," he said, as early as he thought he could. "You young'uns don't stay up too late."

Hannah raised her eyebrows, but didn't follow him to their room.

He waited in bed for her to join him. More than an hour passed before he heard her finally shoo the children to bed. Dusk had darkened their room when she crept in, and he heard her more than saw her disrobe and put on her nightdress.

She slipped into bed beside him, and he reached out to pull her close.

She froze, then whispered, "My monthly has started. Perhaps we shouldn't—"

Zeke sighed. He kissed her neck and rolled away. It took him a long time to get to sleep that night.

Monday morning Zeke awoke groggy and bleary-eyed. Hannah was already up when he roused himself. The twins and Noah were eating hearty bowls of porridge, and Ruth had started baking.

Hannah looked up as he entered the room. "Good morning," she said.

"Morning." He sat at the table.

She brought him a bowl of porridge and asked, "Would you like some meat also?"

"Yes, please."

She fried venison in a skillet and brought him a slice as he finished the porridge, touching his shoulder as she set the plate in front of him.

"Thank you."

After he ate, he and the twins went to the barn to gather their tools for the day. He'd arranged for other men to meet them on an uncleared portion of his claim to fell trees to take to the mill—Daniel Abercrombie, Devlin Feeney, and whichever other ex-soldiers Feeney could find who'd work for a share of the timber price. The wood should bring in enough credit to pay the men's wages and also whittle down Zeke's account at the Abernethy store in town.

Noah begged to accompany them. The boy's arm was fully mended after his fall, and the weather looked like it would be clear, so Zeke agreed. The eight-year-old skipped about the barn while his older brothers worked.

"If you're big enough to come with us, scamp," Zeke said, "you're big enough to carry a saw. Help Jonathan and David load the wagon."

Noah obliged with a grin.

They reached the woodland and found Daniel already waiting. Feeney and two friends of his arrived soon after. The men and boys worked all morning felling trees and bucking the limbs. Then they rolled the logs to the side of the field, ready to haul to the mill when Zeke had a free day or the weather was poor.

Hannah and Ruth brought the noon meal, though the women couldn't drive the wagon very close to the wooded field because the road stopped a few minutes' walk away. They hauled two baskets of food from the wagon to where the men worked. After he ate, Zeke rested awhile, his hat over his face to block the sun. Conversation from the others droned around him as he dozed. He was as happy as he'd been since before Pa died. It finally felt like his family might survive together, like he might be able to raise his siblings successfully.

And Hannah was the reason, he realized. She'd run their household through the spring, and now she was his wife—a man couldn't have it much better.

Hannah and Ruth soon left, but Zeke's good mood lasted through the afternoon. And through another night of lying wakefully beside Hannah.

The next day Zeke and his younger brothers returned to the field to fell logs again. "We got more'n enough for a trip to town already, don't we?" Jonathan complained to Zeke as they set out.

"Weather's still good," Zeke said. "I want to get as many trees cut as I can while it holds. We can haul logs in the rain, but it ain't no sport cutting wood in a downpour."

They drove the wagon as close to the field as they could and unloaded their tools. With their arms full, they traipsed through the woods to the area they'd cleared the day before.

Zeke dropped his tools, stunned. The pile of logs they'd left the day before was considerably smaller. "Someone's taken our wood."

"How could they?" David asked. "Them logs is too heavy to move without a wagon. Ain't no way to get a wagon in here."

"A determined man with a friend might roll 'em out to the road." Zeke gazed about the clearing, looking for how the theft could have been managed. "Look." He gestured at crushed underbrush making a rough path out to the road from behind the pile of logs. "That's where they went."

"Who woulda done such a thing?" Jonathan asked. "It's stealing. We worked hard for that wood."

Daniel trudged into sight along the path carved by the thieves. "Sorry I'm late."

"Did you notice, Daniel?" Zeke asked. "That trail you're on. 'Tweren't there yesterday."

Daniel frowned and looked around. "What happened to your logs? Half of 'em are gone."

"You don't know?" Zeke didn't want to suspect his friend, but Daniel's father wanted Zeke's land. Maybe old Samuel had taken what part of it he could get. Maybe Daniel had helped. "You seen your pa recently?"

Daniel shook his head. "Not since church Sunday. You seen him there, too." Daniel squinted at Zeke. "You think he stole the wood?"

"Who else would've done it?" Zeke asked. "You ain't heard him talk about it?"

"No, sir," Daniel said, sounding indignant. "Pa's a hard man, but he ain't a thief."

Zeke frowned, then picked up the two-man saw. "Well, let's get to work now. I'll have to go to town tomorrow to talk to Mac about it. And to sell the logs I got left. Might drop by your pa's claim first."

Chapter 46: Hannah's Woes

It had only been a week since her wedding day, Hannah mused as she cleaned house with Ruth on Wednesday morning. Every day seemed worse. Zeke came home Tuesday afternoon upset about someone stealing logs. She didn't blame him for being angry because of the theft, but his surliness lasted all evening. The twins and Noah fled to play in the barn after supper, and Ruth tiptoed around him in silence.

"How do you plan to find the thief?" Hannah asked.

"I rode through Samuel Abercrombie's land today. Didn't see nothing. But I still think he took the timber." Zeke sighed. "I'll go see Mac tomorrow. Ain't much he can do, I suspect. Not unless someone sees the culprit with the logs and tells me."

"Did you post a guard on the wood tonight?" she asked.

"Daniel's there now. I'll go back at midnight. And I'll take as much of the remaining wood as I can with me to town tomorrow. Be sure it ain't all stolen."

So Zeke left their bed at midnight and returned at dawn just long enough to rouse the twins to accompany him for the day. They'd left Noah with Hannah and Ruth—"You might get hurt," Zeke told the complaining lad. "Hauling the logs is too hard for you."

"When will you be home this evening?" Hannah asked.

"Don't know. Depends on what McDougall says." He clapped his hat on his head and left without another word or touch.

The first week of marriage had not brought the closeness she'd hoped for. It didn't help that she'd turned him away in bed, but a woman didn't have much choice at certain times, did she? Another question she wished she could ask Jane.

Zeke and the twins had not returned by suppertime, so she fed Ruth and

Noah, then took out paper and quill to write Jane.

> *June 25, 1851*
> *Dear Jane,*
>   *I am married. Ezekiel Pershing and I were wed a week ago in a lovely ceremony at his sister's home. Faith and I carried wildflowers, and I wore my best dress. I had trimmed my old bonnet with new ribbon.*
>   *We are settling into our life together. Zeke added onto his house—one room for us, and another for his sister Ruth. If Faith comes to live with us, which I hope Jacob will allow, then she can share with Ruth. They are good friends already.*
>   *Adapting to married life would be easier, sister, if you were here to confide in, as we used to when we were girls. I miss your loving advice and affection. There are times when I feel so alone in Oregon . . .*

Hannah's eyes stung with tears and a lump formed in her throat. Her letter had turned too gloomy—she couldn't send it to Jane. She hid it away in her trunk, planning to continue it when she was in a better frame of mind.

Zeke and the twins did not return until after dark on Wednesday, and Zeke left by himself in the pouring rain early Thursday morning. All Zeke told Hannah was, "Mac and I talked to the sheriff. Talked to the mill owner, too. But unless the logs are found with the thief, ain't nothing the law can do."

The twins told Hannah the details of their day at breakfast on Thursday after Zeke left. The three Pershings and Daniel Abercrombie spent the morning loading as many logs as possible into both Zeke's and Daniel's wagons, then they hauled the two wagons to town. Zeke sold the timber at the mill and told the mill owner to be on the lookout for similar wood.

But the mill owner had said, "Hard to tell one batch of pine from another. You ain't marked it in any way, did you?"

"Never thought to," Zeke told the man, and the owner just shrugged.

Jonathan and David hadn't been privy to the conversation between Zeke and Mac, nor to what the two men told the sheriff. "We went to see Faith while Zeke and Mac did all their palavering," Jonathan told her. "But her pa didn't want us to stay. So we offered to help in the stockroom, and then he was a lot nicer."

"Yes," Hannah said, smiling at the boys. "That sounds like Jacob. He appreciates free labor."

Zeke came home drenched Thursday night. He'd been notching the bark on the remaining logs in the clearing to mark them as his. He went to bed and was asleep before Hannah joined him.

Hannah's concern for Zeke continued through Friday. The day was sunny, and he worked in the fields again, this time clearing timber on Daniel's land. Samuel Abercrombie had been there also, helping his son. Zeke seethed that evening when he told Hannah about working all day with the man he thought had stolen from him.

"How did you handle it?" she asked him quietly.

"Stayed as far away from him as I could."

Zeke turned in early, and Hannah followed him into their room. He took off his shirt, and she moved toward him. "My monthly's done," she told him. He put his arms around her and buried his face in her neck. "Come to bed," she whispered.

His loving was tender, but as quick as the week before. She felt a stirring of pleasure as he entered her. But he finished and fell asleep almost before she recognized that what she felt was arousal, that perhaps there was something more to marriage than she'd experienced thus far.

The following Sunday, Hannah joined Esther and Jenny after the service. "How's our blushing bride?" Esther asked.

"Just fine," Hannah said.

"Hard to see how you could be," Esther said, "with all the goings on over the stolen timber. Daniel's been talking of little else."

"Mac also," Jenny said. "What a despicable thing for someone to do."

"It has kept Zeke preoccupied," Hannah said. She didn't want to talk about the timber—how could they ignore Zeke's suspicion that Esther's father-in-law was the culprit?

"Not too preoccupied to keep you happy, I hope," Esther said. She leaned toward Hannah. "You are happy you married my brother, ain't you?"

"Of course," Hannah said. Wives shouldn't tell tales about their husbands to other women. And she certainly shouldn't complain to Zeke's sister or to Jenny—the woman he'd first proposed to.

"Well, you're not blushing," Esther said. "So my brother must be doing something wrong."

"Now, Esther—" Jenny said.

"Well, he must be," Esther insisted.

Jenny left, then Esther whispered to Hannah. "Come see me tomorrow afternoon. I want to talk with you."

Hannah wondered what Esther had to say to her, but she agreed to visit.

Monday afternoon, after she and Ruth did the laundry with some help from Noah, Hannah and the two children set out for Esther's house. "Esther invited us," was all Hannah could say in response to Noah's question about why they were going.

When they arrived, Esther gave them all pie and milk. She sent Ruth outside to pick peas with Noah, Jonah, and three-year-old Cordelia and put Sammy and Abigail down to sleep. Then she turned to Hannah. "Now we should be able to talk a bit," Esther said. "Though Cordelia might be back inside soon. She tries to go all day without a nap, but can't always make it."

After handing Hannah a mug of tea, Esther said, "So tell me what's wrong between you and Zeke?"

Hannah shook her head. "I can't talk about my husband behind his back."

Esther snorted. "He's my brother. Even if he's older'n me, I know he ain't perfect. Is he treating you right?"

"Of course." And Hannah remembered using the same words in the churchyard the day before when Esther asked if Zeke kept her happy. Tears welled in her eyes—what was happiness in a marriage anyway?

"Oh, Hannah," Esther said, and took Hannah into her arms.

Hannah wept, for what she didn't know. Finally, she raised her head off Esther's shoulder. "I'm sorry. There's no reason for me to cry."

"Well, there's always a reason," Esther said. "I take it Zeke ain't satisfying you in bed."

"What do you mean?" Hannah said, drawing away from Esther.

"Then he isn't. If he was, you'd know what I meant." Esther sighed. "'Tweren't never a problem for Daniel'n me. We were kissing and such almost from the day we met. 'Twas a good thing we found a preacher when we did." She sighed again. "But then, that's why we got three kids in less'n three years of marriage."

Hannah didn't know how to respond to Esther. The younger woman seemed to know so much more than Hannah did. So she listened as Esther said, "You tell that brother of mine what you like and what you don't."

"What do you mean?"

"When he touches you. In bed. Tell him."

"Well, there isn't much time to talk—" Hannah managed to say.

Esther broke into laughter, loud peals of it, but it sounded loving, not taunting. "So that's the problem." She pressed Hannah's arm. "Then you tell him to slow down. To make you happy first."

"What do you mean?"

"Just tell him," Esther said. "Then come talk to me again."

Chapter 47: Suspicions

Zeke had spoken again with Mac at church on Sunday. "Any news in town about the theft?" he'd asked.

Mac shook his head. "I stopped by the sheriff's office yesterday. He hadn't heard anything."

"Did he talk to Abercrombie?"

"Sheriff said Abercrombie denied having anything to do with it. Same as he told you."

Zeke exhaled deeply. "Who else could it be?"

Mac shrugged. "Stealing doesn't sound like something Abercrombie would do. He's a bully and I could see him getting into a fight, even at his age. But he has some sense of honor."

Zeke spat on the ground. "Then why is he trying to take my land?"

"Now you and Hannah are married, I'll file another motion with Judge Quinn tomorrow. We'll see if we can get the case dismissed. Maybe that will flush out whether Abercrombie had anything to do with your missing logs."

The clouds Monday morning seemed likely to burn off by midday. Zeke, the twins, the two Abercrombie brothers, and Feeney were logging again, when Mac rode his black stallion into the field. Mac dismounted, saying, "Hannah told me you'd be here. I passed her on the road toward Esther's house—she said she was headed there for a visit."

"What's happening?" Zeke asked, wiping the sweat from his forehead with a handkerchief.

"I filed the dismissal motion with Judge Quinn. Took the time for a little *ex parte* conversation." Mac grinned.

"What's that mean?"

"It means I talked to him without Abercrombie or his lawyer there. I told the judge you were married now and it was time to put this foolishness to an end."

"What'd the judge say?"

Mac shrugged. "He couldn't tip his hand, but he agreed he'd set another hearing date for two weeks out, after Abercrombie's lawyer has had a chance to respond to my motion. But there isn't anything to debate—you're married, the law says you can keep the full claim."

Zeke nodded. "Thanks, Mac."

"How're you and Hannah doing anyway?" Mac asked, as he turned back to his horse.

Zeke glanced around. Jonathan and David were nearby—too close to have any man-to-man conversation with Mac. "Just fine," he said.

After supper Zeke told Hannah and the rest of his family, "Mac's going to get Abercrombie's lawsuit dismissed."

Ruth clapped, and Hannah said, "That's good news."

"Yes." Zeke rolled a cigarette. "But that probably won't stop Abercrombie from doing something else—like stealing more timber."

"Are you sure it was him?" Hannah asked.

"Who else could it be? He's the only man in the territory with a grudge against me." Zeke licked the paper on the cigarette and lit it.

"What about Mr. Feeney?" David asked. "He's an odd sort."

Zeke considered. He didn't know Feeney well, but the man worked hard and seemed pleasant enough. "I'm paying him a fair wage. Why would Feeney want to steal from me?"

"I don't like him much," Jonathan said.

"That's because he orders you around when you ain't working," Zeke said with a grin. "Sometimes he catches on to you sooner'n I do."

Hannah rose. "I'm turning in," she said, lighting a candle from the oil lamp, then heading to their room.

Zeke finished his smoke, then followed Hannah to bed. He undressed and climbed in beside her, taking her in his arms. He kissed her, then stroked her scarred thigh and moved his hand up under her nightgown to cup her breast.

As his loving progressed, she whispered to him, "Slow down, Zeke."

He pulled back, trying to see her face in the dark. "Am I hurting you?"

He felt her shake her head. "No. But I might enjoy it more if you took more time at it."

"I didn't think women liked this sort of thing."

She gave a soft, throaty laugh. "I haven't had much of a chance to find out, have I?"

So Zeke tried to take her slowly, until he couldn't wait any longer. Afterward, he asked sleepily, "Was that better?"

"A little," she murmured.

The week continued clear and warm, though each morning began with hazy clouds that faded after the sun rose. Tuesday was July 1, but Zeke noticed the changing of the month only because his younger siblings talked about the Fourth of July celebration in town planned for Friday. The sown fields needed weeding, so he and the twins and Noah left off their timbering and switched to hoeing.

After three days of long, monotonous work, the boys were ready for a holiday. Truth be told, Zeke was also. Though he probably needed a long nap more. His daily labors took a toll on his body, then bedding Hannah tired him further, even if he couldn't resist the time spent with her each night. She let him do whatever he wanted to her body, urging him to continue some things and to slow down others. He tried, he really did, but he was so tired, he couldn't always take the time she wanted him to.

A high haze blanketed the sky on the morning of the Fourth, but Zeke thought the thin layer of cloud would dissipate by midday, as had happened earlier in the week. The family was in a cheerful mood as they piled baskets of food and blankets into the wagon.

"There ain't room for everyone," Jonathan complained. "Can I ride Red to town?"

"I want to ride," David said.

"I was going to ride him. But you two both can, if you keep him to a walk," Zeke said. He wouldn't mind sitting beside his wife, though Red could use some exercise.

"I'm hoping to bring Faith back with us," Hannah said. "If you don't mind."

What was one more young'un in the house? Zeke shook his head. "Fine by me, if your brother permits it."

By the time they reached town, crowds had already gathered in Abernethy Green. The Pershings spread their blankets beside Esther's family, though Zeke frowned when he noticed Samuel Abercrombie and the rest of the Abercrombies on the other side of Esther. Stood to reason, since she was an Abercrombie by marriage, but he didn't like being so close to the man he suspected of stealing his wood.

Other friends were nearby also—Doc and Mrs. Tuller, Mac and Jenny, the Binghams who had also attended the school Hannah taught. Zeke tried to ignore Abercrombie by spending his time talking to the others.

The women served the food as potluck, and Zeke heaped his plate. He stood by Mac and asked, "What's going on with the lawsuit?"

Mac shrugged. "Abercrombie's lawyer filed a short response. It doesn't say much. Not much he can say. I suspect we'll get the case dismissed at the hearing."

Hannah and Jenny joined their husbands. Zeke noticed Jenny's figure was thickening. He glanced at Hannah, taller and thinner than Jenny—he'd married a handsome woman, he realized. When he'd first met her, he focused on her sharp tongue and limping gait. Now he knew how her body looked under the dark dresses she usually wore, how she softened when he kissed her, how her voice smiled at him when she whispered in the dark.

Jenny would always be his first love, but he and Hannah could make a life together. It could be a good life. And he hoped he would soon see Hannah's waist swelling as Jenny's did now.

Chapter 48: Fourth of July Fireworks

After days of seeing only family on the farm, Hannah relished the throng of people at the Fourth of July celebration in Oregon City. She talked with Jenny and Esther, who assured her the afternoon would bring a wonderful parade, followed by cannon and rifle salutes to the nation, the governor, the soldiers, and anyone else the town fathers thought deserving of a volley. And then the fireworks would start.

The food was as plentiful as at the parties earlier in the summer to celebrate Zeke's and Hannah's nuptials. Hannah and Ruth brought more than enough provisions for their family, but all the families shared potluck, and she enjoyed eating something other than her own cooking.

After they ate, Hannah found her brother Jacob and asked if Faith could return with her to Zeke's farm.

"She hasn't packed any clothes," Jacob said.

"I'll go home right now and put some things together," Faith said, her face beaming, and she rushed off before her father could respond.

"You stop, young miss," Alice called after her. "I need your help."

Jacob put a hand on his wife's arm. "Let's give the girl a week or so," he said. "You and she been arguing day in and day out. Maybe some time away will let you both settle." He turned to Hannah. "Bring her back a week from Sunday?"

Hannah smiled and nodded. "Of course."

Alice glared at Hannah, but said no more. Soon Faith returned with a bundle, which Hannah told her to put in Zeke's wagon.

The haze of the morning never dissipated, and the clouds hung warm and heavily above them. By the time the parade began, Hannah felt sated with food and conversation. She and Esther sat on a blanket with baby Abigail napping between them. The Pershing children ate from all the dishes she brought, as well as from those Esther and others prepared. Noah whined he was tired, so she told him to rest on the blanket with her, but at the first bugle blow he raced away to see the parade. The other children, including Faith, followed him. Only the baby remained with the adults.

"Don't you want to watch the parade?" Esther said, as she rose to follow her older children.

Hannah shook her head. Standing didn't appeal to her. "If you like, I'll stay here and watch Abigail for you."

Esther sighed. "That would be a blessing. She's such a little thing, but carrying her all the time weighs me down. Will you be all right alone here?"

Hannah gestured at the crowd. "I'm hardly alone. I'll be fine."

After Esther left, Hannah smiled at the baby sleeping beside her. Perhaps she'd have a little one of her own at next year's Fourth of July. The way Zeke carried on each night, it wouldn't take long to find out if she could have children.

As she thought of Zeke, he appeared standing above her. "May I join you?" he asked.

She smiled and waved him to the spot Esther had vacated. "What about the parade?"

He sat. "I've seen it before. You and the baby made a pretty picture here."

"Thank you." He rarely complimented her, though she wondered if he'd been referring to her or the baby as "pretty." "Who's in the parade?"

"Just about every group in town you can imagine. Every regular Army platoon. Every volunteer regiment. Every club."

"Why aren't you marching?"

He shrugged. "Pa used to march with the Army veterans. But I ain't much of a joiner. All I want to do is farm." He sighed. "But Abercrombie seems bent on keeping me from it."

"You don't have any proof he's the thief," Hannah said.

"There ain't no one else it could be."

She ached to correct his grammar, but now they were married she was determined not to belittle him. Still, she would make sure their future children spoke correctly. She'd already improved Ruth's grammar immensely. And she tried with Noah and the twins.

Zeke lay on the ground beside Abigail and soon fell asleep. His chest rose and fell, while his face relaxed in slumber. He was a nice-looking man. Not the handsomest man she'd known, but pleasing. She thought of what his hands and body did to her in the dark and wondered what it would be like to lie with her husband outdoors in the sunshine. She blushed at her own licentiousness and reached to push Zeke's hair out of his eyes. He mumbled, but didn't wake.

He didn't sleep long, and awoke before dusk arrived. As the sun turned the clouds pink and then red, men set up the munitions and announced the fireworks show would begin. Zeke's and Esther's families returned to their blankets. The children shouted and squealed as gunpowder cracked and lights flashed. Abigail startled at the noise, and Esther gathered her clan to return home.

Noah, professing to no longer be sleepy, convinced Zeke and Hannah to stay until the show ended. Hannah leaned her head back onto Zeke's sturdy shoulder and watched the sky light up. His arm came around her, and she felt as safe and protected as she ever had.

In the dark they packed up the wagon. The twins rode Red again, and Zeke drove the others. Hannah sat beside him, and Faith and Ruth chattered behind them. Noah succumbed to sleep by the time they'd left town.

Hannah gazed at the stars overhead, leaning into Zeke as she had on the green. His solid form soothed her, and she began to doze like Noah.

When they reached home, Zeke told the twins to care for the animals and wagon, and he carried Noah into the cabin and up to the loft to the boy's bed. Hannah, Ruth, and Faith brought the baskets and blankets inside and washed the dishes and pots. By the time they were done, the boys and Zeke were all in bed. Hannah gave the girls a candle and took another to light her way to bed.

"I've waited for you," Zeke said from the bed.

In the candlelight, Hannah put on her nightdress and crawled in beside him. She reached to blow out the candle.

"Leave it," he said, running his hands from her breasts down to her hips.

He kissed her and stroked her as she'd been teaching him she liked. Slowly tonight. Slowly. Until her hips rose to meet him, she arched against him, and pleasure filled her.

"So that's what Esther meant," she murmured after Zeke finished and she nestled against his sleeping form, drowsy and replete. "No wonder she thought I would blush."

For the next several days, Hannah returned to her routine on the farm. After taking Friday off for the Fourth of July celebration, Zeke did not want to spend time in town for church that Sunday. Hannah acquiesced, though she took Faith, Ruth, and Noah for a picnic Sunday afternoon while Zeke and the twins worked. Otherwise, she and the girls handled the household chores, and Noah went to the fields with the men whenever Zeke would permit.

The days were monotonous, but the nights . . . . Hannah smiled at her chores whenever she thought of the nights. She grew bolder, and so did Zeke, and the nights became their private oasis, a refuge from the tedium and concerns of everyday living.

Or that's how she thought of it. She wondered what Zeke thought, but he never said, he just turned to her as soon as they were both in bed. Her body felt like it was singing, but something seemed lacking in the daytime, and she pondered whether all husbands and wives kept such a distance between them.

The following Sunday she insisted they should attend church services. "I told Jacob I'd bring Faith back today," she said. "She's been here ten days."

"Do I have to go home?" Faith asked. "Please, may I stay?"

Hannah put an arm around her niece's shoulders. "I'd be happy to keep you, and I'll tell your father so. But it's up to him."

Faith packed her bag, and they went to town. Faith sat in the same pew as the Pershings, though Jacob and his family were there also. After the service, Hannah talked to her brother. "Faith is enjoying her time with Ruth. Mightn't she stay?"

Jacob hesitated and turned to Alice. "Another week wouldn't hurt, would it?"

Alice sniffed. "I suppose not."

Faith beamed, and the matter was settled, Hannah thought. But as Hannah started away to speak to other friends, Alice called after her, "Don't turn the girl away from her family. We'll be all she has when your marriage to Zeke Pershing is in ruins."

Hannah stumbled, her weight on her bad leg as the words struck her.

Recovering her balance, she turned back to Alice. "I think my marriage is built on a better foundation than yours," she said quietly. But she wondered again—was the physical act of marriage and a focus on children not their own enough to carry a couple through a lifetime?

"Well!" Alice exclaimed. "I think I need Faith at home after all."

Jacob shrugged at his sister. "Perhaps it would be better if Faith remains in town for a while."

Faith gave Hannah a stricken look, but Hannah told her niece, "You must do what your father says."

On the ride home, Zeke seemed upset. "What's wrong?" Hannah asked.

"Hearing in Abercrombie's lawsuit is tomorrow. Mac wants us both there."

"That's no problem for me. I'm happy to attend."

"The case is likely to get dismissed," Zeke said, then exhaled deeply. "But Mac says there ain't nothing can be done about the missing timber."

"You might need to let the timber go," Hannah said.

"It ain't right. The man's a thief."

Mac had correctly predicted the outcome of the hearing. The judge questioned Zeke and Hannah, but as soon as they confirmed they were married, he told Samuel Abercrombie and his lawyer he had no choice but to issue a writ dismissing the case.

"There's another matter between the parties," Mac said. "Regarding stolen property."

Abercrombie stood and shouted, "Now look here, McDougall! You done sicced the sheriff on me for no reason."

The judge shook his head. "If there's another problem, file a new case. All I'm prepared to address this morning is the land claim."

Tuesday evening, Zeke came home from the fields in a dark mood. "What's wrong?" Hannah asked.

"More timber gone. Everything we cut yesterday. And there's trees felled we ain't cut. They're gone, too."

"Who—?"

"It's got to be Abercrombie. He's mad he can't get my land. So he's taking my trees instead."

Chapter 49: More Timber Missing

The weather turned beastly hot that week. Zeke and the twins worked in the fields on Wednesday, the day after he'd discovered the missing timber. Feeney and two of his ex-Army pals labored with them.

"Ain't you going to tell McDougall about it?" Jonathan asked as they stopped for a drink of water.

Zeke spat. "He says he can't do nothing. I'll see him next time I'm in town." He turned to the hired hands. "You men seen anything?"

Feeney shook his head. "We worked on those logs with you all day Monday. Sure was a shame to lose 'em. High quality timber."

"All the wood on this claim is high quality. Tall, virgin trees. Not scrubby like on Douglass Abercrombie's land." Zeke wiped his forehead. That was why he suspected Samuel Abercrombie. He didn't think Daniel was involved, and he hated to blame Douglass, though the man had a reason to regret his poor choice of timberland.

"We'll let you know if we see anything," Feeney said, taking a hoe to the next row of corn. "And you let me know if you need one of us to guard the wood."

"Guess we'll have to post guards when we can't get the hewn logs to town right away," Zeke said. A man ought to be able to trust his neighbors enough to leave timber on his land for a day or two, but not when a thief skulked about the territory.

Zeke and his brothers had agreed to work Daniel's land on Thursday. That morning they arrived at Daniel's claim right after breakfast.

"God damn it, Feeney," Zeke heard Daniel shout as he and the twins rode into the yard. "What'd'ya mean the wood's gone?"

"We cut them trees with you on Tuesday, boss," Feeney said. "But they's gone this morning. We passed your timberland on our way here. The logs are gone."

"Let's go look," Daniel said.

Zeke told his brothers to start hoeing Daniel's wheat field, then he rode to Daniel's timber claim with Feeney and Daniel. When they arrived, Feeney pointed out the tracks where logs had been dragged away. Several sets of hoof marks and boot prints dotted the area also.

"Just like on my land," Zeke said.

"Well, then, it ain't Pa," Daniel told Zeke. "He wouldn't steal from me. Pa can be mighty tetchy, but he wouldn't steal from kin."

"Don't be so sure," Zeke muttered. But he had to admit old Samuel Abercrombie tended to stick by his sons. Still, Zeke fumed all day as the hot sun beat down on his back while he hoed Daniel's fields. And he fumed more as he and the boys rode home and did their evening chores. Who could be stealing the logs?

After supper, Hannah asked Zeke what was bothering him. "You've been quiet all evening," she said. "What's wrong?"

That was one thing he didn't like about having a wife. She always wanted to talk. Zeke preferred to mull problems over in his own head, without jabbering about it. "Nothing," he said.

"Daniel Abercrombie had some of his logs stolen," David said. "Mr. Feeney noticed 'em gone this morning."

Hannah gasped. "Then it's not only your timber missing."

"Seems not," Zeke said, resting his stockinged feet on the stool in front of his chair. He'd taken off his boots when he entered the house.

"Samuel Abercrombie wouldn't steal from his own son, would he?" she asked, setting a mug of spiced tea beside him.

He had to admit having her dote on him was pleasant. Made up for some of the complications of having a wife. Evenings were less busy—the twins and Noah did most of the after-supper chores while he sat. Hannah and Ruth sewed or read after they washed the dishes. Faith had returned to town, and Ruth and Hannah seemed to miss her.

"Well, what about Mr. Abercrombie?" Hannah repeated.

"I don't know." Zeke sighed. "If it ain't him, who is it? No one else in these parts has it in for me."

"Wouldn't someone want the logs for the money? They're worth a pretty penny." Hannah settled into her chair next to his and picked a shirt from her mending basket.

"Of course they are. Californians buy all the logs we Oregonians can produce. And my timber was already hewn and burled. Saved whoever took 'em a lot of time."

"People in Oregon aren't any different than elsewhere," Hannah said. "I'm sure there are some who'd be happy to take advantage of someone else's labor. And if they're stealing from other men's land also, it might not be someone with a grudge against you."

Zeke harrumphed. "Could be anyone, if that's the case. My money's still on Abercrombie." He sipped his tea and wondered how he could catch the bastard in the act.

No more lumber turned up missing the rest of the week. The days remained hot and dry, though thin clouds drifted across the sky in the late afternoons. Sunday morning, July 20, Hannah hurried the Pershing family to church. Zeke would have preferred to stay home, but he also wanted to talk to Mac about the theft of Daniel's timber.

After the service, Samuel Abercrombie strode over to Zeke. "You heard 'bout Daniel's logs going missing, ain't you?" the large man bellowed as he neared. "I ain't done it, and I ain't stole your wood neither. Proof is, I had some stolen last night."

"You?" Zeke asked incredulously. Was the man lying? Had he moved his own timber to reduce the suspicion on himself?

"Yeah, me." Abercrombie crossed his arms across his beefy chest. "Passed by my clearing on the way here this morning. Everything I cut yesterday was gone."

"So who do *you* think done it?" Zeke asked, standing his ground. Out of the corner of his eye, he saw Mac approaching.

"What's going on, Abercrombie?" Mac asked.

Abercrombie spat on the churchyard ground. "Pershing here thinks I'm stealing from my own land and my own son."

"I ain't said that," Zeke protested.

"But you're thinking it." Abercrombie turned to McDougall. "Daniel had logs stolen last week. I had more stolen last night. The Pershings and Daniel were felling trees last Wednesday. Thursday most of Daniel's wood gone missing. Then yesterday I cut wood with Douglass on my claim. 'Tweren't there this morning. I wonder if Zeke here ain't stealing from my family what he thinks I stole from him."

"Now wait a minute." Zeke's hands balled into fists. Abercrombie outweighed him by fifty pounds, but he was thirty-five years younger. If he could keep out of the way of the man's fists for a few minutes, he might be able to take the old bastard.

"Who else knows about the wood?" Mac asked.

"All them Pershings do," Abercrombie said. "Zeke and his whole family. Any of 'em coulda told anyone."

"The same goes for your family," Zeke said. "Daniel and Douglass both know. And Feeney and his crew have worked for both of us."

"Feeney?" Mac said. "My tenant?"

Zeke nodded, trying to relax his hands. "He's hiring himself out all around the valley. Does good work. Brings in his Army buddies when we need more laborers. Quite a few ex-cavalrymen in these parts now. Robert O'Neil was one of the early ones."

Mac nodded. "O'Neil's a good man. Feeney seems to be, too. Most of the regular Army types are used to long hours and hard work. And they do what they're told."

"Feeney's the one told me when my second lot went missing," Zeke said. "Seems like a reliable fellow."

Abercrombie spat again. "I ain't had any trouble with him. Nor my sons neither. And Feeney didn't work with me yesterday."

"Have you talked to the sheriff?" Mac asked.

"Not since the second theft," Zeke said. "I wanted to see you first."

Mac shrugged. "Why don't the two of you—and Daniel, since he had wood stolen also—go see the sheriff this week? Or I can talk to him tomorrow and send him out your way."

"Would you mind doing that, Mac?" Zeke asked. "We're pretty busy on the farm."

"All right by you, Abercrombie?" Mac said. "I'll ask him to see you and Daniel also."

"Fine." Abercrombie squinted at Zeke. "But don't you tell him I stole from you. I ain't done it."

"I'll tell him what I know," Zeke said.

After Abercrombie left, Mac said to Zeke, "Do you have a minute more? I have a favor to ask."

"What's that?" Zeke said.

"I need to make a trip to California. My friend Nate passed away in San Francisco. I'd left him with my power of attorney over the assets I acquired there. I need to make other arrangements."

"What can I do?"

"I can't take Jenny and the children. And with her in a delicate condition . . . " Mac's voice trailed off, then he resumed. "I know it's awkward for you with her. But you've been a good friend for a long time, and I trust you to watch out for her."

Zeke swallowed. He did feel awkward around Jenny. But he couldn't refuse Mac's request. And he thought Hannah liked Jenny also. "All right," he said. "When do you have to leave?"

Chapter 50: A Surprise for Hannah

On the way home from church, Hannah listened to Zeke describe his discussion with Samuel Abercrombie and Mac McDougall about the stolen timber. She didn't know what to think—could Abercrombie have set this up? It seemed less and less likely. While he might conceivably have taken Daniel's wood, would he have moved his own logs? Maybe Douglass had helped him—Zeke thought Douglass too dependent on his father. But it all seemed highly improbable. Who else might have stolen the wood?

Monday she and Ruth were too busy with laundry for her to worry about the stolen trees. The sheriff stopped by the claim while she and Ruth were outside with the washtub. She pointed the lawman toward the field where Zeke planned to work that day.

That evening, Zeke told her, "Sheriff don't know anything. He come to see me first. Hadn't even talked to Daniel or his pa yet. I asked him to come back after he done so, but I ain't seen him again."

Esther had invited Hannah and Ruth to join her and Jenny McDougall on Tuesday. "We're having a quilting," Esther told Hannah after church on Sunday. "Rachel's coming, too. And Harriet and Louisa Abercrombie. I might invite a few other women also."

"I don't have anything to quilt," Hannah said.

"Bring whatever scraps you have," Esther said. "We'll piece together a baby quilt for Jenny. Ruth'll know what to do."

Hannah and Ruth cut up some old shirts and packed them to take to the quilting. Tuesday Hannah packed bread and cheese for the men to take with them to the fields, then she and Ruth drove the wagon to Esther's. Most of the other women were already there, even Jenny had driven from town earlier in the morning.

Hannah sat in the corner near Jenny, while Ruth found a place near her

278

sister Rachel. Annabelle and Rose Abercrombie had come with their mother, but Ruth didn't chat with her former schoolmates. Esther's children milled around on the floor beside the women's skirts playing with wooden blocks.

"Thank you for letting Zeke check on the children and me while Mac is gone," Jenny whispered to Hannah.

"Where is Mac going?" Hannah asked, surprised.

"To California," Jenny said. "Didn't Zeke tell you?"

"No," Hannah said slowly. It surprised her not only that Mac was traveling so far, but also that he wanted Zeke to be responsible for his family in his absence. She remembered her first encounter with Zeke—when the man who was now her husband had struck Mac. Zeke had seemed like such a reprobate at the time.

Jenny explained Mac needed to check on some property, and she didn't want to travel with him. "I'd love to go to California sometime," Jenny said with a sigh. "Mac says it is beautiful. But not now. Not until the baby comes. Maria is teething again, and William will have school in the fall."

"How long will Mac be gone?" Hannah asked.

"I don't know," Jenny said. "I've told him he must be back before the baby is born. He was such a help for me with William."

The conversation flowed around Hannah, but she spoke only when someone asked her a direct question. Just how long would Zeke be keeping an eye on Jenny? And how involved would his responsibilities be? And why hadn't he said anything to her?

Esther said something about Daniel's dirty boots, which made the other women laugh. "Douglass is even worse'n his little brother," Louisa said. "Annabelle, Rose, and I all tell him to clean 'em up afore he comes inside, but he don't listen."

"They both get it from their father," Harriet Abercrombie said. "Samuel ain't never seen the need to scrape his boots afore entering a house. I tried to teach them boys, but my words never were enough to overcome his example."

Hannah listened to the women gossip about their husbands. She never wanted to become a wife who complained about her husband's bad behavior. But dirty boots in the house was a far less grievous offense than Zeke's assenting to look after another man's wife—particularly when that wife was a woman he'd formerly asked to marry him. She stole a glance at

Jenny—was he over his infatuation with this woman or not?

On the wagon ride home with Ruth, and through the late afternoon while they cooked supper, Hannah continued to fret over Zeke's failure to tell her about Mac's departure. When he and the boys arrived home that evening, she was ready to ask him. She headed for the barn as soon as she heard them arrive. "Boys, you go on inside and clean up," she told them. "I need a word with Zeke."

Zeke turned to her, looking exhausted. But she had no sympathy tonight. "What is it, Hannah?"

She paused a moment, waiting for David to haul the door shut. "Why didn't you tell me Mac had to travel to California?"

"I don't know. Why does it matter?"

"*Why does it matter?*" She didn't like the shrill tone in her voice, but she plowed ahead. "Because you'll be spending time with Jenny, I hear."

Zeke looked at her, puzzled. "So? I've spent lots of time with Jenny over the years."

"*That's* why it matters," Hannah said. Now she sounded like a fishwife. "Because all I've heard since I got to Oregon last October was how you and Jenny were sweethearts. How you planned to marry her, until Mac returned." The lump in her throat made it hard to swallow.

"But you're my wife now."

Second choice, she thought to herself. Jenny was prettier. Jenny didn't limp. Jenny was small and beautiful and happy. Everything Hannah was not. A sob escaped her.

"Hannah, it's nothing," Zeke said, taking her by the shoulders. "Mac and Jenny are my friends. We've been through a lot together. I can't turn 'em down. Not when Mac asked me to watch out for her. I thought you liked Jenny."

"I do," she wailed. "But—"

"Do you want me to tell him I won't? Because if that's what you want—"

"No." She inhaled deeply and sighed. "No. You can't do that."

"That's right," he said. "I can't."

Mac left on a ship bound for California on Friday. Hannah took her family to church again on Sunday. She smiled pleasantly as Zeke led her to talk with Jenny and the McDougall children after the service. She held her head up when others in the congregation gawked at the spectacle of Zeke handing Jenny into one wagon, then turning to Hannah to help her into another.

She didn't complain again to Zeke, but found herself holding back tears as she cooked. She tried to hide it from Ruth, but the girl asked one day, "What's wrong, Hannah? You seem sad these days."

"I'm fine, Ruth. Merely a bit tired."

Ruth chuckled. "It's almost like you're having a baby. Esther always gets tetchy when she's first expecting." Then the girl grinned at her. "Are you?"

"Oh, Ruth. That isn't likely—" Hannah stopped. Could it be? It had been five weeks since her monthly. There'd only been the one since her marriage.

Oh, could it be? Her soul jumped. "Time will tell," she said to Ruth. "Don't you say anything until I know."

Chapter 51: To Catch a Thief

Every year, Zeke sweltered for a week or two during the height of the Oregon summer. This year, the heat hit during the last week of July and into early August. He and his brothers worked outside every day, and by midafternoon they were soaked in sweat. The grubbiness of farm work hadn't bothered Zeke in earlier years. But now the children lived with him. Living alone, he'd always been neat, but now Hannah imposed a standard of cleanliness he hadn't maintained since his mother died. So he made the boys wash up when they returned home each evening, and he made his ablutions with them.

As he scrubbed his face and hands on Friday, August 1, beneath a hazy summer sky, Zeke pondered the timber thefts. He hadn't missed any more wood, but then he hadn't cut any more either. Maybe he should try to trap the thief—at church this Sunday, he could announce he'd be felling timber in the week ahead. He'd stand guard after the logs were cut to see what happened.

He wouldn't tell anybody about his plan, not even Daniel. He trusted Daniel, but not the rest of the Abercrombies.

While Hannah talked with Jenny and Esther and other women after the Sunday service, Zeke made sure all the men present knew he'd be logging on Monday. Then Zeke joined Hannah and Jenny, and he asked Jenny how she was doing. She and her children seemed fine. Watching out for her, as Mac requested, wasn't much of a burden, and he didn't understand Hannah's reluctance to have him take on the obligation.

As they drove home after church, Hannah asked, "Why'd you tell everyone you were cutting timber? You don't usually talk about your farm work."

Zeke shrugged. His wife was an inquisitive woman. "Just making small talk, I suppose."

"Most men around here are working the fields these days. Why do you want to log?" Jonathan asked from behind the wagon bench. "Logging's hard work in this heat."

"Trees bring in cash money," Zeke said. "I want to pay down my account at Abernethy's store. The balance is growing mighty high, and will likely stay there till after harvest, if I don't sell some lumber."

The twins grumbled, but followed him to the timber stand on Monday. They felled trees all day, then rolled the stripped trunks to the edge of the clearing.

In the evening when Hannah went to bed, Zeke followed her into their room and told her he'd be standing guard over their timber during the night.

"Is that why you made it known you'd have more lumber this week?" she asked, arching her brow. "Why didn't you tell me?"

"Didn't want it to get around."

She frowned at him. "You can trust me, Zeke. And your brothers. You haven't told them either, have you?"

He shook his head. "I can handle this."

She sighed. "You're not alone anymore. Please don't keep me out of your worries."

"I'll be going now." He kissed her cheek. Then he found his rifle and left.

He hiked to the clearing in the warm night air, and settled himself behind some brush, rifle in his lap. The quarter moon shone bright above him in the clear night sky. He wondered whether its light would encourage or dissuade the thieves.

Through the night he dozed fitfully. In the morning, the logs were still there.

Zeke stumbled groggily back to the cabin in time for breakfast Tuesday morning. The rest of the household was rousing, and he and the boys did the morning chores while Hannah and Ruth fixed the meal. After he returned from the barn and washed his face, Hannah shook her head as she handed him his plate. She looked a little pale.

"What's wrong?" he asked her.

"Just wondering what happened last night."

"Nothing."

"Are we logging again today, Zeke?" David asked.

He shook his head. "Got to work on Daniel's claim. Told him Sunday we'd spend today with him."

"You ain't shaved this morning," Noah piped up.

"You haven't," Hannah said to the boy.

"I probably won't," Zeke said, rubbing his scratchy cheek. "We got to get going."

"Can I come?" Noah asked.

"May I," Hannah said.

"Not today," Zeke said. "It'll be a long day. And it's hot. You'd be better off at home today."

As he, Jonathan, and David walked to Daniel's claim, Zeke cautioned the twins, "Don't tell anyone I was watching the timber last night."

"Is that where you went?" Jonathan said. "Hannah wouldn't tell us where you'd gone."

"You see anything?" David asked.

"No."

They weeded and tilled Daniel's cornfield until dusk. As they worked, Daniel asked Zeke, "How's Jenny doing?"

"Seems fine," Zeke said. "At least, she did on Sunday, last time I seen her. Why?"

Daniel shrugged. "My ma said something about you spending a lot of time talking to her."

"You know Mac asked me to."

"That's what I told Ma. She understands. I think she heard something from some of the other women."

Zeke scratched his stubbly face. "Bunch of old biddies, if you ask me."

Daniel grinned. "You said it. But don't tell my ma I agreed with you."

Zeke watched his timber again that night. The partial moon was barely visible behind high thin clouds, and he hoped the thieves would show their faces tonight. He sat upright with his rifle in hand, trying to stay awake after the long day of field work and little sleep the night before. Still, he nodded off, and soon slept deeply.

When he awoke in the morning, his logs were still there.

His plan was not working, and he couldn't spend every night in the field like this. He'd have to haul the logs to the mill.

After breakfast he sent Noah to find Feeney to help them. "He'll likely be working on Mac's land today," he told the boy. Zeke and the twins headed to the timber pile to start loading the wagon.

Feeney showed up an hour later with two of his Army pals. "Why'd you send the boy out after me? 'Tain't safe for him to wander the woods 'round here."

Zeke raised his eyebrows. "Noah's lived here four years now. He knows all the farmers here 'bouts. Knows the land pretty well, too."

"Don't you worry about wild animals?" Feeney asked. "Boy don't carry no weapon."

Zeke chuckled. "You heard him coming from far off, didn't you? Any wildcat or bear'd likely run from him afore he got close. But I'll caution him."

Feeney shrugged. "He's your charge, not mine. Now, what we doing today?"

They worked until early afternoon loading the logs into the wagon, then Zeke sent the others home and drove the wagon to the sawmill. After he negotiated a price with the mill owner and arranged to have a credit placed on his account at the store, he turned his empty wagon toward home.

As he passed by the McDougall home on the bluff, he decided to stop in to see Jenny. He was grubby and tired, but she'd seen him look worse than this when they traveled the prairies and mountains. She was home and offered him tea. They sat for an hour reminiscing and chatting, until her clock struck five.

"Sorry," Zeke said, jumping up. "I gotta get home. Hannah'll wonder where I am."

Chapter 52: The Plot Thickens

Hannah spent most of her waking hours wondering if she was in fact pregnant. She worried about everything and seemed on the point of tears at least once a day, which was unlike her. Her breasts were heavy and tender, and she had little appetite. No nausea yet. She decided not to say anything to Zeke for another month. Perhaps her monthly would come in the meantime.

"Please don't tell Zeke," she begged Ruth. "There's time enough later on."

Ruth shrugged. "Once you start puking, he'll know."

"Do you think I will?" Hannah asked. "When does that start?"

"For Esther, it was almost immediate. Rachel never did have morning sickness. Made Esther mad as a cornered skunk 'cause Rachel got off so easy."

Hannah sighed. It seemed no two women were alike. And she had only twelve-year-old Ruth to talk to. She couldn't discuss her pregnancy with Esther or Jenny yet. Not before she told Zeke.

On Thursday, August 7, Hannah and Ruth went to Esther's house again to continue working on the quilt. Esther had issued the invitation after church on Sunday.

"Don't you want to come to our cabin?" Hannah had responded. "We have plenty of space when Zeke and the boys are out."

Esther sighed. "I'd like to get out of my house," she said. "But with four little ones—" She waved her hand to show defeat. "It's too much trouble to pack 'em and their diapers and toys up for the day."

"All right," Hannah said. "We'll be there. What can I bring?"

"Bring a pie," Esther said. "That'll help feed us."

Many of the same women gathered on Thursday who had attended the earlier quilting. Hannah found herself sitting beside Louisa and Harriet Abercrombie. Harriet seemed rather officious to Hannah. Still, the older woman had done a good job of raising her stepsons. Both Douglass and Daniel seemed to love their stepmother, so Hannah respected her. But she had little use for Louisa.

Hannah listened absentmindedly as Louisa prattled on, until Louisa said, "By the way, Hannah, what was Zeke doing at the McDougalls' place in town yesterday?"

"I beg your pardon?" Hannah wondered if she'd heard correctly. She knew Zeke had been in town the day before to sell his timber, but he hadn't mentioned stopping by Jenny's.

"Douglass saw him coming out of the McDougall house about five yesterday."

"Oh, he was probably checking in on her. Mac asked him to make sure she and the children were fine."

"His wagon was there earlier when Douglass got to town," Louisa said. "Well, they're old friends, you know. Don't you worry. I'm sure there's nothing to it."

Hannah wouldn't have made anything of it, if it weren't for Louisa's disclaimer and Harriet's arched eyebrows and pursed lips.

When the women paused for refreshments, Hannah found a place to sit by Jenny. "I hear Zeke stopped by yesterday. Is everything all right?"

"Oh, he mentioned it, did he?" Jenny said, smiling. "Yes. It was very kind of him. We talked about our trip in forty-seven while I fed him tea and cakes. He misses his mama, you know. She was a wonderful woman."

"I'm sorry I didn't know her," Hannah said. "All her children remember her fondly."

"Very strict," Jenny said. "Something like you—she ruled her home, even when all she had was a couple of wagons on the trail."

Hannah laughed. She couldn't help liking Jenny, even while she worried about her friend's relationship with Zeke. "You think I rule my home?"

Jenny laughed also. "You ruled the school, and then Zeke's house. You're a strong woman, Hannah Pershing. Zeke is fortunate to have found you."

Despite Jenny's praise, Hannah couldn't help wondering why Zeke hadn't told her he'd gone to Jenny's house. But she didn't want to let on she'd heard gossip about him. It seemed Jenny didn't see anything in his visit, and Hannah hated to come across as shrewish. So she shook it off and said nothing.

Friday morning she awoke feeling queasy, but the feeling passed when she ate a little porridge. She almost welcomed the sensation as another indication she might be pregnant. She craved certainty, to have proof of the child she yearned to have. But she also hoped she wouldn't have nausea as badly as some women did when they carried a child. How would she ever run the house and family if she were incapacitated?

After Zeke and the twins left, Hannah took Ruth and Noah to pick vegetables over at the garden she'd started on the McDougall claim. Devlin Feeney was living in the cabin, but Mac had given her permission to harvest the garden she'd planted. "Feeney won't have time," Mac said. "Just leave him some corn, and I'm sure he'll be happy to let you have the rest."

The sweet corn was almost all harvested, but the beans and carrots and other vegetables were ripe and plentiful. The potatoes would soon be ready, she noticed when they arrived. She and the children picked as much as they could carry, and she sent Noah inside the cabin with a basketful of carrots. Surely Feeney could manage to cook those.

As they walked back home, each carrying two baskets, Hannah thought she saw movement through the forest along the road. "Who do you think that is?" she said, speaking as much to herself as to Ruth and Noah.

"Oh, it's probably Mr. Feeney," Noah said. "He told Zeke he needed the next few days on Mr. McDougall's claim. Couldn't work with us for a bit."

"Mmm," Hannah said. "What's beyond those trees?"

"Don't know," Noah said. "Want me to go see?" He ran off before Hannah could say anything and thrashed through the trees. He came back in a minute, panting, and said. "Yep, it's Feeney."

"Mr. Feeney," Hannah said.

"He's hoeing feed corn with a couple of his Army pals. Grain looks about ready to harvest." Noah skipped ahead, then turned to say. "Zeke says ours is a few weeks out yet."

In the evening over supper, Hannah told Zeke they'd seen Feeney. Zeke nodded. "He told me Mac wanted him to handle everything in the fields while he was away. He ain't been able to help us much recently. Mac's claim is keeping him pretty busy."

"Doesn't it seem strange Mac asked you to check on Jenny but not on his fields?" Hannah asked.

Zeke shook his head. "I got plenty to do with my own land and helping the Abercrombies. I worked Mac's claim when he was in California before. Feeney's welcome to it this time."

Saturday Hannah and Ruth put up the vegetables they couldn't eat immediately. They canned tomatoes and corn and beans, keeping heavy pots of water boiling on the stove as they worked. The heat made Hannah's face flush, and she felt nauseated again. Once when she rubbed her stomach, Ruth asked her how she felt. "I'm fine," Hannah said, willing the nausea to pass. After she took a few deep breaths and fanned her face with her apron, it did.

Around midday, Hannah heard a knock on the door. She wiped her forehead and hands and went to answer it. "Mr. Feeney," she said in surprise, when she saw the ex-Army man, hat in hand, outside the cabin.

"Morning, ma'am," he said. "Came to thank you for the vegetables. It was right nice of you to pick 'em for me."

"You're welcome," she said. "There was more than enough for all of us." She gestured inside. "Ruth and I are canning today—there's far too much to eat. Would you like some corn relish or canned beans to take home?"

"No, ma'am," he said. "I have plenty. I just came to warn you."

"Warn me? Of what?"

"Well, I seen your boy run through the woods as you was headed home. Thought you oughta know—there's been more bears seen in these parts."

"Bears?" Hannah remembered the shooting lesson Zeke had given her and Faith because of bear sightings earlier in the year. She'd never seen a bear, and she didn't want to.

"Yes, ma'am. With the berries ripe now, them bears are out and about. You be careful. They ain't likely to bother you if you make some noise, 'less you get between a mother and her cub. But it'd be best to have a gun with you." He squinted. "You know how to shoot?"

She nodded. "I don't know what I could hit, but I can fire a rifle well enough."

"Safest to stay on the roads," he said. "Don't go wandering through the forest and fields. And keep your young'uns on the roads, too."

"Thank you, Mr. Feeney. I certainly will."

When he left, Ruth said, "Something about that man I don't like."

"But it was kind of him to warn us," Hannah said. "Have you heard anyone else talk about bears recently?"

"No," Ruth said. "But I don't want to see one close up. I'll stick to the roads."

Chapter 53: Zeke Begins to Wonder

The weather remained warm and dry through Sunday. Zeke refused to go to church, wanting the time for his farm. "Take Ruth and Noah, if you want," he told Hannah. "But Jonathan, David, and I need to work."

Hannah shook her head. "We'll stay home also. Unless you want me to go to town to see Jenny."

"No need," Zeke said. "I saw her midweek."

"So I heard at the quilting," Hannah said. "Louisa Abercrombie was eager to tell me. And then Jenny did as well." It sounded to Zeke like she meant to accuse him of something shifty.

But if she'd known since last Thursday he'd visited Jenny and didn't say anything, she'd been hiding the matter as much as he had. Zeke hadn't meant to keep it from her. Mentioning Jenny hadn't come up when they talked. What was a man supposed to tell his wife anyway?

Then Hannah said, "Mr. Feeney stopped by here yesterday."

Another thing she'd kept from him. "Why didn't you tell me last night?" Zeke asked.

"Maybe I should have. He said there are bears in the forest. They're out to pick berries."

"Could be. Did Feeney see one?"

"He didn't say so. Just warned us. Told me to keep Noah from running through the woods."

Zeke grinned. "Good luck with that."

"Then you aren't worried about bears?"

"I'll have a word with Noah," Zeke said, though he wasn't too concerned. Noah knew better than to get in a bear's way. "What else did Feeney say? Anything about when he could work with us again?"

"No, he didn't mention that."

"I'll stop by Mac's claim this morning. See if I can find Feeney. I need all the help I can get going into harvest." Zeke and his twin brothers couldn't handle the harvest by themselves. In prior years, Pa and Robert O'Neil had helped, and Zeke helped on Pa's claim also. With Pa dead and O'Neil living farther away this year, Zeke would struggle. The Abercrombie men also worked with Zeke on occasion, but the Abercrombies had their own land to harvest. Without the extra labor of Feeney and the other Army men, some of Zeke's crops would get left in the fields.

Zeke called the twins and gave them instructions for the day, then he set out for McDougall's claim to find Feeney. The ex-soldier wasn't in the cabin, so Zeke headed to the fields. When he heard the thunks of axes and men shouting, he turned toward McDougall's forested land. Soon he saw Feeney and two other men felling logs.

"What's going on?" he shouted at Feeney.

"What's it look like? We're clearing timber." Feeney leaned on his axe. "What're you doing here?"

"Came to see if you'd be able to work with me this week," Zeke said.

Feeney shook his head. "McDougall wanted me to clear this field. Need to get it done afore he gets back."

"In the middle of harvest?" Zeke was surprised. "Seems cutting wood could wait." He'd been timbering his own land, but only because he wanted to catch the thieves.

Feeney shrugged. "Just doing what I was told. Maybe I shoulda done it sooner, but now I need to get this field cleared and the timber to the mill afore McDougall returns."

These directions didn't sound like Mac. McDougall was usually hell-bent on handling the most important tasks first. Clearing another field could wait until winter—far less critical than getting the wheat harvested. "What about his wheat?"

"I'll get to it." Feeney spat. "You wanna give us a hand here?"

Zeke shook his head in disgust. "Got my own crops to harvest. Come see me if you get the time."

It seemed odd, Zeke thought again, as he returned to his claim to start work. A niggling suspicion grew—could Feeney be taking Mac's wood for himself? Was he the thief?

Zeke had little time to wonder about Feeney through the next week. It rained a couple of days, but most days were fair enough to work from breakfast until dusk. He and the twins stayed busy.

Zeke talked to Noah about watching out for bears. The boy's eyes lit up at the mention of a grizzly, and Zeke could tell his little brother hoped to encounter one. "Bears are nothing to scoff at, Noah," Zeke admonished. "I seen one kill a dog once." He remembered Samuel Abercrombie's hound lying limp after it cornered a grizzly during their journey west. Poor mutt hadn't deserved its fate. "'Tweren't pretty."

To keep Noah under control, Zeke took the boy with him to the fields most days. The young'un couldn't handle a scythe yet, but he picked up after the threshers and ran errands. Even Hannah and Ruth helped with the cutting and gathering some days.

Jenny had helped harvest crops in the years when Mac was in California, though Zeke hadn't liked to see her toil so hard. Now, he felt the same way about Hannah. When she paused for a breath and to wipe the sweat off her face one afternoon, a pang went through him. He'd feel that way about any woman, he told himself. But even as he tried to minimize his concern for Hannah, he remembered her softness curled against his side the night before. He wouldn't let anything bad happen to her. Any man would do the same for a wife. "You and Ruth best get back to the house," he shouted across the field. "Time for supper'll be here afore long."

She nodded wearily, beckoned to Ruth, and the women left.

The next day, Thursday, rain threatened all day and the air was humid. The three Abercrombie men worked with Zeke in the morning, then he and the twins went to Samuel's claim with the Abercrombies in the afternoon.

"That bastard Feeney ain't been no help to us," Samuel complained as he heaved a basket of threshed wheat into his wagon. "You seen him?" he asked Zeke.

"Not since Sunday," Zeke said. "He and his pals were cutting Mac's logs."

Samuel spat a stream of tobacco juice that barely cleared his belly before hitting the ground. "He's been logging more'n he's been farming."

"Think he's our thief, Pa?" Douglass asked, with a raised eyebrow at Zeke.

"Could be," the older Abercrombie said.

"I sat out two nights watching," Zeke said. "Didn't see anyone."

"Just you?" Daniel said. "Your plan might've worked better with a team of us."

Zeke shrugged. "Maybe we could try it again. But where? Wood's been stolen from several claims now."

"Maybe you did it backward," Samuel said. "You watched the wood. Might be we oughta follow Feeney instead."

By evening on Thursday when the men stopped work, rain started to fall. "Should we watch Feeney tonight or wait until tomorrow?" Zeke asked.

Samuel Abercrombie squinted at the sky. "This rain ain't gonna let up. And Feeney ain't likely to wanna be out in it neither. Let's try tomorrow. We'll meet after sunset on the road to McDougall's claim."

Friday was cloudy, but it didn't rain. After supper, Zeke took his rifle and met the three Abercrombies near McDougall's claim. They scouted the cabin where Feeney lived, but couldn't see any sign of his being there. So Zeke led them toward the field Feeney had been clearing.

They sneaked through bushes and trees still wet from yesterday's rain until they could see the cleared field. "There's the logs he was cutting," Zeke whispered, gesturing toward a pile of tree trunks stripped of their limbs. "That was last Sunday. Why hasn't he moved 'em to the mill yet?"

"You see him or his pals?" Daniel whispered back. "Or should we have ourselves a look?"

They listened for a full minute. Nothing but the wind rustling the branches above them. "Daniel, you're with me," Zeke said. "Douglass, you give a hoot if you hear anything."

Samuel muttered but didn't stop the younger men when they crept forward.

Zeke and Daniel reached the logs and walked around them. At one side of the pile, Zeke saw a log with his blaze on it. "That's mine! He stole it," he hissed.

Daniel squatted beside it and rubbed where Zeke had stripped the bark away. "How do you know?"

"I know," Zeke said. "Let's go find him."

"Find who?" Feeney's voice came from the far side of the clearing. "What're you doing here, Pershing? And young Abercrombie, too?"

Zeke stood. "You're the one been stealing logs in the valley."

Feeney stepped forward. His two ex-Army friends stood behind him. "Seems you're the ones trespassing," Feeney said. "You wouldn't be taking McDougall's wood, would you?"

"I marked this log," Zeke said, motioning at the log he'd seen. "You stole from me."

"Mark?" Feeney moved beside Zeke and kicked the log where the bark had been removed. More flaked away. "You call that a mark?"

"I'll have the sheriff here in the morning," Zeke said.

"I don't think so," Feeney said, drawing his pistol. "I think you and Abercrombie here will head on home. Say nothing of this, or your wives and children might get lonely."

Zeke couldn't aim his rifle, nor could Daniel. Not with Feeney already having the draw on them.

From the darkness behind him, Zeke heard Samuel Abercrombie shout, "Put the gun away, Feeney. I got a Winchester aimed at your chest. And Douglass'll git one of your pals. Don't matter much to me which one he decides to shoot."

Feeney lowered his pistol but didn't reholster it.

"Now, Daniel and Zeke, you come on over here," Samuel said. "Nice and easy. Let's nobody git shot tonight. Even if I'd like nothing better than to plug you, Feeney."

Zeke backed up slowly, Daniel right with him.

When they reached Samuel and Douglass, Samuel shouted again, "Let's all go home tonight. Have the sheriff sort this out in the morning." Samuel kept his gun trained toward the clearing as they left.

"We going home, Pa?" Douglass asked when they returned to the road.

"Hell, no," Samuel said. "We're getting the sheriff out of bed now."

Chapter 54: What Hannah Tells Zeke

Hannah stayed awake most of Friday night while Zeke was gone. He'd told her he was going with the Abercrombies to watch Feeney. Feeney was an unctuous little man, she thought, but Samuel Abercrombie was a bully. Would Zeke and the two younger Abercrombies be able to manage Samuel and Feeney?

Zeke took his rifle from above the door when he left, which only worried her more.

She sent the children to bed when the hearth fire died down, but she stayed in the main room sewing by lamplight, Zeke's dog Blackie at her feet. Her stitches were uneven because she couldn't concentrate.

Hannah took out her paper, quill, and ink and moved the lamp to the dining table. She sat and wrote Jane:

> August 15, 1851
> Dear Jane,
>   What I had always hoped might happen has come true. I am with child. It is early yet—I do not anticipate the blessed event until the spring. Early April, I think.
>   And yet, my life is uncertain. My husband is out this evening hunting a timber thief. Someone has been stealing logs from farmers in the valley.
>   You might wonder how men can steal huge tree trunks without anyone seeing, but perhaps that gives you an idea of how

isolated one home is from its neighbor. And much of the land is uncleared, still in forests that rise to a hundred feet above our heads.

The question to ask instead is how we can maintain civilization in the midst of this primeval wilderness. And this is the world into which my child will be born . . .

Once again, Hannah realized her letter was too depressing to finish, at least until she knew the outcome of Zeke's surveillance. The clock struck midnight, and she put away her writing materials. She put on her nightdress and climbed into bed. Alone. And she tossed and turned until dawn.

Zeke didn't arrive home until after Hannah and the children were awake. She was groggy from lack of sleep, but willed her stomach not to rebel as she fried bacon while Ruth made flapjacks. When Zeke stumbled into the house, it was on the tip of her tongue to say, "Take off your boots." But when she saw the fatigue on his face, she said instead, "Sit down." She left the bacon to pour him a cup of coffee.

He mumbled his thanks.

"What happened?" she asked.

"We saw Feeney and his pals," he said, after taking a long drink of the hot liquid. "They had some of my logs on Mac's claim."

"Did you get the sheriff to arrest them?"

He shook his head.

"Why not?"

"They had guns. We was glad they didn't shoot us. Samuel and Douglass got the draw on 'em."

By this time, all the children were gathered around Zeke. Noah's eyes widened at the mention of guns. Jonathan and David grinned, and Ruth gasped.

"What does that mean—got the draw?" Hannah asked.

"In this case, it means Samuel and Douglass had rifles on Feeney and his crew. Feeney and his men couldn't shoot me without getting shot themselves."

At this, Hannah and Ruth both gasped, and Hannah plopped into the chair beside Zeke's.

"So then what?" David asked eagerly.

"We left."

The boys all groaned. "You let 'em get away?" Jonathan exclaimed.

"We went to town. Woke up the sheriff. He sent us home, said he'd go find Feeney today."

"Well, it's in the sheriff's hands then," Hannah said. "That's good, isn't it?"

Zeke shrugged. "Don't know. Feeney might move the wood by the time the sheriff gets there."

Hannah smelled burning bacon and rushed to the stove. She dished up the meal food and the family ate. The boys questioned Zeke further, but Hannah could think only of her coming child—would it even have a father, given Zeke's propensity to confront his enemies?

Then Zeke rose, "Come on, boys. Let's get to work."

"Zeke, you're exhausted," Hannah said.

"Me being tired don't stop the corn from spoiling in the fields." He picked up his hat and rifle and turned to the door. Before he left, he said, "If the sheriff stops by, tell him I'm in the south field."

Hannah saw nothing of the sheriff all day Saturday. She started at every sound as she and Ruth baked and cleaned the house. They took the midday meal to the fields, and Zeke shook his head when she asked if he'd heard anything.

That evening when Zeke and the boys returned, they ate a quick supper. Zeke went out to the barn to do the evening chores, and Hannah followed him.

"Did you hear anything from the sheriff this afternoon?" she asked.

He nodded. "Sheriff Thomas stopped by. He'd been to McDougall's claim. Found Feeney at the cabin, alone. Feeney said we'd threatened him last night, said the Abercrombies and I tried to take logs he'd cut. I told the sheriff about the marks I'd made, but he just scoffed at me—how could he tell I'd cut the bark, not someone else, he said."

"So you don't have any proof it's Feeney?" Hannah asked.

Zeke snorted. "Not according to the sheriff."

"What happens next?"

"Feeney even told the sheriff Abercrombie might've been the thief—old Samuel's been flashing money in town, apparently."

"But you don't think it's Abercrombie anymore, do you?"

Zeke shook his head. "No. We'll all be on the lookout for Feeney now. I took my gun to the fields today. Won't be without it from now on. And you keep a rifle handy in the cabin."

Hannah wondered whether she should tell him now. It was sooner than she'd planned. But a babe coming might make him more careful. "Zeke, I'm having a child."

He turned and stared.

"We'll have a baby in early April." She smiled at him and waited for him to speak, hoping he would be as happy as she was.

He swallowed hard and his Adam's apple bobbed. "I'm pleased, Hannah. I am." He swallowed again and touched her cheek. "Now let me do the chores and get to bed. I'll have to get as much grain harvested as I can, if we'll soon have another mouth to feed."

Chapter 55: Zeke Is Overwhelmed

Zeke realized immediately he hadn't handled Hannah's news well. A baby! Even the thought overwhelmed him. As the oldest in a large brood, he knew well how each new young'un changed the family. He didn't remember Joel's birth, but he remembered the others—Esther, then Rachel, then the twins, and Ruth, then Noah . . . and finally Jonah, whose coming killed their mother. Actually, he had another sibling also—Frankie, Jr., his half-brother, now presumably back in Illinois with Amanda and her offspring.

Each child brought a juggling of relationships, of chores. Each caused sleep deprivation and noise and a jockeying for Ma's and Pa's attention.

And now he would be a father.

He'd known responsibility since childhood, watching over his younger siblings whenever his mother or father told him to. And recently he'd felt the anxiety of providing a home and food and care for the young'uns since his father's death and Amanda's abandonment.

But now he would be a father. He would be this child's parent. He had the obligation of caring for Hannah and his child.

Hannah. The image of his mother heavily pregnant with Jonah flashed into his mind. She'd suffered as they traveled by wagon across the plains and into the mountains. Zeke had been scouting ahead of the wagon train when Jonah was born, and he wasn't there when his mother died. He'd arrived in time for her burial—his father distraught to the point of incoherence, his three sisters in tears, his brothers not knowing how to react. He'd had to be strong then.

Could he be strong if Hannah suffered? *When* Hannah suffered, for he knew all women suffered in childbirth, even when they survived.

Zeke finished his chores, then returned to the house. He'd been up for two days now, he needed sleep. Hannah was already in bed when he staggered into their room. He undressed and crawled under the covers beside her.

She stiffened, so he knew she was awake. He leaned over her back to kiss her cheek, then took her into his arms, spooning around her.

"Are you feeling well?" he murmured.

"Most of the time. Once I'm up. Some mornings are bad."

"I'm sorry."

She turned toward him. "What do you mean, you're sorry?"

He sighed. "I'm not sorry about the child. I want the baby." He held her tighter. "I want you well. I want our family strong and healthy. I want our fields harvested. I want Feeney behind bars. I want it all, and I don't know how to get it."

She touched his cheek. "I'll be all right."

He kissed her mouth and made gentle love to her. "I'm not hurting you, am I?" he whispered as he entered her.

"No," she whispered back.

Afterward, he fell asleep immediately.

The next morning Zeke woke to the smell of frying ham. He dressed and shuffled into the main room, then outside to the privy. When he returned, Hannah set a plate in front of him. "We're going to church today," she announced, "whether or not you need to farm."

Zeke frowned at her. "All right."

"We need the Lord's blessing on this family."

He wondered what brought on her sermon, but he didn't ask. "That's fine. I'll be able to learn what's going on with Feeney. I'll bet Abercrombie's been hounding the sheriff."

They got to town too late for Zeke to talk to Abercrombie before the service, but he corralled the man afterward. "Any news?"

Samuel spat and shook his head. "Damn sheriff won't do a thing. Nothing to go on, he said."

"So what comes next?"

"Tomorrow I'm going to the sawmill owner. Put him on notice."

"I done that already," Zeke said. "First time I was missing timber."

When he finished his conversation with Abercrombie, Zeke drifted back toward Hannah, who was talking with Esther.

Esther threw her arms around his neck. "Hannah told me," she said. "You're going to be a father!"

Unable to resist Esther's enthusiasm, Zeke smiled. "Yes, I guess I am."

"You'll be such a good pa to your child. You've been a first-rate big brother." Esther prattled on about all the times he'd helped her when they were small. Zeke glanced over his sister's head at Hannah, whose eyes shone with humor as she folded her arm across her belly. There was no sign of the coming child yet in her shape, but he recognized the protective gesture his mother and sisters—and Jenny—had made when they were carrying. Hannah's arm brought home the reality of his impending fatherhood more than his sister's words did.

"With your babies joining mine and Rachel's," Esther continued, "we'll have a whole passel of little Pershings, though yours'll be the first of ours to bear Pa's family name." She turned to Hannah, saying, "What will you name your child?"

Hannah shook her head. "Zeke and I will have to talk. And mind you," she said to Esther, "don't let on to everyone yet. It's far too early—they'll know soon enough."

"Not everyone," Esther said. "Just family."

The following week remained hot and hazy. Zeke worked in the fields as much as he could, even when temperatures soared and the air turned sultry. The twins complained, and he ordered Noah back to the house after Hannah and Ruth brought the noon meal. The boy went willingly enough to avoid the heat.

Now he knew Hannah was pregnant, Zeke refused to let her work in the fields. He took Ruth aside and told her to watch out for Hannah. "She's doing fine," his little sister assured him. "No different than Esther and Rachel."

But Hannah was carrying his child, and he wanted her safe. "You do the heavy lifting around the house," he told Ruth, though he hated putting the burden on the twelve-year-old, who was several inches shorter than Hannah.

By Friday, he needed to get to town. Rain threatened again, and he had grain to take to the mill before it rotted. He also wanted to see Sheriff

Thomas. He took the twins in the wagon with him as a treat for their hard work.

They delivered the grain to the mill, then Zeke drove the wagon to the sheriff's office. He went inside, the twins tagging along, their eyes agog at being in the presence of a lawman.

"Any news, Sheriff?" Zeke asked. "About Feeney and the timber?"

The sheriff shook his head. "'Fraid not. I doubt you'll ever see your wood again."

"I don't expect to get the missing logs back," Zeke said. "But I don't want to lose any more."

After the sheriff's office, Zeke and the boys went to Abernethy's store. Zeke bought what he needed, and added candy for all the young'uns. He handed extra ropes of licorice to Jonathan and David immediately. On a whim, he threw a length of lace on top of his pile. "For the little lady?" the clerk asked with a grin.

"I reckon so," Zeke said.

He left the store and decided to stop by Jenny's house on his way out of town. He tried to coax the twins into coming with him, but they wanted to wander the riverbank. "Can we meet you at the McDougalls' house later?" Jonathan asked. "We won't be long."

Zeke didn't think the boys could get into too much trouble, and he knew they'd hate sitting in Jenny's parlor. "All right," he said, handing David his pocket watch. "Be there in an hour."

Zeke found Jenny and her children at their noon meal. She offered him food, and he sat gratefully to a heaping plate. As he ate, Jenny made sandwiches to save for the twins.

"You know much about Feeney?" he asked her. "The man Mac hired to farm your claim?"

"No," she said. "He'd known Robert O'Neil in the Army, but Robert didn't know Mr. Feeney's background. Only that he'd done all right in the cavalry."

"He's the one stealing our timber."

Jenny gasped. "How do you know?"

"Caught him with it the other night. But there's no proof now—the wood's gone." Zeke took a bite, chewed and swallowed, then asked, "When's Mac coming back?" Jenny's pregnancy was far enough along she'd started to look uncomfortable.

"Soon, I hope. But I haven't heard." She sighed. "I'm sure he'll be here before the baby, or he would have written. Mail from San Francisco is better now than it used to be. Usually only takes ten days or so."

"If Feeney bothers you, you'll let me know, won't you?"

She nodded.

"Do you want me to get someone to stay with you?" Zeke asked. "Ruth? Or one of the twins, if you'd rather have someone who can shoot?"

Jenny shook her head. "I hired an Indian maid to help with the children. And Feeney has no reason to do me harm. We'll be fine."

Chapter 56: Faith Comes To Stay

Hannah got the children ready for church Sunday morning. Zeke insisted he needed to stay on the farm, but he told Jonathan and David to go with her. The two boys bickered over which of them would drive the wagon, until Hannah was tempted to insist she'd do it herself. Finally, Zeke ordered Jonathan to drive to town and David to drive home.

Zeke had been solicitous since she'd told him she was with child. He motioned for Ruth to help every time Hannah stood from the table during meals. When he'd returned from town on Friday, he'd told Hannah he'd seen Jenny, and volunteered Jenny had an Indian girl working for her now. "Do you need someone?" he'd asked. "Beyond Ruth, I mean."

She shook her head. "We can't afford to pay anyone."

"I paid you when you were housekeeping for us. I'd manage if you need the help."

"I'll get along." She paused, then said, "I'd still like to have Faith come live with us. Maybe the baby is a good reason to ask Jacob again."

Zeke nodded. "If you think that's best."

"Are you worried about the expense?"

He shrugged. "I offered to hire someone. She'd be cheaper than a maid—it'd only be her food, wouldn't it?"

"Yes," Hannah said. She hadn't thought of paying her niece, and she knew Faith would be glad to escape Alice's tyranny. "But if you don't want me to ask her—"

"Go ahead," Zeke said. "We all like Faith. She'll be a help to you. And to Ruth also."

After the church service, Hannah asked her niece, "Would you still like to come stay with us?"

Faith's face lit up. "Oh, yes, Aunt Hannah! Whenever you want me."

"How about now? Shall we ask your father?" Hannah couldn't help smiling back at her niece.

But Jacob was not at church. Alice stood talking with a couple of other women who lived in town, and Hannah walked over to join them. "Good morning, Alice." She nodded a greeting to the other women.

After no more than a few words of chit-chat, Alice said, "I suppose you know your husband is still carrying on with that McDougall woman."

The two women murmured good-byes and sidled away, leaving Hannah and Alice alone.

"If you mean to tell me Zeke stopped by Jenny's home on Friday, I'm already aware of that," Hannah said. "And how did you hear of it?"

Alice waved her hand as if how she heard were of no importance. "He remained there over an hour." Her voice turned snide. "Alone."

"Mama Alice—" Faith interrupted from behind Hannah's shoulder.

"It's all right, Faith," Hannah said, still facing her sister-in-law. "Zeke has given me no reason not to trust him, and I have no intention of discussing his actions with you. I came to ask if Faith might stay with us for a while. Zeke and I would enjoy her company. And Ruth and the others—"

"I can't let her live with that man," Alice said. "You ain't known him as long as we have. He never could keep his hands off Jenny McDougall."

"Mama Alice!" Faith exclaimed.

"Maybe I should speak with Faith's father about her visiting," Hannah said.

"Jacob is home with the grippe today. I doubt he'll be out of bed for days." Alice sniffed, then added, "With him ill, I need all the help I can get. We should be getting back to him. Faith, find your brothers and sister, and let's go home."

Faith gave Hannah a wild-eyed glance, then followed her stepmother.

Hannah was furious with Alice, but she could do little to help Faith until she talked to her brother. She decided she would make a trip to the store in a few days, when he would likely be over his illness and working again.

It rained on Monday, and Tuesday the rain turned to a thunderstorm. By midafternoon the yard was nothing but mud, and Hannah and Ruth struggled to do laundry in the house. Noah played with wooden soldiers underfoot, too fretful to be much help.

"There ain't—isn't room to hang enough clothesline in here," Ruth complained. "And with all the clothes inside, we can't even move around."

"Once it's all hung, we'll have a good reason to rest, then, won't we?" Hannah said, struggling to keep the mood light. But there'd be more filthy clothes to wash as soon as Zeke and the twins returned.

A knock sounded on the door. Ruth shrieked.

"Who could that be?" Hannah dodged around the hanging laundry to the door and opened it. "Faith!" she said, "What are you doing here? Come in, come in. You're soaked to the skin."

Faith entered the cabin and stood just inside the door, her skirt streaming water and her hair hanging down her back. She clasped a small carpetbag to her chest. "I've come to stay," she said.

"How did you get here?" Hannah exclaimed.

"I walked."

"All the way from town?"

Faith nodded.

"Did your father say you could? And why did you come in the middle of the storm?" Hannah took the bag from her niece and led her to a chair by the stove. "Sit down and dry off."

"I ran away," Faith said. "I couldn't abide Alice any longer. She has been spiteful ever since church on Sunday. You know she can't stand you, nor me either." Tears welled in Faith's eyes. "I told her she'd never replace my mother, and she slapped me! So I came here. Don't make me go back."

Hannah looked at Faith's face more closely. One cheek was redder than the other and looked like a bruise might be coming. "I'll have to let Jacob know you're here. He'll worry."

"I'll take a note to town!" Noah shouted. "Let me go."

"Not until the rain lets up," Hannah said. "Then we'll see."

The storm continued until early evening, though sunset came so late Hannah thought Noah might be able to ride the mule to town and get back before full dark. But she hated the idea of sending the little boy out by himself. "Let's wait a bit," she said. "Maybe the twins will be back in time to go."

A horse nickered in the yard, and Hannah opened the door to find another visitor. "Jacob!" He stood in the doorway, his old mare and wagon behind him.

"Is Faith here?" he asked.

"Yes, come in out of the rain." He didn't look as bedraggled as Faith had after her long walk, but he was wet enough. "Are you well? Alice said you had the grippe."

"I'm fine." But he coughed as he spoke. "Where's my daughter?"

"Here, Pa." Faith came out from behind the hanging clothes.

"Sit, Jacob," Hannah said. "I'll put on the kettle for tea."

Jacob ignored her and asked Faith, "Why did you run, daughter?"

"Oh, Pa!" Faith launched herself into her father's arms, sobbing. "She hit me."

"Alice? What did you do?"

But Faith was crying too hard to speak.

Hannah sighed. "Faith said she told Alice she'd never be her mother. Then Alice slapped her."

Jacob's shoulders sagged. "The two of them have never hit it off."

"Let her stay here awhile," Hannah said. "We'd like to have her."

Jacob shook his head. "I don't know. My family's so torn already. Ever since Beulah died."

"I could use her help," Hannah said. "I'm with child. I'm a little queasy in the mornings."

Faith gasped and Ruth grinned. Even Noah looked pleased.

And so did Jacob. "Then this life is working out for you, Hannah? It's not too hard for you?"

"It's hard," she said. "That's why I could use Faith's help. But I have more hope for the future here than I had in Ohio."

Jacob nodded. "Then Faith can stay for now. We'll see what happens in a couple of weeks. Maybe by then you'll be feeling better."

Chapter 57: A Letter to Mac

Zeke and the twins came home after dark on Tuesday, exhausted after working with the Abercrombie men. "Faith is here," Hannah greeted him as he entered the cabin. "Jacob agreed."

He looked beyond his wife. Faith smiled from a chair beside Ruth. "Welcome," he said. He was too tired to inquire what had happened.

"I need your help," he said to Hannah. "I want to send a letter to Mac. Ask him if he gave Feeney permission to cut timber."

"Isn't it a little late for that?" she asked.

He shrugged. "Better late than never."

"Why do you need my help?"

"My hands ache from the work today, and your penmanship is better than mine. I'll tell you what to write, while I eat."

She served him and the twins each a venison steak with bread and gravy on the side, poured him a cup of coffee, then went to get her writing instruments.

Zeke watched Jonathan and David eyeing Faith across the room. "You boys behave," he said so only they could hear. "I don't want no trouble between you and Faith. She's Hannah's niece and Ruth's friend. She's family."

"Yes, Zeke," the boys muttered.

Hannah sat beside Zeke, and wrote as he dictated between bites. "Dear Mac, your man Feeney has been seen with timber from several claims in the area, mine included. He says you ordered him to cut wood, and he ain't done—"

"Hasn't," Hannah said. "Shall I write that?"

Zeke remembered their first kiss, when he'd hauled her up against him after she corrected his grammar. The memory made him grin at her.

She blushed. Maybe she remembered also.

"Fine," he said. "Feeney says he hasn't done nothing—"

"Anything." She turned redder.

She remembered. He let his grin turn wicked. "—Anything wrong. Sheriff Thomas won't do anything to stop him." Zeke paused for Hannah to catch up with his words. When she stopped writing, she looked up. He caught her eye, and she smiled.

"What comes next?" she asked.

"Maybe we should finish this in the morning. I'm beat," Zeke said.

"I think not, Mr. Pershing." She dipped her quill in the ink bottle. "Pray continue."

"Where was I?" Zeke asked, not taking his eyes off her.

"'Sheriff Thomas won't do anything to stop him,'" she read.

"Unless you let the sheriff know Feeney lied about your orders, I suspect we will continue to lose timber. Please send word. Respectfully, Zeke Pershing."

She wrote as he spoke.

When she finished, Zeke turned to the young'uns. "Time for bed soon," he announced. Then to Hannah, "I'll post the letter tomorrow. I'm turning in soon as I drink my coffee."

"I'll be there after I clean up the dishes." Hannah rose and put away her writing materials. Then, as she removed his plate from the table, her breast brushed against his shoulder.

Clouds still hung overhead Wednesday morning, but the thunderstorms had passed. Zeke sent the twins out to weed the feed corn, telling them, "Come home and help Hannah and the girls when you're done."

He saddled Red and headed to town. As he rode, he thought of the night before. Hannah's blushes foretold a fine time of lovemaking, and he'd drifted off to sleep with her in his arms. He would have to let her correct his grammar more often.

This morning she'd arisen before he did and had breakfast ready by the time he'd shaved. So many young'uns in the house made for noisy meals, reminding him of his own childhood home in Missouri. No babies in his cabin yet, but that would change soon, he thought with satisfaction.

When he arrived in town, he posted the letter, hoping it would be on its way to California soon. But the postmaster couldn't predict which ship would carry the mail. The man shook his head, saying "Hope the next boat'll take it. But it depends if there's better paying cargo. Mailbags fit in wherever we can put 'em."

Before leaving town, Zeke stopped in the sheriff's office. "I've written McDougall to ask about Feeney," he told the lawman. "If he writes back Feeney ain't—" Zeke stuttered, remembering Hannah's reaction to his poor grammar. "—ain't supposed to be cutting wood, will you arrest the bastard?"

"I'd have to bring him in, that's for sure," Sheriff Thomas replied. "But without McDougall here to testify, don't know how long I can hold him. And the judge might not trust a letter as evidence. In the meantime, don't you take the law into your own hands, Pershing. Send for me if there's any trouble."

Zeke nodded, but he knew it would take too long to get the sheriff if anything happened. He'd have to rely on himself and his neighbors.

He hoped McDougall would get back soon. Mac said he'd return in time for Jenny's confinement, but that was still a few months off.

Zeke decided there was no point in stopping by Jenny's house again. He'd just seen her on Friday, and she wouldn't have any news of Mac. Besides, Zeke wanted to get home to Hannah. He'd enjoyed flirting with her the evening before—and see where that had led? He would happily repeat that experience, he thought with a grin.

Zeke went to Bramwell's store to talk to Jacob before heading home. He'd been surprised to find Faith at home last evening, but he'd forgotten to ask Hannah about it. Jacob Bramwell stood behind the counter in his shop, his two sons stocking shelves.

"Hannah is pleased to have Faith visit," Zeke said.

"I'm glad you can take the girl," Jacob said. "I love my daughter, but she and Alice are like oil and water. Hard to have them in the same house."

It wasn't only Faith—everyone had difficulty with Alice's sharp tongue—but Zeke kept that thought to himself. "I'll take a pound of sugar and some lead for shot," he told Bramwell. "When will you get another shipment of calico?"

Bramwell grinned at him. "You buying cloth for my sister? She's mighty particular."

Zeke shook his head. "I ain't that stupid. I'll bring her to town when you get new dry goods stocked. She can do her own shopping."

"I'm pleased to hear she's carrying," Jacob said. "She told me yesterday. That's another reason I left Faith with her. Hannah pretends to be strong, but I worry about her."

Away from Alice, Jacob wasn't a bad sort. He cared about Hannah, even if he'd tried to send her back to Ohio. Zeke put the purchases on his account and left.

For the rest of the week, Zeke labored from morning until full darkness on his own farm or helping his neighbors. Jonathan and David accompanied him each day. When he was on his farm or Daniel's, he took Noah as well. Hannah made no complaint, seeming comfortable to have Ruth and Faith with her.

When they started threshing the wheat, she asked if she and the girls could be of any help. He shook his head. "I don't want you working in the fields. It might harm the baby."

Ruth said, "Ma used to help back in St. Charles. And she was always carrying."

"How would you know?" Zeke said. "Noah's the only one younger'n you born in Missouri."

"Ma told me. She used to tell us stories of Missouri while we walked on the prairie."

Zeke couldn't respond—he'd been driving wagons or scouting with his father most of the time, not walking with his mother. All he knew was he didn't want Hannah doing fieldwork, and he told her so.

"I'd be fine with it, Zeke," she said. "My leg is so much stronger since I moved to Oregon. Here in the country, I work the muscles every day." She smiled. "Maybe I should have traveled to Oregon with Jacob's family."

Zeke thought of Hannah limping along the trail. He'd seen others with infirmities on the journey. He recoiled from the notion of Hannah struggling under such conditions. For the first time, he wondered how his mother had felt—heavy with child and in poor health. He should ask Esther if Ma had complained while they traveled.

Chapter 58: Peace Disturbed

After Faith's arrival, Hannah settled into a contented routine. She'd always enjoyed her niece's company. The months when she'd taught school and lived in the little McDougall cabin with Faith had been one of the happiest periods of her life. Despite the hardships of living in the wilderness, she'd felt useful and competent, and she'd grown fond of the children she taught. Even Annabelle Abercrombie and Jonathan and David Pershing had been sociable young persons, though they'd tried her patience at times. They'd merely been suffering growing pains.

The Friday morning three days after Faith came, Hannah washed the breakfast dishes while Ruth dried them, and Faith swept the floor. The two girls nattered about this and that, nothing serious. Hannah listened with half an ear and daydreamed about the child she would soon have to tend and cherish—a baby to give her life purpose.

She was ill every morning these days, but the nausea passed after she ate a slice of bread or a biscuit spread with a little butter or jam. By the time the rest of the household had eaten, she could keep a little meat or porridge in her stomach.

Hannah and Zeke had settled into a comfortable understanding also. She took care of the home, and he managed the farm. She kept the girls busy, and sometimes Noah, while Zeke supervised the twins in the fields. Hannah and Zeke spent their days mostly apart, but their nights—oh, their nights! She welcomed the growing intimacy she felt with Zeke in the dark of their room, though it seemed so disconnected from the reserve they displayed toward each other in daylight.

Despite Zeke's taciturn nature, he was solicitous of Hannah's well-being. He ordered Ruth and Faith to help her every time she stood. His presumption would have annoyed her, had it not been so clear he acted out of concern for her. So she smiled when he protected her, feeling affection instead of irritation.

Affection. Hannah stilled her hands in the soapy dishwater when she realized the turn her thoughts had taken. When had she begun to feel affection for Zeke?

She'd seen good qualities in him before they married—his devotion to family, his diligence. He wasn't an educated man—his grammar was atrocious, and she wondered whether he'd asked her to write the letter to Mac because his spelling was equally bad. He could be violent with other men—she'd known that since the first time she'd laid eyes on him in the churchyard when he'd struck Mac. When had her emotions shifted into tenderness?

She thought of his hands on her body, coaxing sensations she'd never felt before. His child grew in her womb, a child she welcomed—even cherished. And she hoped Zeke did also. Her hope for the child was not merely for her sake, but also because she believed a baby would bring her closer to her husband. She wanted them to become the family she had yearned for since girlhood, the family she had despaired of ever securing.

Sometime since their wedding day she'd grown to care for this man. Now, standing before the dish tub, she longed for his strength beside her and his arms around her. Her day was brighter when they were together. She wanted a lifetime of days with him.

She loved him.

Saturday morning the skies opened with yet another rainstorm. The weather had been cloudy or wet all week, and Noah was fractious. "Why can't I go with Zeke?" he whined.

"He and the twins need to work fast," Ruth said to her little brother. "You slow them down."

"I do not," Noah shouted.

Hannah looked up from her needlework. "Have you checked for eggs in the barn?" she asked.

"Did that right after breakfast," Noah muttered.

"How about cleaning the chicken coop?"

"Did that yesterday. It don't need cleaning again."

"Doesn't," Hannah said, with a sigh. She would just as soon Noah left the house, if he was going to be so cross. "If you don't mind getting wet, you could gather berries."

"Can I?" His face lit up, and she didn't remind him to say "may I." "The rain is letting up a bit."

"Take a hat," Hannah said. "And a mackintosh. It's warm, but the woods will be wet."

The boy left eagerly, slamming the door shut behind him.

"Is he safe in the woods?" Faith asked. "Jonathan and David told me there are bears around."

Ruth sniffed. "They just wanted to scare you like Mr. Feeney did. We haven't seen any bears recently."

"Recently?" Faith asked in alarm.

"We saw a couple of black bears last year," Ruth said with a shrug. "But Noah knows enough to watch out."

Two hours later, Noah came pounding into the cabin. "Take off your boots," Hannah said without turning to look at the boy.

"What is it, Noah?" Ruth cried. Her anxious tone made Hannah turn around.

Noah's face was white, except for two bright red patches on his cheeks. He was shaking.

As fearful now as Ruth, Hannah dropped her mending and went to the boy. "Noah, tell me what happened," she said in her best teacher's voice.

"M-M-Mr. Feeney."

"You saw Mr. Feeney?"

Noah nodded. "H-He had a gun."

Hannah's stomach rose to her throat. "Are you hurt?"

Noah shook his head. "He told me to go home. Now. Or he'd shoot. He let off a shot toward me. I ran."

She shut her eyes and shuddered. "Where were you?"

"On Mr. McDougall's claim. They got a big blackberry patch. I remembered it from last year."

"Did anything else happen?" Hannah smoothed her hand over the boy's hair and down his back. He was still breathing hard and shaking. "Did he hurt you at all?"

"No." Noah shook his head again. "Just told me to go home, not to come back. Ever."

Noah calmed down after he drank a cup of hot tea, but Hannah fretted all afternoon. When Zeke came home, she went out to the barn to meet him. They seemed to talk more easily alone in the barn, without any children around.

"Feeney threatened Noah today," she told him. "With a gun."

Zeke's lips thinned. "Where's Noah?"

"He's all right," she assured him. "Just scared."

Zeke finished feeding the mules, then went into the house. Hannah trailed behind him. Zeke sat beside Noah and questioned the boy until the story had been told several times. Then Zeke clapped his hat on his head, picked up his rifle, and said to Hannah, "I'll be back after I've talked to Feeney."

"No, Zeke!" Hannah grabbed his arm. "You shouldn't."

He glowered at her. "What am I supposed to do? Let him harm my family?"

"Don't go by yourself."

"I'll get Daniel to go with me," he said through gritted teeth. Then he left.

Chapter 59: Confrontation

Zeke saddled Red and trotted to Daniel's claim, the sun glowing low above the hills to the west. "We're going after Feeney," he shouted to Daniel, who was working on a fence in his yard. "Now."

Esther came out of the house. "What's wrong?" she asked, frowning.

"Feeney shot at Noah. He can't menace our kin."

Esther sucked in a breath. "Be careful, Zeke."

"I can't just let it go, Esther." Zeke turned to Daniel. "Are you coming or not?"

"Don't get yourselves killed." Esther's hands twisted the dishtowel she held.

Young Jonah stood beside her with eyes wider than a full moon. "You gonna shoot him, Zeke?" the boy asked.

"Hope not," Zeke said. "Well, Daniel?"

"Soon as I saddle up," Daniel said. He gathered his tools and headed for the barn. When he returned with his mare, he asked, "Should we take Pa, too? And Douglass?"

Zeke didn't like Samuel Abercrombie, but the man could be a strong ally when he chose to be. And a good shot. Douglass also had a better aim than Daniel. Zeke nodded. "Not a bad idea."

"Please take care of yourselves," Esther said. She pulled Daniel to her and kissed his cheek.

Zeke and Daniel rode to the senior Abercrombie's cabin. Daniel knocked on the door and walked in. "Pa," he said. "Feeney's threatening the Pershings."

Samuel squinted at Zeke, who stood behind Daniel. "What's that to me?"

"He pulled a gun on Noah."

317

Samuel tugged on his beard, frowning. Then he gave a single nod. "Bastard's done enough to harm folks in our wagon company." The older man brought his gelding from the barn and mounted, his rifle in the saddle sleeve. Then the three men fetched Douglass at home, and all four rode to McDougall's claim.

"All I want is to let 'em know they can't bully the young'uns," Zeke told the Abercrombies. "No shooting unless we have to. But I don't trust Feeney or his pals."

They arrived not long before sunset and spread out through the barnyard facing the cabin, all four still mounted with rifles drawn. "Get out here, Feeney," Zeke yelled.

Feeney appeared in the cabin doorway, gun belt on his hip. As he did, Zeke noticed two of the Irishman's cronies. One had a rifle barrel sticking out the downstairs window. The other, partly concealed by the corner of the house, aimed a pistol toward them.

Zeke nodded toward each of Feeney's pals, signaling the Abercrombies where their foes were. The Abercrombies nodded back—they must have seen the armed men also. Confident the Abercrombies would cover him, Zeke focused his attention on Feeney.

"I came to warn you, Feeney," Zeke said. "You threatened my brother. Shot at him, he says. I won't let it pass. Anyone in my family gets hurt, or any of the Abercrombies or their kin, you'll pay."

Feeney grinned. "And you think you can make that happen, Pershing?"

Zeke didn't want the situation to escalate, but he wanted to make his point to Feeney. "Sheriff's on to you. He's just waiting for you to cause a problem so's he can lock you up."

Feeney spat into the yard. "Don't you threaten me, Pershing. Or your house might turn to ashes in the night. I got more men'n these." He taunted, "Think your bride'll relish being burnt again? Maybe her other leg this time?"

Zeke saw red. His head pounded with the need to shove Feeney's words down the man's throat. It was all he could do not to jump off his horse and do battle after the threat to Hannah. She carried his child, and he *would* protect her. But getting himself killed wouldn't help any of his family.

"Should I fire at him now?" Samuel murmured. "My finger's itchy."

Zeke saw a movement from Feeney's man at the corner of the cabin. As the man raised his rifle, Samuel let off a shot that ricocheted off the log wall.

A bullet zinged past Zeke from the downstairs window, and dust kicked up beside Samuel's gelding. The horse danced, but Samuel kept his mount under control.

Samuel shot back at the window, and a barrage of bullets came from Feeney and his two cronies. Daniel and Douglass emptied their rifles as well.

Zeke shot at Feeney, who dove into the cabin. Then Zeke wheeled Red away toward the road. "Let's go," he shouted at the Abercrombies. "We done what we came to do." He glanced back at the cabin as they rode away, yelling, "If you scare my kin again, Feeney, there'll be hell to pay." Another shot from the cabin followed them.

Bent low over his pommel, Douglass groaned, "I'm hit."

Zeke and the Abercrombies galloped down the road. About a quarter mile from the McDougall claim, they paused, horses blowing heavily. "Where'd he git you?" Samuel asked his older son.

Ashen and shaking, Douglass held his left side. "Through the back. Maybe got a lung." He wheezed and spat blood.

"We got to get him home, Pa," Daniel urged. "Fast."

Douglass swayed in the saddle, and his father and brother flanked him as they rode toward his claim.

Zeke rode behind the Abercrombies. Had confronting Feeney over the threat to Noah been worth it? The injury to Douglass made it seem a bad idea. "I'll go for Doc Tuller," he said. "Then head to town for the sheriff."

"Git the doctor," Samuel said. "Once I see to Douglass, I'll deal with Feeney myself."

"No, Pa. Let the law do it," Daniel said. "Feeney's men won't hesitate to shoot us again. They might think twice about challenging the sheriff."

Zeke kicked his gelding into a canter and rode to Doc's claim, leaving the Abercrombie men to argue. He'd do as he said—send Doc Tuller to care for Douglass, then get the sheriff.

He found the doctor home and told him about the shooting. "I don't know how bad Douglass's wound is, but he was coughing blood."

"Damn fools," Doc muttered as he hitched his horse to the wagon. "Can't wait for the lawmen to do their jobs. I thought you had more sense than this, Zeke."

Zeke shook his head. "He threatened my brother."

"Damn fools," Doc said again.

By the time Zeke reached the sheriff's office, the halfmoon shone murkily through high clouds. He woke the deputy on duty. "Where's Sheriff Thomas?" Zeke demanded.

"Home in bed," the deputy said.

"Wake him up! A man's been shot." And Zeke explained the situation with Feeney and his two cohorts.

"I'll tell Sheriff Thomas in the morning," the man said sleepily.

"No, now! You need to get him now."

"Too dark to do anything tonight," the deputy argued. "If there's three of 'em as you say, be too dangerous. One of 'em could easily get the drop on us. Don't want to get another man shot."

Zeke wondered what it would take to get this deputy riled up. "I want to see the sheriff first thing in the morning."

"It's Sunday. Don't know what his plan is."

"Sunday or not, if I don't see him by breakfast, I'll roust him out of bed myself." And Zeke headed home.

When Zeke arrived, Hannah was in bed but not asleep. She sat up and asked what happened as he stumbled to undress in the dark.

"Feeney and his pals shot Douglass Abercrombie."

She hissed in a breath. "Are you all right?"

"I'm fine."

"And Douglass?"

"I don't know. I'll look in on him tomorrow."

"What about us?" she asked. "Are we safe?"

"I'm hoping the sheriff gets Feeney and his gang in the morning."

"And if he doesn't?"

He couldn't see her face, but he heard the fear in her voice. "I'm your husband, I'll protect you. And the young'uns."

"Zeke," she said. "I'm not feeble. Don't keep anything back from me. I can help you guard our children."

Our children, she said, which stabbed him in the gut. Only Faith was related to her—the rest were all *his* kin. And far from being feeble, she was the strongest woman he'd ever met. "Sheriff'll be here in the morning," he said as he crawled into bed and hugged her warmth.

"Then what?" she asked.

"We'll have to see. But Feeney said he'd burn our house down." He felt her gasp more than heard it. "So if Feeney ain't arrested, we'll need to keep an eye out. If you see him around, shoot him. Find out what he wants afterward."

When they arose Sunday morning, Zeke could tell the shooting and Feeney's threats weighed on Hannah's mind as much as on his. It saddened him to see her worried and to know he had to warn the young'uns also.

While Hannah and Ruth cooked, Zeke summoned the others. "Devlin Feeney's made threats against our family," he told them. "I don't want any of you outside alone, and don't leave either Hannah or Noah alone neither."

"Should we keep a rifle handy?" Jonathan asked.

Zeke sighed. These young'uns weren't old enough to bear such responsibility. "Just know where the guns are," he said. "I don't want to scare you, but Feeney means business. His men shot Douglass Abercrombie last night."

"We've all shot varmints before," Faith said. "We can do it again." Despite her brave words, her face was ashen. Even the twins seemed subdued this morning.

They were all eating when Sheriff Thomas knocked on the door. Zeke let him in and led him toward the table.

"I been to see the Abercrombies already." The sheriff nodded his thanks when Hannah poured him a mug of coffee. "Douglass is dead."

Zeke dropped into his chair. "Dead?" He'd had no idea Douglass's wound was so serious. He should have gone to check after talking to the deputy the night before.

"Bled out. Dead by the time Doc got there last night."

"I need to go see them—" Zeke stood. Douglass's family—Louisa and the girls—they were his kin, too, through Esther.

"Best wait awhile, son," the sheriff said. "That family's in no frame of mind to talk. Daniel stayed the night, had a devil of a time keeping his pa from going after Feeney again." He squinted at Zeke. "What in tarnation made you seek 'em out anyway? You knew they was thieves."

"Feeney threatened my brother."

"Well, now a man's dead. And I've got to get a posse together to go after Feeney. You want to be a part of it?"

Behind him, Hannah moaned softly. But he had to do it. He had to avenge Douglass. He nodded at Sheriff Thomas. "I'm going."

Chapter 60: Dealing with Death

Hannah's heart fell when Zeke announced he would be part of the sheriff's posse. She'd been scared witless the evening before when he'd gone to confront Feeney. Now, after Douglass Abercrombie had been killed, he'd left her again. Was there any end to men's need for violence and revenge?

Feeney had treated Noah despicably, but she hadn't felt the need to challenge the thief. As a woman, she knew the importance of being careful and keeping herself and the children out of his way. A part of her wished she hadn't told Zeke about the incident. But even if she'd kept silent, Noah certainly would have said something. One way or another, Zeke's pride would have required him to call out Feeney.

The children stared wide-eyed at each other while Zeke prepared to leave. Hannah could tell Jonathan and David itched to go with their older brother and Sheriff Thomas. They'd watched attentively as Zeke cleaned his rifle and filled his powder horn.

Jonathan volunteered to check Red's saddle, but Zeke shook his head. "I'll do it myself," he said. Then Zeke kissed her cheek, ruffled Noah's hair, and headed for the barn.

After Zeke left, she rose from the table. It was Sunday, but she had no intention of taking the children to town for services. "Well," she said, more cheerfully than she felt. "Let's clean up breakfast. Ruth and Faith, you do the dishes. Noah, make the beds. Jonathan and David, one of you sweep the floor, and the other pump the butter churn." The boys started to protest, so she gave them her best schoolmarm frown. No one said a word.

When the morning chores were done, she announced, "Now we need to prepare a meal to take to the Abercrombies. Louisa won't want to cook and people will be dropping in. If she and her girls can't use the food, their relatives can." With a pang, she remembered Esther was sister-in-law to the deceased. Daniel and his father had been present when Douglass was shot. They must rue their participation in the confrontation with Feeney, which resulted in such a tragic loss for their family.

And poor Louisa Abercrombie. Hannah had not agreed with the woman's handling of her daughters during the school year. Louisa had too quickly allowed Annabelle and Rose to neglect their studies. But however lax she'd been as a parent, she'd done nothing to deserve widowhood. And in such a violent way.

By noon, they had several loaves of bread, a tub of butter, and a stew ready to take. Hannah sent Faith and Ruth to the cellar for preserves and pickles. "Jonathan, please harness the mules to the wagon. And David, get the pistol and extra bullets. Put them under the wagon bench."

"What do I do?" Noah asked.

"See if you can find any eggs in the barn, while I get my bonnet."

When they were ready, they piled into the wagon. Hannah and Faith sat on the wagon bench. "Watch out the front," she told her niece. Jonathan and David, you sit in back and watch. Ruth and Noah, you each take a side. Shout if you see anyone approaching or any sign of Mr. Feeney."

She snapped the reins, and they rode in silence to Louisa Abercrombie's house. Hannah felt as heavy and somber as the gray clouds above her. She peered through the trees as they traveled, feeling as if Feeney and his men must be searching for them, but she couldn't leave Louisa and the girls unattended.

They arrived to find several wagons in the yard outside Louisa's cabin. Hannah recognized Esther's wagon and mules. Another looked like the doctor's. She couldn't identify them all, though she guessed one probably belonged to Samuel and Harriet Abercrombie.

They climbed out of the wagon, and Hannah supervised the carrying of the food to the cabin door. She knocked, and Esther opened the door. "Come in," she said soberly, her cheeks streaked with dried tears.

Wailing sounded from inside. "We've brought a meal," Hannah said. "But if you have a crowd, we won't stay."

Esther shook her head. "More folks won't cause any harm. It's bedlam here already."

When Hannah entered, she saw Louisa sitting in a rocking chair crying loudly. Annabelle and Rose sat on the floor at her feet. The girls sniffled less volubly than their mother, and they looked up at Hannah and the Pershing children.

Harriet Abercrombie, Samuel's wife, bustled about the hearth. Daniel and Samuel Abercrombie were nowhere to be seen, though Doc and Mrs. Tuller and another couple Hannah didn't know sat at the table.

Hannah beckoned to the children to take the food to Harriet. "Use this whenever you want," she told the older woman. "The stew needs another hour or two on the fire before it'll be ready."

Harriet nodded grimly. "Thank you."

"I'm so sorry about Douglass," Hannah murmured. "His passing will leave a hole in your family."

Harriet's eyes filled. "He was a sweet boy," she said. "My first child. Though I only had the rearing of him after my sister—Samuel's first wife—died when he was ten."

Hannah turned to Esther. "Where is Daniel?"

Esther motioned with her hand wordlessly.

"He and Samuel both went with the sheriff," Harriet said. "We tried to stop them, Esther and I, but Samuel insisted."

"And made Daniel go with him," Esther said.

Bile rose to Hannah's throat. If Samuel Abercrombie was with the posse, she feared there would be more gunfire, placing Zeke's and the other men's lives at risk. "May we wait with you?" she asked.

Hours passed. Nothing changed but the volume of Louisa's sobbing. Douglass's body was laid out on the bed in the corner of the room. Harriet and Esther must have washed it, because it bore no sign of blood or injury. "Funeral's tomorrow," Esther told Hannah. "Though the men left before making a coffin."

Jonathan stepped forward. "Are there boards in the barn, Esther? David and me, we could build a casket."

Esther stared at her brothers. Then she nodded. "That would be a right nice thing to do, Jonathan."

The twins dashed outside, and Noah trailed after them. Hannah asked Annabelle, "Would you and Rose like to help? It would be good for you to get some fresh air. Faith and Ruth, you, too?"

Annabelle smiled, and she and Rose followed the boys. Faith and Ruth went also.

After a bit, Hannah went to check on the children. The Pershings and Faith were busily working. Even the girls held hammers and pounded nails, though Jonathan had apparently appointed himself head carpenter. Rose assisted half-heartedly, but Annabelle sat on a bale of hay in the corner of the barn and wept softly, her earlier smile replaced by tears.

"I'm sorry for your loss," Hannah said, putting a hand on Annabelle's shoulder.

The girl turned her face into Hannah's lap and bawled. "I'm an orphan," she sobbed. "And I'm ugly. Without my pa, we'll starve. And no boy will ever marry me when we're poor."

Hannah's lips twitched, but she didn't argue. Annabelle's self-centered fears were understandable in the wake of this tragedy. She held Annabelle and made soothing sounds.

Where was Zeke? Hannah hugged Annabelle a bit closer.

Chapter 61: The Posse

Zeke rode behind the sheriff toward the McDougall claim. At a crossroad leading from Oregon City, five men waited for them—two deputies with badges and three men from town whom Zeke recognized but could not name. They'd been deputized for the day, as Zeke had been. With a hand signal, Sheriff Thomas started the full posse down the road to confront Feeney.

Horse hooves pounded behind them. Zeke turned around—Samuel Abercrombie on his large gelding and Daniel on his mare galloped toward the posse.

"What are you doing here?" the sheriff shouted at the newcomers. "I told you to stay home."

"'Twas my son killed," Samuel bellowed. "It's my right to avenge him."

"I'm the law," the sheriff yelled back. "Leave it to me."

Samuel spat tobacco juice and said nothing. Daniel sat on his horse beside his father, grim-faced.

Zeke walked Red toward the Abercrombies. "Wouldn't you rather wait it out?" he asked Samuel. "Your families can't stand to lose another man."

"You're the only Pershing man left in these parts," Samuel retorted. "You got a wife and young'uns depending on you. But you're here."

Zeke had no response to that.

The sheriff stared at Samuel and sighed. "If you're coming, you'll do as I say." Then he turned his horse and signaled for the men to follow him.

When the posse approached the McDougall claim, Sheriff Thomas directed them to circle the cabin. He sent Zeke and the Abercrombies to the back. "Your task is to cover that window in the upper story. It's the only escape on this side. Make sure no one tries to get out. Or decides to open fire from it. Don't come 'round front unless I shout for you." He beckoned to Zeke and told him, "You keep the Abercrombies back here. They ain't got no business shooting today."

Zeke nodded. He positioned himself with Red at the tree line behind the McDougalls' cabin, where he could see a portion of the barnyard. Samuel and Daniel were on the opposite side of the cabin, also at the tree line.

The only other men Zeke could see were a deputy and one of the townsmen, both stationed on the side of the barn nearest Zeke. From his location, he hoped to hear what was happening, even if he couldn't see much.

"Feeney!" the sheriff shouted. "Come on out. Let's do this peaceably. No more bloodshed."

Zeke didn't hear the cabin door open, but he heard Feeney call, "What'd'ya want?"

"Where are your pals?" Sheriff Thomas asked.

Feeney said something unintelligible from where Zeke sat, though the sheriff responded, "Get 'em out here."

Then Zeke heard Feeney ask, "What's this about, Sheriff?"

"Hear tell there was a shooting here yesterday," the sheriff said. "Man died afterward."

"Pershing and them Abercrombies was trespassing. I had every right to shoot. They all rode off alive, far as I could see." Zeke had wondered how Feeney would interpret the confrontation the day before. Now he knew.

"Get your men out here," Sheriff Thomas said.

"What are you going to do? Lock us up for defending ourselves?" Feeney asked.

"I plan to take you to town. We'll see what happens next. A man's dead. Shot in the back. I can't let it go, Feeney."

A gun cracked, followed by a yowl. Then more shots. The two posse members Zeke could see raced forward to the corner of the barn nearest the house. The deputy dropped to the ground and crawled forward. The townsman covered him from the corner, his rifle poking around the side of the barn.

"Windham got shot," someone called. Windham was one of the townsmen, Zeke remembered. "He's winged."

While concentrating on the conversation between the sheriff and Feeney, Zeke had taken his attention off the upstairs window. Glass shattered, then a sharp crack sounded as a bullet whizzed past his ear.

He looked up. A windowpane was broken out and a rifle barrel showed through the opening. He fired his pistol up at the window. Where were the Abercrombies? He couldn't see them. Another bullet zinged past him.

Zeke tied Red to a bush, then raced across open ground to the backyard privy. With the privy between him and the house, he reloaded and fired again at the window. A man cried out, but Zeke couldn't see anyone inside.

He darted toward the cabin and along its wall to the front. Once Zeke had a view of the barnyard, he saw Sheriff Thomas with a rifle pointed at Feeney, whose hands were raised. A townsman—Windham—writhed on the ground. Samuel and Daniel Abercrombie stood on the far side of the cabin, weapons drawn.

"Where are your other men?" Sheriff Thomas shouted, poking his weapon in Feeney's gut.

Feeney smirked.

"I think I wounded a man upstairs," Zeke said.

"Hell," Sheriff Thomas said. "Now we have to go in and get him. What's the cabin like inside?"

"I'll go," Zeke said. "I know it well." He described the basic layout of the cabin's interior.

"Then you're with me," the sheriff said. He told one of the deputies to keep a gun on Feeney.

"Where's the third bastard?" Zeke asked. "Feeney has two men always with him."

"Got away," one of the townsmen said. "Had a horse nearby, I guess. Heard one crashing through the woods anyway."

"Then there should only be the one man inside," Sheriff Thomas said. He went in first, and Zeke followed.

They dashed across the room to the bottom of the ladder to the loft. No sound from above. "I'm going up," the lawman whispered, his gun above his head. "Cover me."

Zeke shot into the loft ceiling while the sheriff climbed the ladder.

"He's passed out," the sheriff called, and Zeke climbed far enough to poke his head over the loft floor. Sheriff Thomas kicked the man, who groaned. "Help me get him out of here," the sheriff said.

They carried the wounded villain down the ladder and dropped him on the ground outside. Sheriff Thomas motioned to the deputies. "Tie him up," he said. "Then load him on a horse." He gestured at Feeney. "Same with him."

While the deputies worked, the sheriff frowned at Zeke and the Abercrombies. "I didn't call any of you, though I guess I'm glad of your help."

Zeke shrugged. He'd done what he thought best, but he didn't blame the lawman—Zeke had ignored Thomas's instructions, even if he'd helped by shooting the man in the loft.

After Feeney and his wounded crony were trussed and mounted on their horses, and Windham helped on to a horse as well, the sheriff sent his two deputies to track the escaped man. He ordered the two uninjured townsmen to accompany him and the prisoners back to Oregon City. "Shoot 'em if they look crosswise while we're riding," he told the townsmen. "And you," he said to Zeke and the Abercrombies, "go on home. No need for you to come to town."

"What'll you do with 'em?" Samuel asked. "They killed my boy." His voice cracked.

"We'll let the judge sort the matter out tomorrow." Sheriff Thomas raised his hand and motioned for the posse to begin the trip back to town. With a pang of loss, Zeke remembered his father gesturing in the same way to set the wagons rolling on their trek to Oregon. So much had changed in four years.

He retrieved Red and followed Samuel and Daniel toward their claims.

Zeke wanted to return straight home, but he decided he would pay his respects to Louisa first. Daniel said Esther and their children were at Louisa's, and Zeke wondered if Hannah had gone there also.

Sure enough, when they rode into Douglass's yard, Zeke's wagon and mules were hitched along with a few others.

The womenfolk all looked up when the three men entered the cabin. Esther rushed toward Daniel. "What happened?" she asked.

Sewing basket in hand, Hannah sat beside the Abercrombie girls, with Ruth and Faith nearby. He caught her eye, and relief showed in her smile.

"Sheriff took Feeney and one of his men to jail," Samuel said, dropping into a chair. "Other man got away." The big man nodded when his wife handed him a mug of coffee.

"Anyone hurt?" Hannah asked quietly.

Samuel took a swallow of the coffee. "One of the henchmen was shot, but he could still ride. Same with one of the posse members."

Hannah stood and motioned to the younger Pershings. "We'd best get home," she said to Louisa. "We'll see you for the funeral tomorrow."

Zeke went out to see to the wagon, while Hannah gathered his siblings and Faith. Then they drove away, Zeke and Hannah on the bench, and all the young'uns behind them, except for Jonathan, who begged to ride Red.

When they were about halfway home, Hannah asked, "What will happen to them now?"

"To Feeney and his gang?" he asked. "They'll—"

"No," she said. "What will happen to Louisa and her girls?"

Zeke sighed. "I reckon the Abercrombies will take care of 'em. They've always stuck together."

"But without a husband . . . in this wilderness . . . ." Her voice trailed off and he thought she stifled a sob.

"Hannah, I'm fine—"

"This time, Zeke. You're fine this time. But what happens next time?"

He shrugged. There was no point in wondering about next time. It would come when it came. Meanwhile, he worried about how to protect Hannah and the young'uns from the man who'd escaped.

Monday a sparse group of settlers attended Douglass Abercrombie's funeral. The Abercrombies and Pershings made up about half of the mourners, though the Tullers and Binghams were there also. Sheriff Thomas was present and had brought Jenny McDougall from town.

After Douglass was laid to rest, Zeke approached the sheriff and asked, "Any sign of Feeney's pal who got away?"

The lawman shook his head. "Tracks disappeared into a nearby stream. My deputies couldn't find him. I sent 'em out again today. We'll get him." He displayed more confidence than Zeke felt.

That afternoon, Zeke stayed close to home, doing odd tasks, fixing tools, and making other repairs. His excuse for not working in the fields was that the skies threatened rain. And sure enough, a thunderstorm hit in the evening.

On Tuesday he knew he needed to get back to harvesting grain, even with a murderer at large. He took the twins with him, but refused to let Noah come. They worked within shouting distance of the house all day, returning to the cabin for the midday meal.

By evening he'd made a decision—he would send Hannah and the young'uns to town to live until things settled down. He couldn't farm his land and still protect them adequately. After supper, he announced to Hannah, "Think I'll move you to town for a while," he said.

"Zeke!"

"You can live with Jenny. You and she can watch out for each other. The twins and I'll stay here through harvest."

"I'm not leaving the three of you here."

"You and Ruth and Noah will go. Jenny has room. And Faith. You'll have a grand time in town. Go to the stores and stock up for winter."

"When I moved to Oregon, I knew it would be rough," Hannah continued. "I can fend for myself and the children while you're working."

"You'll all be safer with Jenny."

"We aren't the only ones at risk," she said. "Even if we're in town, Mr. Feeney's friend might hurt someone else instead. You can't protect all the neighbors."

"The neighbors ain't my charge," Zeke said as he washed his hands in the basin by the stove. "You are."

Hannah frowned at him. "Your sister lives nearby. Her relatives. Your friends. You keep more people in your heart than just those of us in this house, Zeke. I know you do."

Zeke's shoulders tightened. Didn't she understand? She was his wife and she carried his child. He'd taken on responsibility for everyone in this house. She and the children were his concern, above all else. They would not be harmed as long as he lived.

"Zeke, I'm not going."

He set his jaw stubbornly. She'd go.

Chapter 62: The McDougall House

Hannah couldn't get Zeke to change his mind. He insisted she, the girls, and Noah move to town. Wednesday morning he ordered them to pack some clothes, then he loaded their bags into the wagon.

She argued, "Jenny doesn't even know we're coming. How can we simply appear on her doorstep uninvited?"

"Jenny won't mind." His face showed no sign of weakening.

Hannah threw up her hands. She'd confessed to herself she loved him, but that didn't mean she had to agree with every obtuse and simple-minded notion he had. She could have refused to go, she supposed. But in the mood he was in, he probably would have placed her in the wagon bodily.

She and Zeke rode to town in silence. Behind them, Noah, Ruth, and Faith spoke in whispers.

When they arrived at the large McDougall house on the bluff above town, Zeke lifted her down and said, "It'll be all right. You'll be safe here."

She sighed, and preceded him to the front door.

Zeke knocked, and Jenny's young Kalapuya maid answered the door. The girl curtsied and said, "I get madam."

Jenny soon appeared. "What a surprise!" she said. "How nice to see you all." Then a puzzled expression came over her face. She must have noticed their baggage, Hannah thought.

"We need your help, Jenny," Zeke said.

"All right." Jenny stepped back and ushered them into her front parlor, where they all sat. "What is it, Zeke?"

Hannah remained silent. This was Zeke's doing, let him explain.

Zeke glanced at her, then cleared his throat, and said to Jenny, "Feeney threatened our family before he killed Douglass. He's in jail now, but one of his men is still loose. Can Hannah and the children stay with you awhile?"

Jenny's hand covered her pregnant belly. She gasped.

"I'm sorry, Jenny," Hannah said. "We shouldn't bother you. We'll return home."

"No," Jenny said. She turned to Zeke. "Will they be safer here?"

He nodded. "You're closer to the sheriff. I don't think Feeney's pal will come to town after them. Not when the twins and I are still on the claim."

Hannah stood. "You don't mean to say you're using those boys and yourself as bait, do you? You think that man will come after you to avenge Mr. Feeney's capture?"

"Now, Hannah—" Zeke ran a hand through his hair.

"Because I won't tolerate it. I'll have Jonathan and David in town also."

"Someone has to tend the livestock and fields. It'll take all three of us through harvest."

"And I'm not staying here through harvest," Hannah responded. "You said a few days."

"Sit down, Hannah."

"Not until you're reasonable," she said, but she sat, realizing she was causing a spectacle in front of Jenny.

Jenny reached out and touched Hannah's arm. "Truly," she said. "It's all right. I'd welcome your company. Maybe the situation will get sorted out soon."

"I don't want to put you and your children in any danger," Hannah said.

Jenny smiled. "I think Zeke's right. You'll be safer here than on your farm."

Zeke stood. "Then I'll be getting home."

Hannah followed him to the door. "You'll be careful, Zeke?" She clutched his coat front with both hands. "You and the boys?"

He leaned over and kissed her cheek. "We'll be careful."

She watched as he vaulted into the wagon and drove away.

Jenny was a gracious hostess and made Hannah and the children feel welcome, despite Zeke's having foisted them on her with no invitation. Within an hour of their arrival, she had Faith and Ruth stewing a fruit compote and baking sugar cookies and Noah bossing young William and

Maria in the playroom. Jenny and Hannah sat in the parlor with their needlework, and Jenny regaled Hannah with the gossip of town.

Jenny's home was more luxurious than Zeke's farmhouse, with large rooms and finely finished woodwork. But even so, Hannah missed Zeke and the farm with all her heart. She didn't know if it was because of the coming child, her newly discovered love for her husband, or the roots she'd put down in the wilderness. All she knew was that despite her pleasant surroundings and company, loneliness consumed her. At every sound, she startled, wondering if he'd returned for her and the children. At night, she reached out under the sheets for his warmth, only to find the bed empty of any comfort.

Two days went by. Jenny's amiable company was interrupted Friday after the noon meal. Alice came to visit.

Hannah had gone to see Jacob in his shop Wednesday afternoon to let him know she and Faith were in town. He was surprised, but did not suggest Faith return to his house. He only asked, "Are you safe enough?" She assured him they would be fine.

On Friday Alice was greeted with a tight-lipped smile from Jenny and a small nod from Hannah. Alice sat with them in the parlor and immediately demanded Faith be sent home. "She should not be here," Alice said. "Not when I have need of her help in her father's house."

"I spoke with Jacob Wednesday," Hannah said. "He did not indicate she should come home."

"He had not talked to me. He might manage the store, but *I'm* in charge of our household. Faith's assistance is required."

Hannah barely looked up from her mending. "Did Jacob inform you I am with child and am grateful for Faith's support?"

Alice sniffed and gestured at the well-furnished parlor. "I'm sure you are in great need of support here."

"Faith is welcome to stay as long as Hannah and the younger Pershings do," Jenny said. "She is an engaging girl and a pleasure to have as a companion." As Jenny spoke, peals of laughter came from the kitchen where Faith and Ruth busied themselves making meat pies. Jenny continued with a smile, "She and Ruth are preparing our supper now. I expect we shall have some treat in store for us."

"Well, I never!" Alice exclaimed. "You're using my stepdaughter as your cook. As if you don't have the means to hire more servants of your own."

"The girls are enjoying themselves," Hannah said, putting down her needle and rising. "Perhaps you can return for another visit next week."

"Next week! I must insist Faith return home now." Alice rose also.

Jenny stood with them. "It's been a pleasure, Alice." She took Alice's elbow to guide her to the door.

"Get your hands off me, you whore!" Alice's face reddened and her eyes flashed venom. "You're no better'n the strumpets setting up in Portland these days. I hear tell you took up with McDougall afore you were married. Then Zeke. God only knows what you did to lure Mac into making an honest woman of you."

Hannah's bones chilled at her sister-in-law's words. "Alice!" she said, her voice reflecting the cold she suddenly felt in the room. "That is enough. You've insulted Jenny once too often in her own home. Please leave. Now." Hannah pushed the bitch—she could think of no other word to describe her sister-in-law—into the hallway and out the door.

After Hannah slammed the front door behind Alice, she took a deep breath and turned back toward the parlor. The house was quiet, no more giggles from the kitchen, no sound from Jenny.

She stepped into the parlor to find Jenny sitting, hands folded around her rounded belly, her white face staring down at her lap.

Jenny looked up when Hannah entered the room. "I need to tell you a story," she said.

Hannah closed the door behind her and sat beside Jenny. "Don't tell me anything you'll regret."

Jenny shook her head. "No. It's only right you should know. You're Zeke's wife. Alice has slandered him, and there is no cause." She exhaled slowly. "The story begins back in Missouri." She stopped and swallowed visibly. Hannah took her hand.

"There's no easy way to say it," Jenny began. "I was raped by several men. In my stepfather's tavern. I was just fourteen. Afterward, I was desperate to escape my home, and Mac rescued me. He took me from a place where I'd been defiled and brought me to Oregon."

Hannah had known pain and she'd known evil, but nothing to match what Jenny described. "I'm so sorry."

"There's more," Jenny whispered. "William is the result of my violation. Only Mac knew at first. Until Doc and Mrs. Tuller guessed. Even now, only they and Esther and Zeke know the truth. No one else. I never want William to know."

Hannah squeezed Jenny's hand more tightly. "You can trust me."

"Mac and I didn't marry then, in forty-seven. We claimed to be married as we traveled. Then he asked me, and I refused him. I could not abide the thought of relations with a man, even Mac." Jenny stared at the ceiling and blinked back tears. "I came to regret my decision, but he was gone." She smiled bleakly at Hannah. "He left me after we came to Oregon."

"But he came back."

"Yes." Jenny's smile turned brighter. "He did. And we married last October. The day we met you."

"And Zeke?" Hannah felt for Jenny, but her bigger concern was Zeke. What role had he played in all this? How much of the story had he left out? He hadn't told her Mac and Jenny did not marry until after Mac's return from California.

"I've told you the truth. Zeke has been a good friend to me. My protector, even before he knew my story. Both on our trek to Oregon and later after Mac left William and me. Then, when Zeke found out Mac and I were not wed, he asked me to marry him. At the time I thought Mac would never return."

"But you turned Zeke down. Why?" Hannah wondered what she would have done in Jenny's situation. Why hadn't Jenny wanted him?

Jenny shrugged. "I was in love with Mac, not Zeke." She rose and walked to the window, staring outside. "I hesitate to say this because Zeke is now your husband. But you should know. Zeke did not seem to want William. That was the other reason I turned him down." She turned back toward Hannah. "You shouldn't worry. He said it was the circumstances of William's birth. I'm sure he'll love his own child when it comes."

But would he? Hannah wondered. He said he wanted their baby, but he'd sent her away to stay with Jenny.

Chapter 63: Zeke Wonders About Love

Zeke missed Hannah while she stayed in town with Jenny. He missed her cooking, he missed her conversation with the young'uns, he missed the comfort of her next to him at night. He and the twins came home to a cold supper in the evenings, though they made a hearty breakfast before heading to the fields at first light. They took food for midday with them and didn't stop their harvesting until the dusk was so deep they could barely see to return home.

On Sunday, September 7, though the day was clear and he should have continued his labors in the fields, Zeke took the twins to town. They left early enough to stop by Jenny's house and escort Hannah, Jenny, and the children to the Methodist church.

"We're coming home with you after the service," Hannah announced, when they were in the wagon on the way down the hill toward the center of town.

"You're safer with Jenny." Zeke didn't turn toward his wife but felt her stiffen beside him as he spoke.

"I don't care," Hannah said. "A wife's place is with her husband."

"I won't have it."

She sniffed. If Hannah was the type to "humph" she would have. Zeke's lips twitched at the thought, until he heard her speak. "I will not be persuaded by your 'lord and master' attitude. The 'obey' in my wedding vows did not mean I have to put up with pig-headedness."

"What about Ruth and Noah? And Faith?" If she didn't care about her own safety, would she risk the children's? "How will you protect them when I'm away?"

Now she did "humph," followed by, "And how will we protect them from the evils of town? My sister-in-law is as bad as anyone associated

338

with Mr. Feeney."

"What happened with Alice?" Zeke looked at Hannah in consternation. Sitting on the other side of his wife, Jenny sat stone-faced.

"I'll tell you when we're home." Hannah didn't say another word about her stay with Jenny.

After the service, Hannah went directly to the wagon. Zeke hurried after her. "Are you feeling all right?" he asked.

She nodded. "I just want to get home, Zeke. Please."

She wouldn't back down—he knew her well enough by now. "All right," he said. "We'll take Jenny home and gather your belongings."

She smiled at him for the first time that day.

In their room that evening, Zeke resumed his argument with Hannah. "I should take you back to town after you see to the house and laundry for a day or two. You're safer there."

"I don't care about my safety," Hannah replied. "I care about being with you."

"You've got to be responsible. We need to keep the young'uns safe. I can't watch out for any of you when I'm away from the house."

"We've already discussed this. I don't belong with Jenny. I belong with you."

Their argument went round in circles until he gave up. He couldn't force her to live away from home any longer.

Then Hannah recounted Alice's insult to Jenny and Jenny's tale of William's parentage. "She said you knew all this," Hannah said, "or I wouldn't be telling you. I promised Jenny I would keep her story to myself."

Zeke rubbed a hand over his face. "Yes. I knew. I also told her I wouldn't say nothing. That's why I didn't tell you." He wondered if he'd made a mistake keeping secrets from Hannah. But what did it matter to her who William's father was? Hannah had known he'd asked Jenny to marry him—which was all she needed to know.

"Jenny said . . . " Hannah's voice trailed off, then she frowned and said, "She said you didn't want to act as William's father, that you didn't want her child."

"It wasn't like that—" It hadn't been. He'd worried the boy might turn out to be like the rapist who fathered him. He hadn't been overjoyed to take on another man's child, but now he was raising his own siblings willingly, wasn't he? He knew where their blood came from, and the coming baby was his own blood kin.

"Do you want our child, Zeke?" Her voice quavered.

"Of course, I do!" How could she think otherwise? He took care of his own, and she was his, as was his child.

"I have to know you want it." Now she spoke firmly.

Zeke moved toward her. He took her in his arms, but she stood primly, schoolmarm to her core. He kissed her forehead and placed his hand on her belly. "Yes, I want our child. Boy or girl, brown hair like you or blond as Esther or anywhere in between."

She looked at him solemnly. "I've come to care for you, Zeke. I don't know when I began to love you, but it happened. Maybe during our nights"—she blushed—"or maybe during the days as I see you toiling for our family. But I do love you, and I love our child. That's why I have to be here with you. And I couldn't bear it if you did not want our child."

He stared at her, speechless. Love? She loved him?

What did that mean? He cared for Hannah, maybe he felt more for her than he'd felt for Jenny.

Hannah saw to his meals and household, she tended his siblings, she joined him in passion and carried his baby. He farmed and hunted and cared for the land and animals. He'd be damned if he let Feeney or his men touch her. Did that amount to love, or did love require more?

She seemed to want him to respond to her last words. He leaned over and kissed her, tenderly touching her lips and tongue until tenderness bloomed into fire. It was the only response he could think to give.

In the morning, Zeke rose wearily. He and Hannah had made love long into the night. He'd cherished her body and she'd received him joyfully. Or so he thought. But in the morning as she dressed she seemed quiet, reserved—almost as prickly as she'd been when he first met her.

There were so many sides to Hannah. The tetchy schoolmarm. The busy housekeeper. The tall, proud woman who wouldn't let a disfigured leg keep her from learning or doing anything. The woman who loved him—there was that word again, "love"—who loved him in the night.

Zeke took his brothers to the fields and they labored in silence piling the corn into sheaves. The work gave him time to think. Did he love Hannah? Some of the couples he'd known best in his life came to mind—his parents, Esther and Daniel, Jenny and Mac. He didn't feel about Hannah the way any of those pairs seemed to feel about each other.

He thought Pa and Ma had loved each other. Pa was devastated when Ma died, unable to cope, even though they'd been separated so often while Pa was in the Army. Pa took to drink after Ma was gone—he couldn't manage the wagon train, couldn't care for the young'uns. He'd married Amanda to have a woman tend to them.

Zeke didn't think he'd turn to drink if Hannah died, not like Pa. Though his heart pounded at the notion of Hannah dying—she could, after all, die in childbirth, just like Ma.

And Esther and Daniel—they'd had eyes only for each other almost from the day they met. Even Zeke had seen that, and as her older brother, he'd almost come to blows over Daniel's infatuation with his sister. It had been a good thing the young couple had married quickly.

Mac and Jenny? Even now, Zeke clenched his fist, remembering the fury he'd felt upon Mac's return from California almost a year ago. He could still feel the snap of Mac's head when Zeke punched him for abandoning Jenny . . . and for returning to steal Jenny away. But Zeke had come to realize Jenny had never been his. He'd hoped she would be, but she'd always been Mac's. She'd loved Mac even when he left her, even when she didn't think Mac would return.

If Hannah left him, how would he feel? Zeke paused at the end of a cornrow to mull over that notion. If she left him, he would be destroyed, more so than if she died. Was that love? Or was it responsibility—she was his, and he would care for her? He'd told her so, and he'd tell her so again. She and the child, they were his to care for through all their days. That was one certainty in his life. But was it love or obligation?

Chapter 64: Mac Returns

The week after Hannah returned home passed quietly. Zeke was finishing the harvest, and he took the twins and often Noah with him to the fields. Ruth and Faith stayed in the cabin with Hannah, except on Friday. "Rain's threatening," he told Hannah that morning. "I need the girls to help gather the corn also. Can't let it sit in the fields once it's cut. It'll rot."

"That's fine," Hannah said, wiping her hands on her apron.

"Will you be all right alone?" Zeke's face wrinkled in worry.

"I won't be alone," she said. "I'm going with you to help with the corn." The work would be hard, but the farm was hers also. After all, Zeke married her so he could keep it all.

"Not in your condition."

"Women have been having babies for a long time, Zeke. I'll be fine." She packed bread, cheese, and ham for a noon meal, along with ginger water. But when they got to the field, Zeke parked the wagon in the shade, and then told her to keep her sunbonnet on, despite the clouds.

"Stay in the wagon," he said. "You can empty the ears from our bushel baskets into the big ones for the mill. The rest of us will gather the corn."

She rolled her eyes, but kept silent.

It never did rain, but by supper time they'd harvested the last of the corn from the last of the fields. Hannah was exhausted, even though she hadn't labored nearly so much as the others. Ruth's cheeks were flushed, and sweat stained Faith's dress. The boys were even more disheveled.

"That's done," Zeke said as he took up the reins to drive home. "Tomorrow I'll haul the grain to the mill."

He went alone to town on Saturday, telling Jonathan and David to stay near the house, in case Feeney's man appeared.

"I thought I'd visit Esther today," Hannah said. "I haven't talked to her since before I stayed with Jenny."

Zeke shook his head. "Not today. You'll see her at church tomorrow."

Rather than argue, Hannah stayed home. She and the children saw no sign of anyone. When Zeke returned in the evening, he announced, "Mac's back in town. Heard it at the steamboat dock. I ain't seen him yet, but tomorrow I'll talk to him about Feeney stealing the timber and shooting Douglass in the back. I wonder if he even got my letter."

Hannah looked forward to church on Sunday. She wanted to thank Jenny again for her hospitality and offer congratulations on Mac's safe return from California. And she would welcome any news Mac brought from back East—the reports in the *Spectator* always seemed old by the time they were published. Mail service to California was much more frequent than to Oregon.

It took longer than Hannah wanted to get everyone ready to leave. When they reached the church, they had to rush inside to be seated. Jenny, Mac, and their two children sat in a pew farther forward. When the congregation stood for the opening hymn, Jenny clung to Mac's arm, smiling at him. Mac held a squirming Maria, the toddler reaching to be set down. William, recently turned four, leaned against Mac on the other side from Jenny and grinned up at his father. Mac tousled the boy's hair.

This was the boy Zeke hadn't wanted? Hannah thought anyone would be captivated by William's impish grin. In the months since Hannah had arrived in Oregon, the boy had grown from chubby baby to tall and lean. She touched her stomach, thinking of her own child. Would she have a son or a daughter? Short or tall? Curly hair or straight?

After the service, she and Zeke joined the McDougalls. Mac told stories of his two months in California. "I was able to find another agent to manage my affairs after my friend's death," he said. "And I hired an attorney to sell off Nate's assets. That was easy enough. Settling Nate's granddaughter Susan took more time. She was distraught at losing him."

A wry grimace crossed Jenny's face. "But you found her passage back to the States," she said. "For which I'm glad."

Mac laughed and put his arm around Jenny's shoulders, pulling her to him despite the public setting. "You're not jealous, sweetheart, are you? I have no interest in Susan."

"But you did once."

"Not after I realized I loved you." Mac dropped a kiss on his wife's cheek. Hannah couldn't help but smile, wishing Zeke would show affection for her publicly like Mac did for Jenny.

But Zeke seemed intent on discussing Mr. Feeney. "Did you get my letter?" he asked Mac. "Your tenant Feeney stole timber while you were gone. Several landowners in these parts lost logs to him. And when the Abercrombies and I called him on it, he threatened us and our families. Then he and his pals shot Douglass. Killed him."

"Jenny told me." Mac looked stricken. "Poor Douglass. And his family."

Zeke related all that had happened and ended by describing how Feeney had been arrested but one of his men got away. "I'm worried Feeney's man'll follow through on the threats," Zeke said. "Feeney threatened to burn down my house."

"What proof is there Feeney was the thief?" Mac sounded like the lawyer he was.

"You know I suspected old Abercrombie to begin with. But then I notched my logs and found some of them on your land along with other logs Feeney said were yours. He claimed he and his cronies cut it all at your request."

"Not so," Mac said, frowning. "I told him to farm the crops, but once our new house was built I had no reason to cut any wood. I didn't tell him to do any logging. I can harvest the timber in future years. Prices of old wood will keep rising as more people come to Oregon."

"Then we need to tell the sheriff," Zeke said. "Feeney's claiming we had no right to accuse him. Said his men shot Douglass in self-defense. Though he was hit in the back."

Hannah clutched his arm, worried the situation with Feeney would escalate.

"Tomorrow morning. First thing." Mac shook his head. "I'm sorry I chose such a bad tenant. Feeney seemed an amiable sort, but if he's a thief and a murderer, he should stay in jail. Whether charges are filed or not, I won't have him back on my land."

"I'll go with you," Zeke said. "Sheriff knows what Feeney done, what he said about Hannah." Hannah wondered again what Feeney had said— Zeke only told her Mac's tenant had threatened them. "I want to be there to see him locked up for good. And Abercrombie wants him hung for murder."

Hannah waited anxiously all Monday for Zeke's return. At dawn he'd ridden away through the fog, intending to meet Mac and the sheriff in town. She wished she could have accompanied the men, so she would know what was happening, but she was certain neither man would allow it.

She kept the children close to home. The twins complained, but she insisted they do chores in the barn. "Muck out the stalls," she said. "You've let them go this week because of the harvest."

By the noon meal, the haze lifted and the skies were clear. After they ate, she shooed the girls and Noah outside to play. "Stay in the yard," she told them. "And keep the door open. Shout if you see anyone." She placed the loaded rifle just inside the door, hoping she wouldn't need to use it.

The sun had dropped below the trees but not yet set when Zeke returned. Noah shouted, "Zeke's home!" and Hannah went to the doorway. Her husband's face was grim.

"What happened?" she asked.

"Let me put Red away. Then we'll talk." He took the gelding into the barn, the children all following him. Hannah trailed behind the others.

"Did you shoot anybody?" Jonathan asked.

Zeke shook his head. "No. Wait till we're in the house. Then I'll tell the story."

The children all whined in disappointment, but Zeke stayed silent until he was seated inside with a cup of coffee in his hand.

"Mac talked to Sheriff Thomas. Told him Feeney had no business cutting timber. That meant Feeney lied to the sheriff. So Feeney and his pal will stay locked up."

"What about the other man?" Hannah asked.

Zeke shrugged. "No one's seen him. Sheriff and his deputies are still looking, but with Feeney in jail, I don't think they'll look very hard for the other man. They'll only try the two they caught."

"So there will be a trial?" Hannah wasn't sure if that was a good thing or not. It would keep Zeke and the other men stirred up for weeks.

Zeke nodded. "For theft. And murder—though these two will probably say the third man shot Douglass."

"When will the trial be?" she asked.

"Whenever we can get the judge to hear it. Shouldn't be long." Zeke stretched his legs out toward the stove. "Though Mac says the bast—men might get off. As I said, there ain't no proof who shot Douglass. And there ain't much to show whose timber Feeney took. But Mac can testify he ain't given Feeney leave to cut wood, and I can testify Feeney said the wood was Mac's. That might be enough to convict him of stealing Mac's timber, even if we can't prove no other stealing."

"So it's over."

He looked at her. "Let's hope so."

Chapter 65: Locked Up

With Feeney in jail and the harvest finished, Zeke should have felt at ease on Tuesday. But he worried. Despite the fine fall weather, he worried. Would the sheriff be able to keep the murderers locked up, or would some lawyer get Feeney and his men out?

Zeke spent the morning with his brothers, plowing under the corn stubble. In the afternoon they helped Daniel Abercrombie gather the last of his corn. Daniel's father worked with them also.

"Fine crop, son," Samuel Abercrombie told Daniel. "'Bout the best I seen since we left Tennessee. Now we need to get onto harvesting Douglass's fields." His voice cracked when he mentioned his older son's name.

"I'm pleased with my yield," Daniel said. "How'd you do, Zeke?"

"Can't complain, least not about my grain. Though my yield ain't quite as good as yours." Then Zeke told them Feeney's trial was scheduled.

"Glad them sonsabitches is locked up," Samuel said. "You shoulda come told us soon as you heard. I want the bastard hanged for killing my boy."

"I needed to talk to Hannah and the young'uns. They were threatened also." Zeke pushed his hat off his forehead and wiped the sweat from his brow. "I know Hannah was worried."

"If the judge don't hang Feeney, I'll see to it myself." Samuel spat a stream of tobacco juice.

Zeke shook his head. "McDougall ain't even sure they'll stay locked up. Says Feeney'll try to claim self-defense on Douglass's death."

"The hell with self-defense!" Samuel bellowed. "Have McDougall come talk to me. I'll tell him what's what. We was there. We know what Feeney and his men done. And we all seen them logs. We heard Feeney say he got 'em from McDougall's own land. How the hell can McDougall say there ain't no evidence?"

"He didn't say there weren't no evidence," Zeke said. "Just that it were weak. Feeney can claim it was all a misunderstanding—that he thought Mac wanted him to cut the timber."

"And our logs? Yours and mine? And Pa's?" Daniel said. "We all had wood stolen. You and me, we marked ours. We seen it there."

"Sheriff didn't think it'd hold up in court." Zeke shrugged. "Says anyone coulda notched the wood."

"The judge'd better listen to us," Samuel blustered. "Damn shame when a man can't get the benefit of the timber on his own land."

By Wednesday morning, Zeke was so antsy he decided to ride into town to check on Feeney himself. Other neighboring farmers thought Feeney would stay locked up until trial and then hung, but Zeke had heard Mac and the sheriff debate the evidence. Mac argued hard against Feeney, and Zeke chimed in as well. But Sheriff Thomas had been doubtful—and he'd seen more lawbreakers than Mac and Zeke combined.

"What's the word, Sheriff?" Zeke asked.

The lawman chewed on the end of a cigar and squinted up at Zeke from his chair. "About Feeney? He's still behind bars. And his man with him."

"Good to hear. They got a lawyer yet?"

"Yep." The sheriff rocked back on the rear legs of his chair. "The man's new in Oregon, but says he had a thriving law practice back East. If that's true, I wonder why he bothered to come here. Unless he was running from the law himself."

"Is he going to try to get Feeney and his man out afore trial?" That was Zeke's biggest fear—that Feeney would be free and full of anger. Hannah might not be safe yet.

"That's what every criminal's lawyer tries to do." Sheriff Thomas didn't seem concerned.

"Do you think he can?"

The lawman shrugged. "All's I can say is, I'll let you know if the judge orders me to let 'em out. And I'll keep an eye on 'em as long as they're in these parts."

"Won't they have to stick around for their trial?" Zeke asked.

"That's what the judge'll order 'em to do. But if I was in their boots, I'd hustle down to California. Start over there."

His conversation with Sheriff Thomas left Zeke feeling unsettled. It was fine to have Feeney and his crony locked up, but one of Feeney's outlaws was still free, and the jailed men could be let out. He didn't trust the sheriff to let him know in time to stop Feeney from hurting Hannah or the young'uns. So he stopped by Mac's law office before returning home.

"Talked to the sheriff," Zeke said as he entered.

"And?" Mac leaned back in his chair, just like Thomas had, though his expression showed more concern than the lawman's.

"Feeney's got a lawyer trying to get him out of jail."

Mac nodded. "I expected as much."

"Yeah, me too." Zeke sighed. "But it don't make me feel any better 'bout it. Ain't there any way we can make sure he stays locked up?"

Mac shook his head. "Doubtful. Not if Feeney promises to be here for his trial."

"When will that be?"

"Don't know." Mac sat forward, his front chair legs slamming onto the floor. "A prosecutor's been named, but he doesn't know anything about the case. I thought I'd go see him tomorrow. Tell him what we know. His next steps should be to investigate on his own, prepare the case." Mac shrugged. "If he isn't too busy, it should only take a couple of weeks."

"Can he tell the judge to keep Feeney in jail?"

Mac shrugged again. "I'll ask the prosecutor. Make sure he knows about the threats to your family. The threats, plus Douglass's death, ought to give the judge pause to let Feeney go free."

"What can I do?" Zeke felt helpless. A farmer had little power once the lawyers got hold of a matter. Maybe he should have let Abercrombie shoot Feeney when he wanted to. Whether Hannah wanted violence or not.

Maybe he was obsessing over Feeney. But how could he live with himself if Hannah or the young'uns got hurt?

Chapter 66: Showdown

Zeke came back from town on Wednesday afternoon looking glum. "What's wrong?" Hannah asked him, trying to keep the fear out of her voice. "Has Mr. Feeney been released?"

"Nope. He and his man are still in jail. But Mac and the sheriff can't tell me they'll stay there."

She breathed a sigh of relief. They were out of any immediate danger. "No sense fretting about them getting out unless it happens."

"I can't help worrying. I got to keep you and the young'uns safe."

Hannah wished Zeke saw his family as more than an obligation, a burden to watch over. She knew he cared for them, but sometimes she wondered if *he* knew it. His actions portrayed his affection, but it would be nice to have him say the words sometimes. In the meantime, there was supper to eat. "Stew's ready," she told him. "Go wash up, and get the boys to do the same."

Through the evening meal, the children peppered Zeke with questions about the "bandits," as Jonathan and David had taken to calling Feeney and his gang. "You don't think them bandits will escape, do you, Zeke?" Jonathan asked.

David scoffed. "There ain't never been a jailbreak in Oregon yet."

"But there could be," Jonathan insisted. "And one of 'em's still loose."

Noah's eyes widened as his brothers bantered. Faith and Ruth stayed silent, but Ruth bit her lip and merely pushed the food around on her plate.

"Shush," Hannah finally told the twins. "You're scaring the others."

They muttered, but started teasing each other about the harvest dance in mid-October. "You gonna dance with Annabelle Abercrombie?" David asked Jonathan.

"Weren't planning on it."

"Wasn't," Hannah corrected. "I wasn't planning on it."

At that, both twins chortled. "Didn't expect *you* to dance with her, Hannah," David said, snickering.

Hannah raised an eyebrow at his insolence, but smiled as she did so.

Later that night, she lay in Zeke's arms after he'd made gentle love to her. He whispered drowsily, "God help me, Hannah, if anything happened to you or the babe."

The rest of the week passed smoothly, the weather clear and pleasant. With the hard work of harvest over, Zeke and the boys had time to hunt and fish. On the Saturday after Feeney was arrested, the whole family— Hannah thought of the Pershing children as her family, and Faith fit seamlessly into the Pershing clan—packed food for the noon meal and went to the creek.

"We should think about school for the children," Hannah said to Zeke as they watched the boys fishing and the girls berrying. Blackie raced from one child to another, begging for attention.

"Can't you teach 'em?" he murmured. He dozed beside her with his hat over his face.

"I suppose," she said. "But I have the household to look after."

"You managed Jenny's cabin while teaching last year."

Hannah laughed. "If you think cooking for Faith and myself is the same as for you and all your kin—"

He rolled over and laid his head in her lap. "Don't worry. If you get Noah to do some lessons, that'll be enough. Ruth knows plenty, and she and Faith can keep up their reading together. The twins know everything they need to."

It went against her nature to let children forgo their education. School had been a haven for her growing up. "We could send Ruth to town to the girls' academy. Jacob may want Faith to return there for the fall term."

"How much is the fee?"

"I don't know. I'll find out."

Zeke wriggled as if to get more comfortable. "I expect we could send Ruth to school in town, if she wants. Though she's likely to want to set up her own household soon."

"Soon! She's twelve." The idea of Ruth marrying so young horrified

351

Hannah.

"I didn't mean this year, but in a couple of years. Esther married at fifteen. Rachel was barely fifteen. Too many single men in Oregon for Ruth to stay with us for long."

"And do you think the twins should marry as well?" Hannah bristled at the notion—the twins couldn't even remember to wash their hands before eating.

Zeke shook his head against her skirt. "They need land afore they can marry. Or some other way of supporting a family."

She ran a hand over his hair. "Like you had."

"They won't be able to claim as much land. But since I can keep the whole six hundred forty acres, we'll have enough to get 'em started. And Noah, too, when he's ready."

"And that's why you married me."

He squinted up at her. "You knew that." He patted her belly, which hadn't yet begun to swell. "Look at how well we've done together. It's been a good match. And when I perfect my claim in November, we'll be set."

Hannah sighed, then smiled down at him. "Yes, Zeke. We'll be set."

Sunday services and fellowship on September 21 passed with more talk about Feeney and his gang. The Abercrombies were there, and Samuel asked Mac when he expected Douglass's murder to be avenged. Mac said the trial would likely be held the first week in October, two weeks hence. Until then, there was nothing Abercrombie or Zeke could do.

As they drove home after church, Hannah told Zeke again not to fret. "I'll quit worrying when he's locked up for good," he responded. "Or dead. And not before." She didn't say anything more after that.

On Monday, Zeke decided to take the twins hunting. "We need to start salting meat for the winter," he said. "Will you be all right with the girls and Noah? I'd leave Blackie, but he's a help in the field."

"I'm sure we'll be fine," she said, smiling at him, glad he felt able to leave her. "We're doing laundry today. You'd be happier if you're out of the way."

"Let the girls haul the washtubs," he said. "Or do you want me to leave one of the twins here?"

"We can do it," Ruth assured him. "We've been dragging those tubs around all year, ain't—haven't we?"

"Go on," Hannah told him.

"Keep the extra rifle handy," Zeke said as he left.

The women worked all morning, and Noah grew increasingly cantankerous. "Wish I coulda gone hunting," he complained. "I don't get to go nowhere. This is women's work. Can I go fishing?"

"By yourself?" Hannah asked.

"I'm eight and a half," Noah boasted. "I been fishing since I was four."

"Let him go, Hannah," Ruth said. "He'll be cross as a grizzly if he stays."

"I don't want him encountering any wild animals," Hannah said. "I thought the bears were fishing also—fattening themselves for winter."

"I'll be careful, Hannah," Noah whined. "I won't let no bear catch me."

"Any bear," Hannah said, knowing she'd lost the argument. "Stay on this side of the creek."

After Noah left, Hannah and the girls finished the washing and hung the laundry out to dry. "Let's go inside and sit a spell," Hannah said. "Do some mending until the clothes dry."

High thin clouds kept the afternoon sky hazy, and the girls welcomed the chance to sit inside. They gathered their needlework and began to sew. Faith and Ruth chatted amicably. Hannah rocked as she darned Zeke's socks, thinking she would soon need to cut down some of the boys' shirts into baby clothes. She wasn't a good knitter, but could probably manage a few small garments. Perhaps Esther could teach her new stitches.

"Zeke! Hannah! Help!" Noah's voice shrilled from outside.

Hannah jumped from her chair and raced to the door, Ruth and Faith right behind her. She pulled the door open and gasped.

Feeney had his arm around Noah's neck, a pistol at the boy's head.

She stopped the girls from following any farther. "Stay here," she hissed. "Get the rifle." Her knees quaking, she went outside and called, "Let the boy go, Mr. Feeney."

"Found him wandering in the woods. Ain't I told him before it ain't safe?" Feeney grinned. "Seems I was right."

"What do you want?" Hannah's heart pounded, louder than the clothes flapping on the line. She had no defense against a gun and wanted to run inside and bolt the door, but she couldn't leave Noah alone with the man.

"Can I give you something to eat?"

"Well, ma'am, that might be nice. But what I really want is a horse. Where's your husband?"

"He's away at the moment, but should be home any time now." The Lord would forgive a lie in this situation, surely. Hannah swallowed the bile in her throat. "Please put your gun down, Mr. Feeney. You're scaring Noah."

"You wanna take his place, Mrs. Pershing?" Feeney chortled vilely. "Or I could take one of those girls you got inside."

"Let the boy go, and I'll help you saddle a mule. The horse is gone." If she could keep her wits, Feeney might bargain with her. Could she get him to leave? Though Zeke had told her to shoot Feeney if he showed up. "While we saddle the mule, Noah can go inside and help his sister prepare some food for you to take." She took a step into the yard.

Feeney squinted at her, then cuffed Noah away. He turned the pistol toward Hannah, motioning her toward the barn. "All right, then. Let's go."

Hannah said to Noah, "Get Ruth to pack meat and bread in a towel and place it outside the door."

"Some cider, too, if you have it," Feeney said.

"I think we have some ginger beer," Hannah said. "Put a bottle in the bundle of food."

Noah nodded vigorously and dashed for the door.

Hannah moved toward Feeney, wanting to take his attention off the children. "How'd you get free, Mr. Feeney? Did your lawyer get you out?"

"Lawyers." Feeney spat. "My man on the outside came for us."

A jailbreak then, Hannah thought. Feeney would be desperate to get away. If she helped him, he would leave, and he wouldn't come back. "Let's saddle the mule. He isn't used to carrying a man, but he's done it before. He should take you away faster than if you walked."

"Well, I surely hope so. I ain't planning to stick around in these parts. Killed a deputy getting out, so all the lawmen in the territory will be gunning for me."

Her skin crawled as she entered the barn ahead of Feeney, his gun and menacing grin blocking her exit. She motioned toward the saddle and bridle, but he waved the pistol at her. "You do it, Mrs. Pershing. I ain't taking the gunsight off you till I leave."

So Hannah saddled the mule. "Where are your men, Mr. Feeney?"

"Could be anywhere. We split up once we was out of jail."

Hannah handed the reins to Feeney.

He shook his head. "Lead him on out. Tie him to the fence."

She did as he instructed.

"Now go get my food."

The bundle was right outside the door, and she picked it up. "Tie it on the saddle horn."

"Our rope is in the barn."

He motioned with the pistol for her to go get it. As she returned to the barn, he followed her. She reached up for a skein of rope looped over a hook on the wall. She turned around, and Feeney punched her in the stomach. She grunted as the air left her lungs.

He pressed himself against her, shoving her into the wall. Her head snapped back and hit the hook, gashing her scalp. Her vision blurred from the sharp pain.

She tried to push him away. When she finally got her breath, she gasped, "I've done what you wanted. Let me go." Feeney's breath stank and his body smelled fetid. Bile rose to her throat and she stifled a retch.

"Pershing owes me for getting me locked up. I know how he can repay me." His gun hand pressed the pistol to her temple, while the other hand crept up her body, then down again.

If she fought, he'd shoot her. If she stayed still, he'd rape her. Fear lanced her belly, sharp as a pain. How could she get away?

Feeney stuck his tongue in her mouth and pawed her with one hand, keeping the pistol firmly against her head with the other. Blood trickled down her neck from the cut in her scalp. Still pressing his weight against her, he quit groping and wrestled with the buttons on his pants. "You undo 'em," he groaned, tapping the gun against her scalp. "Now."

Her fingers fumbled at the buttons until they were undone, but she refused to pull out his member—she wouldn't touch it. He moved his legs apart to free himself. *A chance!* She kneed him in the groin.

He yowled, the gun went off, and he fell to the ground. Had he shot himself? Hannah didn't stop to check, she ran toward the house, her bad leg throbbing from the blow she'd dealt Feeney.

Faith stood in the doorway, rifle in hand. "I heard the shot," she said. "I was coming after you."

"Give it to me," Hannah said and took the rifle.

Feeney staggered in the barn doorway, pants still undone. He raised the pistol in his hand toward them.

Hannah shot, and Feeney went down, grabbing his thigh.

Hands shaking, Hannah reloaded the carbine, then trained the rifle on Feeney's writhing body. She hadn't killed him, but he wouldn't be riding off either. "Get his gun, Faith," she said. "Ruth, the rope's on the barn floor. Tie him up."

When Zeke and the twins returned an hour later, Hannah sat on the cabin stoop. She braced the carbine on her lap, pointing it across the barnyard at a trussed and moaning Feeney. Faith, Ruth, and Noah sat around her.

Faith had bandaged Hannah's gashed scalp, though the wound still pulsed and ached. But Hannah had not told the children about the stabbing pain piercing her gut.

Chapter 67: Tragedy

Zeke had never been so frightened as when he saw Hannah sitting on the front step of their cabin with a bandage around her head and a rifle in her lap, the young'uns beside her. Heedless of the deer carcass lashed to Red's saddlebags, he kicked his mount forward, leaving the twins and Blackie behind. He rode into the barnyard and vaulted off the gelding, leaving the reins to dangle.

He ran to Hannah and knelt beside her. "What happened? Are you all right?"

She pointed toward the barn.

Only then did he see Feeney writhing on the ground, tied like a hog for butchering and bleeding from his leg. "How did he get here?" he asked.

"Says he escaped. He had Noah. I shot him." Hannah started to shiver, and Zeke lifted her into his arms. There was more to the story, he was sure, but he'd find out after he saw to Hannah and dealt with Feeney.

The twins ran into the yard, Blackie at their heels. The dog barked and snarled at the wounded villain. "One of you take care of the horse and meat," Zeke shouted. "The other keep the gun on Feeney." Then he carried Hannah into the cabin and laid her on their bed. "Are you all right?" he asked again, touching her bandaged scalp.

"I banged my head. Just get rid of Mr. Feeney, please," she murmured, still shaking.

Zeke looked around the room helplessly, not wanting to leave her alone.

A shout sounded from the yard, and he rushed outside. "Ruth, go sit with Hannah." The girl went inside.

Mac McDougall rode up on his stallion. "Feeney escaped. I came as soon as I heard. Sheriff told me an hour ago. A deputy died in the melee."

"Bastard's right there," Zeke said, gesturing. "Don't know what happened—I just got here myself. Hannah says she shot him. She's hurt."

Mac dismounted and knelt beside Feeney. "He's still breathing, more's the pity. I'll take him back to town. You stay here with your family."

Zeke noticed one of the mules saddled and tied to the fence. "What's the mule doing there?" he asked.

"Feeney wanted to use him to escape," Faith said.

Zeke turned to the twins. Jonathan gaped from the barn doorway, while David pointed Hannah's rifle at Feeney. "Jonathan, bring out the other mule." After the boy complied, Zeke tied a rope around Feeney's thigh to slow the bleeding. He and Mac heaved the cursing murderer onto the mule's back like the sack of manure he was.

Zeke ran a hand through his hair. "Where's the rest of his gang?" he asked, not directing his question to anyone in particular.

"Sheriff doesn't know," Mac said.

"Feeney told Aunt Hannah they'd all run in different directions," Faith said. "We haven't seen any sign of them."

Zeke was torn. He wanted to stay with Hannah, but with two of the villains still loose, Mac shouldn't take Feeney to town alone. "Can you young'uns take care of things till I get back?" he asked.

Noah whimpered, but Faith put a hand on the boy's head. "We'll be fine," she said.

"We'll stand guard," Jonathan said. David nodded.

"Faith, you help Ruth with Hannah. And tend to Noah." Zeke led Faith and Noah inside. Hannah lay on the bed with her eyes closed. Ruth sat beside her and held her hand. "Mac and I need to take Feeney back to jail," he said. "Will you be all right?"

Hannah didn't open her eyes, but pursed her lips and nodded.

Zeke returned to the yard, then rode Red toward town, leading the mule laden with Feeney. Mac rode behind them, rifle in hand. When they arrived at the sheriff's office, Zeke stormed inside, leaving Mac to guard Feeney. He found Sheriff Thomas and his men discussing the search for the escapees. The lawmen shouted and cursed in frustration and concern over the murdered deputy.

"We have Feeney outside," Zeke announced. "My wife shot him." Zeke made no effort to keep the pride out of his voice at Hannah's courage and resourcefulness.

"Well done," Sheriff Thomas said, surprised. "Rumor has it one of his pals was headed toward Portland, and I sent a man after him. But I hadn't heard about Feeney or his other companion. We'll have at least one man to hang for the killings they've done."

The men went outside. "She done us all a favor," the sheriff said as he examined Feeney's bleeding thigh. "But it's too bad she didn't shoot him dead," he added. "Now we still gotta have a trial."

Zeke told Sheriff Thomas what he knew about Feeney's visit to his farm, but he couldn't answer most of the lawman's questions. "If you need more information, come talk to Hannah tomorrow."

"I'll be there," Sheriff Thomas said.

Zeke left Mac and the sheriff and headed home with the mule in tow behind Red.

When he arrived back at his claim, Zeke found the twins and Noah sitting outside. David still held the rifle as he had when Zeke left. "What's going on?" Zeke asked.

"Faith's inside," Jonathan said. "Ruth went to get Esther."

"Why?" Zeke asked.

"Hannah's sick."

"Take care of Red and the mule," Zeke told the boys. He went inside and stood in the bedroom doorway. "What's wrong?" he asked.

"She's losing the baby," Faith said, in tears. "I don't know what to do."

"Did you send for the doctor?" Zeke asked, kneeling beside an ashen Hannah, her head still in a bloody bandage.

Faith shook her head. "Just Esther."

Zeke went to the barnyard. "Jonathan, go get Doc Tuller. Or his wife, whichever one can come quickest. Take Red." The horse was tired, but Hannah's well-being was more important. Then he returned to Hannah, who moaned in pain.

"How long has this gone on?" he asked Faith.

Hannah whispered, "Pain started after Feeney attacked me."

"He what?" She hadn't mentioned any attack before. "Tell me what happened."

"I saddled the mule for him, so he could get away." She grimaced and paused. "He hit me. In the belly. My head struck the hook."

"Hannah!" He wanted to be soothing, but he heard the anguish in his voice. She could have been killed. "But you'll be all right," he said. She had to be.

"The baby!" she sobbed.

"Let's wait till Doc Tuller gets here."

She shook her head, thrashing on the bed. "It's gone. I know it is."

Esther came. Doc Tuller came. They couldn't do anything. By late evening, it was over.

As the doctor packed his bag to leave, Zeke asked, "Will Hannah be all right?"

Doc nodded. "Most women recover fine after a miscarriage." He shrugged. "Sepsis is possible. Just like after a birth. But this early in pregnancy, it don't usually happen."

"Will she have another child?"

The doctor frowned at Zeke. "It's way too early for you to be thinking about another one. She needs rest."

"But will she?"

Doc snorted. "I don't know. No doctor knows whether a woman'll get pregnant. With her leg . . . and her head wound . . . medicine simply can't answer these questions. And some women ain't built to carry children to term."

Through the night, Hannah slept, and Zeke sat by the fire, dry sobs escaping. His thoughts about love and obligation and Pa's drinking after Ma died returned to him. He would have been devastated to lose Hannah. All his doubts about what she meant to him vanished.

He loved her.

The gray skies the next morning matched the mood in the Pershing cabin. Zeke puttered about the house and barn, fixing things that didn't need fixing. He kept all the boys outside, and told Ruth and Faith to be quiet as they cooked and washed dishes.

Hannah stayed in bed.

Esther came over in midmorning, carrying five-month-old Abigail, not yet weaned. "How is Hannah?" she asked.

Zeke shrugged. "She don't say much."

Esther went into the bedroom, and Zeke heard the women murmuring. After a short time, his sister came out, wiping her eyes. "She's fine, really," she told Zeke. "Just sad."

"She told me her head hurt," Zeke said.

"It does, but losing the baby—that's what hurts her most." Esther sighed. "And me—" She gestured at the baby on her hip. "Seeing Abby don't help. It's everything she'll never have." Esther's voice caught as she spoke.

Shocked, Zeke said, "Doc didn't say we couldn't have another."

"That's not what Hannah thinks. She's convinced she'll never carry again."

Had their chance for happiness been taken from them forever? Zeke's heart rebelled. He'd only just acknowledged to himself his love for Hannah. Was it too late? She must know he'd love her whether she had children or not.

After Esther left, he crept into the darkened bedroom and sat beside his wife. "Hannah."

"Mmm?" she said sleepily.

"I love you."

At that, her eyes opened and she glared at him. "You don't have to say it, just because I lost the baby."

"It's not your fault," he said, stroking her cheek. "Feeney—"

"I never expected to carry a child. Maybe I wasn't meant to. My leg—"

"Your leg has done you fine, all the time you've been in Oregon. Look what you can do now—keep house, tend a garden, shoot—"

"Shoot?" She almost spat the word. "What good did shooting Feeney do me? Our baby's gone."

"You saved Noah and the others. You saved yourself."

She turned her head away. "And lost our child."

He knelt where she had to look at him. "It's you I love. It's you I can't live without."

She closed her eyes and wouldn't talk to him. Zeke thought she went to sleep after a bit, but he stayed beside her, praying as he hadn't prayed since Ma died. He prayed for Hannah to get over this loss. He prayed for them to have another child. He prayed for Feeney to rot in hell.

But as he prayed, the thought didn't leave him—Feeney might have cost him Hannah as well as the baby. Their new love might not survive the death of the unborn infant. Zeke sat beside his wife, holding her hand. He didn't move until Ruth called him for the noon meal.

Chapter 68: Empty

Friday, September 26, dawned bright and clear. Hannah managed to drag herself out of bed and begin preparing breakfast. She grieved the loss of her child bitterly—her sorrow colored even the sunshine and blue sky. She noted those things dispassionately, unable to feel any pleasure in the fine day.

It had just been four days, she told herself. Four days since Feeney attacked her, since her womb had emptied. Surely she was entitled to grieve more than four days.

The household swirled around her, hushed but active. Zeke and the boys were preparing the fields to plant winter wheat. Faith and Ruth talked in low voices and stifled their giggles as they did housework. She couldn't begrudge the rest of the family their pleasures, just because she was unable to feel any joy herself.

Zeke came to bed at night and folded her into his arms gently. She wanted to lean on him, to respond to his caring, but she couldn't. She was angry. Angry Zeke hadn't been there when Feeney came, though there was no reason he should have been. Angry he'd taken Feeney back to jail while she bled out their child, though he hadn't yet known of the loss. Angry he'd said he loved her—how could he love her when she didn't love herself? She had no value as a wife or mother, she couldn't keep the child she'd conceived. He'd said the words merely to make her feel better, and instead his concern made her feel worse.

Zeke came up behind her Friday morning as she fried bacon and whispered in her ear, "Glad to see you up." He squeezed her shoulders.

She froze, unable to respond, or even to grunt an acknowledgment.

He left her and sat at the table. "Ruth, is the cornbread ready?" he asked. Ruth brought him the bread and honey, and he turned his attention to the meal.

When Hannah slid bacon onto his plate, he nodded. "Thank you," as if she was a stranger.

She wanted to scream that she was his wife, that they'd lost a child. She wanted to demand that he cry with her.

After Zeke and the boys left, she told the girls, "I'm going to the barn to see if Noah missed any eggs." When she got to the barn she slumped onto a pile of hay and sobbed.

She was ashamed of her tears. They reminded her of how Amanda Pershing hid in her darkened bedroom after her husband died. Amanda abandoned her children and stepchildren, until Hannah and others stepped in to help. Even then, the woman ran away as soon as she could.

Now, running away seemed like an excellent plan, if only Hannah had somewhere to run.

Hannah accompanied the rest of the family to church on Sunday, but she played no part in getting the children ready. She wasn't sure who had supervised the boys' washing and hair combing—Zeke? Ruth? No matter, they were all in the wagon at the appointed time. She sat beside Zeke as he drove, not touching her, though he glanced at her from time to time. The children talked quietly in back, only Noah showing any exuberance.

After church, she told Zeke, "I'm going to sit in the wagon until you're all ready to leave."

"Are you tired?" he asked, frowning.

She shook her head. "I just don't feel like talking." Every woman she saw seemed to be pregnant or carrying a baby—a joy she didn't think she'd ever experience again. Doc Tuller had given her little hope.

Jenny stepped over to the wagon. Jenny's child must be due in a matter of weeks, Hannah thought with a pang.

"I'm sorry for your loss," Jenny told her.

"Thank you," Hannah said numbly.

"I haven't lost a child myself," Jenny continued. "But I've seen the anguish it causes. Hatty Tanner—she and her family lived on the claim with me when Mac left—she had a stillborn daughter. Named her Jenny, after me. Little Jenny Tanner, who never drew a breath, is buried under a tree on our claim."

Hannah remembered seeing the grave. She nodded, but the lump in her throat prevented her from saying anything. She closed her eyes, saddened that she hadn't even had the benefit of a prayer over her baby's grave—it had been too early. Jenny patted her hand and left.

Her brother Jacob approached the wagon. "I heard you've suffered a loss," he said, his words brusque, though his expression seemed sorrowful. "I'm sorry."

She nodded.

"Our mother lost a child, too. Did you know? After Jane and before you. I was a boy at the time."

Hannah shook her head, feeling a pang of devastation over a sibling she'd never known existed. "I didn't know." Did the failure to carry a child run in her family?

"If there's anything I can do . . ." Jacob's voice trailed off.

Hannah saw Alice moving toward Jacob from across the churchyard. She couldn't bear to talk to her sister-in-law now. "Thank you, brother. I'll be fine." She waved to Zeke to hurry him in collecting the children. "We'll be off for home soon," she told Jacob. "I appreciate your concern."

In the following week, as September became October, Hannah continued to feel blue. She went about her daily chores, determined not to collapse as Amanda Pershing had. But more and more the thought came to her—she didn't belong in Oregon. She'd never belonged, and she should leave.

She told herself she wouldn't run away, that she couldn't—she had nowhere to go and no one to turn to. Would Jacob help her leave? When she'd first arrived, her brother had been all too eager to help her return to Ohio. But the money he'd intended for her ticket had gone into lumber for Zeke's house addition. Could he help her now?

On Thursday, Jenny and Esther arrived with baskets of mending. Hannah had intended to bake bread, but when the women arrived, Faith told her, "Ruth and I can make the bread. You sit and sew with your friends."

Esther settled her baby Abigail to play on a blanket. "She turns over now, and tries to scoot, but she can't move very fast. She'll be fine beside me on the floor."

Hannah tried to smile. She'd been happy to attend Esther during Abigail's birth in April, but now the sight of the infant filled her with sadness. She choked back a sob.

Esther and Jenny gossiped while the three women sewed. Hannah dutifully brought out her mending, but she contributed little to the conversation. She didn't care about Louisa Abercrombie's new dress, nor about Doc Tuller's graying hair and his wife's increasing girth, nor about the harvest dance the following Saturday. She would not be dancing anytime soon.

When the women were ready to leave, Esther hugged Hannah. "It'll get better," she said, shaking Hannah's shoulders gently. "Grief always does. A body can't stay sad forever."

Jenny followed with another hug. "There is happiness after tragedy, Hannah. You'll be happy again, I know you will."

That evening, Zeke sat smoking a cigarette by the fire, complaining to the twins it would likely rain the next day. Faith read *The Old Curiosity Shop* by Dickens, Ruth knitted a sock, and the boys played marbles on the floor. Hannah watched them all, feeling distant and alone.

She should write Jane about her loss. Her last letter had been filled with hope. Now she would have to report that motherhood was not in her future after all.

Hannah found her paper, ink, and quill.

October 2, 1851

Dear Jane,

Last week my hopes of a blessed event next spring were dashed. My unborn angel has been called to its heavenly home, and I am distraught.

I now wonder whether I should ever have made this disastrous trip to Oregon. I feel no more settled now than I did after my arrival a year ago.

Hannah set her quill on the table and put her head in her hands.

Had it truly been a year? Almost—she'd arrived in mid-October 1850. So much had happened. She'd taught school. She'd kept house for Zeke, then married him. She'd loved Zeke and his siblings. She'd grown to see the beauty in the land. But now? Now it all seemed lost to her. Despite her friends' assurances, she saw no hope for happiness.

How could she stay married to Zeke knowing she couldn't give him a child?

Chapter 69: Love Lost

Feeney's trial began on Monday, October 6. Zeke attended with Mac McDougall. It was just two weeks after Feeney attacked Hannah and she shot him. Just two weeks after she'd lost the baby.

Feeney was the only man tried for the murders of Douglass Abercrombie and the deputy, the attempted murder and attempted rape of Hannah, the kidnapping of Noah, and the theft of timber. His two cohorts had disappeared. Zeke suspected they'd fled as the sheriff speculated.

A few days before the trial started, the prosecuting attorney had come to the farm and spoken with Zeke and Hannah. "We're trying the man for as many crimes as possible," the lawyer told them. "I want him to hang."

Zeke nodded. He wanted the man dead also.

"But you'll need to testify, Mrs. Pershing," the prosecutor said. "I can try to keep your boy Noah out of it. But Feeney confessed to you and he injured you, and you'll have to tell the jury about what he said and did."

"All right," Hannah said. "I'll testify."

The attorney's face reddened. "I know you suffered a bereavement, ma'am. I can't do anything about the loss of your child under the law. But he'll pay for the rest of what he's done." The lawyer asked her in detail about Feeney's actions, preparing her for her testimony at trial. Zeke went rigid with rage as he listened while Hannah recounted in a monotone how Feeney trapped her in the barn. Zeke tried to take his wife's hand at one point, but she brushed him away.

On the day the trial began, Zeke sat in the courtroom, preparing to hear evidence that would again make him livid. Samuel and Daniel Abercrombie and Mac McDougall were also present.

Sheriff Thomas testified first. He told of Feeney's first arrest and escape from jail. The lawman hemmed and hawed when describing the escape—

how Feeney's pal took the keys from the deputy, then one of the villains killed the deputy. Zeke's anger returned as he heard how incompetent the sheriff's office had been. If the deputy hadn't been overpowered, Hannah might not have been hurt. They would probably still be expecting their child in the spring.

During the two weeks since Feeney attacked her, Zeke had watched Hannah sink into deep despair. After the first few days, she resumed her chores, seemingly determined to behave as if nothing had happened. But Zeke knew she was distressed. Once he'd awakened in the night and heard her weeping into her pillow. He'd reached out to her and whispered, "It's all right, love," but she'd shrugged him off, just as she had when the prosecutor talked to her.

Zeke took the stand and testified about his timber losses and the confrontation with Feeney on McDougall's claim when Douglass was shot. Samuel and Daniel Abercrombie gave their evidence as well, Samuel's anger palpable as he spoke. Mac McDougall avowed he'd never authorized Feeney to cut wood. That part of the trial seemed wrapped up by the end of the day on Monday.

But the morrow would bring Hannah's time on the witness stand. Zeke again wished he could spare her the ordeal—she would hate describing her near-rape to a roomful of men. But to prove Feeney's guilt beyond a reasonable doubt, she would have to do it.

As Zeke rode home, he mulled over the events of the past year. It wasn't much over a year ago that Jenny rejected him. Then he'd met Hannah, argued with her over the young'uns, hired her as a housekeeper, married her. The life he'd built with Hannah was far richer than what he'd dreamed of with Jenny. But perhaps the happiness he'd begun to enjoy with Hannah had been taken from him before he even knew he had it.

Tuesday morning, Zeke and Hannah drove silently into town. She sat beside him, as rigid as when the prosecutor questioned her the week before. "I wish you didn't have to do this," he said.

She sighed. "No way around it. I'm the only one who heard Feeney confess to killing the deputy."

Zeke wanted to tell Hannah how he felt about her, though it didn't come easy to him. "I love you, Hannah. You've become my world."

A wistful smile touched her lips, and she leaned against him briefly. "I know you're trying to help, Zeke."

"Can we find our way back?"

"Back where?" she asked.

He shrugged. He didn't really know what he was trying to say. "We were happy before, weren't we?"

She stared toward the cloudy sky, her eyes bright.

"I've been happy with you, Hannah."

She looked at him and brushed away tears. "I'm not a wifely person, I suppose. I never thought I would be, and I'm not."

"How can you say that?" Her remark surprised him—she'd been everything a wife should be. Kept the house and young'uns. Worked in his fields. Warmed his bed and conceived his child. She'd won his heart—she must know she had.

"I never thought I'd marry. My leg. The baby. It's God's way of telling me I've grasped for too much."

"Hannah, if anybody deserves—"

She waved a hand to silence him.

When they arrived at the courthouse, Zeke tied the mules to a post and escorted Hannah inside. She was the first witness of the day. As the prosecutor took her through the events with Feeney, she told her story quietly, but with poise, ending with how she'd escaped the man and shot him. Zeke was proud of her composure, though he ached when he stared at her pallid face, wishing he could speak in her place.

He glared at Feeney who sat in the front of the courtroom next to his attorney. When Hannah described the blows to her head and belly, Zeke almost jumped the bar between spectators and lawyers. And at her account of Feeney's attempted molestation, Zeke wanted to pound the man's face into jelly. He'd been able to punch Mac for abandoning Jenny, but Zeke could do nothing to Feeney for assaulting Hannah.

"Any cross-examination?" the judge asked Feeney's lawyer.

The attorney shook his head and stayed seated. If he hadn't, Zeke would have wanted to kill him, too.

After Hannah's testimony, she walked past Zeke and out the door. Zeke followed her.

"Let's go," she said. "Jenny said we could wait for the verdict at her house."

Mac came out of the courtroom behind Zeke. Mac bowed to Hannah. "A brave job, Hannah. You've assured the prosecution's victory, I believe."

"Hannah said Jenny has invited her to your home," Zeke said.

Mac nodded. "You'll both be more comfortable there. I'll stay and bring news of the verdict as soon as it's read."

"Please, Zeke." Hannah grasped his arm, her fingers white.

"All right." He escorted her to the wagon and drove to the McDougalls' house.

Jenny led them to the parlor, and she made conversation with Hannah. Zeke prowled the room, unable to sit. He wanted to do something, but with the law involved, he was powerless.

The noon hour passed, and Jenny invited them to eat. Zeke heard the children upstairs, but they remained unseen. "What about your children?" Hannah asked Jenny as the three of them sat at a table loaded with food. "Don't they need their meal also?"

"The maid will feed them," Jenny said. "I didn't think you'd want—"

"To see them?" Hannah interrupted. "Of course, I want to see them. I can't avoid young children forever."

Jenny smiled. "Then we'll visit the nursery after we eat."

After they finished the meal, the women went upstairs, and Zeke sat outside on the porch smoking. He rolled a cigarette, lit it, puffed until it was gone, then rolled another. As he finished his third cigarette, Mac rode his black stallion up the hill and into the yard.

Zeke stood from his perch on the porch railing. "Well?"

"Guilty," Mac said as he dismounted. "On all counts. Come help me put Valiente away." He led the stallion toward the stable behind the house.

"Will he hang?" Zeke asked.

Mac nodded. "The jury had no doubts. They deliberated for less than an hour. The judge pronounced the sentence immediately after hearing the verdict."

"When will it be?"

Mac shrugged. "Not long. They hanged the Cayuse who killed the Whitmans just days after they were found guilty."

"Then it will be over." Zeke sighed in relief. "And our lives will go back to normal."

The hanging was set for Thursday. Zeke went to town for it, but refused to let Hannah or the children attend. "I'm only going to be sure it's done," he said. "It ain't something I want any of my kin to see."

He'd never seen a man hanged, and he didn't relish it now. But as he'd told his family, he needed to know for certain Feeney wouldn't trouble them again.

It was quick. Feeney dropped from the scaffold, twitched twice, and was still. When the doctor—not Doc Tuller—pronounced Feeney dead, Zeke's stomach turned.

After the hanging, Zeke stopped by Abernethy's store to check for mail. The clerk handed him a letter for Hannah that looked like it was from her sister. Then he rode home, shivering despite the October sun above him. Death, even Feeney's death, was a chilling event.

What a year it had been—losing Pa, regretting Jenny's refusal to marry him, seeing Hannah as a convenient solution to his problems, and now realizing Hannah was more dear to him than anyone in the world had ever been.

Yet she seemed to have lost her grit along with their child. How could he reassure her and let her know they could still have a happy life? All the success he might have in farming wouldn't be worth a penny if he didn't have Hannah by his side.

Chapter 70: A Decision

The death of Devlin Feeney gave Hannah no comfort. She still saw him, felt him, smelled him every time she closed her eyes. When she recalled his attack, her head throbbed again as it had when she'd struck it against the hook on the barn wall. Her stomach wrenched with pain as it had when he punched her and later during the hours of her miscarriage. She felt again the despair of losing what she'd most desired.

Zeke told her the hanging was done, but didn't describe it. And she didn't ask for details.

"I brought a letter from town," he told Hannah and dropped it on the table. "From your sister perhaps? Must've been sent afore she heard we was—were—married. It's addressed to Hannah Bramwell. I hope she sends you good news." He planted a kiss on her head, and went outside.

Hannah glanced at the letter—Jane's handwriting, though the script seemed shakier than usual. Was Jane ill? She broke the seal and unfolded the letter.

July 1, 1851
Dear Hannah,
    I need you—Charles is dead.

Dead? There was too much death in this world, Hannah thought in despair. She'd left Cincinnati in part because of Charles. Jane knew nothing of Charles's aggressions toward Hannah. Or, at least, Hannah prayed her sister had not been aware of her husband's roving eyes and hands. Now Charles was gone—no great loss, in Hannah's estimation.

She continued reading:

He took fever suddenly last week, and suffered only three days with a most putrid inflammation of the brain before he breathed his last. He was insensible almost from the first sign of illness, and left me no instructions on how to manage the store or his other affairs.

I am distressed and cannot cope without you. Jacob and his children, it seems from your letters, do not need you.

Hannah paused and closed her eyes. Jane must not have received Hannah's letter about her marriage to Zeke—Jane didn't mention Zeke or his siblings at all. Hannah sighed and resumed reading Jane's letter:

You must return home as quickly as you can. My house is in shambles. And without any attention, the store will go to ruin.

I cannot bear to leave my room to see anyone other than the doctor, who has come to see me twice daily. Otherwise, I would have no one to lean on in my distress.

You must come home,
Jane

Hannah's hand shook as she finished the letter. Poor Jane! Her sister suffered from the vapors at the slightest inconvenience, and the death of her husband would surely send her into hysterics for weeks.

But what could Hannah do? She was married. She'd pledged her life to Zeke. She and Jane had discussed Hannah's leaving at length before Hannah left Ohio—Jane had known they would probably never see each other again. Hannah could not leave Oregon.

But how would Jane cope without her? What duty did she owe her grieving sister?

Wasn't her greater duty to Zeke and the rest of the Pershings?

Days passed, and Hannah plodded from task to task, befuddled in her grief over her lost child and bewildered over how to respond to Jane. She found no meaning in her chores and no joy in the turning leaves on the alders and maples.

The children were good to her—careful not to be too loud, eager to help with housework. But their very goodness tried her patience—particularly the boys, who tiptoed about the cabin unlike their usual boisterous selves. Their attentive behavior proved she was damaged, proved she could no longer tolerate the rough-and-tumble family and life she'd come to love.

Love her family she did. And she wanted them to love her as she had been before the miscarriage, not as she was now.

With each new morning, she awoke pondering her future. How could she stay with Zeke when she'd failed him as a wife? How could she leave after pledging her troth to him?

The only person who needed her was Jane. She would have to return to Cincinnati. With Charles dead and no longer pursuing her, Jane's home would be a refuge. She could leave behind the demands of marriage and the daily reminders her body had betrayed her, had killed her one hope of bearing her own child.

Sunday, October 19, was the anniversary of her arrival in Oregon. Monday, October 20, was the anniversary of the first time she'd seen Zeke—the day he'd hit Mac in the jaw and she'd shrunk from his violence and coarseness.

In the past year, she'd come to see Zeke as so much more than the first impression she'd had of him. As a loving son who grieved his father. As an older brother who assumed responsibility for siblings he had no idea how to care for. As a husband who could make her body sing, the body she'd seen only as a liability since her childhood injury.

How she wanted to stay with them, these Pershings! They were her family in ways her own parents and siblings had never been. But how could she? She'd failed them, and she doubted she would ever provide Zeke with a child.

Doc Tuller hadn't said so directly. He'd come to see her again after the trial. She'd asked him, as she had on the day of her miscarriage, "Will I bear another child?"

"Give it time," he said.

But she knew. She'd never expected to become pregnant, but she had and she'd felt the promise of joy. Then, thanks to the evil Feeney, she'd lost her chance.

So on Wednesday morning, after Zeke and the twins left to hunt, Hannah told Faith and Ruth, "Mind Noah, and stay near the house. I'm driving to town."

"Can't we go?" Noah asked.

Hannah shook her head. "I have business with my brother. You stay here. I'll be quick as I can be."

She drove to Jacob's store and went inside. "May I speak with you privately, Jacob?" she asked, seeing his sons stocking shelves.

Jacob took her into the back room. "What is it, Hannah?"

"I need to borrow money for a ticket home."

"A ticket?"

"To Ohio."

Jacob stared at her. "You can't go back. You're married to Zeke Pershing now."

Hannah choked back tears. "I know you gave Zeke lumber for the house last spring instead of my ticket home, but I can't stay. Jane needs me—Charles has died."

"Charles? Dead?"

She showed him Jane's letter. "So you see, I must go to her. Please, I'll pay you back for the ticket."

"Has Zeke hurt you?"

She gaped. "Zeke? No. Of course not."

"Then why are you leaving?"

"I can't be the wife he needs."

"You're married. One spouse can't leave the other." Hannah wondered if Jacob meant to imply he'd leave Alice if he could. "You can't leave. Not even for Jane."

"My life here is hopeless, Jacob. And Jane needs me."

They argued, but finally he agreed a visit to Jane's home might be a good thing for both sisters. "But you'll have to return to Zeke after a bit," he said. "The steamship leaves daily for Portland. There you can buy a ticket to California, then back East. When do you want to leave?"

"I'll pack a bag and be back tomorrow," she said.

"Have you told Zeke?"

She shook her head. "But I will."

That afternoon Hannah sent the girls and Noah to check for melons and vegetables in the garden on the McDougall claim. "I don't know if there'll be anything left this late in the season," she said. "But no one is living there now, so we might as well get the benefit of what Faith and I planted in the spring."

When she was alone, she packed a satchel of her belongings as well as the trunk she'd brought from Ohio. It sat at the end of the bed, filled with odds and ends, which she managed to store elsewhere in the cabin. She tried not to leave any signs she was planning her departure. She wasn't sure she would be able to follow through with it in the morning.

What would she tell Zeke?

The children returned from the McDougall claim with a small melon and some beans. "Simmer the beans with bacon," she told Ruth and Faith. "Noah, scoop out the melon, and we'll stew it with apples and nutmeg."

Zeke and the twins returned at dusk with several ducks to pluck and dress. When the birds were ready, Hannah fried two of them. "You can roast the others tomorrow," she told Faith. She felt a pang of regret at leaving her niece, who would probably have to return to town to live with Jacob and Alice.

"Where will you be?" Faith asked, laughing.

"Sorry, I'm just muddle-headed today," Hannah said, feeling her face redden. She glanced at Zeke, but he hadn't heard her slip of the tongue.

She waited until the children retired for the night, then went into her bedroom and sat on the bed. Zeke came in a few minutes later.

"Zeke—" she began, staring at her hands in her lap, unable to look at him.

He sat beside her, turned her face to him, and kissed her. "I love you, Hannah Bramwell Pershing. Do you believe me?"

She buried her face in his shoulder and sobbed.

"Hannah," Zeke said, cradling her close. "I'm sorry about the child. But whether we have children of our own or not, we have a family. You've made us a family. Don't cry. Let me love you."

And so she did. Afterward, Zeke slept, while she nestled in his arms.

How could she leave?

Zeke and the twins were gone when Hannah awoke Thursday morning. She panicked. She hadn't told him, yet she had to leave in time to get the ticket from Jacob. After breakfast, she sat at the table and wrote,

> Zeke,
>   I cannot be the wife you need.
>   I am returning to Ohio to visit Jane. With her husband dead, she needs me. I will write you when I reach Cincinnati.
>   All my love,
>   Hannah

She sealed the note, then asked Faith and Ruth to help her load the trunk into the wagon. "Why do you need it, Aunt Hannah?"

Cringing at her lie, she said, "I have some things for Jacob." Then she hugged the girls and Noah, and said, "Be good." She grabbed her satchel, and heaved it into the wagon.

Chapter 71: Homecoming

Zeke left Hannah in bed on Thursday morning. He'd made love to her the night before for the first time since she'd lost the baby. She'd responded but seemed distant, and afterward he thought he heard her crying softly as he drifted off to sleep.

He wanted to stay home with her. Maybe he could get her to laugh. Or maybe she would correct his grammar—she hadn't done so in weeks. But he'd made a commitment to help Samuel Abercrombie clear another field. Daniel would be there, but with Zeke and the twins, the job could be accomplished twice as fast.

After hitching the mules to the wagon, Zeke, Jonathan, and David rode toward old Samuel's farm. As he drove, Zeke thought of all the winter tasks he needed to do. With the harvest in, he should have more time at home. But the farm always needed work—clearing land like Samuel wanted them to do today, cutting timber, tending the winter wheat. And he should lay in more meat—venison and birds, maybe buy a hog to butcher.

He would be able to prove his claim in November, after four long years of labor. Thanks to his marriage to Hannah, he would have title to the entire six hundred and forty acres he'd claimed. He estimated he had about eighty acres cleared now, enough to support the family, but not enough for many luxuries. If he could clear more land and hire a man to help him and his brothers next year, he might be able to make a profit. Maybe even build a bigger house, a frame house like Mac's, instead of a log cabin. There was no end to what a man could do with six hundred and forty acres.

"Pershing!"

Zeke looked over his shoulder. Jacob Bramwell trotted on his mare toward the wagon. "What brings you out from town?" Zeke called.

"Why aren't you with Hannah?" Jacob yelled.

"I told Abercrombie we'd help him."

"Didn't she talk to you?" Jacob's voice was harsh. "About leaving Oregon?"

"What?"

"Go home, Zeke. Now. She may already be on her way to town. She wanted me to loan her the money for a ticket. I was coming out to try to talk her out of it."

Zeke's gut seized. "Where would she go?"

Instead of answering, Jacob dismounted and offered his reins to Zeke. "Take my horse. It'll be faster than the wagon."

"Boys," Zeke shouted at his brothers as he hefted himself onto Jacob's mare. "Follow me home. Bring Jacob. We'll sort this out." But even as he spoke, Zeke feared Hannah wouldn't let herself be sorted out.

Zeke galloped the mare home, wondering what he would find when he arrived. Would Hannah still be there? Or would he be too late? If she was gone, he resolved to go after her, to follow her until he found her. Wherever she had gone. He couldn't bear to lose her.

When he got to the barnyard, he saw Hannah in the smaller farm wagon, his gelding Red prancing in the unaccustomed traces. Her bag perched on the seat beside her, and her big trunk sat behind in the wagon box.

"Where are you going?" he shouted.

Hannah's face blanched. "I'm supposed to meet Jacob in town this morning."

"He's on his way here." Zeke said. "I just left him. He told me to talk to you. What's going on?"

"I left you a note."

"Never mind the note. Tell me." Zeke dismounted and tied Jacob's mare to a fencepost. Then he leapt onto the wagon bench beside Hannah. Out of the corner of his eye, he saw Ruth, Noah, and Faith watching them from the cabin doorway.

Hannah whispered, "I can't stay here, Zeke. Jane needs me."

"The hell you can't. You're my wife. You ain't going nowhere unless I say so." He shouted, but his belligerence came from fear.

"You can't keep me here. I can leave if I want."

If she'd punched him as hard as she could, she couldn't have hurt him more. "You said you loved me." His voice cracked.

"It's because I love you I have to go. I'm not the wife you need."

"That's for me to say, not you." She couldn't leave him. Not when he was about to prove up his claim, not when their lives lay ahead of them.

"I'm returning to Ohio. Jane needs me."

"There's nothing for you in Ohio. You told me so. Jane must have friends to help her."

"It's the only place I can go." She gestured at the house, at the children. "I can't stay here. I'm not fit."

"Of course, you're fit. I love you," he said. "You know that."

"Zeke, please don't make this harder on me. I have to leave."

"I ain't letting you go, Hannah." He grasped her shoulders.

Jacob and the twins drove the wagon and mules into the yard. The three of them stared at Zeke and Hannah from their wagon, while the other three children watched from the cabin door.

Zeke turned Hannah to look at them all and waved his hand. "We're your family, Hannah. You belong here."

"No—"

"Tell her," he called to the young'uns. "Tell her we need her."

At that, the five children raced to the wagon and climbed in the box. Ruth threw her arms around Hannah. "Please don't go, Hannah. You have to stay." the girl said. Faith hugged Hannah as well.

"We do need you, Hannah," David said, his voice choked. Jonathan nodded.

Noah squirmed between Hannah and Zeke and climbed in her lap.

Jacob got out of the other wagon and tied up the lead mule. He walked over to Hannah also. "Seems they don't want you to go, sister."

"I told you not to tell them."

"You said you'd tell Zeke. You didn't." Jacob coughed. "A man has a right to know what his wife's doing."

"I'm not fit for life on the frontier," Hannah cried. "I can't handle the work. I can't bear a child. I should tend to Jane."

"You taught me my sums," Noah said. "And I'm learning my timeses." His lower lip trembled. Zeke picked Noah off Hannah and set the boy on his own lap.

"If you won't stay," Zeke said, "we'll all move to Ohio." He hadn't thought through what he was about to say, but as he spoke, it seemed right.

"If you don't like it here, we'll all go there. Or I'll visit your sister with you. We love you and we want to be with you. We won't let you leave us." He felt Noah wriggle and nod in agreement.

"Don't be silly," Hannah said. "Your farm is here. You've made a life here."

Giving up his claim would hurt, but Zeke could handle it. "My life is with you, Hannah. I can farm anywhere."

"Your land—"

"There's other land. I can start again." And Zeke realized he *could*. He could farm wherever land was available. He could work for another man farming. But he'd never find another wife like Hannah. So he told her, "You're what makes my claim worth having. You and the young'uns. The land is only important because it keeps us together. We're family. We need to stay together."

Chapter 72: Hope Revived

When Zeke galloped into the barnyard, Hannah's heart leapt. She hadn't wanted to confront him about her departure, though she knew she should have. Now she couldn't escape—they would have to talk. What she had to say would hurt him, and she shuddered at the thought of wounding Zeke.

When he asked where she was going, she told him. His blasted arrogance in proclaiming she couldn't leave because she was his wife infuriated her. He ignored what she said about Jane. They argued until Zeke turned her toward the children. "We're your family, Hannah. You belong here."

They swarmed her, all those children. Her family, he called them. Her defenses melted. It wasn't fair for Zeke to bring them into it. This should be between her and her husband. But when Zeke told her his family was her family, she began to believe he was right.

Jacob added his two cents, just as he had the day before in his store. Though, like Zeke, he took a typically male perspective when she chastised him for telling Zeke of her plan. When she declared she wasn't fit, her family fought back.

And then Zeke said, "If you won't stay, we'll all go to Ohio."

That stunned her. Zeke's land was a part of him. He'd poured his heart into this farm. He'd married her for it. "Don't be silly," she said. "Your farm is here. You've made a life here."

"There's other land," he said. "I can start again. You're what makes my claim worth having." She'd waited so long for him to say these words, for him to see her value apart from the land.

He continued, "The land is only important because it keeps us together. We're family. We need to stay together."

Family. She wanted to be a part of this family so badly. She loved each

383

of the children—her niece Faith who fit with the Pershings like she'd been born to them, the unruly twins trying so hard to become men, Ruth growing from girl to woman before her eyes, and Noah who looked like she imagined Zeke had looked at eight.

And Zeke. Her happiest moments had been when she curled in his arms each night, when he entered the cabin each evening after a day apart, when he—deliberately, she knew—used poor grammar to rile her. She yearned to stay, to build a life with him. Could she? Should she?

Would he really abandon his land and accompany her to Ohio? "Your claim will be proved up in just weeks," she said.

He nodded. "I'd be giving up four years' work." He squeezed her shoulders. "But you're worth it, Hannah. I have decades to farm. I want to spend those decades with you."

His eyes said he meant it. A sprig of hope poked through her despair. She wasn't a quitter. If Zeke was willing to move for her, she would have to stay in the West for him. Jane would have to manage on her own. "All right," she said. "I'll stay."

One of the girls sobbed, Jonathan gave a cheer, and David threw her carpetbag to the ground.

"Get her trunk, too!" Noah shouted. "Take it inside quick, afore she changes her mind."

As she smiled at Noah's statement and the pandemonium around her, Zeke leaned over and kissed her. When she was breathless, he whispered into her ear, "We're a family, and you're part of it. You ain't going nowhere."

"You aren't," she said, grinning at him now. "You aren't going anywhere. And neither am I."

He got out of the wagon, lifted her down, and carried her into the cabin.

Chapter 73: One Year Later

Hannah sat at her table near the fire, paper and ink in front of her and quill in her hand. With her foot, she rocked a cradle beside her.

October 21, 1852
Dear Jane,

My dearest wish has come to pass. I was delivered of a baby girl yesterday morning, two years to the day after I first encountered Ezekiel Pershing under less than auspicious circumstances.

Zeke and I have named her Hope. She cannot replace our niece of the same name, who succumbed to smallpox with her mother three years ago. But my daughter Hope fulfills the promise of the life I have built on the frontier.

As I write, she sleeps with little whimpers in a cradle Zeke made from a tree felled on our land. My heart spills over with joy, and my thoughts are drawn to the old hymn:

The Lord has promised good to me,
His word my hope secures;
He will my shield and portion be
As long as life endures.

It has not been an easy year since the murderer's brutality deprived us of our first child. Yet Zeke and I have been blessed in so many ways. At last, I feel secure in the home we have made with his siblings and our niece Faith . . . and now with Hope.

My life is not what I dreamed of when we were girls. It is infinitely richer. I pray that you find hope and joy as well.

My love,

Your sister Hannah

THE END

Find more books from Theresa Hupp at
https://www.amazon.com/Theresa-Hupp/e/B009H8QIT8

Author's Note and Research Methods

This book is a work of fiction. Although its events are imaginary, I have tried to stay true to Oregon history in 1850-51. The Donation Land Act of 1850 reduced the number of acres single men could choose. At least one news account talked about the rush of many men to marry to avoid losing half their claims, though I found no documentation of how many men actually had their claims reduced nor any statistics on how many couples married to avoid the problem.

Gold was discovered in the Rogue River Valley in southern Oregon in 1850. Many prospectors migrated there from California or from northern Oregon.

Farming and logging have been important economic activities in Oregon since the territory's earliest history. Many of the early land claims encompassed both farmland and timberland, and I've tried to show the importance of these two industries in this novel.

One resource I used in researching *My Hope Secured* was *The Oregon Spectator*, a local newspaper of the era in Oregon City. Each month, the Spectator reported on the weather, which provides one level of verisimilitude in my novel. I also used *The Oregon Spectator* to find other daily events in Oregon City in 1850-51. The entire archive of *The Oregon Spectator* (1846-1855) can be found on the Historic Oregon Newspapers website at https://oregonnews.uoregon.edu/lccn/sn84022662/issues/.

I also read large sections of Hubert Howe Bancroft's multi-volume *History of Oregon*, as well as other sources of information on 19th-century farming methods and timbering.

On a personal note, I discovered some old family history while researching Oregon history. In 1852, one of my ancestors, Cyrenus (that's how his name is usually spelled in family records) Hooker, was the first person murdered in Polk County, Oregon. Like the murderer in my novel, my ancestor's killer was hung just a few weeks after his conviction. You can find out more in "The Murder of Cyrenius C. Hooker," by Thomas Branigar in the *Oregon Historical Quarterly*, Vol. 75, No. 4 (Dec.1974), pp. 344-359, and in *Legal Executions in the Western Territories, 1847-1911*, by R. Michael Wilson (2010), p. 155 et seq.

I take responsibility for any historical errors in *My Hope Secured.*

Discussion Guide

These questions are intended to help book clubs and other reading groups discuss *My Hope Secured*. Students might also use them as essay topics.

1. What did you learn about daily life on the frontier in 1850-51? What surprised you? What would you like to know more about?

2. How did roles of men and women differ on Oregon farms? How did their roles overlap?

3. How did courtship and romance differ in 1850-51 from today? What similarities did you notice?

4. What did you think of the portrayal of childhood in *My Hope Secured*? How did childhood differ in the 19th century from today?

5. What did you think of the practical reasons Hannah Bramwell and Zeke Pershing had for marrying?

6. If Zeke and Hannah made choices you didn't like, why did you disagree with their decisions, and what would you have done instead?

7. How did the difficulties with communications between the West and the settled United States contribute to the plot? What in your life might have been different without today's instant communications?

8. How have you handled people like Samuel Abercrombie?

9. How did the criminal prosecution of Devlin Feeney differ from criminal trials and sentencing today?

10. For those of you who have also read my earlier novels, how do you think Zeke has developed? Do you like him more or less in *My Hope Secured* than in earlier books?

11. Which character was your favorite in *My Hope Secured*? How did this person change and develop through the story?

12. Where do you see these characters in five or ten years?

If you enjoyed **My Hope Secured**, *you might also enjoy my other novels,* **Lead Me Home**, **Now I'm Found**, *and* **Forever Mine**.

All books are available on Amazon and Barnes & Noble, or find them here:

https://www.amazon.com/Theresa-Hupp/e/B009H8QIT8

Acknowledgments

I am fortunate to be part of several writing groups, including the Sedulous Writers Group, Homer's Orphans, and Write Brain Trust. The knowledge and expertise of the authors in these groups have helped me develop my writing, and I appreciate them all.

Norman Ledgin, a founding member of the Sedulous Writers critique group, passed away during the final editing of this novel. I owe a huge debt to Norm for his faithful input until just days before his death. His suggestions over the past several years have made me a better writer.

My thanks as well to early readers and editors of this book, specifically Darlene, Sylvia, and Priscilla.

I am grateful to all these friends and colleagues for their help. This community of writers and readers has made *My Hope Secured* a better book than if I worked in isolation.

About the Author

Theresa Hupp grew up in Eastern Washington State and the Willamette Valley in Oregon. Her ancestors include 19th century emigrants to Oregon and California, and she now lives in Kansas City, Missouri.

Theresa is the award-winning author of novels, short stories, essays, and poetry, and has worked as an attorney, mediator, and human resources executive.

A #1 bestselling novel about the Oregon Trail in Amazon's Kindle Store, *Lead Me Home* (2015) tells the story of Mac McDougall and Jenny Calhoun on their wagon journey along the Oregon Trail. *Now I'm Found* (2016) follows Mac and Jenny through the early California Gold Rush days. *Forever Mine* tells the story of the Oregon Trail trek from other members' points of view, which provide additional perspectives on the journey.

Theresa has also published a bestselling financial thriller under a pseudonym, as well as an anthology titled, *Family Recipe: Sweet and saucy stories, essays, and poems about family life*. In addition, Theresa has written short works for *Chicken Soup for the Soul*, *Mozark Press*, and *Kansas City Voices*. She is a member of the Kansas City Writers Group, Missouri Writers Guild, Oklahoma Writers Federation, Inc., and Write Brain Trust.

You can follow Theresa on her website and blog, http://TheresaHuppAuthor.com, on her Facebook Author page, http://facebook.com/TheresaHuppAuthor, and her Amazon page at http://www.amazon.com/Theresa-Hupp/e/B009H8QIT8. You can also subscribe to Theresa's monthly newsletter through her website.

Readers' Praise for Earlier Books

Lead Me Home:

> . . . *on the challenging Oregon Trail of 1847 . . . the going is slow and scary and dusty behind a team of oxen. . . . [Hupp] takes us on this journey and shows how her characters cope and grow under these difficult circumstances.*

> . . . *an incredible story, amazingly and beautifully written.*

Now I'm Found:

> *Hupp has done extensive research on . . . traveling the Oregon Trail and prospecting for gold in the California mountains. The descriptions of those closely related periods of history are exciting backgrounds for a tender love story.*

> . . . *A love story served well by the pioneer notions of courtship, loyalty and marriage. Hupp does history and fiction well!*

Forever Mine:

> *Hupp researches her books with care, plots them well, describes the land beautifully, and makes the people of these books come alive with vivid characterizations.*

> *For any true lover of the western and the hardships of the pioneers who were willing to put their life in danger. . . .*

All Theresa Hupp's books are available online at Amazon or Barnes & Noble, in paperback or ebook formats.